PAY OR PLAY

PAY OR PLAY

a novel by Jon Boorstin

SILES PRESS   LOS ANGELES

First Siles Press Edition

10 9 8 7 6 5 4 3 2 1

Epigraph from Cavafy, C. P., translated by Edmund Keeley and Philip Sherrard,
C. P. Cavafy Collected Poems, revised edition 1995, copyright © 1975 by Keeley/
Sherrard, reprinted by permission of Princeton University Press.

Library of Congress Cataloging-in-Publication Data

Boorstin, Jon, 1946-
Pay or play / Jon Boorstin.
p. cm.
1. Motion picture industry—California—Los Angeles—Fiction.
2. Screenwriters—California—Los Angeles—Fiction.
3. Hollywood (Los Angeles, Calif.)—Fiction. I. Title
PS3552.O64396 P3 2000   813'.54—dc21   99-089202

ISBN 1-890085-04-9

Cover design by Wade Lageose

Printed in the United States of America.

SILES PRESS
3624 Shannon Road
Los Angeles, CA 90027

For
Eric and Ariel

*For some people the day comes
when they have to declare the great Yes
or the great No.*

—C. P. Cavafy

I

The Big Yes

ONE

The 101 flows cleanly through the Cahuenga pass, dammed on the sides by steep canyon walls, but where it pours into Hollywood it trails a swath of urban waste in the death zone below the high-water mark of its cacophony: rubble-strewn parking lots, graffiti-scrawled self-storage units, double-barred boarded-up bungalows. There, one piece of forties flotsam looms among the freeway jetsam—the Chateau Maison. A massive if decaying homage to the palaces of the Loire valley, too big to tear down, too freeway-close to inhabit sanely, it offers under its slate mansard roof a haven for impoverished transients who would rather have Hollywood at their feet than a good night's sleep.

Since many come to Hollywood in this frame of mind, the Chateau is usually fully subscribed. But many a one-month lease is abandoned after a week. The constant internal-combustion pounding defeats the most efficient earplugs, jolting inner organs through sheer bone conduction, crushing the romance from the Hollywood adventure.

The longest-lived tenant was a massively obese woman who inhabited a ground floor apartment in the perpetual shadow of the 101; she'd grown old with the building, and she'd been stone deaf for thirty years. And then there was Elmo.

Elmo had been living at the Chateau for almost a year, in a bare apartment just below the roof. It was easy to tell his apartment from the freeway—it was the only one with the windows open. Elmo savored the breeze blowing over the bare oak floors with its odors of engine oil and eucalyptus and dog shit. He fed off the freeway roar pounding deep in his thorax like a second heart, pumping raw energy through his body.

Elmo worked all the time, writing his screenplay, except when he was stuck. When he was stuck he'd leave the Chateau, thin as a shadow in black T-shirt, black tennis shoes, and black blue jeans, and haunt one of the cheap rerun houses video can't kill,

3

the Bijou or the Carmel or the Vista, where he'd sit in the third
row, letting the movie wash over him, waiting for breakthrough.

At this moment Elmo was leaping up the seven flights of stairs
to his apartment, panting more from excitement than from effort, pulling himself along by the handrail in his desire to get
back to work. He'd been stuck a long time, longer than he'd
ever been stuck before. Seventy-one hours. And now he had it.

He had just seen a double bill, *Terminator* and *Predator,*
eleven times. By the fifth time, the large, speckled, scratched
images had assumed a life of their own, each new scene pregnant with the possibilities of actual experience; by the eighth,
time collapsed into a frenzied stew of payoffs and setups,
crashes, chases, battles and beheadings; by the eleventh, the
churning film grain boiled from the frame onto his face and
arms, seeping through his flesh, percolating to his brain, breaking him through.

He sat down at the typewriter and cranked in a page. He
typed quickly, in bursts. The "b" stuck, jamming the keys, and
he would poke at them and curse, and try not to use it. His
grandfather had left him only a few thousand dollars. A computer would have cost him four months living, minimum. He
couldn't spare the time.

Elmo was happiest at breakthrough. He lived for that click in
his brain when the movie in there snapped to life and jerked him
by his endocrine system, the same "aha" spasm that made Ein-
stein forgo straight razors and struck Kepler dumb when he'd
deciphered the music of the spheres. That click in his head didn't
mean he was a genius, of course. It was a chemical reaction,
pure and simple, shared by crack smokers and schizophrenics
and presidential assailants. But Elmo rode it for all it was worth.

Particularly this time, because this was the big one. After a
year of writing and rewriting, the work had reduced to a single
knot, an undigested growth deforming the climax of his story.
He'd hacked and pounded mercilessly for weeks, pushing the
lump this way and that, but never cleaving it clean off. Now he
had the lump in his grip. He could drain the mass.

Elmo clattered on, burning with breakthrough but serene in
his vision. For Elmo knew he had what it took. It was only a
matter of time. And if he couldn't make it—couldn't have that
life breakthrough like those story breakthroughs that drove him
on—well, he had a plan. If he was still here in three years—two
years now—still clacking away, invisible, he'd lean out the open

window, inhale the scents of engine oil and eucalyptus one last time, and launch himself onto the beckoning freeway.

This scene, odd though it might be, was at that very moment being played out with only minor variations in thousands of shacks and walk-ups among the beaches, canyons, and slums of Greater Los Angeles. With two crucial differences. First, most of the others would compromise with life's inevitable disappointments. If they didn't break through, they'd try to write for television, and if that failed, they'd end up selling real estate or bartering ad time for syndication; their lives, if less glamorous and ego-gratifying, would yield up other, perhaps greater, compensatory satisfactions. Raising a family, for instance. Not Elmo. Elmo was a clenched fist. He'd punch through or crush trying.

The second difference was much rarer in Hollywood than truly suicidal singleness of purpose, for this town, like Washington, lures those convinced they're touched by the finger of God. In the Chateau alone there was at that moment at least one other who was dead serious about suicide as a solution to career frustration. A third, a young would-be Janet Jackson, would drive her Toyota into a bridge abutment on the Simi Valley Freeway, but it would never be clear if hers was an incandescent act of desperation or the failure of her hydraulic system.

The second difference, and what truly set Elmo apart from all those others with a burning desire to be set apart, was that his script was very, very good. Not adequate, not a good writing sample, not promising; better than Shakespeare for these purposes, or even Ben Hecht, it was a tough, crazed poem of freedom and self-expression through ultra-violence against tremendous odds, a cathartic paean to nihilistic action that grabbed you by the throat and hauled you panting and screaming through ninety minutes of sex and violence that would play as well on the Upper East Side of Manhattan as the red-light district of Bangalore.

Elmo had a winner.

TWO

At three A.M., Rodeo Drive was dead as Wall Street. Only patrol cars prowled. In the mercury vapor gloom, the cuboid buildings glowed dully, like bank vaults. Save one: wedged between two purveyors of leather sundries, so exclusive they carried no names, a narrow sliver of tower rose in contravention of all zoning laws, klieg-lit brilliant white: Consolidated Creativity. Bo—everyone called him Bo—had collected air rights to the parking lots along Beverly Drive and used his singular influence with the city council to convert a blind alley into this, his architectural monument, lit day and night as a beacon of pride and profit.

But even Consolidated was deserted at three A.M. In the lobby, a guard watched two of Bo's clients in prison blues duke it out with toothbrush shivs on a tiny TV; behind, in the narrow atrium, the trout stream burbled peacefully.

In the far reaches of the lobby, on the Camden Drive side where the trout stream began in a four-story waterfall, a compact young man, Jack Doberman, sat with a shopping cart full of manila envelopes. Jack had positioned the cart to block the humidifiers which were programmed to spray a nocturnal fog over the ferns and rushes; now the mist was seeping into the envelopes, loosening those it didn't soak beyond repair. Jack would open an envelope, glance briefly at the contents, move to the next, swatting at the occasional mosquito that rose from the muddy banks of the stream.

Jack was night man in the mail room, ninth circle of hell for his chosen profession. In a business that was all buzz and contacts, he came to work after the action died and left before it came alive; no amount of eager enterprise would call him to the attention of his betters. But Jack told himself he didn't mind, for now. He'd made it into Consolidated, that's what mattered, and he'd done it without any ins. He had no relatives in the business except a cousin who worked at 20-20 Video in Studio City. He

6

hadn't gone to Harvard, though when he was growing up in Sherman Oaks he'd tell girls he went to the tony Harvard School when playing hooky from Grant High. He'd phoned Bo's office every twenty minutes for a month and a half, and when one of the mail room guys, a Yale Law grad, quit because he couldn't take the pressure, Bo thought it would be fun to reward such demonic persistence.

Jack picked up a soggy envelope. It dissolved in his hands. A leather-bound, gilt-edged tome fell into the stream. He fished it out and opened it. The rag paper took water well. *Leeuwenhoek.* He peeled away a cover letter: "Dear Sirs," it read:

> Most people only think of Leeuwenhoek as the inventor of the microscope, but he was in fact a renowned poet, swordsman, and lover. Only one man has the charisma to portray him—your client, Klaus Frotner . . .

Jack tossed it on the shredding pile and picked up another. This time the envelope held, and out slid a slim item laser-printed on onion skin, its red silk cover embossed in pink *Eternally Yours.* A note was attached on scented paper:

> Klaus Frotner IS Anatole Dubois/Thaddeus Strong/Kent Ramsey/Franklin Strick/Montgomery Frost/Jason Mark!

He leafed it idly; it was the tale of star-crossed lovers, fated to die tragically in each other's arms only to reunite in another incarnation. And another, and another. He slipped the script back into the envelope, licked it closed, and stamped on the outside in large red letters:

RETURNED UNOPENED. CONSOLIDATED CREATIV-ITY DOES NOT READ UNSOLICITED MATERIAL.

He tossed it on the return pile and picked up another.

Jack knew the odds. Of tens of thousands of scripts written every year, only a handful were good enough to jump-start the juggernaut; of those, at least nine out of ten were name-brand product. But he had to feel he was doing something, playing some angle, or he'd go nuts before he could wangle himself off the night shift. The first few weeks he'd gone through the Dumpster, looking for deal memos, but all the good stuff was shredded. Now each night before he returned to sender he'd see what shit floated to the top.

Jack knew nothing about writing, but he figured that was a plus. The rest of the food chain weren't fucking lit professors. The thing he was looking for, whatever it was, had to play in his head like a movie, a movie that made him forget the mosquitoes and dead phones of the night shift. If a script did that, he'd have his club to beat the business with.

Jack looked at the next envelope. The address was a nearly illegible scrawl, blurred by the mist. The cheap envelope turned to mush in his hands. *The Agonizer.* He flipped through the thin, waterlogged copier stock, typewritten with heavy black cross-outs. Who the hell used a typewriter anymore? No cover; just a letter addressed to Bo. The "B" was sort of twisted. Maybe it was "Do." Christ.

Then he began to read.

THREE

Dawn sun was just hitting the top floors of the Chateau Maison, bathing Jack in a dirty golden glow as he skipped up stairs in the Armani suit he'd bought from profits scalping Oscar tickets, his suede shoes making expensive schlupping noises on the worn carpet. It was early, but what the hell.

Jack bounded to the door, knocked briskly, and spoke in his best cop voice. "Mr. Zwalt? Elmo Zwalt?"

Eventually, the door opened. Jack faced a wraith in Jockey briefs, so extraordinarily thin his pale chest seemed translucent in the sunlight. They eyed each other. Jack jumped right in.

"Jack Doberman. Consolidated Creativity." He thrust a card into Elmo's hand. The card was a cut-and-paste job, but he figured Elmo wouldn't miss the "CC" hologram of authenticity. He didn't. Elmo took the card and opened the door wider. He seemed to be expecting him.

"One minute, Jack." Elmo waved a fat calligraphy brush and returned to the kitchen table, where he dipped it in India ink and bent over a half-finished drawing. Jack followed him in, and gravitated to forty other sketches tacked to the wall, flapping in the morning breeze—the *Agonizer* opening, laid out beat for beat, comic-book style, drawn with a sure sense of composition and a forceful line. Jack whistled. "Shit on a stick."

Elmo tacked up the new frame. Even then, rush hour was starting. Traffic noise was so loud, Elmo seemed to move in pantomime.

"Congratulations, kid." He called Elmo kid, though Elmo was a couple of years older than he was.

"What?"

Jack shouted over the din. "Congratulations. Your script has attracted the attention of Klaus Frotner."

"I know. I sent it to him."

"You sent it to me." Jack indicated he was holding the damp pages. "I should be having this conversation with your agent."

9

"I don't have one."

Jack feigned surprise. "Can I close the windows? I can't hear myself think." Jack went around the room shutting windows. The roar diminished to a coronary throb.

"Anyone else told you they liked the script? Schwarzenegger? Willis?"

"I didn't show it to them. I want Frotner."

Better and better. "So Klaus is the only person you've sent the script?" Elmo didn't bother to answer. "What about directors? Cameron? Verhoeven?"

Elmo waved at the drawings that now hung limp on the walls. "I'm directing it myself." He went into the bedroom for his black jeans.

Perfect. "Frotner'll tell you nobody directs Frotner first time out of the box."

"But he likes the script. When he sees the storyboards, he'll want me."

"Where'd you learn to draw like that?" Jack figured writing was like talking, but you had to learn how to draw.

"I was on my back for a year and a half with acute asthma. I wrote off for a correspondence course. But mostly I traced every Spider-Man and X-men I could find." Elmo leaned forward and clasped his hands. "I don't think you understand. I'm not a writer. I—ever since I lay in that hospital staring at the ceiling I've been seeing movies in my head. Writing it down's just the closest I can get in words to what's in there. Those pictures—that's closer, maybe. In some ways. But you need the words too. I see this movie. I see it. I see Frotner."

"I know you do. The way you write it, I see it too." Jack could tell Elmo wasn't making a bullshit speech. He was just telling him who he was. He had two arms, he had two legs, he saw movies in his head.

"I have movies to make. And I'm going to make them. Or—" Elmo paused, stuck. He couldn't think of an alternative.

Jack sized up Elmo and weighed his options. He could play it sweet and grand or he could go for the cojones. His instincts told him Elmo was a guy you kicked in the groin.

"The script is fucking brilliant. Those drawings are fucking brilliant. You're fucking brilliant. You're the man to direct this picture. But I'll level with you, kid. They'll sit on a cattle prod before they let you do it."

"Who's they?"

"They—all the fat asses who'll want to cash in on your picture. Klaus, for one. Bo, for another. Why should he let you direct when he's got a stable of studs who'd butt-fuck each other for the chance?"

"It's my script."

"They'll give you a million dollars. More—"

"But this isn't about money to me, I told you—"

"Fuckin' A it isn't. Your script's worth more than money. It's a fucking career and they know it. They'll make nicey-nicey about 'best efforts' and 'directing pay or play' and 'next time for sure.' They'll say whatever you want to hear but they'll fuck themselves in the ear before they let you direct it."

Elmo sat down. This had the sickening ring of truth. "What can I do, then?"

"Check that card I gave you."

Elmo looked for it; before he could track it down, Jack shoved another at him. "Check that out."

Elmo stared at it.

"That look right to you?"

"I never saw a Consolidated card before."

"It's junk. A Xerox ripoff."

Elmo's pallor vanished. Crimson anger suffused his pale chest. "You're not with Consolidated?"

"Hell yes. How'd you think I got your script?"

"I don't know. Maybe you stole it."

"I picked it out of the garbage at Consolidated."

"What are you, then, some kind of janitor?" The card bent double in Elmo's fingers.

"You think a guy like Frotner reads something he gets in the mail?"

Elmo started to quiver. "Give me my script back."

Elmo lunged for the script. Jack danced out of his way. "So I'm no fat-cat agent. If I was, I'd pat you on the back and screw you out of the deal 'cause I'd have other fat-cat clients I'd want to deal in, and I'd be scared shitless of crossing Frotner. Here, take your fuckin' script." He tossed it at Elmo. Elmo smoothed the crumpled pages.

"Look, Elmo, I'm like you. I'm at the starting gate. I know my game and I got nothing to lose—as long as I stick with you. Klaus can karate-chop his dick off for all I care. You're my rocket ship. You make me your agent, I'll get you your bundle and you'll direct the picture. I swear on my mother's womb."

"Why should I believe you?"

" 'Cause I'm here."

Clutching the script, Elmo went to the refrigerator to think this out. He opened it and pulled out what he had, bananas and peanut butter. He'd discovered if you put bananas in the fridge they'd turn black, but they'd last longer. "I'd have to pay you a commission, right?"

"You don't direct, you don't owe me jack shit."

Elmo peeled a banana and spread it with peanut butter. High-protein snack.

"Want one?"

Sensing victory, Jack stuck his finger in the peanut butter jar. "One other thing. This is going to be a bitch, you can bet on it. Bo didn't get to be Bo being a pussy. They'll play serious head games with you. You gotta hang in there and do what I say, or you'll screw yourself."

Elmo listened solemnly. Jack licked the peanut butter from his finger and went on talking. He had fuckin' great instincts.

FOUR

Klaus was greeting the sun with his morning karate kata, knee-deep in the Pacific. He was a late riser, but since the sun didn't top the Malibu hills until nine-thirty, he had the satisfaction of a dawn ritual at a sane hour.

Klaus was a big man, but he photographed bigger. He had short, skinny legs for such a massive torso, and a chunky head with Tatar cheekbones and the square mandibles of a fashion model. He had considered calf implants, but now that he was who he was, he didn't need them. He just made sure his pants were superbly tailored. The studio restructured his Levis for him.

Klaus slid through the water with barely a ripple, carving the air with fluidity and power. He was a truly graceful man, and at his happiest when moving intricately, when his brain ceased to be the dominant organ and became instead a servant of the system, a proprioceptive conduit of instinct, balance, and pattern.

There were rumors, which pleased Klaus, that before he surfaced in Hollywood he'd been a contract killer for the Yakuza in the Balkans. Though not a violent man, Klaus liked to think that in another time and place he could have been a killing machine. Instead, his skills and sangfroid had made him sensei to the stars and finally to Bo, a karmic confluence that launched him into the firmament and made Bo millions in the process.

Except when he was in violent motion, Klaus's grace did not transfer to the big screen. As an actor he was undeniably stiff; his fans said he had the dignified reserve of a Gary Cooper, but his detractors called it the Rock Hudson syndrome, just plain bad acting. His detractors were eloquent and widely read, but his fans were legion. Klaus's great asset for the manufacture of movies was his review-proof appeal.

Klaus finished in an alpha trance, face to the sun, sea at his back. When he opened his eyes he saw a compact young man

13

waiting for him on the beach, wearing the silk jacket and crimson jockey cap of a Consolidated messenger. The young man held out a towel. Klaus didn't take it.

"This is a private beach." Klaus talked in clipped tones, in what might be construed as a mysterious mid-European accent.

The messenger touched his cap. He was trying to appear servile, but there was a cockiness in his stance he couldn't hide from Klaus. "I'm sorry, sir. They said to wait in the house, but I saw you down here and, well, Bo said it was urgent, and when Bo says it's urgent, I figure it's urgent." He said "Bo" with the requisite mixture of relish and awe, as if conjuring the name would give him a share of the mantle.

Klaus took the towel. "Never come on this beach again."

"Yessir."

They climbed a wire-mesh staircase and traipsed along a chain-link catwalk to the house, perched on steel pylons over the ocean, Frank Gehry's answer to the Pacific. When Klaus had dried off, the messenger took the towel and held out a script. Klaus looked at it with distaste.

"What's so urgent about a damn script?"

"Bo said you had to read this right away."

"Did Bo tell you why?"

The messenger seemed to find this question absurd. "No sir. Didn't he call you?"

They entered the living room from the deck. The room was a glass box with chicken-wire awnings, and the furniture was from Gehry's corrugated phase. The cardboard coffee table and easy chair were piled with scripts. Klaus was between projects, in that narrow launch window when an actor's commitment really meant something, and the town knew it. He couldn't have lunch without the parking valet slipping an action movie into his Humvee.

A strikingly beautiful woman in a thong bikini was reclining on the corrugated sofa, intensely leafing through scripts. She was long-limbed, sleek, and muscular, with thighs that could crush walnuts, and her skin was absolutely flawless, as perfect in life as the airbrushed throats used to sell perfumes in fashion magazines.

"Did Bo call, Inga?"

"No."

Klaus sighed and took the script from the messenger's hand. *The Agonizer.* There was no note attached.

"Who's directing this thing?"

The messenger gave him a blank look.

"Okay. Thanks."

He tossed the script on top of a pile and poured himself some fresh lime juice. When he looked up, the messenger was still standing there.

"Beat it."

"I'm supposed to stay here while you read it."

Klaus stared at the messenger. He considered tossing him out, or having him tossed out, but the kid's intensity was kind of touching. If he was for real, not some crazy who'd mugged a Consolidated courier, he was going to do or die for old Bo. Klaus might have to break bones to get him out of there.

He picked up a phone and punched an auto-dial button: "It's Klaus. For Bo."

"Bo is in transit, Mr. Frotner. I'll try his car." The woman's voice had a lilting quaver that told him she was one of his fans.

"Use the hot line, honey."

"Of course, Mr. Frotner."

Klaus waited, gauging the messenger the way he might gauge a karate opponent. Ignoring the body language—the boy stood calmly enough—boring into the eyes. Klaus thought he detected a narrowing there, a tension, but that might come from simply being in Klaus's presence. It happened often enough.

"Bo is passing through Benedict Canyon, Mr. Frotner. He'll be cut off for a few minutes."

"I'll hold."

"Very good, Mr. Frotner."

Klaus thought he saw the messenger's eyes flash. The kid picked up the script and turned to Inga with a disarming smile.

"Maybe you'd like to read a few pages while we're waiting."

"Don't, Inga."

"Why not?"

"Something's fishy."

"Christ, Klaus. Give the kid a break."

Inga was on page eight when Bo emerged from the canyon. By then who the kid was didn't matter.

FIVE

Back in his Armani duds, Jack stepped into Bo's personal elevator with a nod to its crimson-liveried operator. Adrenaline made his feet swell. This was it. *Mano a mano* with the best of the best.

He'd never been in this elevator before. He'd never been in an elevator with an operator, for that matter. He was disappointed. He'd expected gold, thick carpet, maybe marble or brocade. This was a seamless rectangle of black granite, dimly lit, like the inside of a pharaoh's tomb. No buttons even. The operator just pressed a place on the stone and up they went.

With no place else to rest his eyes in the blank darkness, Jack fastened them on the wrinkled neck of the old geek in red. Somebody'd said he was the father of a major player at the agency Bo left to form Consolidated. Rumor was he'd tossed his son out of the house at fourteen and had never been forgiven. Bo'd salvaged him in an act of charity and a kick in the pants at his old boss. Perfect.

The dim elevator opened onto blinding white. Dazzled, Jack blinked and stumbled out. In the harsh glare he thought he detected a white-robed receptionist behind a white desk. Groping toward her, he heard a muffled "bong" and felt a cool blade try to sever his shinbone. Glass table. Eyes teared with pain, he laughed. Now the tomb elevator made sense. Jack bet when Bo rode, it was nice and bright.

Jack heard a smooth Brit accent behind him. He wheeled and collided with tweed. "This way, sir. Bo awaits you."

Neat, thought Jack. He'd expected to sit on his hands for a long half hour. Bo really knew how to keep you off balance. Jack limped after the tweed into a low, dark corridor. Dizzying white wiped to black, and purple blotches swam in Jack's head. Tweed paused, Jack kept going, rubbing his nose in expensive wool. Purple blotches were joined by green ones, as Jack's pupils dilated enough to make out more dim black granite.

Tweed gave a gentle shove and he was bathed again in dazzling white.

Jack's retina played Ping-Pong with fireballs. He heard ominous swishing sounds. Fighting the impulse to rub his eyes, he moved in their general direction.

"AIYA-KIII!!!!"

A swift breeze rippled his nostrils. He recoiled, hand over face. Through fingers and floating color bubbles he made out Bo, dressed in the simple white yukata of the martial artist, gesturing with a samurai sword.

Damn that flinch. Down one.

Bo was an ordinary-looking guy of middling height, middling weight, not handsome but not put-down ugly either; his features had the bland, neutral quality of a good frat buddy. He'd been an apt aikido student, and Klaus had taught him well, but he had none of Klaus's grace when he moved. The gestures were precisely executed, but in the jerky by-the-numbers way that comes when mind tells body what to do.

His unimpressive presence was no secret to Bo. He had an exact sense of his effect on others. He knew that what set him apart was not physical, but spiritual. His bland envelope was swollen with ferocious energy. He wasn't hyperactive, he didn't talk fast or shout or do three things at once; his energy was bottled inside, under pressure. When he spoke, he spoke quietly; when he handled his sword, he moved exactly as he was taught; but this man meant it. His sword wielding wasn't ritual exercise, it was practice murder.

One piebald blob before Jack's eyes resolved into a large mottled melon on a lacquer pedestal. Bo was waving his sword around the object; he paused, muttered a Zen blessing, head lowered. Then he looked at Jack. He held up the sword.

"Do you know what this is?"

"A samurai sword."

"This is a bar of iron that's been heated to an exact temperature, beaten in a prescribed pattern, and cooled by expert hands, heated and beaten and cooled again and again, thirty thousand times, until it's one molecule thick at the cutting edge and tough enough to slice through bone."

Bo cut complex patterns in the air. Jack wanted to back off but knew better. To make up for his previous lapse, he moved in half a step.

Bo picked up a gray slab and tossed it to Jack. It was a metal ingot. "A bar of iron's worth a few pennies, and it's melted down for horseshoes. Once the experts are through, it's priceless, and it lasts a thousand years."

Bo gestured at the ingot, then at the sword. "That's the script. That's the movie."

Bo held up the sword. "Making a movie is a spiritual act. It depends on trust. Teamwork. Sacrifice. And we don't even have a bar of metal to fall back on. We have only our honor. Our sacred word."

"I thought the script was the bar of metal. That's something to fall back on."

Bo ignored the comment, though the sword slashed closer to Jack in its dance. "You have abused the sanctity of the word. You have endangered my relationship of trust with one of my closest friends—one of Consolidated's most cherished assets. By rights you should be horsewhipped and thrown in the street."

For emphasis, Bo brought down the sword. It flitted past Jack's cheek as Bo wheeled a half-turn, slashing the ceremonial melon once, twice. The pieces stayed neatly in place.

Jack figured if Bo was this upset, he'd struck gold. He wasn't afraid of being tossed in the street. If Bo wanted him fired, he'd have been fired by minions. The minions who hired him. In this world it's all about who needs who more. Right now Bo needed him or he wouldn't have wasted that melon.

"Look, Bo, I did just what you'd do in that situation. The bottom line is we've got Klaus's next movie. It's our package."

Bo reverently wiped the sword and placed it on its stand.

"A swordsmith carries water for three years before he's allowed to touch iron. He heats iron for four years before he's allowed to beat it. You have been practicing my craft for a few months and you want to make a movie."

"All I want is to be part of the team."

"And what do you bring to the table?"

"Elmo Zwalt."

Bo looked confused for an instant. Then it passed. "The writer."

"Yeah."

"You've got the script locked up?"

"The writer."

Bo touched a medallion on his yukata and talked into the air. "Conroy, get me Elmo Zwalt." Bo must have heard something in the bug in his ear, because he replied: "Zwalt. *The Agonizer.*"

"He's my client, Bo. Talk to me and I'll talk to him."

Bo ignored him. He stood, hands at his sides, absolutely still, waiting for the call. Conroy must have had trouble finding Elmo's number. One minute passed, then two. Bo just stood there, frozen in place, eye on an imaginary horizon. Damn, thought Jack, the man is good.

Then Bo heard something. "No. Put it on the speaker."

Elmo's voice rang out with six-track clarity.

"Hello? Hello?"

Jack managed a "Hello, Elmo—" before Bo cut him off.

"Mr. Zwalt, this is Bo. Of Consolidated Creativity. How are you today?"

"I'm fine, Bo."

"Do you know who I am?"

"Sure, Bo, everybody does. You're the most powerful man in Hollywood." Elmo gave a nervous laugh.

"Well, you have written a fine script. You have a very bright future. I would like to help you find that future. Frankly, with my help you would find it faster than you might otherwise."

"That's very kind of you, Bo, but I've already got an agent. I thought he was with you."

"And who might that be?"

"Jack Doberman, sir."

Jack smiled. Hang in there, kid.

A slight vertical line creased Bo's brow. He seemed genuinely perplexed. "I don't think you quite understand what I'm saying, Mr. Zwalt. I'm offering to represent you myself. Personally."

"That's very kind of you, but like I said, I already have an agent. Isn't he with Consolidated?"

"Can you hold for one moment, please?" He touched the hold button on his medallion.

Bo thought this out. If he said Jack was a pirate, wasn't even a registered agent much less a Consolidated man, he might scare the guy off Jack. But then again, he might not. His fabled instincts told him Elmo might not do the logical thing; besides, Elmo was so new to the business, he might actually feel scruples about changing agents. Jack might run off and take this guy with him.

Bo didn't doubt he'd be able to get Elmo back on board eventually. But there was movement here. A major star wanted to make a movie out of this script right now. The important thing was to keep the train on track until it built enough momentum to smash any obstacle in its way.

Besides, Jack was right, he did remind him of himself. The guy had broken all the rules, pulled a major coup in the process. Bo didn't see any reason to set Jack up in business against him. There was always that one-in-a-million chance that the guy was enough like Bo that he'd be starting the next Consolidated. Then Bo's dad could be operating Jack's elevator. No. Better to keep him here, under his own eye and thumb. Then he could play out the Elmo game in its own sweet time without holding up the train.

He turned to Jack. "You told him you were a Consolidated agent?"

"I just want on the team, sir."

"It's Jack. Jack . . ." Bo snapped his fingers and pointed at him.

"Doberman, sir."

Bo punched his medallion. "I have Jack Doberman here in the office with me."

"Hi, Elmo. How's it hangin'?"

"Hi, Jack. Everything's going just like you said."

"Jack confirms that he has agreed to be your agent. But you can rest assured that we are a team, Mr. Zwalt. Our collective talents are at your disposal to ensure that your talent is put to best use."

"That sounds great, Bo."

"Call Jack anytime, tell him what you need, and Consolidated will see that you get it."

"Thanks, Bo."

Bo hung up. He held out his hand to Jack.

"Congratulations. You are now the youngest agent in the history of Consolidated." Consolidated was eleven years old.

Jack grinned and shook his hand. Bo put an avuncular arm around his shoulder and led him to an artfully selected granite boulder. A stream sprang to life beneath the boulder, dropping through lesser agents' offices to the lobby below. Jack told himself it wouldn't be long before he moved into one of the coveted stream suites.

Bo knelt against the boulder, a samurai at rest. As he found his position, the room's brilliant white light magically faded to a warm sunset glow. Jack tried to match Bo's pose and ended up in an uncomfortable half squat. Bo winked conspiratorially.

"So, master agent, what do you think we can get for your script?"

"I figure with Klaus's firm commitment it's worth three and a half million. Let's ask four."

Bo smiled. He liked this kid. "What about a director?"

"I say we make the script deal first."

Bo's smile vanished. "You're holding out on me."

"Bo, Bo—"

Bo cut Jack off. "Don't tell me—he wants to direct," said Bo, laughing.

"You don't understand, Bo. He really wants to direct. And I'm gonna see he does."

"They all really want to direct, Jack." Bo relaxed against a concealed foam pad. This was going to take longer than he expected. "*Chai,* Conroy."

Tweed-suited Conroy appeared noiselessly on his tabi split-toed socks, bearing a lacquer tray with steaming bowls of Lap-sang souchong.

SIX

It was a piercing clear morning. On a day like this, Homer would usually savor the vista from the top of the hill, at least if he didn't look toward the college: nothing but white mounds, thickly furred with barren, prickly stands of oak and maple and hemlock, and tiers of dark green pine rolling into the distance.

Brave words and sentimental postcards of sleigh rides and sugar maples notwithstanding, most natives loved Vermont in the summer and put up with it the rest of the year. Numbing cold gets tiresome after a month or two. Homer, however, thrived on the muffled solitude, the clean tingle of the limpid air in his nostrils, the burn in his fingertips. Most days he even enjoyed chopping firewood. But Homer hated getting to the top of Mucklinberg Hill before the salt truck.

Derek, the driver of the truck, had been fighting with Bonnie Mamalok again about his route. When they were on the outs he made a point of salting the hill last thing, since Mucklinberg State Junior College lay at the bottom, and Bonnie, when she wasn't chairing the town council, worked there. This didn't bother Bonnie much, since she rode a big-wheeled Bronco shod with Sno-Trak Grabbers, but the four-wheel drive was out in Homer's old Subaru, and though his tires were theoretically snow tires, they'd been driven year-round so long, they were indistinguishable from ordinary radials. They didn't even make that humming sound anymore when he ventured on the interstate.

The hill was a sheet of ice. Homer considered parking and sitting for an hour or so till the sun softened it up, or trekking the last half mile on foot. But he was already late for his meeting with Dean Planck, and he had too much stuff to carry. So he slipped the Subaru into first, holding the shift in place so it wouldn't pop out, and took his foot off the clutch.

The car nosed downhill. For a few yards the tires held, then he floated free. He crunched the car into reverse. The tires whined as the car picked up momentum anyway, so he jammed it back into first and tried to match tire speed to the trees whipping by. He felt the tires not exactly grip, but turn in synch with the countryside as the slipping squeak diminished to a silky whir.

Homer was enjoying himself now. He felt like the pilot of a lunar orbiter, man and machine against the elements, floating along, keeping that whir soft and smooth by judiciously goosing the accelerator as the car picked up speed. He smiled as he keyed up for reentry.

At the bottom, where the hill tapered off, the road took a sharp right turn; just after the turn the driveway to the college went off to the left. Hitting the flatter part of the road, Homer felt his tires, matching orbital speed, cling for a few seconds to the slick surface, long enough for him to throw the car into a controlled slide around the right turn. Floating again, he jammed himself into reverse, and what friction there was skewed the car left, rocketing it through the battered gates of Mucklinberg State Junior College, where it careened to a stop against a stanchion in the parking lot.

The Subaru door opened and Homer put his foot gravely on the ground. "One small step for a man." He noted with satisfaction that the new dent in the Subaru's nose was on top of the dent from last time.

A hot Cambridge design team had shaped Mucklinberg College in the redbrick modernist idiom of the palmy sixties. In the years since, the bricks had sweated mineral salts, turning them patchy white, as if from fungus; when South African sanctions pushed copper to an all-time high, the copper roof had been stripped off and sold, replaced with tar and asphalt. Now the place stood blotchy and bald, its condition a memorial to the new multinational economy and the lack of a Vermont state sales tax.

Homer found its deficiencies vaguely reassuring. They made him feel more like he belonged. It wasn't that he felt incompetent, but it was comfortable to know he could relax and do his work without a bunch of high-powered types chasing after his job. It was the only conceivable work within a hundred miles of his farm.

The college had been laid out with the imperial bureaucracy

of a growing education system in mind. Homer trod once-pol-
ished concrete floors that led through a drained secretarial pool
past barren lairs of minor functionaries, to where Bonnie sat
guarding Dean Planck's office. She was a square woman in a
helmet haircut, typing away, cursing the gloves on her hands.
The building was a heat sieve. In these tight times it was kept at
a nominal fifty-five degrees, but in the mornings or when it was
cloudy you could see your breath. Homer's came in plumes
from the door.

"Uh, Bonnie, think you're gonna work things out with Derek
sometime soon?"

"Sonofabitch would rather paint than work. Claims he needs
the morning light. I told him choose between life and art, or salt
the fucking roads before the fucking sun comes up." The phone
rang and Bonnie answered it. "Dance department. Hang on."
Homer liked Bonnie, but her energy and authority filled him
with awe. There was nothing much Planck could do to Homer
except fire him, but Bonnie handled everything from vending
machine refunds to complaints of sexual harassment. She typed
a quick line and cursed.

"You should try cutting the fingers off those gloves."

"My nails'd fall off. The capillaries are rusted shut." She
jerked her thumb at a closed door. "Plankton's waiting for
you." Another line rang. She picked it up. "Film department.
Hang on." She returned to her typewriter.

Homer found the dean huddled over his electric heater reading
a deconstructivist film journal. Gloveless, he noticed. Mack
Planck was doughy, a TV weatherman gone to seed, but he was
tough.

Homer held out a sheaf of papers. "Here, Mack: 'Film Production for Television,' 'Video Production for Television,' and
'Film and Video Production for Television.' I thought I sent you
copies a month ago."

Planck ignored the offering. "You did."

"So what's the crisis?"

"Those are the same lesson plans you gave me last year."

"I'm teaching the same courses—"

"You always teach the same courses."

"I always give you the same lesson plans."

Mack snorted. "Don't you get bored doing the same thing over and over?"

"Not particularly." The truth was, Homer never worried whether he was bored or not. It was his job. He got to be with people, which he liked, and he earned enough to keep the farm going. Well, not going, exactly, since it wasn't really a farm, but enough to keep it from falling apart. "An actor'll play Shakespeare year after year."

"This isn't Shakespeare. This is teaching kids not to point a vidicon tube at a bright light."

"They learn that the first week."

Mack's voice took on a frustrated edge. "Dammit, you're a smart young man. You should be beating down my door with new ideas."

"I don't understand, Mack. You've never brought this up before."

"These are parlous days, Homer. Innovate or die. That's the message of the times."

"But you keep saying we're broke."

"That's the point! New ideas create new revenue. Look at the Department of Media-Meteorology. We didn't even have one when I came here, now we're number one in the country."

"Aren't we still the only one?"

"The point is, we've got more weathermen on the air that any college in the country, and that didn't happen all by itself. I made it happen. Do you know how?"

"No."

"I looked around. I asked myself what in God's name we had going for us in this godforsaken frozen hellhole. First I saw nothing but ice and rocks and pine sap. Kids whose biggest ambition was to stay warm. I got discouraged, sure, but I didn't give up. I said to myself, there has to be something, some one thing I had going for me. And there it was! Staring me right in the face!"

He waited. Homer looked blank.

"The weather! We get more weather in a month than Los Angeles gets in a decade!" He clapped Homer on the back. "It's out there, waiting to be found. All it takes is vision! Look around! Come back with a winner." And he pushed Homer out the door.

Homer must have looked exceedingly confused, because Bonnie stopped typing and eyed him sympathetically. Homer found this disconcerting. Bonnie wasn't long on sympathy. She never let emotions get in the way of her work.

"Do I have vision, Bonnie?"

"Vision? What do you need vision for?"

"I'm supposed to come up with a revolutionary new class. Something that'll put us on the map and save the department."

"Spineless worm."

Homer looked hurt.

"Not you. Plankton." Bonnie rummaged through some papers on the desk. "I have the budget for next semester. We've been cut twenty percent." She found a sheet and tossed it to Homer. "Plankton's decided you're the twenty percent."

Homer looked at the sheets of numbers. He didn't see his name on it anywhere. "What about Meerschaum? He's not even trimmed."

"Come on. Plankton plays racquetball with him twice a week. Besides, critical studies doesn't cost anything. It's just a room and some chairs. You're a high-overhead item."

"But what will happen to . . . what about all the equipment and tape and stuff?"

"Plankton's phasing out the film side, folding video into media-meteorology."

"If I can come up with something really good, maybe Planck'll be able to find the dough."

"That's a crock, Homer. All that vision crap's just his chickenshit way of trying to make you feel responsible for his dirty work." Bonnie patted his arm compassionately. " 'You don't need a weatherman to know which way the wind blows.' " At least now he knew why she was being so nice.

Homer walked back to his car in shock. Sure enough, the weather had changed. It was leaded over now. There was no chance the ice would melt off Mucklinberg Hill. He'd have to wait for Derek to show up with the salt truck. Or the sun to come out. Whichever came first.

SEVEN

The Pacific loomed pale and pastel as Jack's Mercedes hurtled off the Santa Monica Freeway and on up the coast. Elmo was slouched down riding shotgun. Jack wanted to tell him to get his fucking feet off the dash, but he knew when to shut up. Elmo was in deep thought, and Jack had learned it wasn't a good move to break him out. It could make him sulk. If Elmo sulked now, it could ruin the whole game.

Besides, the Mercedes was leased anyway, and it was a fuckin' E class 300. He wouldn't have it for long. He'd demanded an S500, figuring they'd give him a 420, but Bo had hung tough and he'd had to settle. At least it wasn't C class. But Bo knew he'd have walked if they'd tried to force a fuckin' tin toy yuppie jerkmobile down his throat.

The negotiation had been a motherfucker. Still, he'd done about as well as anyone could. They were going to submit Klaus and *The Agonizer* as a fixed-price package to the majors— Klaus's next picture, take it or leave it, forty-eight hours to respond. He'd made Bo ask a million more for the script than he'd wanted to, and lock in Elmo as director. Sort of. All Elmo had to do was get Klaus's okay.

He wondered if Elmo knew what a long shot that was. Klaus must've really gone for the script, because he didn't rule out Elmo right off the bat. Maybe he was going along with the Elmo idea until the script was nailed down and then he'd can him. Maybe Bo told him to play it that way. That's what he'd tell him if he was Bo.

He'd pointed all this out to Elmo, to cover his own ass, but Elmo had been remarkably serene. "Just get me in a room with Klaus. Let me tell him my movie. Once I've laid it out for him, he'll have to have me." Elmo's attitude made Jack very nervous.

The pisser was, Elmo'd hung tough on Jack's "you don't direct, you don't owe me shit" pitch. Jack had been counting on

27

Bo to bail him out of that, since it meant a few hundred grand less for the agency, but Bo'd taken to the idea. He'd used it as a tourniquet to squeeze Jack. "You're the super-agent," he said, "make him director or face the consequences." And then he made him take the E300. Christ. Everyone knew Bo got started by offering a few key clients commission-free service, to get the ball rolling. But this was different.

When they passed Topanga Feed and Supply, Jack took a chance and worked on Elmo a little.

"Elmo?"

"Yeah?" Elmo dragged his sneaker as he sat up, leaving a crescent smear on the passenger-side air bag.

"Elmo, can I give you some tips on how to handle Klaus?"

"I'm fine, thanks. I've got it all worked out."

"What's your angle?"

"I don't want to talk about it. It's like a performance. I've got to get up for my performance." Elmo slumped back in the seat and focused inward.

At Broad Beach, Jack parked on the road. He hadn't seen Klaus since his messenger ploy and figured it should stay that way until things firmed up. Elmo got out of the car, clutching his storyboard in a black portfolio. He would have headed off without a word, but Jack grabbed him by the arm.

"Remember. The guy's a movie star. He didn't get there by being wrong a lot. Listen to him." Elmo just smiled and gave him the thumbs-up sign. Jack hung on. "This is a date, Elmo. You've gotta seduce him. Be charming. Say yes. Whatever he wants, say yes. Get him into bed and worry about the rest later."

"No problem, Jack."

"Swear to me!"

"Don't worry about a thing."

When Elmo'd crossed the street, Jack turned up Lou Reed full blast on the CD and tried to pray. Trouble was, he didn't know who to pray to.

The Norwegian houseboy led Elmo into the glass cage living room. Elmo liked the stark modernist look, the waves rolling in beyond the deck, the trafficlike pounding of the surf. He ran a finger along the velvety nubs of the corrugated cardboard coffee table. Klaus had taste. He felt even better choosing him for *The Agonizer.*

The sliding glass doors were shut. Out on the deck he caught the naked back and oiled legs of the most perfect woman he'd even seen, but he didn't let that distract him. He knew he'd see a lot more like her soon enough. The houseboy'd said Klaus was swimming and he didn't know when he'd be back. Elmo wanted to lay out the pictures while he still had time. He pushed the coffee table against the sofa to give himself more room.

Elmo opened his portfolio and knelt on the asphalt floor. He laid out the pictures one by one, squaring them up with care. In spite of himself, Elmos was excited at the thought that in a matter of minutes he would be telling his movie to Klaus Frotner, a man he'd never met, but whom he felt he understood better than his own father. Although he'd just written the words Klaus would speak in his next movie, Elmo couldn't shake the feeling that Klaus, not writers, gave voice in his films, that Klaus really was the man Elmo saw in his movies, strong, terse, and bold, conduit and embodiment of Elmo's rawest macho fantasies. The thought that Klaus would soon be listening carefully to Elmo's concoctions, soberly discussing them, was heady tonic. Surf pounding in his head, Elmo lovingly laid out the deft, expressive drawings on the very asphalt Klaus trod. The India ink lines took on a massive obsidian sheen. The asphalt melted away.

Peace flooded Elmo as he entered the Zone. The Zone was why he wrote, really. Land of the Breakthrough. Every day at his typewriter he'd try to will himself into the Zone, with ritual coffee-drinking and pencil-sharpening and crap-taking. If he was lucky, after an hour or two of torment he'd feel the comfortable slide into his own head, and find peace, blind to the world until he'd exhausted the brain chemicals that fueled the state. Here he was master, creator and consumer of his own wonders; here there was no barrier between himself and his creations, not the slightest delay between impulse and image.

Elmo was god, or, rather, a pantheon of gods, Erato, Ares, and Eros, and Hephaestus at the forge, smashing, shaping, fucking, soaring, slipping, sinking into dark terrors, crashing through crystalline worlds.

Elmo pored over his drawings, and experienced his movie as never before. The movie in his head had always felt real in its own way, but he'd always been aware it was locked inside his brain. Now the story unfolded all about him in bold, bright color and piercing detail.

Elmo saw Klaus jump ship from the Amazon river freighter, elude the crocodiles, and crawl into the forest, where he lay naked and half dead, laced with welts from the gunrunner's pistol-whipping. He saw the Xavanti children discover him, and mistake the welts for tribal markings of a mythic tribe; he saw Klaus nursed back to health in their compound, under the suspicious eye of the healer-sorcerer Itangi; he saw Klaus, strong again, naked as the rest of them, strangle an enemy with his own bowstring.

A large drop of water landed on Klaus with a "plop," turning his biceps into a runny, tearlike blob.

"Make yourself at home."

Elmo looked up to see Klaus looming above him, bare-chested, primeval, a towel girding his loins. He flinched, then huddled protectively over his drawings. "You're dripping."

Klaus pulled back. "Sorry."

"That's all right." Elmo felt an instinctive pang of rage, being ripped from the Zone like that. He wanted to strangle the guy, or better yet shut him out and dive back in. With wrenching effort he pasted a smile on his face and held out his hand. "An honor to meet you."

Klaus didn't miss the flicker of fury that rippled across Elmo's brow. It made him wary. He knew the type. Head-up-his-ass dreamer. "Mind if I sit down?"

Elmo laughed nervously. "No. Of course not."

Klaus pushed the coffee table away from the sofa, watching the pale, scrawny guy scurry to get his drawings out of the way.

"Great place you have here. That surf sound really gets in the blood."

"Like it? I'll turn it up." The beautiful woman had entered from the deck. She was wearing a Brazilian thong and nothing else, her breasts very round and very firm, the small, perfect nipples standing up like brass percussion caps. She adjusted a dial on the wall and hissing surf boiled into the room. Now Elmo could tell it came from quad speakers. "Stereo mikes under the house," she said.

"Christ, Inga, will you put something on?" Klaus tossed her his towel, revealing his own string bikini. She draped the towel casually over her shoulders as she settled next to Klaus on the sofa and continued. "You've written a first-rate script, Mr. Zwalt. Well-structured, and it really delivers. A Klaus Frotner film has to have a certain pace, it has to build a certain way, and you've caught that perfectly." She smiled, showing finely sculpted teeth. Klaus took the cue.

"I wanted to talk to you about the girl, though," said Klaus. "She needs work. She's plenty ballsy. I like that. But you gotta make her more vulnerable. We've gotta feel a warm heart beating under that tough skin."

Elmo looked at Inga and wondered how vulnerable she was. Not as vulnerable as she wanted to be. "She's a nun. She's been raped. That's pretty vulnerable."

"But she kills the guy with a broken bottle."

"You'll see," said Elmo. "We'll get the right woman, she'll have that vulnerable edge. It'll be fine."

"I was thinking Inga would be good for the role."

Elmo looked at the two of them. He knew what Jack would say—agree, agree, worry about it later—but looking at those two nearly perfect, nearly naked bodies, he knew it wasn't going to be that easy. Klaus's guard was up, and she—well, she was queen bitch goddess perfecto, but vulnerable she wasn't. She wasn't in the movie in his head.

Klaus read his look and didn't like it. "You have a problem with that?"

Elmo had only one hope. Drag them into the Zone. That's what he'd been planning all along, and that's what he had to do. "Look, Klaus, why don't I just tell you the movie from the beginning? We can talk about the other stuff later."

"I read the script. You don't have to tell it to me."

"Let me show you the storyboards. I'll kind of act it out as we go along."

Klaus liked storyboards. It was reassuring to be told exactly what to do. But this guy was beginning to piss him off. "No. Let's talk about the nun."

Elmo ignored him. He started spreading the pictures again. "Just listen—"

"No. You listen. I've done eighteen pictures. Before I could call the shots I did them with all kinds of directors. Drunks and fag lechers and bullies and burnouts. But the worst kind was the know-it-all. Know-it-alls don't listen, see, and they turn into screamers on the set, and they always end up fucking it all to hell."

"But let me lay it out for you. It's beautiful—"

Klaus began to gather up drawings as fast as Elmo put them down. Elmo grabbed his wrist. He shook Elmo off. "Out."

Elmo stared at this massive, square-jawed man clutching his movie in a fist and showing him the door. Until then he'd never doubted the outcome of the meeting. It was just another step in making his movie. Now he knew he'd never had a chance. This Klaus wasn't the tough but fair guy in the movies. This Klaus was taking his movie and telling him to fuck off.

"Give me my movie!" Elmo lunged for his drawings. Klaus whipped them out of reach. Elmo took a swing at Klaus. Klaus went into action.

Jack lay on the beach, basking like a lizard in the hot sun. A wave rolled gently under him, wetting his ass. He arched and the wave ebbed. Drawing back, its cold fingers gripped his ankle. He tugged his foot and looked down. The wave was dragging him out to sea. He clawed burning sand. Nothing to grab. A pelican honked—

Jack was jolted awake by a loud rapping noise and a bloody hand smearing his windshield. The honk was Elmo, trying to say Jack's name through a nose the size of a tangerine.

Jack swung the door open. Elmo slid in, groaning and cradling his ribs. Jack grabbed a handful of Kleenex and went to work on the nose, but Elmo pushed him away. "I'b fibe."

"Want to tell me about it?"

"Doh."

Jack didn't say anything. What was there to say? It was painted in blood on the poor schlub's face. Klaus and Elmo had "creative differences," and from the look of Elmo, they weren't the sort an agent could patch up. How could a guy so smart be so stupid? God, he hated being at the mercy of artists.

Jack took Elmo to St. John's Hospital, where they said he had a broken nose and some cracked ribs but was basically okay. Jack had worried Elmo'd want to sue Klaus, and pointed out whatever he'd get wouldn't be worth what he'd lose queering the script deal, but Elmo hadn't been interested one way or the other. He'd sunk into a silent funk. So Jack drove him back to the Chateau, telling Elmo how he'd be able to move into Bel Air or the Palisades in a couple of weeks, and helped him upstairs to his room.

Jack spent the rest of the day trying to get through to Klaus. Nothing worked. Bodyguards chased him off the beach, and when he parked outside the house for an all-night vigil, Malibu cops escorted him back to the Santa Monica line.

Next day, Jack reluctantly returned to Consolidated. He didn't have an angle on this yet, and he didn't want to deal with Bo until he did. But he figured he'd better put on a positive face, act like everything was okay until he could work out his next move. He knew he didn't have much time.

He didn't have any time. Consolidated security met him at the door with a terse note in a slim envelope, telling him his services were no longer required.

The garage wouldn't give him his Mercedes back, so Jack took a taxi to the Chateau. He pounded on Elmo's door until Elmo opened it. Elmo was dressed the way Jack had left him, same black T-shirt stiff with blood. He must have slept in the damn thing. Elmo let Jack take him into the bedroom, strip him, and stick him under the shower. He stood on one leg under the stream, head twisted to one side to keep the water off the bulbous plastic-wrapped splint on his nose. Looked like a mangy flamingo at the zoo.

Jack dried him off and helped him into clean clothes and gave him the pep talk of his life. How he shouldn't let the bastards get him down. They still controlled the script. Fuck Klaus. Fuck Consolidated. They hadn't put it out to bids yet. Take it to Willis, take it to Schwarzenegger, take it to Mel Gibson, they'll all want it. Jack had promised Elmo would direct, and by God he would. He'd see.

Elmo listened patiently but didn't say anything. Finally he looked straight into Jack's eyes and said matter-of-factly, "I'm going with Bo."

"But what about our deal, Elmo?"

"What about it? You promised I'd direct. You said Klaus would be in it."

"Did I take a swing at him? Was that my fault?"

Elmo stared at Jack, stony. "You broke your promise."

This was taking the worst possible turn. Jack stuck his face so close to Elmo's, his nose brushed Elmo's cast. "Look at me, Elmo. I do not hear the word 'no.' 'No' is not in my vocabulary. As far as I'm concerned, I'm still representing you."

"I told you, Bo's my agent."

"Fuck Bo. I wasn't getting paid fuck-all for repping you anyway. You can roll over and let them fuck you in the ass on this, but I'm not. I'm gonna get you that directing gig."

"But you're not my agent—"

"I don't give a fuck. I'm getting you that gig."

"What are you going to do?"

"Just answer me this—if I get you that gig, will you be my client?"

"Directing Klaus?"

"Whoever the fuck you want."

Elmo shrugged, then winced from the pain in his ribs. "Sure, Jack. That was the deal. But I don't see what you can do about it."

Jack patted Elmo gently on the shoulder with a confident grin. "That's all I want to hear." Then he headed downstairs to catch the bus on Vine, wishing he knew what he was going to do next.

EIGHT

The farm had all the charm of a failed housing development. A half-mile washboard ribbon of frozen dirt ended in a rutted staging area which Homer's Subaru shared with a rusty snowmobile, a gravity pump, and a puke-green propane tank. The house itself, a slippery trudge away on the nearest hillock, was a living catalogue of cost-effective building materials familiar to slum dwellers from Soweto to Rio, but less appropriate for this wintry clime—plywood, particle board, and corrugated fiberglass, heaped in ungainly piles around a tiny core cabin hewn in more idealistic times from logs of local pine. Unlike the shacks of the favela, real glass paned the windows, but from the outside it was impossible to tell, since the windows were double-glazed with sheets of polyurethane held in place by duct tape.

The door opened and Homer skidded down the walk toting an ax and an empty five-gallon water bag. He didn't bother with the pump, which was bled for the winter, but went straight to the snowmobile. He gave the rip cord a fruitless yank, then another. When five minutes of furious whipping wouldn't get the beast to kick over, he took his ax and his plastic bag, and telling himself he should return to the house for his snowshoes, headed off across the open field toward the creek. Every couple of steps a boot broke through the crust, leaving him up to the knee in soft snow. Raising the foot, he'd have to break back out of the crust; wrenching free, often as not, sent his other boot through to the knee. His tracks looked like a series of small explosions, boot prints through a mine field.

Homer's breathing came hard. Even with the thermometer in the teens, it was hot work. Yet, as he lumbered along, Homer found himself humming a tune: "I've been working on the railroad." This wasn't like talking to Dean Planck. He could see the point of this. He needed water; he was getting it. Walking over his own field to his own stream.

Near the stream, the going got tougher. Tiers of springy wil-

lows, bent under snow, blocked his way. A boot would catch in
the tangled mass. Tugging would release elastic branches into
his face, lashing his cheeks and packing gobbets of ice down his
collar.

He bulled through to the creek and paused to catch his
breath. The snow inside his parka was melting into his sweat,
forging long underwear and wool shirt into a single soggy mass.
But his feet were still warm in the felt-lined boots, and the satisfying prickle in the tips of his fingers told him he was wearing
good warm gloves on a damn cold day.

The sun was gone over the hill. Snow bounced blue twilight
up into the trees, suspending them, shadowless, plum gray
above the lilac fields and the frozen stream that glowed with a
lavender sheen. Homer found it deeply relaxing to study the
implacable geometry of the place, the shapes molded and sited
by simple, absolute laws he would never understand. He'd like
to make a movie about this stretch of stream, he thought. Follow its changes over a year. He could sit out here day after day
and it would count as working.

Homer woke from his squatting reverie when his outboard
boot slipped, skidding onto the ice with all his weight, and
crashed through an air bubble into water moving too fast to
freeze. He shrieked and cursed and shoved the plastic bag into
the hole. At least he wouldn't have to use the ax.

While Homer thawed out, Frances and Ham cooked dinner.
Frances was a tall, erect woman, old enough to be Homer's
mother; in fact, she was his mother. Ham was Homer's grand-
dad. Frances and Ham both cooked, because Frances was a veg-
etarian and refused to prepare meat, and Ham needed meat or it
wasn't a meal. Frances and Ham divided up the propane range,
two burners each, and both boiled water and made soups on the
woodstove to save gas. Occasionally Ham would use Frances's
spoon or get bacon grease on her skillet, but over the years
they'd worked out a modus vivendi, and between the two, Homer always had enough to eat, if he wasn't too picky about veg
or nonveg. All he had to do was draw the water. And clean up.

During the Nixon years, Abby, Homer's father, had come out
from Boston to find a new, truer life in the woods, and in Mucklinberg he'd met his soulmate in Frances, a local girl of like

mind. Frances had been a hippie, but a media hippie. She wasn't one of those spoiled, big-city, middle-class kids disaffected with their parents' materialistic values, looking to return to the land. Her father, Ham, was a scion of the Green Mountain State, a sixth-generation Vermonter. The biggest city she'd seen before she met Homer's father was Burlington. But she'd known all about the hippie revolution, she'd seen *Monterey Pop* and the TV coverage of the march on Washington and the days of rage in Chicago. When Abby wanted to start a fledgling commune, she'd volunteered Ham's land to do it. Ham had bitched and moaned, but he wasn't about to call the cops to chuck out his own daughter, even if she was building a shantytown on his property.

Ham complained, but in truth the newcomers, the ones that stuck out the winter at least, were closer to his own way of thinking than the local kids who dreamed of running off to B.U. on a hockey scholarship. Sticking it out is relative, though, and by the second thaw communal friction and remorseless cold had reduced the noble experiment to a decent well and a pile of warping lumber. By the time Homer was born, Frances and Abby were a conventional binary couple, homesteading on Ham's place.

Abby was a man of limited experience but ample vision and energy. Ham used to say he got tired just watching him. When the commune fell apart, Abby decided he'd build his dream home with his own hands. Abby drew plans for an elaborate, multistory house, with running water and central heating and huge Thermopane picture windows and a double-height living room. He spent one backbreaking summer digging and pouring foundations. That winter, felling trees, one fell on him.

Frances and the baby moved back in with Ham, but she'd refused to abandon Abby's dream. With Ham's help she'd pieced together what she could on the foundations, and when Ham's roof collapsed one particularly snowy winter, they'd all made the place their home. Fortunately for Frances, living room and loft had been completed before the pine tree buried Abby. They were built of squared tree trunks, reasonably well chinked, though the double-glazing had never been installed, and rents in the plastic sheeting let fingers of cold air reach through the windows into the room.

Frances kept Abby's majestic plans prominently tacked on the wall for inspiration, but in twenty-three years they'd managed only to rough out the other spaces with scavenged building materials. That worked all right for a month or two in summer, but most of the year the add-ons were too cold even for raccoons and foxes. For all her talk, Frances wasn't much of a builder, and Ham didn't see the point. They'd all been too busy earning a living to earn construction money. Anyway, they couldn't agree on which major project to undertake first. Raise and roof a real bedroom or two? Pipe in running water? Electricity? Heating? Pave the drive? Double-glaze? Finish the kitchen? The projects all hung in the air, to be completed next summer, summer after summer after summer, until they'd become so accustomed to what they had that they might have actually resented any change. Homer in particular. This was the only home he'd ever known. Though he would look at his father's plans and dream of an easier, more elegant life, he was living the only way he'd ever lived, and he knew he was where he belonged.

That evening Ham and Frances were giving each other the silent treatment. Ham had discovered a letter in the mail from a junior college in Arizona, rejecting Frances's bid to be their women's basketball coach—her last real job being PE teacher and pan-athletic sports maven at Mucklinberg College in the pre-cutback years. Frances was pissed off that Ham opened her mail, and Ham was hurt she'd want to run off to Arizona. Neither one should have been surprised—when Ham got to the mail first he always opened everything, and Frances was constantly scheming ways to flee to warmer climes—but such behavior would always spark a sharp exchange, and then the two would clam up for the evening.

This suited Homer just fine. It meant they wouldn't grill him on what he was going to do now that Planck had as good as given him the ax. He knew what they'd say, and he didn't need to hear it, thank you very much. Ham would go on for half an hour about how it took grit to make a living in this state, and how Homer should have learned a practical skill like finish carpentry or foundation work instead of fooling around with film, because then at least they'd have a place to live they could call a proper house, and Homer'd have work besides. Frances would get on his back about sending out résumés to places like Florida and Texas, with growing economies, relatively speaking, and no fuel bills.

After a sepulchral dinner, Frances went outside and fired up the generator so she could watch some TV. The furry hills soaked up whatever faint signals were beamed their way from Burlington, so all she could get on the best of nights was a grainy image of channel two, the local CBS affiliate. But Wednesdays it didn't bother her, because Wednesday was *Entertainment Tonight* night. Frances liked to watch the latest gossip about the aristocracy of beauty and talent. Ham would mutter about the impending end of civilization and bitch about generator whine, but Homer enjoyed it in an anthropological way. It reminded him why he was glad he lived far from hustle and glitter of all description.

Tonight the hostess posed dramatically atop a rushing superhighway. She pointed to a scummy pile of decaying masonry and shouted over traffic noise about a poor slob who'd lived in that hellhole for a year while writing a script he'd just sold for three million dollars. Homer couldn't have lived there for a week. He wondered if the guy's hearing was permanently damaged, and if it was, if the guy thought going deaf was worth three million dollars.

A strangled jingle, almost buried in generator jangle, intruded on the roar of video traffic. For a moment Homer thought the generator had thrown a bearing. Then he remembered the telephone. Ham said when the phone rang it sounded like someone throttling Tinker Bell.

Homer had installed it last summer, bootleg. He'd spliced into the line at the road, and unspooled half a mile of cable that dropped off his friend Nat's phone-company truck through brush and fallen trees to the farm. Now that Ham was getting older, it had seemed like a good idea. It was kind of reassuring, when he and Frances were both away from the farm, to know Ham wasn't completely cut off. The problem was, squirrels liked the taste of plastic insulation and the tingle of low-voltage phone current on their incisors. In summer the line was often as not chewed through in a couple of places and out of service. In winter it was buried under four feet of snow, and relatively safe; on the other hand, the squirrels were hungrier.

If it was ringing, the phone must be working. Homer picked it up, pleased and a little excited. Since the phone wasn't exactly legal, few people had their number, and those that had knew not to count on getting through. When the phone rang, therefore, it was likely someone they knew well with a matter of import. Unless it was the woman Ham met in Burlington, but she didn't call until the bars closed. And Ham swore he'd kissed her off.

It had to be one of a couple of people, but Homer still couldn't recognize the caller. Squirrels had dined on enough insulation so the voice was buried under surging layers of static. He could tell it was a woman, though. Homer shouted at her to speak up, and she shouted back, until he could just make her out. It was an interesting effect, he thought. Like a drowning person yelling over storm waves breaking on a gravel beach.

"John!" The voice said. "John!"

"No!" Homer shouted back. "Homer! Homer!"

"John! John!"

"Homer! Homer!" Homer thought it must be a wrong number, but as he was hanging up he realized the voice wasn't saying "John" exactly. "John? John?" he screamed.

The voice cranked up a couple of decibels. Now it sounded suspiciously like "Job! Job!"

"Job?! Job?!"

"Job! Job!" That was it! He pressed his ear closer to the phone and shouted: "Job?! Who?! What?!"

The voice screamed a phone number, numeral by numeral, and he screamed it back to be sure. When he shouted for more info, he heard something like "Fuck this!" and the line went dead. Frances and Ham were staring at him.

"I think I've been offered a job."

"What?" "By who?" Ham and Frances tended to talk at the same time.

He waved the phone number he'd written down. "I don't know, but I've got their number. Maybe I'd better give them a call."

"Why talk to them if they can't hear you?" said Francis while Ham was saying, "What are you going to tell them? You're calling from Antarctica?"

Frances turned back to her program. Homer pocketed the number and joined her. She poked him in the ribs. "Maybe it's Hollywood calling."

Ham cackled. "Maybe they want to offer you a million dollars."

A woman was being interviewed now. Even through the electronic snow Homer could tell she was exceptionally beautiful, with the aquiline nose, wide, full mouth, and regal skull of a fifties high-fashion model. The bones bespoke extraordinary sophistication, but the eyes, ah, the eyes were the eyes of a startled fawn, looking out on the world with disarming childlike wonder. Homer was entranced. He strained for her name: Annette Foray. She was an executive at Studio Pictures.

Annette spoke with all the grace and poise her appearance promised. She was delighted Studio had bought this script. It was a lot of money, but it was a very good script. A good script was the secret to a good movie, and people went to good movies in droves and droves, so this particular script was actually a bargain. She said it with such a dazzling smile that Homer was convinced he'd been told a fundamental secret of moviemaking, and sure that she'd made a very good bargain indeed when she bought this first-time script for a paltry three million dollars.

NINE

Annette was draped over a deco chair, staring at the Chief's well-tailored back, planning her next move. Darius stood in deep carpet, hands clasped behind, dwarfed by a huge window flanked with massive arras drapes, peering out at the parking lot. His office was designed by an Oscar-winning art director back in the thirties, when Studio Pictures was synonymous with Hollywood; walls rose to a ceiling beyond eyeshot and light cascaded from hidden coves above.

This was a room built by giants for giants. Under normal conditions Darius Fo was an imposing man, tall, large of girth, more barrel-chested than obese—though fine dining had puffed out his thighs and thickened his jaw—but the room shrank him; Annette always thought that here in his office he seemed to be not a titan of industry but a supporting actor in a Depression-era picture about the fabulously rich—the hero's befuddled father, or the wicked pol in sheep's clothing, or the kindly banker who won't make the hero's loan.

Annette, on the other hand, was leading lady all the way. Immaculate in a Hepburn-style man-cut suit, hair coiffed to subtly enhance the contours of her shapely chin, she exuded star presence, perched on the edge of the overstuffed streamlined sofa, tapping her teeth with a Mont Blanc pen.

She wanted this one. It was a lifetime ago that Studio had been at the top of the heap—the last year they'd made twenty pictures was the year she was born—and over the previous couple of decades Studio had been bought and sold in a wily series of de-accessionings that stripped it of its film library, its fabled props, wardrobe department and sets, and most of its back lot, until all that remained was this single imposing office structure, a commissary redolent with Hollywood history, and a clutch of soundstages. Darius Fo had swept in on the latest influx of capital, with the most recent mandate to reclaim the glory days, but all he'd put in the pipeline so far was a wacko-in-the-army film, a circus picture, and a dog picture. Now Bo himself had thrown them this dynamite Klaus action number. Well, thrown was an exaggeration. Bo'd known that Darius was desperate to stake his claim as a serious player, and he'd squeezed him for a million more than the rest of the market would bear. (The final price had been four point two million, but at Darius's insistence they admitted only to three.) This was Darius's roll of the dice. And for all the talk of deep pockets, Annette knew he didn't have the wherewithal to roll them twice.

With so little action and so much at stake, Darius would be reluctant to interpose Annette between himself and the making of *The Agonizer*. But if it was hers and it saved Studio, which it just might, she'd be right where she wanted to be. On the fast track to running one of these places. Not bad for a Vassar girl. Attend a Seven Sister, run one of the seven majors. She liked the sound of that.

And when you thought about it, she really belonged in the middle of the process. She was a people person—that's why Darius had hired her. She specialized in managing the difficultly talented, and success here would depend on keeping Klaus happy. Who could do that better than she? But bringing Darius around was another matter. Darius didn't like to be pushed. If he sensed how much she wanted it, he'd screw her out of it.

Now was her moment. They were picking a producer for the project. If Darius went with one of his old cronies, the guy would give her a fatherly pat on the behind and tell her to play elsewhere. If he picked one of the younger, more pliable types, she knew she could make herself indispensable.

She had a list of producers in front of her, but she wasn't looking at it. She had brought it in to appear thorough, but they both knew all the names. It was a short list. Everyone on it had been hired by Darius in the past three months, and they were all getting at least a third of a million dollars a year from Studio, so far for doing mostly nothing.

"So," she said. "What about Milton?" Milton was an old fart. Leading with Milton would show she wasn't being self-serving. And Darius would never go for the first name anyway. "Milton handled *Death Squad* very well, and that had some of the same elements."

"Elements?" Darius made the word sound vaguely disturbing.

"Klaus Frotner. And difficult locations."

"Um." Darius waved his hand noncommittally.

Better toss out another crony. "There's Herman. Mr. Taste Police. He's not afraid to get in the director's face if it's not good enough."

"I suppose so."

"Freddie, then." One last old guy. "Freddie did those Schwarzenegger pictures. He's your biggest overhead item."

Not a word this time, just a wave. Good. Time to go for it. "Francine, maybe?" She could work with Francine. "Francine's a tiger. She'd deliver."

"Think so?"

"She always has."

Nothing.

"Wesley? Wesley would kill for this." If Annette got him this, he'd kill for Annette.

Darius just rocked back and forth. Annette hated this game. It reminded her of Battleship. She had to drop names on Darius, and he'd tell her when she scored. Darius didn't want her suggestions, he wanted her to read his mind. Then it would be her idea, and she'd be responsible if it didn't work out. Unless, of course, he really didn't have a clue, which was always possible, in which case she was working for a moron. Or he could be leading her on, acting like a moron to make her drop her guard. You never knew with Darius. Nobody knew. She just knew this stupid game had no up side for her.

Darius turned from the window and lay on the sofa, staring at the ceiling with his feet toward Annette. The soles of his shoes had the polished look of leather right out of the box. He must never wear them beyond the thick pile carpet of this room. Unless he put on a new pair every morning. He wiggled them at her. Time for another name. She was nearing the end of the list. She threw out a long shot. "Jason?" Jason was handling the dog movie. He had a couple of teen comedies and a slasher pic to his credit.

The soles clicked together. "Hmmm . . ."

Annette knew that "hmmm." It meant she'd hit his aircraft carrier. She moved in for the kill. "He's not as experienced as Milton and the rest, but he'll give it a younger spin. Of course we'd have to take him off *Wow Bowser*."

Darius grunted encouragingly.

This was too good to be true. "This picture would put Jason in the Show. He'd run over his grandmother to get it."

Darius looked at her for the first time. She realized she'd used an unfortunate turn of phrase.

"You know what I mean."

Darius nodded vaguely. Darius Fo was rumored to have Asian blood in his family (though Fo was an abbreviation of Forenstein), and while he looked Caucasian in every other way, he had the hint of an epicanthic fold about the eye, which made it difficult to tell his smile from his grimace. She pushed on. "Jason would be an excellent choice. He's smart, he's motivated, and most of all you can count on his complete loyalty. He'll do what you want."

Darius nodded. "Why don't you let him know."

Jackpot. Annette couldn't believe her luck. Not her first choice, maybe, but there was definitely the potential for a working relationship. And she had to admit it wasn't that dumb a call. Jason would do exactly what Darius wanted.

She regretted her crack about Jason running over his grandmother, though. She'd meant it in a general sense. Darius must have thought she was talking about Helena. Darius's mother, Helena, was a reclusive woman who lived in a cottage on his compound. Darius and his assorted wives had never taken much of an interest in Jason, and Helena had as good as raised him when he wasn't away at prep school.

TEN

Jason Fo shifted into third and the gears ground. Damn. He was used to stick shifts—he'd always disdained automatics, tending toward Porsches and M-series BMWs—but this was the first time he'd driven a car with the shift on the steering column. First time he'd driven a car with cloth seats, for that matter. Was it the first American car he'd driven? No, of course not. There was Jerry's Z-28 and the old T-bird.

Jason was banging along in a dilapidated clunker, feeling very pleased with himself. He was in the right car going to the right place with the right woman by his side. He smiled at Annette, and she smiled back, a radiant rose in the dung heap of the old Ford.

The car had been a brilliant stroke. His secretary, Lisa, had picked it out at Rent-a-Wreck, but it had been his idea. What better way to arrive at an Oxfam fund-raiser than in a car that epitomized the dilemma of the poor and downtrodden of the earth? Walking would have been better, wearing tire-tread sandals, but walking was out of the question in Los Angeles.

Annette had loved it. As one of the principal organizers of this affair, it was important that she arrive in appropriate style. She'd laughed her melodious laugh and pronounced it perfect.

Jason couldn't believe how well things had been going for him lately. If he'd been a Nichiren chanter or a Catholic or some such, he'd have put it down to divine intervention. But he was more inclined to credit Annette. Ever since she'd sent him *The Agonizer* stashed in a basket of designer condiments, his life had positively taken off.

He'd known the script was on the lot, but he hadn't even bothered to throw his hat in the ring. He had a deep distrust of Darius, based on years of experience. Darius would never give him that kind of break. But somehow Annette convinced the guy to give him his shot. He didn't know how she did it. She was awfully persuasive. The most persuasive person he'd ever

46

met. In this town that was saying a lot. She was probably the only person in the whole town who could get his father to assign him *The Agonizer*.

Of course, she wasn't doing it just to make nice. She needed him too. She wanted in on this, and she figured if he was producing it, she'd be part of the mix. He wasn't about to go around her and deal directly with Darius. So there was a synergy here.

And she could help in other ways. That first meeting with Klaus, for example—smart move, taking it in her office, not his trailer. Now that he was producing the Klaus picture, he'd be moving into the main building, switching office space with Wesley, who was taking over *Bowser*, but it would have been really tacky to meet with Klaus in that déclassé environment. The meeting had gone well too. Klaus had been reserved, but Jason had expected that. Klaus had been pleased by his enthusiasm. And Annette's. Klaus had pushed using Inga as the nun, which they could certainly do, but Jason sensed Klaus wasn't as hot about the idea as he pretended. That was something else Annette could follow up on in her tactful way. They were a team. And it would be his name on the movie: Produced by Jason Fo. She could do it all, it was still his name up there. Not that he wanted her to do it all. No sir.

He downshifted manfully. There was a gratifying crunch, then a less pleasing sound: the metallic snap of a cotter pin shearing. The car began to coast.

Annoyed, Jason steered the heap to the curb. "Linkage snapped. I'll have to call a car." Annette's purse was already open and her cell phone out. She smiled sweetly and put on a nasal Lily-Tomlin-as-Ernestine voice. "Number puleeze." He decided to play it cool.

He flipped his wallet and read her the number of the Lithuanian car company that took him to the airport. When it connected, Annette, still in her Geraldine voice, said, "One moment, puleeze. Mr. Jason Fo calling," and handed him the phone.

Jason, trying to match her gay insouciance, asked the dispatcher for the crummiest car they had.

"We have no crummy cars. All cars first class. Washed every day."

"Well, check around. See what you can come up with."

"Moment please."

Jason smiled conspiratorially at Annette. He noticed the hint of a crease between her eyebrows. "Is something the matter?"

"No, no."

"No, no, something's wrong."

She looked at him, thoughtful. "Is there any point in arriving in a beaten-up limo? If we're being driven anyway . . ."

"You're absolutely right." Driving a wreck, that was a statement. Showing up in a ratty limo was just low rent. When the dispatcher got back on the line, Jason ordered a stretch. Then he called Lisa and had the junker towed.

Annette, in her long black gown and killer heels, pranced into the corner 7-Eleven to get them both a Coke. What class. As admiration surged, he was tempted to spring his breakthrough idea for *The Agonizer*. But when he saw her emerge with a paper cup in each hand, he thought not. Better when they were on more of an upper.

They could have driven right on the lot, but Jason stopped the limo at the gate so he and Annette could walk past the paparazzi. They were a glamorous couple. He was built like his father, a large, athletic man, but without his father's enigmatic manner; his open face radiated the boyish enthusiasm of a USC spirit squadder, which he would have been had he not attended Andover and Harvard. He'd considered dressing down for this affair, but in the end rejected it as condescending to the poor, so he dressed as he always did, East Coast all the way, in J. Press lightweight herringbone blazer and gabardine slacks. Less glamorous but more exotic than the conventionally trendy. He thought there was competitive advantage in looking like he'd just come out from the East, and he was probably right. Don't be fooled by my pep squad grin, he was saying, I'm not from Hollywood, I'm from weightier climes.

Annette wore a simple, unpretentious basic black sheath that might have cost fifty dollars but fit her like it cost five thousand. As the two of them left their limo, smiling and waving at friends, the photographers surged forward. The less experienced, seeing they weren't movie stars, quickly turned to other subjects, but the savvier recognized Annette. They entered the lot through a satisfying barrage of exploding strobes.

Inside, uniformed attendants with light-wands in gloved

hands pointed the way to Stage Two. Stage Two was smaller than Stage One, but still impressive. As Studio execs were fond of pointing out, when the firewall between them was thrown open, they formed the largest soundstage in the world. Until yesterday, Stage Two had housed the prime set for the period circus picture that had just wrapped. The set had been a typical Hollywood anachronism, a Belle Epoque three-ring-circus tent. The candy-striped canvas had been struck, as inappropriate to the spirit of the occasion, leaving an acre of packed brown earth against a forty-foot sky-blue backing, baking under fifty silver quartz-halogen suns. It had been Annette's idea to use the stage, and it was, as so much she touched, perfect. In publicity photos it would look as if they were dining in the Kalahari or the Sudan.

The one thousand diners were arrayed symbolically in three tiers, representing the peoples of the world. Six hundred and fifty, representing the two-thirds of the earth's population who could not afford animal protein, had no tables, and ate their rice and beans off tortillas on the ground. Two hundred and fifty, representing the twenty-five percent who could afford meat once a week, ate lamb curry off tin plates on plywood caterer's tables. A hundred unlucky souls, representing the haves of the world, dined on Spago cuisine off Spode and linen. They had considered not feeding a hundred people, to represent the ten percent of the earth's peoples who go to bed hungry every night, but Annette had vetoed the idea. If people weren't fed, they'd just go to a fancy restaurant after, which would destroy the symbolic value of the occasion.

Seating was supposed to be random, but Jason didn't see any movie stars dining off fine china. He did notice, with some satisfaction, a very glum Wesley at the haves table, toying with the heavy silver and looking all the more absurd because he'd donned a djellaba for the occasion.

Wesley brightened considerably—and Jason felt a pang—when Darius, looking entirely unrepentant, sat beside him with his current wife, June. Darius ignored his attempts at conversation, however, and glanced over at Jason—no, not Jason, Annette. Darius gave her the smallest of nods, and Jason realized he must have asked Annette to put him there. Typical. Darius was so used to being a fat cat, he didn't even see the celestial irony of the situation—he'd forgotten there were people out there who never went to Morton's, or who owned only one house. When that happened, you lost your sense of the market-place, and you were as good as dead in the business. Jason found the thought comforting.

He and Annette ate on the floor. They snaked past a row of kettles, where recent immigrants handed them each a tortilla and ladled onto it their meager ration of rice and beans; then they were seated near the sky backing, where they would photo-graph best, beside a clutch of movie stars and the Oxfam repre-sentatives, two gaunt, tense Brits. Jason, who made a practice of reading four papers a day—the *L.A.* and *New York Times,* the *Wall Street Journal,* and *Variety*—put the outsiders at their ease by conversing knowledgeably on the election results in Ban-gladesh and the latest Malaysian breakthrough in genetically engineered rice.

As the Brits warmed to him, Jason felt his face flush with pleasure and his body suffuse with an enveloping glow. He was overcome with the rightness of things. He was at the vortex, the absolute navel of the Hollywood universe, acquitting himself brilliantly, partnered with a gorgeous, regal woman. He was making a splash, and concentric circles of influence and power rippled outward, lapping at the very edges of the room, all the way out to Wesley and Darius, only to recoil back toward the focus, the center of it all, him.

He had Annette to thank for this. He looked at her with a surge of gratitude. Laughing gaily, her slender fingers deftly folded her tortilla. Laugh faded to delicate smile as she took a dainty bite. The tiniest drop of salsa formed on her lower lip. Pursing her mouth slightly, she gently daubed the bead with her exquisite forefinger (napkins being reserved for the rich), then delicately stretched her tongue to lick it up. As tongue touched finger, she caught Jason's eye, and the demure gesture became the promise of something altogether different and more wonder-ful.

When they'd finished their tortillas, Annette rose to speak. The Spago contingent was just receiving its entree, and Annette opened with a quip about execs who have three working break-fasts, and how they could have five if they ate nothing for break-fast like most of the world. It was a brief speech introducing the Oxfam representative, balanced, calm, and to the point. She neatly summed up the peculiarity of their situation, sitting on a soundstage that looked like the Somalian desert, eating rice and beans with their fingers to fight world hunger. "The folks in

Zimbabwe will go to bed just as hungry tonight," she said. "But if our fantasy desert and our mock hunger can make the front pages and the nightly news all over the world, perhaps millions of people who would otherwise ignore the problem will see it in a new light. Hollywood can't feed the starving, but Hollywood can give the world dreams. Why not give the world the dream of a planet without hunger?"

Jason led the thunderous applause. The taller and gaunter of the Englishmen proceeded to drone on for half an hour in a nasal monotone, reciting a withering barrage of statistics about the millions upon millions who constituted the neediest of the earth, and who would almost certainly die without ever seeing a movie. The group at the linen-covered tables, who had dug into their butterfly shrimp and racks of lamb with gusto during Annette's comments, backed off their food as the grim facts mounted. All save Darius, who, Jason noted triumphantly, continued to dine with stolid epicurean precision.

Jason stretched his legs, cradled a glass of white wine, and gazed contentedly out the smoked window of the long limo as it negotiated the narrow curves of Laurel Terrace on its way up to Annette's place on Wonderland Avenue. This is as good as it gets, he thought. Now to spring it.

Smiling his most boyish smile, he poured Annette some more wine and lifted his glass: "To *The Agonizer*. May it leap off the screen as it leaps off the page."

They clinked glasses. He went on. "We haven't had time to talk directors. But I've been digging around."

She eyed him seriously over the rim of her glass. "What have you turned up?"

"The usual suspects are all tied up. Cameron has his deal at Fox, Ridley's on a mega-project that'll take him eighteen more months at least, Verhoeven's got two pictures back to back—"

"Have you tried the second tier yet?"

"I was about to, and then I got a crazy idea. I caught *Spartacus* the other night on cable—"

"Kubrick will never do this. He won't work outside England—"

"Kubrick won't do it because he doesn't have to. He's already proved he can. But if we could get the right guy, a first-class director who's never made a big-budget actioner, it can be his *Spartacus*. He could take the blockbuster material and lift it to another level. Not just *Terminator 2—Lawrence of Arabia*."

Her eyes narrowed speculatively: "Who?"

He leaned in and mouthed the name quietly, with respect: "Chris Parrott."

He could see he'd caught her by surprise. Good. "But he's doing that script he wrote," Annette said. "The one about growing up on the Upper East Side—"

"*Precious Things*. Casting fell through. I've got it on good authority financing will go with it." It was a small picture, and depended on star power.

She was impressed, but dubious. "Why would he go for this?" Parrott was a New York director known for well-acted, depressing dramas and tight, paranoid thrillers; "wrenching" was the term most often applied by critics to his best work.

"Who wouldn't go for a chance at two hundred million domestic? He's never done more than fifty, sixty tops. He pulls this off, he'll double his price, and make a classic besides."

"He won't go for this. He's an intellectual."

"So am I." She was warming to the idea. Time to close for the kill. He beckoned to her conspiratorially. "What would you say if I told you I faxed him the script yesterday, and he loved it?"

She jerked away in surprise. He knew he'd overstepped his bounds in showing the script to Parrott without telling the studio, but he was the producer, dammit. It was a calculated risk. He plowed on.

"Parrott's never handled a film of this scale, but this man is a thorough professional. He takes a budget seriously. Actors respect him. He's a consummate craftsman—he builds a taut movie, he's a master at character and motivation, he understands suspense. He can make *The Agonizer* into *The Godfather* for the millennium."

Annette clutched her glass and peered at him seriously with her big liquid eyes. He saw a new brittleness there, as if they were icing over.

"You've offered him the film?"

"More or less."

She put her hand on his arm. "If you're that high on Parrott, we should hop a plane tomorrow and see what his take is on the project." That new look in her eyes wasn't anger. It was respect.

Wonderland Avenue is a concrete creek running through a

steep ravine, houses jammed like giant boulders between hillside and road. They had pulled into her driveway; the limo tail stuck five feet into the narrow street. The chauffeur opened the door and Annette stepped out. Jason pressed his advantage.

"Klaus will jump at the chance to work with Parrott. He's never worked with an actor's director before."

"Want to come in?"

He thought of her satiny tongue plucking salsa off her finger. "Sure." Walking to the door, he channeled his excitement into his pitch. "Parrott and this script practically guarantees Klaus a nomination—" She put that very finger to his lips.

"I have one rule. No business in the house." She nodded to the driver. "But you can still charge his time to the picture." And she laughed her bright insouciant laugh.

They entered her house. The driver looked for a safer place to stash the car.

Annette's house was built in the thirties, when Laurel Canyon was a mountainous summer hideaway, by a local craftsman who'd lived in it most of his life. It was a small oak-and-redwood gem. Each doorjamb, each rafter, windowsill, post, and beam was meticulously shaped and fitted, an act of love between man and material. Annette had bought the bungalow for the craftsmanship, and because it boasted a rarity for the canyon, a natural pocket of land behind the house, a quarter acre the builder had landscaped with orange and quince and grapefruit trees into a miniature English garden, around a small but serviceable swimming pool.

Jason stood alone in the garden, listening to a raucous chorus of canine howls skirling up and down the canyon. A coyote must be on the prowl, he thought. The dogs are giving chase. His blood stirred. He swelled out his chest. He was giving chase. He hadn't sat back. He'd pushed the envelope. He'd won her respect. This was a city of dreams, and his was coming true—but only because he'd taken charge.

The bedroom French doors opened and Annette stepped out wrapped in a silk kimono. She scowled at the barking. "Those dogs are the worst thing about living in the canyon. One starts, the next chimes in—it travels right up to the top and back down again, for hours."

"Oh, I don't know," said Jason. "It's kind of exciting. The call of the wild." The barking reached a frenzied pitch. "Sounds like they've cornered a coyote. It has an elemental power, don't you think? Nature, red of tooth and claw, fighting its life-and-death battles right in the heart of Los Angeles." He was closing in too. He was about to hop a plane and corner the great Chris Parrott. And Annette would be at his side. He felt like the mighty thunder god Thor come to earth in a herringbone jacket. (He was developing a script based on the Marvel comic.) Immortal, invincible, he strode like a giant among mere flesh-and-blood creatures, with Annette his Mjolnir, the enchanted hammer, poised to leap from his hand at his bidding, stun the enemy, and return.

"Let's have a dip." Annette dropped her kimono. He caught a flash of white, and she was in the water. The pool was painted black, and lit from below. Through the distorting water her body gleamed like a pearl in the nacreous glow. Naked.

Jason tore off his clothes and dived for Annette. When he surfaced beside her, the crazed barking in the hills above had given way to gnashing and ripping and frantic yelps. He growled and grabbed for her. She slipped away. A single piercing shriek, an almost human cry of desperation, echoed through the canyon. Jason lunged, barking like a dog; Annette backed off, laughing and splashing. The canyon rang with the muted snarfles of blood-crazed beasts worrying the carcass of their prey.

A fistful of water caught Jason full in the face, blinding him. When he rubbed it out, Annette was an indistinct fuzzy blob. Damn! He'd lost his contacts. He fingered his eyeballs, trying to push the lenses back into place, but they were definitely gone. Washed off. Annette was pulling away, now no more than a gleam in the night. Jason swam for it. The pale blur became a ball that levitated from the water and unrolled itself into a puddle of light at the edge of the black pool.

As he neared, Jason could make out her vague pulsing form, face to the stars, chest rising and falling from the exertion of the swim. He vowed to laser sculpt his eyeballs.

Jason pulled himself out of the pool. Finally, inches from her, Annette came into focus. Her eyes were closed, her mouth lightly parted; she'd given herself to the cool sensation of water lifting from her skin. He was close enough to make out the swelling of her cornea beneath her silken eyelid. He slipped over taut cheeks to wide, full lips, billowing gently as she breathed. Seen from this distance, the perfection of her parts was astonishing. My God! he thought. This woman is Katharine Hepburn and Audrey Hepburn rolled into one! He closed the final gap for a kiss, and felt her sweet breath warming his lips, but decided against it. Instead, he nosed down her body to explore the rest of her.

This close, any blemish should become an ugly blight, but on Annette the effect was quite the opposite. The occasional mole was an ebony island that set off her astonishing pellucid pallor. Her skin, he now realized, was the secret to her uncanny allure. He peered deep, at faint purple veins pulsing beneath luminous flesh, and he remembered an Attic alabaster urn in the Gardner Museum that he'd looked at the same way, up close with his glasses off. Annette's skin was the exact hue and translucence of the stone, but it was warm, and, he imagined, soft. It amazed him that so cool a white could exude such warmth.

He skimmed over the hillock of her right breast, bulging from its own weight. The nipple loomed steep-sided and craggy in the cool air, like a red-rock mesa, rising and falling as she breathed. When it sank, he placed his mouth where it had been; it rose again, and slipped inside. He licked, and it fell back. It rose; this time he closed his lips, tugging gently. It fell away with a light "plop."

He left her breast and grazed on to her belly button. He was almost surprised she had one. She was too perfect to need a belly button. It was small, and round, with a tiny mole in the center wrinkle of flesh. He kissed the mole. She squirmed and laughed and turned on her stomach.

Her lower back was covered with a light down, fine dark hairs lined up in overlapping rows that flowed together toward the base of her spine. He licked them the wrong way. They stood soft against his tongue. Annette wriggled, and he placated her by licking the other direction. Toward her ass.

He'd never licked an ass before, but this was irresistible. He felt the buttocks with his tongue, and found them warm and smooth and soft and firm, a weight and texture that he instantly recognized as the Source, the mother of all sensation—of warm showers, warm sand, and warm pillows; warm, fluffy pancakes in the mouth, smooth silk shirts on the back, cool, elastic water-balloons in the hand; he opened his mouth wide, until his jaws ached, to swallow the feeling whole; Annette pulled away. He was staring now at the river of fine hairs leading into the ravine between her buttocks. The Laurel Canyon of her ass, he thought, her Wonderland Avenue. I'm on the prowl.

He nuzzled in between the hills, licking the smooth river of light down, until his tongue hit the tiny puckered depression. He pressed his tongue against it, searching for the coyote; it was resistant but elastic; Annette arched her back obligingly, and his tongue poked through, tickling the smooth, moist, and faintly acrid pit.

Annette pressed her ass against his face for a moment, and then flipped over again, brushing his nose in her pubic hair. Her mons was puffy and inviting. All her curves, he noticed, even her most private, were convex. Impossible. She wasn't fat—with clothes on, she had a model's lithe figure—but her body was put together with no dents, only one swelling form blooming from another. He tracked the graceful arc of her inner thigh, licking so lightly, his tongue touched only the fine hairs.

Her privates were a delicious pink, the color of cotton candy. He followed the soft folds with the tip of his tongue, tasting salt and chlorine. She ran her long fingers through his hair. He learned her geography fold by fold, then traced up one side and down the other of the small, slim guppy swimming in her warm, rosy sea.

Annette pulled away. He tried to follow, but her hand closed around him with a rhythmic squeeze, and her face came close to his, and she was gazing at him with huge, awestruck eyes, eyes that widened with wonder each time she tightened her grip. Blood fled his vital organs. His body shriveled until he floated, weightless, moored only by the massive anchor clasped in Annette's dainty hand.

She hopped up, laughing lightly, and skipped over to her kimono. Jason, the thunder god, watched her light extinguish beneath the silk. A painful throbbing told him from that moment there was no such thing as life without Annette.

ELEVEN

Homer huddled in a frigid phone booth, shoveling in his nickels and dialing the mystery number while traffic whizzed by outside. A woman's voice answered.

"Mr. Grant's office."

"Hello?" It probably wasn't the voice that had screamed at him through the static, but he couldn't be sure. "This is Homer Dooley. Did you call me about a job?"

"No."

Homer suddenly felt the cold. "Are you sure?"

"Who are you?"

"Dooley. I work over at the JC."

"What do you do?"

"I teach film."

"Film?" The voice seemed surprised. "Hold on."

He waited long enough that he thought she'd forgotten him. But she hadn't. "Mr. Dooley? Can you come in this afternoon at two?"

"Sure."

"See you then."

"Where are you—" But the voice had hung up.

Homer had used up his change waiting on hold. He dialed the operator. Labored explanation got her to check the crisscross index. The number belonged to Granite Plywood. He sighed. He'd worked there as a kid for a summer, in the glue factory, rendering horse's hooves and making casein from sour milk. He could still feel the fetid smells sticking to his body. Each odor by itself was bad enough, but recognizable at least; together they had blended into a nameless, repulsive aroma of rot that seemed to emanate from his own flesh. He remembered particularly that he'd bought cheap gloves, trying to sock away a few more bucks for school, and the stinking goop had oozed through the leather, staining his hands. The smell refused to wash off, and he'd spent the summer fighting nausea every time he'd lifted his hands to his face. It had cured him of biting his nails, though.

Homer bought himself a good pair of heavy gloves and reported to the mill. It hadn't changed since he'd worked in it, except that since nothing had changed, it was much the worse for wear. The main structure was a long two-story shed of rusting girders and dirty glass, boarded over, where glass had broken, with four-by-eight plywood rejects. It was about fifty-fifty glass and plywood now. The glue department was in an open-air plywood A-frame in back.

Personnel had never heard of Homer. When he told them he was there about a job, they thought he was conning them. They hadn't been hiring for five years. In fact, personnel, payroll, and procurement were all being handled out of one office now. Homer wondered if it was because they all began with "P."

Homer felt a certain guilty relief. If the hardware store wouldn't refund the money for his gloves, they'd certainly give him a credit. He was thinking over what to get with the credit, tending toward a new ax but tempted by the thought of a roll of one-inch foam insulation, when, walking past an open door, he heard a woman on the telephone. It was the voice that gave him his appointment. He walked in just as she hung up.

"Mr. Grant's office?" he asked.

"Who wants to know?"

"Homer Dooley."

"You're fifteen minutes late."

"I'm sorry. I got lost."

"Go on in."

When Homer entered Silas Grant's office, he felt like he was walking into the start of an old crime-busters film, the kind J. Edgar Hoover would introduce from behind his desk as a true tale from the annals of the FBI. The room was built in the forties, and stocked with utilitarian office furniture from that period; it was monochrome, not the grays of a forties movie, true, but mahogany-paneled with a mahogany desk and mahogany, well-hoovered carpet. The desk was flanked by the Stars and

Stripes and the flag of Vermont. Between them, where the window should have framed the Capitol dome, it displayed the crumbling plywood factory.

What made the crime-busters image leap to Homer's mind was the man behind the desk. He looked more like an FBI director than J. Edgar Hoover did—lean, gray, erect, brush-cut, and stern. He eyed Homer suspiciously. Instinctively, Homer straightened his spine. He resisted the temptation to salute. "Homer Dooley, sir."

Silas Grant nodded curtly. "Have a seat."

"That's all right, sir." Homer felt better standing at attention before this man.

"Mucklinberg College tells me you make movies."

"Yes, sir." So the voice that called the farm was Bonnie's!

"They say you do it as well as anyone around here."

"That is very kind of them, sir."

"I need a movie made."

"Yes, sir!" Homer's chin shot back into his Adam's apple. Special Agent Dooley was receiving his assignment.

"Will you sit down, young man!" Homer hopped to the nearest chair.

"Granite Plywood, as you might know, is the third largest producer of plywood in the state of Vermont. It is the oldest continuously operating manufacturing concern, and the second-largest employer, in the northeast quadrant of the state. The virtues of Granite Plywood have never been properly explained to our investors. I would like to have a film demonstrating those virtues for our next stockholders meeting.

"A movie is a great idea, sir."

"However, it is my fiduciary responsibility to ensure that this film is made at a price."

"Well, your first decision, sir, is whether to make it on film or video."

"What is the difference?"

"Well, video is cheaper, because you don't have to buy film and pay for processing. You could get some students at the school to knock out a video for you. It probably wouldn't cost you anything. They'd do it for the experience."

"Are you trying to talk yourself out of a job?"

"No, sir. You asked about the cheapest—"

"Granite stands for quality! My film must bespeak quality!"

The intensity of Silas's retort surprised Homer. "Excuse me, sir, but is quality really that important? I mean, the stockholders are already stockholders. Isn't it enough to inform them about the company—"

Silas cut him off. "Granite Plywood is ninety-five percent owned by myself and my wife."

"Then why do you need a movie?"

"Because I wish to demonstrate the advantages of Granite Plywood to potential investors!"

"Oh," said Homer. "You're trying to sell it."

"Do you want to make this movie or not!"

"Yes, sir. Absolutely. And film is the way to go, sir, if you're looking for quality. Film always looks better."

"How much will that cost?"

"Well, there's film and processing, like I said, and equipment rental, and my time, and a sound man, and postproduction—"

"I will give you five thousand dollars."

Five thousand! It seemed like a lot of money to Homer, but he knew how expensive moviemaking was. He did some quick calculating. If he borrowed equipment from school, and got Bonnie to give him the outdated film they'd been storing since they ran out of processing money, and found a student to run sound for free, and did all the editing and sound transfer and negative cutting himself, then all he'd have to pay for was audiotape and editing supplies, and titles, and developing and printing at fifty-five cents a foot, and the optical track and answer print at a dollar ninety or so a foot. If he could keep raw footage down below five thousand feet and the finished film down to ten minutes, he'd clear a thousand dollars, maybe more. "Okay."

"I expect this to be a film of premium quality."

"Absolutely. First rate, sir." This time Agent Dooley saluted.

"Delivered in three months. I will pay you half when you start, half when you present the film."

"Yes, sir." Twelve weeks. It would be a push, but he could do it. He'd have to put aside the start money to pay for film processing, and take his salary out of the completion payment. Twelve weeks of oatmeal and potatoes.

On the way out, Homer did some rough division. He divided the thousand dollars into the twelve weeks and he came up with eighty dollars a week. He wondered briefly if he shouldn't have asked for a little more money. But if Mr. Grant had wanted to spend more, he would have offered more. Mostly, he was excited. He had a job!

To celebrate, he decided he wouldn't even try to get his money back on the gloves. He'd trade them right in for the foam insulation.

TWELVE

Jason was trying not to be ticked off. It was important to keep your larger interests in view, and in this case larger interests required cranking back the seat in his XJS and catching some rays. So that's exactly what he was doing, baking under the Malibu sun while his fate was being decided a hundred yards away in Klaus Frotner's living room. Or on his beach, maybe. He didn't even know where they were talking.

In a way, he had only himself to blame. He'd squired Chris Parrott out to Malibu for this meeting on the pretense of sociability—everyone knew Parrott didn't drive—but he'd expected to be invited in on the party. He was producing the damn picture, after all. And Parrott had handled it well. He'd looked Jason straight in the eye and explained in solemn tones that first encounters were critical in all relationships, that his first encounter with Klaus—with any actor—was especially critical, since the first impression defines the whole future nature of the actor-director relationship, and the actor-director relationship is the crux of the whole filmmaking process. If they were to have a rapport based on openness and trust, it had to start here, and for that to happen they had to meet one on one, man to man.

These last words were a trifle strange coming from Parrott's mouth. Parrott had a somewhat effeminate air, not exactly a pouf, but a man with a highly developed feminine side, so while the words were perceptive enough, and there was nothing particularly masculine or feminine about the concept, it sounded like a woman talking about meeting a man she planned to seduce "man to man."

Jason smiled bitterly at the thought. It was a seduction, really. Or it better be. Klaus had director approval. It was hard to believe Klaus would turn down a man of Parrott's reputation, but stranger things had happened. Klaus liked men's men. On *Red Death,* Klaus had fired the director, calling him a faggot, and had him replaced with the stunt coordinator, a sky-diving, bull-riding adrenaline junkie who'd never directed a scene involving dialogue. Jason stared at the steel door across Broad Beach Road and wished he had X-ray vision.

X-ray vision made him think of Annette. God, he wished he'd had X-ray vision in New York, when she was in the next hotel room. With all the hurly-burly they'd never managed another tryst. They'd both been so busy. Fuck that, *she'd* been so busy. At least he was pretty sure she wasn't doing it with anybody else. He wondered idly if she'd done it with Darius. He stared hard at the steel door to put the thought out of mind. They'd been in there a long time.

Christopher Parrott told himself he was enjoying this. He loved a tough audience. A tough audience cleared his mind and honed his wits. If Klaus was being difficult, that only made the battle more worth winning.

From the start he'd known he was in for trouble. He'd been kept waiting for fifteen minutes—not twenty, thank God, twenty would have been a definite negative message, whereas fifteen was only a warning shot across his bow—then Klaus had appeared in a bathing suit he'd expect to see on a male stripper, a satin jockstrap really, and sprawled himself on the couch splay-legged. Parrott saw this as a direct challenge to his reputation as a maker of film as art. "You make serious films," Klaus was saying, "I make films where I run around with my cock flapping in the wind. What makes you think you can make my kind of movie?"

Parrott had countered by doing something he almost never did. He removed his blazer. In the heat of battle, he even went the next step and untied the bandanna he wore rakishly at his neck. The irony of that act did not escape him—in Manhattan his trademark bandanna was a sign of his raffish Hollywood roots, but in Malibu it seemed as stuffy as a silk four-in-hand.

But this was form, not substance. Parrott was actually encouraged by Klaus's opening hostility. He read it as a sign of insecurity, and if Klaus was insecure around Parrott, it was because he thought Parrott had something he didn't have, something that he wanted. Parrott's job was to hold out the promise Klaus could get it without putting him off with condescension or pretense. And Parrott was damn good at his job.

Parrott knew it was important to take control from the out-set. He frankly admitted that as a rule he never took a project that was already cast, that the purpose of the meeting as far as he was concerned was to see if he and Klaus shared the same vision of the script and could work together, and if they couldn't, they couldn't, but that he was excited about this proj-ect; he'd never read a script, he said, that so fitted a star as this script fit Frotner. He expanded on the nature of movie roles, with enough humor to show Klaus he wasn't pompous, but with enough intensity to make Klaus feel the gold ring was within his reach, saying that great premises made great movie deals, but great characters made great movies, and here was the rare proj-ect with both; that a great character in a movie wasn't Hamlet or Raskolnikov—he might have gone beyond Klaus here, he feared—but a character that perfectly fit the personality of a great star; that he had studied Klaus's principal films, *Red Death* and the sequels *Blue Death* and *Black Death,* and *Widowmaker,* and *Firewalker,* and *Windwalker,* and that Klaus had been strong, very strong, of course, but that there was an untapped potential he sensed in Klaus, something only hinted at in those earlier films, but there in spades in the *Agonizer* script, and, well, that he'd like to be the director who finally delivered the real Klaus Frotner.

This was said with disarming candor, and it was a measure of his success, he felt, that Klaus did not ask him exactly what special quality was missing in his earlier films. Parrott didn't volunteer it either. His task here was to inflate Klaus and reas-sure him at the same time. Getting too specific would only be counterproductive. Parrott had a fine sense for others' weak-nesses, and Klaus was an easy read: Klaus wanted to be taken seriously as an actor, but he was afraid he couldn't pull it off. Parrott had to make him feel that he, Parrott, could lead Klaus to greatness—but also that he'd only be asking Klaus to do what he always did, only better.

A striking woman materialized at this point, whom Klaus in-troduced as Inga. Her timing was too good. Parrott suspected she'd somehow been listening in. He'd been warned about her, and from what he'd heard was surprised to see her modestly attired in a floor-length muumuu. But she appeared to be on his side. She shook his hand firmly, saying she and Klaus both felt it was time for Klaus to be appreciated as an actor as well as a star, and they hoped Mr. Parrott was the man to do that. Then she asked what he'd do to improve the script.

Parrott knew a trick question when he heard one, and he'd been well prepped by Jason. The game here was to bring her along without appearing to be her patsy. Klaus wanted her dealt with, but not at his expense. So Parrott answered with vague generalities about tweaking Klaus's character, and then—keeping a weather eye on Klaus, to gauge how the game was going—expounded at length on the lack of a credible, sympathetic, vulnerable female presence to counterpoint the male-dominated action; how there should be a woman's role that was strong, dynamic—physical—yet also a tempering force, a yin to Klaus's yang; how the contrast would set off Klaus's inner struggle to better effect, and add another level of meaning to the piece.

Jason jerked out of his reverie when the steel doors opened. Parrott emerged, but not alone: Inga was walking him to the car with her arm through his, and Klaus was trailing along behind. Hot damn! He'd won.

Anxiety abated, Jason's annoyance at being left in the car like some damn chauffeur rose to the surface. As they approached, he went to meet them. Parrott played mein host: "Jason Fo, Klaus Frotner and Inga Thorne."

Jason shook their hands, ticked off. "We've met. At the studio." What did the guy think? Klaus was in his fucking movie and they hadn't met? Though he had to admit they'd met only that once, in Annette's office.

"Yes, of course. But I wasn't sure you knew Inga." Parrott turned to Klaus. "I told Darius I thought he'd made an excellent choice bringing in Jason. He has a real feel for the material." Jason was flattered, as he'd been meant to be, but he was also discomfited by the way Parrott so effortlessly appropriated the project. You'd think Jason was working for him.

On the way back up the coast, Jason got some satisfaction from winding out the Jag's V12 engine and slinging Parrott around a bit. But Parrott grabbed the dashboard and didn't complain, and soon Jason realized that any form of hostility was a mistake on his part, a sign of weakness, so he eased off the throttle and remarked that it looked liked things had gone well. Parrott agreed. Jason resolved to further show his strength by not asking him what had actually happened. Parrott seemed to appreciate his restraint, and took on the conspiratorial tone of one movie *macher* talking to another: "Now," said Parrott, "we go to work on the script."

This surprised Jason. He thought everybody loved the script. But he didn't want to say so; if Parrott saw script problems, Jason didn't want him to think he couldn't see them too. So he merely nodded and grunted.

"Why don't you get together your notes and we can talk it out at length?"

"Sure." This would be a gas, talking script with Chris Parrott. Parrott tapped his arm, as if suddenly struck by a thought. "We can bring in Flaherty, I bet. I think he's got some time."

Flaherty and Parrott. Wow! Flaherty had written Parrott's most respected films, and had two Oscars on his shelf. Did he have a Tony too? Maybe it was a Pulitzer, Jason couldn't remember.

Jason allowed himself a pat on the back. He'd pulled it off. He'd attached Chris Parrott to a Klaus Frotner project. And now he was going to be in with the big boys, in the big time, talking story with Parrott and Flaherty, shaping the kind of movie he'd studied in film class. He resolved to start a diary, just in case this movie was one for the ages.

THIRTEEN

Homer watched, mesmerized. A pine log rolled down the iron ramp and seated itself against the strong blade of the cutter. Grapples grabbed the log ends, like hands holding a giant ear of corn, and revolved the log against the blade, neatly peeling a thin, fragrant strip of veneer; as the papery strip unfolded, the log shrank magically to broom-handle thickness. It reminded Homer of the Woody Woodpecker cartoon of a factory where a whole log was whittled down to make a single toothpick. How much would the cartoon rights cost?

When he'd worked in the glue division as a kid, Homer had just done his job and gone home, but now that he was making a film about it, he had to admit plywood was a fascinating subject. He'd always thought of plywood as one thing, maybe two, if you counted interior and exterior quality. He'd been amazed to learn the sophistication of the medium, the subtle variations of glue and ply, core and veneer. He'd begun to understand what an improvement plywood was over nature. Man had taken a simple idea, juxtaposing wood grains crosswise to each other, and created a new class of fibrous object, stronger, more durable, and more adaptable than anything grown by God.

The problem was, he was shooting more film than he planned. There was so much to show: all the uses of plywood—culled mostly from photos in magazines he found at the library—not just its uses in house construction, but applications in furniture, in van and truck construction, in boat-building and box-making; the history of plywood, which was closely bound to the history of glues, a complex chemical evolution from blood glue to the phenol synthetics and urea-formaldehyde; the way plywood was formed, cold-pressed or hot-pressed into sheets, or pressure-molded into exotic shapes; how plywood worked not just as sheeting but as structural members, I-beams and A-frames, and as concrete forms; and of course the Granite Plywood Company itself, the source of these wonders. Homer had been entrusted with an awesome task, and he approached it the only way he knew how, one step at a time, up the tall mountain, but with growing concern that he was shooting up his film budget before he even got to Silas Grant's part of the story, the Granite factory.

He was finally at Granite, and telling himself to use restraint, film just what he needed, but the processes were so engrossing that he was soon talking himself into a little more of this, a little more of that, and losing track of footage until the film ran out and he had to slap in another four hundred feet. Now the sight of the stripper banished all economizing thoughts. This was the central image of his film. His plywood metaphor.

Homer watched the logs for a long time, trying to absorb the rhythms of the machine. He decided the stripper had to be captured in a single, unbroken shot. He wanted a camera move that would enhance the sensation of mass and velocity generated by the log's downhill roll, and the force and precision of the stripper blade peeling wood. He spent the morning planning and rehearsing a complex pan and pullback.

He could have used some help, but while he'd talked Bonnie out of the film and equipment, he hadn't been able to interest any students in giving him a hand. He couldn't pay them, and they didn't see why they should learn technology that not only wasn't digital, it wasn't even analog video. He could see their point, but it meant he was his own camera assistant and his own sound man.

Luckily he was using an old Auricon, the kind newsmen used before the video revolution. It could be rigged to run "single-system" to pick up sound along with the image like a home movie camera, without a sound technician, albeit with home movie results. Operating the camera without a camera assistant, however, was a trickier problem. The Auricon with its bulky Angenieux zoom was a boxy, awkward device set on an old wood tripod, and to get the shot he had to track the log through the eyepiece while he turned the zoom ring with his left hand, shifted focus with his right, and tilted and panned the camera by manipulating the tripod handle wedged into his armpit. The Auricon was too heavy for the tripod head, so every time he reached a certain point in the pan, the camera wanted to tip over on its nose. It took a lot of practice to tighten his lats at the crucial moment, braking the camera without jerking it, but he finally worked it out. Then he checked to make sure there was a fresh load in the magazine and he was ready to go.

Homer turned on the camera. The log slid instead of rolled and he missed it. He shut off the camera, adjusted his timing, and waited for the next log. Take two: This one came at a slight angle, and was never in frame. He widened a bit for the next one. Take three: The log hung up, and this time he was ahead of it. He figured that each blown take cost him ten feet of film. Six dollars if he processed and printed the roll.

Eight takes later he got what he needed: an extraordinarily symmetrical log rolling right where he wanted it, in focus and in frame. He zoomed out and panned down, miraculously smooth and uncannily in sync with the wood as it hurtled closer, and just at his widest frame he caught the moment of contact with the splitter. The blade bit into the log exactly where he wanted it, and peeled the translucent veneer in a sinuous sheet that filled his viewfinder. Savoring the undulating veneer, twisting and writhing like a scared skate, he felt the rare and extraordinary pleasure of being in absolute, transcendent unity with his subject. Waiting for the payoff, he and the splitter were one—now all that remained was for the sheet of veneer to float away, revealing the tiny toothpick.

A large beer belly entered frame. "This is a hard-hat area, kid. Gotta wear a lid."

Homer knew he should shut off then and there, write off the take, and not waste any more film, but he couldn't bear to. He couldn't sacrifice that feeling of completeness. So instead he panned the camera to pick up the owner of the belly, the foreman, Mel. Mel grinned and waved a stumpy hand at the lens. He was a thirty-year man, missing joints on three fingers, and he liked Homer now that he was convinced that Homer's enthusiasm and curiosity were genuine.

"I can't, Mel. It blocks my move." Behind Mel, the veneer floated away and the slim rod was ejected by the stripper. Homer pointed to the missing payoff to his shot.

"Does the core have a name?"

"That there's called the fitch."

"Why a fitch?"

"So's we can call that stripper tender there a son of a fitch."

In the background the stripper tender grinned. "Fuck you too, Mel."

Homer kept rolling. "Do you do anything with the fitches?" asked Homer. "Sell them for broom handles or anything?"

"Send 'em to the chipper for particle board is all. Want one?

You can have it." Mel picked up the rod as the next log skidded down the chute and held it out to Homer as the grapples moved in.

"Thanks." Homer took it with his zoom hand, pleased. He'd hang it over his editing table for inspiration.

Suddenly there was a rapid series of nasty metallic twangs. Homer saw a flare of light in the lens and felt something hard whistle past his left ear.

"*Shit!*" The stripper tender slammed the machine into neutral and all movement ceased. "Holy Mary Mother of God!" The tender walked out onto the machine and Homer panned over with him. The massive blade had a three-inch crescent-shaped bite out of it. "What the fuck—"

The tender knelt and examined the log. Two dull black knobs protruded. Behind him, he heard Mel's voice. "Fuckin' tree huggers." Homer panned over as Mel straightened up, holding a silver chunk of stripper blade in one hand and a bent black spike in the other. Mel handed him the spike. "Here. Another souvenir."

Still filming, Homer took the spike. His left ear was burning; he stroked it with the hand holding the spike, and noticed a quarter-inch notch was missing from the top.

"Christ, Mel," said the tender, "that coulda nailed your pal's head to the back wall."

Homer felt a little queasy. He couldn't really imagine how close he'd come to dying, but he knew if his camera'd been knocked out, it would have been the end of his film. "Does this happen very often, Mel?"

"Just started a couple weeks ago."

"Hasn't anyone called the police?"

"Boss figures if we don't say nothing, the eco-freaks'll knock it off. They're only doin' it to get on the news. Meantime, lopper crews watch for 'em."

"You tell those spaced-out fuckers to stop smoking dope on the job!" Homer panned back to the stripper tender. He was an ashy gray. "Shit!" He kicked the broken blade with his steel-toed boot. "Shit! Shit! Shit!"

It was midafternoon, an off hour for the Mucklinberg cafeteria, and the room was mostly deserted except for an intense young man with his back to the view, eating french fries and talking into Homer's camera. The cafeteria was a favorite hangout for students, even though the kitchen had been closed down for years. It had been designed as the school's focal point, and it still had most of its big Thermopane windows with their sweeping vista of rolling pine woods. Bonnie had cut a tough deal with a hard-up vending machine vendor, so students had a good choice of machine food. Once a major financial drain on the college, the cafeteria was now a modest profit center, and dispensed the best fries in Mucklinberg.

Homer had chosen the room because the forest made an appropriate backdrop, and because the windows poured soft north light over his subject, Trent Lockwood. Lockwood had been recommended to Homer as head of the militant wing of the local Green movement. Homer liked the way the cool light set off his stiff blond brush-cut and the blue tribal tattoos on his cheeks.

"What you've got here is the inevitable price of violence in our society." Trent rocked as he talked, and Homer was having a hard time listening and following focus at the same time. "Our heroes are guys like Stallone and Schwarzenegger and Frotner—comic-book super-hero super-killers—or real-life guys like Schwarzkopf, who get off on destroying Iraq to save it."

"So you're telling me you deplore this kind of sabotage?"

"Fuck no. I'm saying our killer culture's so blood-crazed, you've got to kill people to get their attention. Look at the Rodney King riots. The power structure beats on the underclass, starves 'em, humiliates 'em, and pretends nothing's the matter until the people rise up and lash out. It's the same with the environment, but trees can't fight back. Acid rain's no different than Xyklon-B, that Auschwitz nerve gas. It's genocide, just like what's been going down in L.A. is genocide, but no matter how much destruction the power structure lays on the forest, trees can't rise up in revolt. So someone's gotta do it for 'em." He waved Homer's spike for emphasis and Homer panned with it.

"Then you think tree-spiking is a good idea."

"It sure got your attention. Would you be here interviewing me if you hadn't had your ear clipped?"

"Are you spiking trees?"

"Tree-spiking is a felony." Trent nodded coyly at the camera. "I'd have to be pretty stupid to admit to a felony while that's on, wouldn't I?"

Homer turned it off. "Do you spike trees?"

Trent polished off his last french fry and rose. "Earth first, bro."

Homer had set up a makeshift editing area in the farm's kitchen, since it was the only room with a table. He'd built two trim bins, big bags in wooden frames, and he'd filled them with hundreds of neatly labeled strips of film suspended from wire nails tacked into the wood. Editing consisted of pasting these bits together in different ways and studying the effect. He'd stick pieces together with a guillotine splicer, a precision-machined aluminum block that held two shots by their sprocket holes while it punched matching holes in a special Scotch tape that cost five dollars a roll. Each time he brought down the splicer head, it made a satisfying thunk. He'd examine the splice to make sure it was even, no bubbles in the tape, and trim the edge with a single-edged razor blade.

It was rewarding work for Homer, craftsmanly and suspenseful. He enjoyed the anticipation, wondering if his edit would have the imagined effect. If it didn't, he'd peel off the tape carefully so emulsion wouldn't peel off too, and then he'd add a few frames, or trim a few frames, or try another combination entirely until he found something that felt right. He viewed the results through a Moviescope he'd hooked up along with a sound amplifier to run off a car battery.

The setup didn't take much power, since he advanced the film by hand, pulling it through the viewer with rewinds he'd clamped to the table, but it was hard to turn the film at exactly twenty-four frames a second. The sound acted as a guide; when he turned too fast, voices sounded like Chip and Dale. He liked to play the film back and forth to get the rhythms right, studying the edit points, trying to make the cleanest, smoothest transitions from one movement to another, or the sharpest, most arresting jumps. When he made an edit that particularly pleased him, he fell in love with it, even if it didn't have much to do with plywood. He had a long stretch of extreme close-ups of the willows and the river behind the house, for instance, which related to plywood only in the most general, pantheistic way.

He was studying the Trent Lockwood footage with Ham and Frances crowding him from both sides, trying to make dinner. It was spaghetti night, and Frances was slicing vegetables which Ham was borrowing uninvited for his meat sauce. Homer turned up the volume to block out their bickering while he ran his film back and forth, back and forth, until Ham told him to shut the damn thing off.

"What does that geek have to do with plywood anyway?"

"Is that the face of a man who spikes trees?" Homer asked, pulling the face back and forth through the viewer. Trent opened and closed his mouth smugly, like a trout.

"What do you care?"

"I have to decide whether to put him in the film or not."

"Stick to plywood."

"But what do you think?"

Ham peered at the face. "That jerk's one hundred percent all show and no go."

"How can you be so sure?"

"You don't live to my age in these parts without knowing the barkers from the biters."

Homer ran the film a few more times. Ham waved his sauce spoon dangerously near the take-up reel. "Turn that damn thing off. He's not gonna change what he said."

Homer knew the image he wanted to start the movie. It was what he called the Crimebuster opening, Silas Grant seated between his flags, welcoming the audience and giving them the ground rules, so to speak. He thought it would add dignity. For his part, Silas was amenable. Homer gave him a general idea what to say, but he didn't want to script him. That would hurt the verisimilitude of the moment, and besides, he figured Silas could come up with something better than anything Homer could write for him. Silas was stiff, but Homer liked that. It made him credible, like the real G-men in crime-busting movies.

The actual shot didn't turn out as Homer had planned. Homer wanted to see the factory out the window, his Capitol dome, so to speak, so he borrowed some five-kilowatt quartz-halogen lights from the college to bring up the light level in the room to match the outside brightness. Silas, normally so confident and in command, was intimidated by the glare of the lights. Instead of being merely stiff and formal, he went rigid. He sat ramrod straight, hands pushing isometrically against the table-top; after every phrase his jaws clamped shut with an ominous click. When Homer suggested he gesture a bit, thinking it might loosen him up, he raised his fist in jerks and brought it down so hard, the desk shook.

Silas Grant's unfortunate performance was further undermined by the fact that the lights were very hot as well as very bright. Silas, wearing a heavy wool three-piece suit, had a pronounced tendency to perspire. The longer Silas talked, the stiffer he became and the more he sweated; instead of a cool, authoritative presence, Silas projected a man with a great deal to hide, afraid he'd be unmasked any moment. Homer tried shooting more takes, hoping Silas would relax into the part, but the longer Homer shot, the stiffer and more sodden Silas became.

Which was doubly bad for Homer, because it messed up the second part of the shoot, what Homer had thought of as the "we get our man" sequence. When Homer had finished the opening shot, and Silas had mopped himself off, Homer turned on the camera again and nodded to the young man who'd been helping him with the lights, whose face had been obscured behind a large straw hat. The hat came off to reveal a blond brush-cut and tribal tattoos.

"Mr. Grant," said Homer, "this is Trent Lockwood. He represents Free The Earth, an ecological movement you might have heard of."

Trent stepped forward. "I accuse you of rape and murder."

Silas jerked himself erect. Ignoring Trent, he advanced on Homer. Homer follow-focused. "What is going on here?"

"You've been having some trouble with tree-spiking—"

"Who has talked to you about tree-spiking—"

"No one. I mean, I saw an accident, and I thought if you talked to Mr. Lockwood here, you might be able to iron out whatever the problems are—"

Silas turned back to Lockwood. "Are you spiking my trees?"

"Those aren't your trees. Nobody owns trees. Trees own us."

Silas barked at Homer. "Turn off that camera!"

"Why don't you just talk to him. I bet you can make him see your point of view."

"Turn that damn thing off!"

Homer wasn't trying to show Silas up. He'd imagined that Silas would as likely show Lockwood up. He just knew that putting the two of them in a room together would reveal a whole new dimension to the plywood question. Now that he'd done it, he wanted to see what would happen. So he kept on filming.

Anyone will tell you that the great archaeologists are the lucky ones. Knowledge and pluck are not enough. So it is with documentary filmmaking. For the documentarian, like the archaeologist, is no better than what he stumbles across. Homer, like Schliemann, was at the mercy of the fates. And Homer was about to discover his Troy.

At that very moment, in the factory outside Silas's window, a spiked log rolled down the ramp toward the splitter. Grapples grabbed the log, rotated it at five hundred revolutions per minute, and jammed it against the splitter blade. The blade shattered, but not before shearing the spike and sending it flying off at a sixty-degree angle to slice through a power conduit near the chipping machine, showering sparks in the air. The chipping machine had been going full out all morning, reducing wood scraps to sawdust, and in the process filling the air with a dense haze of superfine wood particles. Fine wood particles suspended in air have the explosive potential of a fuel-air bomb.

While Silas screamed to shut off the goddamn thing, through the window Homer and his camera saw all the remaining windows blow out of the factory and the center of the roof fly twenty feet into the air, propelled by a gigantic fireball.

The shock wave shattered the office windows and threw Silas and Trent to the ground, out of frame. For a beat the camera caught nothing but the fiery spectacle through the splintered window; then the tops of the two men's heads entered frame as they peered over the sill at the carnage. A smoky mushroom cloud was forming.

Trent was struck dumb. His mouth opened and closed, opened and closed silently, like film of himself running back and forth on Homer's Moviescope. He turned to face Silas. For a moment they stared at each other with the mushroom cloud behind; then Silas gave an animal growl and threw himself on Trent.

Silas was old, but leather-tough. He closed his hands around Trent's throat and squeezed, tendons taut as guy wires. Trent pried one hand off, and Silas grabbed a tobacco jar from his desk, a clay bust of a jolly lumberjack, and pounded at Trent's head with it. The lumberjack's cap flew off, releasing a swarm of black latakia flakes into the air.

Homer, meanwhile, filmed away. He didn't consider intervening. He wasn't being venal or exploitive, it simply didn't occur to him. Through the viewfinder the events took on a disembodied air, as if they were a show being mounted for his benefit. Perhaps if actual violence were being done, he might have snapped out of his cameraman mode, but this had a Three Stooges air about it. Trent weighed twice what Silas did, and the grinning lumberjack was bouncing ineffectually off Trent's big arms; the flying tobacco looked like buzzing gnats, and made the men sneeze.

The lumberjack shattered. Trent pushed Silas away, keeping the desk between them. Trent was scared, but not of Silas. "I swear to God, man, I don't spike trees! I swear to God!" He turned to Homer and his camera: "I never spiked a tree in my life!"

No doubt the facts would come out later, in a court of law. But the camera told its own truth, and anyone who saw that footage knew Trent was incapable of violent action. He didn't need to say anything more. But the camera whirred, implacable.

"I work for the FBI, man," he said. "Call 'em! Ask 'em!"

FOURTEEN

If given the choice, movie people, like most people, prefer to live in comfort surrounded by beauty, and more than most they are able to indulge their life-style inclinations. But film people are artists, and artists are occasionally forced to compromise quality of life for art. Such was the case for the *Agonizer* location-scouting team in Wewak.

The port of Wewak, the largest town in northern Papua New Guinea, consists of five thousand souls of various races and re-solves, hemmed in by a mangrove swamp famous for rabid mos-quitoes and four hundred annual inches of rainfall. Its principal social event is a market held in the square every Thursday, where nearby indigenous peoples peddle their yams, bananas, and copra to a waterlogged clientele. Week-old prawns were available for a price. Wealth is measured in pigs, which are therefore consumed only on those occasions when a first-worlder might open a bottle of fine champagne.

As always, the film people on reconnoiter were staying at the best place in town, but here that meant the Cassowary, a bar with rooms in the back and none of the weathered romance of jungle cantinas—a mildewed, low-ceilinged prefab made of re-frigerated truck panels, floated into the region by a now-bank-rupt mining consortium. Foam-insulated aluminum siding kept the majority of crawling creatures at bay, and staved off the inevitable rot induced by eight months of incessant rainfall.

It was raining, as usual, and the film people were jammed into an old Chevy Impala that was plowing through hubcap-high mud from the Cassowary to the mining compound. The driver was driving very fast, afraid if he lost momentum he would bog down indefinitely; the car periodically hit a rut at·speed, and then the Impala would buck like an angry mule, sending a fan of dirty water flying against the windows on both sides of the street and banging the heads of the travelers inside against the roof.

Every time his head hit the roof, Jason wondered whether it

would be better to walk. Then he would look outside at the mud and the downpour and decide he might as well stay where he was. It had been a long trip. Seventeen thousand miles in forty-two hours. He had lost all track of time. He assumed it must be the wee hours for him, as he was very sensitive to jet lag and his body temperature had just plunged, sending his brain reeling from nausea to stupor, but it appeared to be midmorning in Wewak, and though semicomatose, he was incapable of sleep. His throat tasted of bile. He looked right and noted with displeasure that George Marshall, his thin, laconic production designer, was chipper and alert. On his left, McGinty, his red-faced production manager, snored like a contented sow. Parrott, in the front seat, was unreadable from Jason's vantage point, but when the car pitched he detected a queasy lurching of the skull, which cheered him somewhat. That, and the thought that they would soon be soaring over the weather to some of the lushest virgin forest on the planet.

The film car cleared the mining company guard gate and passed through a twelve-foot chain-link and razor-wire fence into another world. The Chevy scooted through rows of heavy machinery, massed like Allied armor on D day—gargantuan dump trucks, earth movers with eight-foot tires and scoops a man could stand in, and tractor-trailers big enough to haul the earth movers—finally alighting at a trim prefab command center, the Cassowary in better days.

Jason and his compatriots decamped shakily, and stood around the office clutching cups of acrid coffee while McGinty showed their papers and dickered in the back room with a precise gentleman who wore his work clothes like a lieutenant's uniform.

To ameliorate his own misery, Jason pulled Parrott aside, and in a voice filled with managerial concern asked how he was feeling. Parrott wouldn't bite; he only grunted and sat down next to Marshall. Marshall sipped his coffee and inquired of the secretary in cheerful, fractured Papuan if the beans were local. She held up a foil packet of Nescafé.

McGinty reappeared. He wore an inscrutable look that Jason knew meant trouble. There was a problem about the helicopter, he said. Parrott asked if it was safe to fly in this weather, and seemed unconvinced when McGinty said it was; the problem, said McGinty, was that he'd been told there'd be a Bell Jet Ranger, and there was nothing but a Hughes 500. He assured

Parrott that the Hughes was as safe as a Jet Ranger. The problem was, it was a four-seater. Pilot plus three.

They looked at each other for a few beats. Parrott diplomatically said that Jason as the producer should decide who should stay behind.

Foggily, Jason realized this was some sort of test. Parrott knew he'd be going, of course. Marshall, too, that was obvious—he was the only one who'd been here before. They were there because he wanted to show it to them.

No. Even in his stupor he knew it was him or McGinty. McGinty knew it too. He just stood there, grinning noncommittally, his florid face inches from Jason's. The smug son of a bitch. He knew he had Jason in a box. If he bumped McGinty, McGinty couldn't do his job. This was a vicious location, and neither Jason nor Parrott had made a big physical movie before. McGinty might be a drink-dimmed bumbler, but he'd made his share of blockbusters in better days. Jason needed McGinty's expertise, and McGinty had to see the lay of the land to give useful advice.

But if McGinty went, Jason stayed behind, a piece of excess baggage. He knew McGinty hadn't wanted him on the trip at all; that florid sot saw him as a studio boy, a fucking suit, as he liked to call studio people, and thought fucking suits just got in the way of the guys who got their hands dirty making movies.

The basic problem was, he couldn't fire McGinty, and McGinty knew it. Parrott wouldn't let him. McGinty'd worked with Parrott on too many pictures, and Parrott's contract gave him control over cast and crew, subject only to studio head approval; if Jason went to Darius about firing a production manager, it had better be because he was a thief or a flagrant incompetent. Without a smoking gun, Jason told himself, he'd look like a punk kid; Darius would do his usual statue act, and from then on McGinty would ignore him completely.

Jason had to admit that his leverage was in general woefully limited. Parrott had most of the powers normally invested in a producer. It was going to be a Parrott Film, not merely a Film By Christopher Parrott. Parrott even had final cut: Contractually, the studio had to release the film he gave them, and they had to let him do it his way, as long as he kept within the budget. And while Parrott had been very nice to Jason, and they'd spent a lot of time talking about the film, and he'd been welcome at all the casting sessions, and some of the scheduling,

Jason couldn't shake the feeling that everything would have happened exactly the same way if he hadn't been there.

Sure, bringing in Parrott had been a brilliant stroke, creative producing at its best. But Parrott had brought his whole team with him. The team treated Jason with everything from amused tolerance to outright hostility, depending on how much they viewed him as a threat, but they never treated him as a true creative partner, a collaborator. And Parrott kept what he called his sensitive creative areas to himself. He'd insisted on plotting the shooting schedule alone with the assistant director, and, in spite of his intimations, when it came to actually talking script with Flaherty, he'd decided for creative reasons to do that at Flaherty's place in Nantucket, leaving Jason in Los Angeles "to oversee preproduction." Not that the various departments would take his word for anything without first checking it with Parrott.

So Jason stared at McGinty's fat, complacent face and thought how much he'd like to ground the fucker. But Jason reminded himself that he was the producer. The producer had to rise above petty personal jealousies. He had to keep the larger interests of the picture in mind.

When people at parties would ask him, as they often did, what a producer's job actually was, Jason would smile and tell them that the producer's job was to levitate. Let the production manager worry about finding parking for the film trucks and getting a location cheap; the producer must float above the fray. While everyone else got lost among the trees of day-to-day shooting, he would see the forest of the whole movie. He was the keeper of the original vision. The Big Picture. He would see to it the final film was the film they'd started out to make. He'd said this often enough, in fact, that Annette had sent him a museum reproduction of a large pornographic Grecian urn, with a note saying that she was entrusting him with the Big Pitcher. But it was true. Jason found comfort in the thought that even a Chris Parrott needed a producer with vision.

Through the window of the prefab, Jason watched the Hughes 500 ascend into the clouds. The rain beat a muffled tattoo in the mud. A heavy truck rumbled by, shaking him in his folding chair. He clutched his briefcase. It sweated in the clammy heat.

Jason considered using the time to write in his journal. He decided against it. He'd been carrying one around since the beginning of preproduction, unopened, a calfskin-bound volume with gilded leaves, but he didn't feel like starting it just then.

The Hughes paralleled the shore until the toad-green coastal swamp was cut by the brown slash of the Sepik River; then the chopper veered south, following the dirty ribbon at a hundred and fifty miles an hour. Mangrove gave way to nipa palm stewing in brackish waters, then stands of sago palm when the land dried out. Then they left the clouds behind, and were soon casting their shadow on a dense shag carpet of emerald foliage.

Christopher Parrott relaxed, and let himself enjoy the magical feeling of floating over the soft expanse. He still got a thrill from the romance and freedom of chopper flying, zipping along at two hundred miles an hour one moment, then swooping down and hovering when something caught the eye. It was as close as he'd ever get to living out the flying dreams he'd had as a child, when he'd sail high over oceans of rolling wheat, his arms spread like wings, then plummet with gut giddiness until plowed earth rose to touch his face and he could smell the damp soil before soaring back into the blue sky. He'd liked the dreams so much, he'd gone to sleep on his back with his arms out, like Christ or a Sabre jet, to bring them on. Now, of course, he understood their Freudian implications; they were sublimated sexual fantasies of his latency period, Eros channeled into images of omnipotence and abandon. He'd had an extraordinarily prolonged latency; he wondered if that was the source, somehow, of his urge to be a director. The thought intrigued him. He might mention it in his next interview. But as he imagined how he'd frame it, one part of the dream still eluded him. He didn't get the farmland imagery. He told himself that plowed earth, furrowed and smelly, would be feminine sexuality, and fallow fields a symbol of latency itself, but the metaphors didn't resonate in him. The closest he'd been to a farm was the family place in East Hampton.

"That's classic three-tier virgin rain forest." Marshall spoke into his tiny headset; they all wore headsets, so they could communicate over rotor noise. "What Palenque looked like when we shot *Predator*."

Parrott turned his attention back to the problem at hand. He peered down at the forest, and felt a pang for the blackberry patches of the Hamptons. Parrott enjoyed the idea of mastering the wilderness in the abstract, but he wasn't a man who relished actual physical struggle. During shooting he liked to sleep in his own bed, be met at his own door by a car and driven to a soundstage, where he could stand around, nursing a cup of coffee, discussing the day's work with his people, in a place he could control, where he and his actors could feel comfortable and safe. That was the way to get the best work. Once you started wrestling with mountains and rivers, creative energy dissipated on logistical problems.

This current situation was a perfect example. They had hired a location scout who specialized in jungle locations expressly to find them the right rain forest. He had logged almost one hundred thousand miles, and they still didn't have a good solution. It wasn't simply finding vast virgin forest; it was finding forest near a staging area that could feed and house a hundred people for three months in first-world conditions.

The scout had touted Palenque, until he went back down there and discovered the jungle had been mowed down for resort hotels. Catemaco, where he'd placed *Medicine Man,* had been turned into a gigantic cattle ranch. Thick Malaysian foliage had once kept the Japanese army at bay; now Malaysia looked like Southern California, all freeways, condos, and shopping malls. In desperation, the scout had pushed Belem, in Brazil itself, since the action was set in the Amazon, but Parrott had ruled that out—*At Play in the Fields of the Lord,* shot in Belem, had been one long yellow fever epidemic, relieved only by recurrent bouts of dysentery.

So here they were on the island of New Guinea. Irian Jaya, the Indonesian half, was impossible for political reasons. There was strong popular opposition to "outside exploitation" of the area, and while this could no doubt be overcome by judicious bribery, there was always the risk of the arrangement blowing up in their faces in the middle of the shoot. That would be disaster. Papua New Guinea, this half, was in development mode.

Parrott looked down at a chain of barges hauling heavy equipment upriver. The timing was perfect. There had been a big copper strike in the Sepik valley; it was still virgin forest, but large-scale mining was moving in. They could hook in with the mining crews, use their access and their camps, film the movie before the strip mining decimated the jungle. They could even shoot the big finale, the burning of the forest, on a grand scale.

Parrott smiled when he thought of the gasp he would draw from his audience when the camera pulled up, up, up and away, and the screen would be filled with thousands of acres of fiery forest. A gargantuan, promethean vision. And for a good price too: the mining company had to clear the land anyway. Parrott calculated that the equipment on the barges below probably cost more than his whole film.

Parrott was as much a conservationist as the next man. The thought of all that charred jungle pained him. But he was also a realist. The jungle would burn whether or not he filmed it. At least if he filmed it, the world would see the desecration. Then, he told himself, the forest would not have died in vain.

The Hughes alit atop a hill scraped clean by dozer blades. Parrott let Marshall lead them down into the stifling greenery. Parrott was not a man who relished heat. He was a clean man. He enjoyed the crisp feel of a well-ironed shirt. But he had an embarrassing tendency to perspire. His shirt was instantly soaked. He used the tip of the kerchief knotted at his neck to dab at large drops slipping off his nose.

He looked around the jungle, disappointed. It was dark; worse, the light was dull and lifeless, what you'd expect on a leaden winter day, but tinted sickly green. Instead of lush, dense growth, scattered tree trunks sprang at large intervals from damp earth littered with decayed vegetable matter. Vines hung like rigging lines. He pushed one tentatively. Something dark and nasty skittered between his legs. "No sky. No horizon. No foliage. Looks like a Republic Pictures jungle." He looked significantly at Marshall. "You could give me a more interesting forest on a soundstage."

"Three-tier forest is always sparse at the bottom level."

"And this light is flatter than piss on a plate." Parrott held up his hand and looked at it vanish against the background. "I was hoping for a sun-dappled effect."

Marshall squinted upward in the gloom. "We could prune the higher foliage, squeeze some sun down here."

"I don't see flying seventeen thousand miles to shoot on an old Tarzan set."

Marshall had worked with Parrott enough to know where he wanted to be led. "I suppose we could double this on a stage. Depends on the action, doesn't it?"

Parrott perked up. "How much do you think we could do on a stage?"

"The script I have, not a hell of a lot. Some. But the set would have to be massive."

McGinty, who'd been straggling, caught Marshall's last words. "You don't want to build a set. It would cost a fuckin' fortune. You'd save a couple weeks location time at the most."

Parrott looked peeved. "How do you know that? You haven't seen Flaherty's script."

McGinty backed off. "It worked for *Arachnophobia*. I guess it depends on the rewrites."

"I think you'll find that when Flaherty's done, we'll have a more manageable set of locations."

"Great. Then a stage might work."

Back in the chopper, Marshall tapped on Parrott's arm. When Parrott turned, he shouted into his ear; if he used the intercom, McGinty would hear, and he didn't want that. "When can I get a look at the new script?"

"When it's ready, you'll be the first."

Marshall looked worried. "Maybe you can tell me what you're doing. If we're building a set, I should have started yesterday."

Parrott stiffened. He didn't like being pressured. "When it's farther along, we'll let you know." Marshall settled back unhappily.

The chopper banked, and Parrott's throat felt sour. He was beginning to have a bad feeling about this one. It could slip out of control too damn easily. He had a momentary flash, a frightening vision of the giant undertaking, all its tens of millions of dollars and decades of man-years loaded on one of the mining company's huge trucks; the truck was careening downhill, picking up speed, and he was in the driver's seat, spinning a useless steering wheel and stabbing at brakes that didn't respond.

He realized now he'd been fighting the feeling for weeks, since he'd pulled apart the script with Flaherty and taken a hard look at what made it tick. Visions of nine-digit grosses, and the kind of creative freedom they would give him in the future, were all well and good, but first he had to make a film that worked. And that meant trusting his own instincts. He knew that. The problem was, for the first time he wasn't sure his instincts were appropriate.

He'd sensed resistance in Flaherty from the beginning. Joe was too much the pro to actually voice real concern that Parrott couldn't pull this one off, but he'd affected an amused distance from the material which told Parrott he'd disengaged from the project on some basic level.

Parrott suspected that half the time they were talking, Flaherty was thinking about his novel. Normally, this would annoy Parrott, but it would also challenge him to be more brilliant and engaging, to bring Flaherty back to the matter at hand, and Flaherty would usually come around. Come around or tell Parrott to get another writer. But this time Flaherty had been harder to read. He wouldn't pull out and he wouldn't dive in. Perhaps he wanted to pull out, but kept at it because he was getting twice his usual rate, trapped at his trade like an aging gigolo. Flaherty had expensive tastes for a serious novelist. But Parrott had the nagging suspicion that Flaherty's ambivalence had to do with Parrott's take on the material.

Parrott attacked a screenplay through the characters. He didn't know any other way. And once he started digging through *The Agonizer,* he had to admit that the characters were very thin indeed. They were simple, driven mechanisms; the Agonizer himself was a loutish brute who hit first and asked questions later, a super-strong, invulnerable cartoon character. He lacked any of the complexities and ambiguities that made drama involving. Flaherty, of all men, must have seen that. And yet he sensed Flaherty didn't want to do anything about it.

Flaherty didn't say it explicitly, of course. Flaherty always trotted out his best shrink manner when dealing with Chris. He'd listen, nod, take notes, say something supportive and leading. Parrott knew he was being handled, but he appreciated Flaherty's finesse. It made the work more pleasant, and it freed up Parrott's creative juices. And ultimately that was the most important thing. No matter who wrote what, Parrott had to make it his. Parrott had to chew it and swallow it and absorb it into his own body, so that when he directed, what came out had as much of his particular smell and texture as his own shit.

But good shrinks empathize. Flaherty had been maddeningly aloof. Parrott had toyed with the idea of sacking Flaherty and doing it all by himself. He still found it tempting. He was a writer now. Parrott thought fondly of his coming-of-age script, *Precious Things,* of the fall woods outside his study window in the Hamptons, where he wrote it. If only Brad Pitt had said yes. But that was the idea of doing *The Agonizer,* to become Pitt-proof. There were a dozen actors who could play the young Parrott part; after *The Agonizer* Bo could put together foreign money, and he could make *Precious Things* on his own terms. Without having to drop his price. He knew what happened when you dropped your price. It was the beginning of the end.

But Parrott knew he couldn't do the rewrite all by himself. He was too damn busy. So he'd pushed Joe hard, and Joe had given just enough back to make him think it might work.

Parrott had been frank about his fears, and frank about his hopes. This could be his *Lawrence of Arabia* after all. But it needed a character as complex as Lawrence at its center. The more Parrott thought about T. E. Lawrence, the more he thought the man might be a good model for the Agonizer. What was lacking in the script—what was lacking in all Frotner scripts—was a sense of the man's vulnerability. The fire of inner conflict that drove Lawrence. If Flaherty could get the Agonizer's inner pain on the page, Parrott could draw it out of Frotner.

They'd discussed the causes of the pain. Parrott was convinced it had to be tied to the violence. Was the Agonizer, like Lawrence, disgusted by the pleasure he took in sadistic brutality? Or did he, like Lawrence, have a masochistic side? Perhaps his macho posturing was only a way to invite a good beating. Did his fantasies of invulnerability come from denial of death? Or on the contrary, from a death wish? Was the Agonizer's violent nature the result of sexual confusion? Perhaps the Agonizer courted pain to purge himself of sexual ambivalence. Parrott sensed a homoerotic undertone to the male bonding in the script—let Flaherty punch that up, see where it led.

Parrott thought about Flaherty attacking that kind of material, and he relaxed. Flaherty wasn't just a craftsman, he was a tortured soul; once he started digging deep into the Agonizer, asking himself hard questions about the character as a man, his juices would start flowing. Parrott was sure of it. And Parrott's business was knowing people.

Parrott let himself imagine what the script could be like when an inspired Flaherty was done with it. This could be one for the ages. He smiled at the thought of Flaherty, after all his foot-dragging, up on the rostrum of the Dorothy Chandler Pavilion, trim but debauched in his black tie, accepting the Oscar. The two of them would be up there together, of course, since Parrott's contract gave him a share of the writing credit.

FIFTEEN

Mr. Grant's secretary looked up sharply when Homer banged through the door. He was lugging an old Bell & Howell projector, the kind they used in schools before video, and a portable screen.

"Mr. Dooley," she said, "do you have an appointment?"

"No, ma'am. I have something better than that. I have the film!" He waved a skinny pizza of a film can and grinned enthusiastically.

The secretary was not impressed. "Mr. Grant is very busy."

"I know. That's what you said when I called."

"If you had left a number, I'm sure he would have gotten back to you."

"That's what I figured."

"But you didn't leave a number."

"I couldn't."

"You couldn't? Don't you have a telephone?"

"It's kind of hard to explain. That's why I'm here." Homer smiled in triumph, as if all were made clear. The secretary didn't smile back.

"But he isn't expecting you."

"He must see some people he doesn't expect."

"He's very busy."

"Tell him I've brought the film. He'll see me."

She started to say something and changed her mind. Homer thought she looked a little sick. "Are you all right?" he asked.

"I'm fine," she answered with a peculiar stress on "I'm." But she rose and went into Mr. Grant's office, carefully shutting the door behind.

Homer stood patiently fiddling with the flimsy metal legs of the portable screen. They were sticking, and he was worried they wouldn't open all the way. He thought he heard Mr. Grant's voice through the door, loud and muffled. Mr. Grant appeared to be yelling about something.

The secretary returned. She didn't look any better. "I bet you're coming down with something," Homer said.

"Mr. Grant is really very busy, Mr. Dooley."

"I'll wait." He sat down.

The secretary remained standing. "I don't think that's a very good idea."

"That's okay, I've got plenty of time."

She went over to him and tugged at his arm. "Mr. Dooley, please."

"It's okay, really. I'll catch him when he comes out."

Suddenly the woman got angry. "Mr. Dooley, if you're still here when Mr. Grant comes out, he's going to brain you with a heavy object!"

"Brain me?" Homer's genuine surprise fueled the secretary's anger.

"That's exactly what he said. And he means it."

"But why?"

She leaned close to him. "The last time you were here, he was assaulted by a fanatic and his factory exploded."

"Oh." Homer sagged.

His disappointment softened her somewhat. "Mr. Dooley. Exactly what did you expect?"

"I thought I'd show him my movie and he'd pay me."

The secretary laughed incredulously. "You have got to be kidding," she said.

"Kidding? He owes me half my money."

"Chalk it up to experience, kid, if you know what's good for you."

Homer looked at her, helpless. "I can't." In truth, more than the money was at stake. Homer had made his movie for an audience of one. In his mind he'd been secret agent Dooley on the plywood caper, and Grant was his demanding superior officer, tough but fair. He had to please the man, sure, that was the job, but his boss didn't want some yes-man patsy. That wouldn't get the job done. He wanted a man who would stand up for his beliefs, even if the boss didn't like it, because the boss knew that only a man of integrity who followed his own instincts could crack the case.

Homer wasn't about to give up on Silas Grant. With much clattering and banging, he gathered his goods. The secretary didn't stop him when he pushed through the door into the inner office.

Silas grunted when he saw Homer. "You!" His body stiffened and his hand closed over a paperweight shaped like a logging truck. He seemed to squeeze it hard enough to melt the brass.

"I've got your film," Homer said cheerily. Silas glared at him, but Homer plowed on. He had to. "It's a little longer than I'd planned. Plywood was a bigger subject than I thought. I know I told you ten minutes, but I couldn't do justice to the subject in less than forty-two."

"Out."

"The thing is, I was hoping you could give me some money to cover the extra length."

"Out."

"When you see it, you'll see why it had to be longer. Really." Homer looked around the room for the best place to set up the projector. He decided to put it on a low filing cabinet across the room from Mr. Grant. He swung out the projector's feed arms and attached the take-up reel. Mr. Grant watched him, rigid.

"Look, Mr. Grant, I can understand why you'd be upset. You've been through a lot, your factory blowing up and all, and from what I've read in the papers, you weren't even insured, since your policy was canceled after those suspicious fires last year—"

A strangled groan rose from Silas Grant's throat. "Penny!" He shouted.

Homer pushed on, noting with concern that the veins in Silas's neck bulged with purple blood, and his trapezius muscles stood out in knotted deltas: "But I figure that means you need a film all the more. I mean now you really have some explaining to do—"

The secretary stuck her head in the door. "Call security!" Grant bellowed hoarsely. Penny's head snapped out of sight.

Homer had the film threaded up. He figured he'd better not take the time to screw around with the screen, but he noticed a white shade covered the window behind Grant's desk.

"Could you move? Sorry." Homer aimed the projector and clicked the switch. The projector flickered directly into Silas Grant's eyes.

The strobing light broke Silas Grant free. He rose stiffly and stalked toward Homer, hefting the brass paperweight like a blackjack. Behind him, film leader was counting down on the window shade.

Homer adjusted focus and backed away. "Mr. Grant. Give the movie a chance. You'll like it. I'm sure. I'm very proud of it. I think I've really caught the essence of the subject."

A Schubert concerto sifted thinly from the tinny speaker. Grant liked Schubert. He paused in his advance on Homer, and looked back at the flickering shade. Since the explosion, he'd kept it pulled to protect his blood pressure from the view; now it was pink and blue and gold, a forest stream at twilight. Silas Grant's voice floated over the music. "Wood is a natural material. God's material. A complex and powerful substance, beyond the creative powers of man. And yet, wood is not perfect. It is expensive; it is irregularly shaped; it is stronger in one direction than another."

Penny appeared with the guard just as the forest stream metamorphosed into a life-sized Silas. He'd been filmed behind his desk. Projected on the window shade, he was there again, his teeth clicking tensely on the d's and g's: "Plywood is God's tree remade in man's image."

The movie Silas was stiff and sweaty, but the corporeal Silas didn't seem to mind. Both cracked small grim smiles at hearing the phrase. The corporeal one pushed Penny and the guard out the door and settled warily into a chair next to Homer. He still clung to the paperweight.

Homer patted him on the back. Grant flinched. "If I don't like your movie, I'm not paying one red cent."

"That's all I'm asking, sir." Homer relaxed. He knew he'd done a good job. How could Silas not appreciate the work? He forgot about his problems, and became engrossed in the odd spectacle of today's Silas watching yesterday's Silas sitting behind his desk.

The desk-bound Silas gave way to a rapid succession of furniture, houses, boats, and exotic industrial artifacts, all miracles of plywood manufacture, while Grant droned on about its myriad uses. The Granite Plywood factory emerged through the skittering images, artfully photographed in baby-soft dawn light. Granite wasn't, perhaps, the latest in technical wizardry, but it exuded the down-home, funky warmth redolent with old-world craftsmanship of a Jack Daniel's distillery. Homer saw the Silas next to him place his brass logging truck gently on the floor.

Inside the factory, long-haired workmen labored among rich, Rembrantesque shafts of golden sunlight. But the sound track was crudely mixed—Homer had done it himself in his living room. The background noise was harsh and intrusive, abrading the idyllic spell. Silas the spectator scowled.

"They're not wearing hair nets."

"Excuse me?"

"They're supposed to wear hair nets. They're violating OSHA rules."

Homer was concerned. "I didn't know."

"You have to take that out."

It was Homer's only establishing shot. He was shifting things around in his mind, trying to figure out how he could work around it, when his favorite shot appeared on the screen, the central image of his film, the stripper peeling the log into a ten-foot toothpick.

Silas liked it too, until Mel's beer belly showed up, and he waved his stumpy hand at the camera.

"He's missing fingers!"

"It's okay, it's okay" was all Homer could think of to say.

"It damn well is not!"

And then, with a flash of light and the nasty sound of metal tearing, a vicious black spike flew at the camera. It was Homer's favorite moment in the movie. Every time he saw it, it reminded him of the X-winged fighters in *Star Wars*.

For the next week Ham called Homer "Mr. De Mille," and lectured him on the evils of his chosen profession. "If you build a porch and the son of a bitch doesn't pay," he told Homer, "you can always tear down the porch and find a use for the lumber."

Frances wasn't quite so negative. She'd watched enough of *Entertainment Tonight* to know how these things worked. Everyone got screwed on the first film. This was his calling card, she said. He should show it around and make a name for himself.

Homer thought about it, and decided that basically, Ham was

right. He'd be better off chopping wood. At least the work was outdoors, and he was sure of getting paid.

He didn't have much choice anyway. He owed Bonnie two hundred and forty dollars. But first he helped Ham set out traps for squirrel stew.

SIXTEEN

While Jason's fork picked at shreds of soggy chicken in a salad named for a former great producer, his tongue picked at words to explain what producing was all about. Melinda, all two hundred and fifty pounds of her, leaned forward on her elbows, intent; both studiously ignored the small black box between them, capturing his wisdom.

Bringing Melinda to the commissary was a calculated risk, since Melinda considered a first-class lunch a basic perk of her profession, but Jason wanted to link his picture with the great Studio pictures of the past, and himself with the wunderkind producers of its Golden Age. The commissary was vintage thirties, blending the sleek aerodynamics of a portholed Packard with the grim bombast of a People's Palace of Culture. As a symbol of the latest resurgence, Darius had ordered it restored to its former glory; the designer, stripping off decades of paint and partitions, had rediscovered maple and chrome and a historic WPA mural. Jason and Melinda ate in a streamlined booth beneath a heroic gang of chunky, heavily muscled film proletarians, gaffing and gripping towering lights and camera cranes while bull-necked comrades urged them on with megaphones and riding crops.

Unfortunately, the traditional fare of that era was long gone. The solid all-American meat loaf, goulash, and Swedish meatballs, the real sliced turkey breast with cranberry sauce, mashed potatoes, and gravy, the best club sandwich and chicken soup in town, were history, along with the lippy, helpful ladies who'd been mother to the Studio staff for the first thirty years of its existence. Now the restaurant was self-service: a pair of disaffected Salvadoran señoritas doled out wilted salads from thin plastic bowls and gluey entrees from tepid warming pans, chattering in Tzotzil about their boyfriends. Studio staffers ate off the lot whenever they could.

Jason had run a big risk, taking her there. But as he was

explaining to Melinda, that's what producing was about. Taking risks. The Big Picture was important, yes, but the acid test for producers was knowing when to make that leap into the unknown. He was modest, and careful to give credit to the other creative elements in the process, particularly his director, Chris Parrott, and to a lesser extent his writer, Flaherty; but he knew Melinda had been around the business long enough to appreciate what a daring coup it was to pair men like that with Klaus Frotner on an action picture. And that was the essence of producing. Risking a hundred million domestic for three hundred million, while taking a shot at making a really substantial film.

As he walked Melinda out, he could tell by the way she eyed the gelatinous pies and mealy cakes by the door that she was feeling martyred. That wasn't such a bad thing. It gave her a stake in the picture. He offered her a foil-wrapped mint and told her he'd picked her because she understood how hard it was to make a film. She respected the process. He was letting her in early, so she could chronicle the process from the inside. He'd give her access to every aspect of the project. She sucked on the mint thoughtfully, gauging the situation.

In truth, once he'd realized how impractical it was for him to keep a journal, he'd settled on Melinda as a better alternative. She had a warm heart, a kid's enthusiasm for Hollywood, and a regular column in the *Los Angeles Times,* not the bitchy backstabbing kind, but a sincere, empathetic corner of the paper where the trials and travails of the industry were portrayed with insight and understanding. If he brought her aboard, the *Times* would carry periodic updates on his film, reports from location, no doubt a cover story in the Sunday Calendar the week of release. Maybe he could even get her a book deal from the conglomerate that owned Studio.

"People will say you're just *The Agonizer*'s producer because your daddy owns the football."

She was testing him. Good. He smiled boyishly, to let her know he wasn't some thin-skinned defensive insecure jerk. "Producing a film is like committing a murder. You need means, motive, and opportunity. Darius provided the opportunity, sure—everybody needs a break—but the rest is up to me. And, like committing murder, the test is whether I can get away with it." He bore in on her with his baby blues. "How did Darius get his start? His father was a movie star. I'm third-generation Hollywood. There's a story in that. First there were the old moguls, like petty tyrants in their little medieval satrapies, ruling over liege lords on seven-year contracts, producing movies with vassals' labor within their castle walls; then their offspring took over, Renaissance princes, plotting and conniving, fighting over the services of freelance artists, Michelangelos and Da Vincis who moved from prince to prince, making their art for the highest bidder; now there's the likes of me. We're the coming of the Age of Empire—we're working for multinational conglomerates, modern versions of the East India or the Hudson Bay Company, taking resources from everywhere to make movies that span the globe; our films must make not tens of millions, but hundreds of millions, and our audience isn't America's heartland but the world at large—" As he spoke he could see he was losing Melinda. This was too broad a view to interest a journalist. "Anyway, you could do a piece on third-generation Hollywood. Call us the In Crowd or the Third-Worlders or something."

That made Melinda smile. She was a short five-two, and she was craning her neck, watching the landmark water tower glide by behind the high walls of Stage One as they walked to the parking lot. "I always get a thrill when I go on a studio lot," she said. "A soundstage is like a big present wrapped in plain paper, bland and anonymous on the outside but packed with exciting surprises."

Melinda slowed down. The stage door, with the red light over it that flashed during shooting, had a sign in bold block letters reading CLOSED SET ABSOLUTELY NO ADMITTANCE, but the huge loading bay next to it was half open, and she peered into the darkness hopefully.

Jason flashed a conspiratorial smile. "I'll let you in on a little secret," he said. "We've taken One and Two. We're putting them together." His fingers meshed in a symbolic canopy over Melinda's fat face. "The first time in twenty-five years."

"That'll make it the biggest soundstage in the world."

"Keerect. Chris likes the kind of control you can only get on a stage. Let's sneak a peak." He beckoned her inside. She tiptoed after.

There was plenty of activity, but nothing much to see. The room was big enough to hold a production line for 747s. Work lights hung low, leaving the upper reaches of the stage in darkness, while gangs of carpenters sawed and hammered at wooden scaffolding that broke up the flat expanse of floor. Though dozens of men were hard at work, the cavernous gloom and the sheer scale of the space shrunk all the activity to toy size. Jason could tell Melinda was disappointed.

"Chris is a stickler for detail. You're looking at what will no doubt be the most expensive set built in Hollywood this decade."

This intrigued Melinda. "What is it?"

Jason beckoned her closer, and spoke in a hush. "A tropical rain forest."

Melinda was dubious. "For an action picture?"

"You won't know it isn't real. We're building the next best thing to a self-sustaining ecosystem. We'll have sixteen species of snakes, twenty species of spiders, forty-seven species of butterflies. Marshall did a *Batman,* you know, and the Las Vegas set for *Bugsy.*"

He could see her wheels turning. "Do you have any sketches I could use if I wanted to do a story?"

"Well, this is all supposed to be confidential. But I could scare something up. Come over here, I'll show you what it's going to look like."

He led her back to the construction foreman's small trailer just inside the loading bay. The door was closed. He knocked, said "Jason Fo" in a loud, friendly voice. When no one answered, he opened the door and ushered Melinda inside.

He stopped when he saw Marshall and Parrott looking up at him. "Oh. Sorry." But it was too late. They had spotted Melinda. She was hard to miss, all aflutter in the narrow confines of the trailer.

"Mr. Parrott! Melinda Toto. I covered you at Cannes."

Parrott forced a smile. Jason could see he'd intruded on an unpleasant conversation. "Of course. How are you?"

"Jason's been telling me about this film. It sounds really exciting."

"It's a challenge." He eyed Jason, his voice ominously neutral. "If you don't mind, Miss Toto—"

"Melinda. Of course. We can talk later." She backed out, as if in the presence of royalty. Bumping against the door frame, she salaamed vaguely and gave him a coy smile. "This set sounds absolutely amazing. The set of the decade. Jason's after me to do a story about it."

"As a rule, I prefer to talk about the work after the fact.

Otherwise the creative process becomes too self-referential. But call the office."

"I will." She was outside the trailer now.

"Could you spare Jason for a minute, please?" Parrott eyed the door, and Jason apologetically shut it in Melinda's face.

Parrott had been having a difficult morning. Marshall was a courtly man who saw himself in the tradition of the gentleman architect, but Marshall got very possessive about his sets, and Marshall had been dogging him relentlessly about reading the script. He wanted to know the action so he could build his set to fit. He'd been with Parrott long enough to know he wouldn't be fired for pushing Parrott for his own good, and he'd pushed him. Hard.

Unfortunately, Marshall's hectoring only made Parrott more nervous about the project. Flaherty hadn't delivered the rewrite yet, and Parrott didn't want to cut off his options. Anyway, he couldn't admit to Marshall he didn't know what Flaherty would come up with. So Parrott had talked in general terms about a chase sequence through the trees, and a village compound, and a piranha pool, and Marshall was trying to cram it all into the set without knowing how it tied together, designing it while it was being built, which was a crazy thing to do, especially without a script. Finally, he told Chris he knew Chris needed a whiff of catastrophe in the air to get his creative juices flowing, and he respected that, but this time Chris was courting disaster. This was a first for Parrott, but not for Marshall. You don't do big action pictures without storyboards. You don't build a set this size until you know exactly what you're going to do with it.

In his gut, Parrott feared Marshall was right. But he didn't see any alternative. He was just trying to keep all the balls in the air until the script arrived. He had to keep Marshall building, or they'd miss their start date, and then they could lose Frotner, who was the whole reason to do the picture in the first place. He couldn't admit to Marshall he was pushing ahead blind, of course, but Marshall knew, and they were just dancing around the real issue—the start date—when Jason had blundered in with that ink-stained troll. Now Jason was facing Parrott with his bland, accommodating smile, speaking softly so Melinda wouldn't hear through the door. "What can I do for you?"

Parrott gave him a dirty look. "You have seriously compromised this film."

"What, Melinda? She's a cheerleader. I can handle her."

"Perhaps you should ask her to call Klaus and tell him we're shooting the movie on a soundstage."

"You haven't told him yet?"

"No. Of course not. I was waiting for the new script."

"Christ."

"Now he can read about it in the *Times*."

"I'll call her off. It's no big deal."

"How long do you think it'll stay a secret now that you've brought in the press?"

"I don't see how anyone is going to get very excited about our building a set."

"Moments ago you were pushing it to Melinda as the story of the decade."

"I'll handle her. Don't worry."

Parrott sized him up, then sighed. "I'll call Klaus this afternoon."

"He's probably not in town anyway."

Klaus skipped down the boarding ramp from the Warner Bros. G-3, squinting into the sun for his chauffeur, and grimaced when he spotted a gaunt, beak-nosed young man and a matronly woman in tailored suit and Liberty scarf standing by the car. Nils and Barbara. As he approached the limo, Barbara waved and chirped.

"Have a nice time, Mr. Frotner?"

"Windy."

"You have a lovely tan."

"Windburn." He was walnut from the ultraviolet rays in the higher reaches of the Bugaboos, where he'd been helicopter skiing.

"We have a lot to talk about. There's the AIDS benefit, and the *Vanity Fair* cover."

Christ. It was starting already. He ducked in the car. "Let's get out of here. What AIDS benefit?"

"I have to get the luggage." Barbara hovered outside. "Don't you remember you told David Geffen—"

The thin young man poked his head inside. "Mr. Frotner, we have to talk."

"What's the problem, Nils?"

Nils looked back at Barbara and didn't say anything. Barbara held out an organizer and a clutch of file folders, imploring. "I've tagged the really urgent things with red." Klaus beckoned Nils inside. "I'll see you next week, Barbara."

"The luggage—"

"Send it on, for Christ sake."

The chauffeur started the car. Barbara wavered. She had the sick feeling she had to pin him down that instant or he'd be out of town before she could get in the same room with him. She jumped in beside the chauffeur and spoke brightly to Klaus through the open partition. "I'll arrange the luggage by the car phone—then when you're through with Nils we can talk." Klaus ignored her. Nils closed the partition.

The car glided from the private terminal at LAX up Lincoln Boulevard for Malibu. Klaus forced himself to listen while Nils rattled on about the latest crisis. Why did he let people talk him into these things? Klaus Kickers, his franchise storefront tae kwon do operation, had overexpanded into countless deserted minimalls, mostly corner lots, former filling stations; meanwhile, the eager-beaver bullshit artist who'd gotten Klaus on board had started a second company, unbeknownst to Klaus or his accountants, and was using the franchises as collateral to buy up the minimalls and reconvert them to pumping gas. Nils was more impressed than upset. The tax laws that spawned the empty minimalls had changed, he explained, leaving them severe drains on the holding companies that owned them, and the guy had seen his opening and moved fast—

Klaus cut him off. "What am I supposed to do about this?"

"Meet with him. Get him to cut you in on the deal or you'll be holding a fistful of worthless stock while he's cleaning up."

"That's what I pay you for."

Nils shrugged. "He's not doing anything illegal. He's just being a smart businessman. I don't have any clout with him. If you want to make it work for you, you've got to step in, make something happen."

"Talk to him yourself. You make it work, for Christ sake. I'm leaving for Idaho day after tomorrow."

Nils wasn't happy to hear this. "You've got a board meeting for the restaurant next week."

"You do it. I'm not coming back till we start production."

"You've got cash-flow problems. Remember, we leveraged your Ferraris against the clothing company—Ferraris are way down, worth maybe a third what we're borrowing against them—"

"For Christ sake!"

"And we have to discuss Inga's ponies."

"How much can a horse cost?"

"These are trained polo ponies. A string of eight."

"I get ten million when we start production."

"When's that?"

"I don't know. A couple weeks. Check with Consolidated."

"You shooting in town?"

"Papua New Guinea."

Nils was not happy. "That's not even covered by satellite."

"Sorry."

Nils sniffed and swallowed, his Adam's apple bobbing silently. Klaus took small, perverse pleasure in the look on his face: With his beak nose, he reminded Klaus of a banded cormorant trying to force a fish past the metal ring around its throat.

Barbara, spying in the rearview mirror, saw the audience with Nils had ended and purred into the intercom.

"Mr. Frotner, about David Geffen—"

Klaus cut off the intercom. He looked out the smoked window across the broad, stained tarmac of Lincoln Boulevard. A ragged parade of cracker-box body shops, tire stores, and fast-food stands strangled in their own telephone wires. God, how he hated L.A.

Barbara stalked Klaus in the rearview mirror for the next half hour. When the car reached Broad Beach he jumped out before it stopped moving. She pursued him, waving her folders. He mumbled something about talking to her tomorrow and slipped in the door.

Barbara climbed into the back of the limo with Nils, poured herself a scotch, and asked him why they put up with this shit. Nils didn't answer. He never did. She picked some ice cubes from the fridge and told the chauffeur to step on it.

Klaus entered warily. The house was just like he'd left it. Piles of scripts waiting to be read. He retreated into the bedroom.

No Inga. That was a relief. He peeled off his travel leathers, pulled on a thong bikini, and headed out to wash all the shit out of his head. Thank God for the Pacific Ocean.

He was on the catwalk when he met Inga returning from the beach, playing with her towel. A rattlesnake G-string glistened between her thighs. Wearing less than he was. Fuck, she looked hard.

She stroked his neck. "You better use more sunblock. You're skin'll wrinkle like a used Kleenex."

He grabbed her towel and headed for the water. "Thanks."

"You're not going in, I hope."

"What, can't take the cold?"

"The sewer main broke in the storm last week. Didn't you hear?"

"It didn't make the snow reports in Western Canada."

"The bay's loaded with effluent. You'll come out covered in shit."

"I'm already covered in shit."

"No. You're full of it."

He glared back at her. She struck a pose, hip out, bare tit pointing skyward. He flicked the towel. Her nipple resounded with a satisfying "ping." If it hadn't been so firmly attached, he would have snapped it off.

"Bastard!"

He grinned. He was feeling a little better.

Inga spun and jumped, delivering a spring kick to his midsection. He sat with a grunt. She ran into the house, laughing.

Klaus caught up with her in the living room. She tried to keep the cardboard coffee table between them, but he shattered it with a falling-star plunge. She countered with a side kick left, but he caught her ankle and hoisted her into the air. Inga hobbled back two steps on one leg, then lost her footing. As her arms went behind her to break her fall, Klaus's free hand went for her crotch.

She laughed and twisted and lashed out with her loose leg, and Klaus caught that one too, pinning it under his elbow while he tore at the snakeskin patch. The scales split, revealing a hairless white egg with a narrow pink crack. The only part of Inga not tanned gold.

Klaus pushed forward as he worked. Inga writhed like an upended turtle, skittering back on her hands to keep from being scraped along the floor. Klaus used his advantage to reach for his own crotch, feeling the pleasant heft as he neatly uncupped his cock and balls.

The move allowed Inga to pry her leg from under his elbow.

She jabbed hard, toes pointed spearlike, cutting red grooves in Klaus's forearm with adamantine toenails. Klaus kept coming. She twisted around, ass to him, using her free leg to clamber for the cardboard sofa. She almost kicked loose, but he yanked her off balance. Her chest thunked against the corrugated seat of the sofa. He caught her flailing free leg and held her ankles wheelbarrow fashion. From beyond her ass, Inga's pale pouch winked at him. Then she clamped her thighs together. He deftly shifted his grip, taking each leg just above the knee, and pried.

Klaus strained against Inga. He was a strong man, but martial arts had taught him that half the body's muscle mass lies below the waist. Inga's legs bulged against his pressure, blooming power packed in silk.

He inched her thighs apart, and wondered if she was toying with him. He wrenched harder. No, she fought back, but there was an open wedge now, a line of attack. He plunged, driving her into the couch. His balls rubbed rough cardboard as he slipped home.

Inga stopped fighting. She relaxed her thighs, arched her back, and pressed against him. Damn, her ass was hard! He pulled out and rammed home, feeling the gratifying slap of her tight glutes, enjoying the view of this powerful woman splayed helpless before him, pinned to the couch like a squirrel on a skinning board. Inga moaned. Her tapered fingers reached back to stroke his balls—and closed around them.

Inga gave a squeeze, gentle but firm. Possessive. He froze in place. She tightened her grip just a notch. He remembered holding a baby bird like that as a kid. It struggled. He squeezed. Crushed it.

Inga looked back over her shoulder, gauging his reaction as she tightened another notch. His balls burned. He considered pulling out, sudden, but her fingers were long and hard, her nails razor-sharp. Sharp as her timing. She'd pulp that bird.

Oddly, the pain didn't shrink his cock. It made him harder. Inga gazed into his eyes with a wicked grin. Her fingers ground together through his soft bag. The fire congealed into a searing chunk of hot, jagged shrapnel.

Klaus summoned his martial discipline. Pain is a state of mind. Master the negative *chi*. He managed a thin smile.

Inga responded with a deliberate, wrenching twist—clean and efficient, like wringing the last drops from a washcloth.

Angry beasts screamed and slashed inside Klaus's sac. His smile straightened. A muscle in the corner of one eye twitched.

That was enough for Inga. She suddenly relaxed her grip. Sculpted nails gently ruffled his silky scrotum hairs.

Klaus's toes tingled. *Chi* crackled from his heels up his hamstrings to the base of his spine, flooding his sac. The bag imploded. His balls tried to fuse. Mass converted into pure energy, scalding his cock and boiling into Inga.

He fell on top of her, panting. She tolerated his weight for a few seconds, then slipped out from under and nudged the broken coffee table.

"We're gonna need new furniture."

The bitch always talked too soon.

"This cardboard crap is junk," she said. "Like living in a goddamn box factory."

He'd just had the greatest fuckin' come of his life, but he never wanted to touch the bitch again. Not right now anyway.

"Parrott called, by the way."

"Why?"

"Wants to know if I'll play the nun."

"Yeah. Right." This bitch never backed off.

"He just said call him back. I'd do a damn good job in the nun part, and you know it."

"I can sure see you slitting the guy's throat with the broken bottle." Klaus touched his balls gingerly.

"I've been working on my range. Ask Penny." Penny was her acting coach. Klaus called her the Finger-in-the-Dyke.

Klaus grunted. "I'm sure you'd be great."

"Make him test me. You'll see."

"You hate leaving L.A."

"I know. We're in the finals of the Olivia de Havilland cup."

"That's what I'm saying." He had no idea what she meant, probably some arena polo bullshit. But it would keep her in L.A. "You don't want to be sitting for months in some hellhole. It can hurt your health. *Medicine Man* was one long hepatitis epidemic. Half the crew got jaundice. Jaundice turns your skin into construction paper."

"You're not going on location."

"Bullshit."

"Not for long, anyway. François told me you were shooting in town."

"Who's François?"

"The costume designer. We were playing polo."

"How the hell would he know?"

"He said he was told they wouldn't have to prep for distant location. They'd be close to the workrooms—"

"That's bullshit. Who told him that?"

"What's-his-name. McGinty. The production manager. François said he told him they'd be doing most of the shoot on the soundstages at Studio."

"Bull-fuckin'-shit."

"Ask Parrott. And while you're at it, arrange for my test."

Annette was watching a stand-up comic when the phone rang. He'd been on *Letterman*. He had this whole routine about dying of AIDS, and the punch line was he really was dying of AIDS. He was pretty funny, but he wasn't having much impact on his audience, sipping and chatting in their red plush booths, killing time. Half the booths had curtains drawn anyway. Men at work, thirty thousand feet above the Grand Canyon.

This flight always had good entertainment. Comics and singers called Stairway to Heaven's eight A.M. eastbound the Stairway to Stardom—they'd work it for nothing, for the exposure. There was sure to be the kind of audience you couldn't buy for money: record, TV, and movie execs, top agents and lawyers. Annette thought it was all rather silly, though she liked the privacy the booths afforded, and the airline served an excellent foie gras. She and Darius flew Stairway as a matter of corporate policy. The conglomerate owned Stairway, an all-first-class line serving only the coast-to-Gotham run, ergo they flew Stairway to New York. Studio couldn't afford a company jet in any case.

To her surprise, Annette's armrest buzzed. She picked up the phone tentatively. Nobody had this number.

"Annette Foray."

"One moment please." Pops and crackles.

"Annette. This is Bo."

"Bo! What's up?" Darius buried his nose deeper in *Time*.

"I'm afraid we have a serious problem here." Bo never wasted time on small talk.

"What's that?"

"My client Mr. Frotner was led to believe he was shooting an all-location picture, of a quality consonant with his previous endeavors. Apparently we were misled."

"What do you mean?" When Bo talked legalese, it meant there was real trouble.

"Mr. Frotner has just learned *The Agonizer* is going to be filmed on a soundstage. He feels that will destroy the artistic integrity of the endeavor and he says this constitutes a breach of contract."

"You mean no one told Klaus we were shooting on stage?"

Klaus's voice cut through: "Damn fuckin' straight!"

"Klaus? Are you there too?"

"What does it matter where I am? I thought we were doing *Lawrence of Arabia* in the rain forest. It's gonna be Tarzan of the fuckin' apes on the back lot."

"I'm sure there were sound creative reasons for the decision."

"You should know," said Bo. "You must have approved it."

"We approved it because it makes financial sense, but the decision wasn't made for financial reasons. It was a creative decision. It didn't come from us. It came from the creative team."

"Well, you better unmake it, or find yourself another Agonizer."

"Klaus, please, let's discuss this like rational human beings." Klaus had a lot to lose if he pulled out of the project. But it could happen. He could put himself in a position where he had to back out to save face. She had to find him a way to save face. "I can't believe you weren't consulted."

"Believe it."

"Have you brought this up with Parrott?"

"I don't call Parrott. Parrott calls me. And he calls me before he builds the fuckin' set."

"Suppose I call him, have him call you now? I'm sure he'll have a very reasonable explanation—"

"Too fuckin' late. We make this movie his way or we make it my way."

She briefly considered the crushing cost of scrapping the set, but Parrott had made it clear he had no intention of spending months in New Guinea. She had to get Klaus and Parrott back together. They were the twin engines that powered the picture—

Darius, who had been watching placidly, waggled his finger at her.

"Just a minute," Annette said, hitting hold.

"Let me speak to him," said Darius.

Darius never volunteered for anything. Certainly not to take her heat. It made her suspicious. "It's okay. I can handle it."

"Give it to me."

She took Klaus and Bo off hold. "Darius wants to say a few words."

"I'm always happy to hear what Darius has to say." This was a new experience for Bo too.

Darius had the phone. "You're right, Klaus. We fucked up." There was beat of silence. Annette could sense Klaus cooling down. She leaned close to Darius to hear through the earpiece.

Darius continued. "Don't dump this on Parrott's lap, though. It was the producer's decision."

"That little snot-nosed prick?" said Klaus.

"You should be aware you're talking about Darius's son," said Bo.

"I don't give a fuck. He's a major fuckup," said Klaus.

"I'm sorry to say I have to agree with you," said Darius. "It is inconceivable to me that a producer would make such a basic decision without consulting the star of his film."

"He gets his break and all of a sudden he thinks he's George fuckin' Lucas."

"I took a chance on him. The opportunity may have gone to his head."

"Damn fuckin' straight."

"I'll tell you what. I positively guarantee you he won't make this kind of mistake again."

"How are you gonna do that? Bug his phones?"

"As of now, he's off the picture."

Silence at the other end. This shut up even Klaus.

"I appreciate that it must be hard for you to sack your own son," said Bo.

"Klaus is right. It's the only thing to do. I'll tell him myself as soon as we're back from New York."

"How do you feel about that, Klaus?" asked Bo.

A surly pause. "That should help."

"I'm sorry, we can't scrap the set, though," said Darius. "We've sunk too much into it."

"It's only money," said Klaus, though with less spirit than before. "If the picture's a hit, nobody'll give a damn what it cost."

"We're backed up against the start date. We couldn't switch

over to a location shoot and make you pay or play on schedule."

Bingo. Annette could sense Klaus retreat. Not Bo, though: "You're contractually committed to paying Klaus ten million dollars in three weeks, or he's a free man," he said. "I hope you're not trying to renegotiate at this late date."

"You know me better than that, Bo. I'm just trying to deal with this set situation."

Annette chimed in, cheek to cheek with Darius. "Klaus, I'm sure when Chris explains the way he plans to use the set, you'll think it's a terrific idea."

They all made nice, and Darius hung up and returned to his copy of *Time*. Annette looked at the man with renewed respect. He had cut to the heart of the matter, and found a solution that didn't drive a wedge between Parrott and Klaus.

But she knew who would have to give Jason the bad news.

SEVENTEEN

The Academy of Motion Picture Arts and Sciences has its own building of raked concrete and bronze glass, paid for by Oscar broadcasts, on Wilshire Boulevard just beyond the posh part of Beverly Hills. It tries to be imposing and solid, but it's too shiny and the corners are too sharp, a slick architect's model made large, like a bad Hollywood movie both timid and pretentious. The Nominating Committee for Documentary Features meets in a small screening room on the third floor.

There is no documentary division to the Academy, as there is an editing division, or a writing division, or a directing division. The Selection Committee consists of whoever has the time and the inclination. In the interest of fairness, selecting members must view all entries, so the committee consists of Academy members willing to watch the sixty-plus films that have either played for a week in a Los Angeles theater—a favor granted by certain arthouses owned by Goldwyn or the Laemmles—or won a film festival award. In a town where documentaries are a form of court-ordered punishment for drug-abusing producers, the Documentary Committee is a small and peripheral group of devotees, for the most part septuagenarian film technicians and unemployed social-activist actors.

The disparate mix creates an ideological split. The old-line white belt, white shoe crowd who've spent their lives smoothing edits and layering sound tracks value sleek technique. The actors value character and social import. Like many capable but underutilized members of the film community, these are frustrated people with time on their hands, so there is much wrangling, intensified by the fact that Academy rules state that "subject matter" is supposed to be ignored. The film is to be judged on filmmaking merit alone. This causes bitter arguments between the old pros and the actors—the pros accusing the actors of being incompetent in technical matters, and the actors saying that if a film moves them, then it must be well made.

The final resort of the old pros is to denounce a film as not being a true documentary. The actors cannot counter such a charge. Consequently, the few documentaries that actually find an audience, films like *Thin Blue Line* or *Roger and Me* or *Crumb* don't survive the nominating process, not because they're unworthy, but because they're not a documentary in some absolute, ideal sense. Committee purists maintain the errant filmmakers impose too much of their own personality on the subject matter.

What remain to be judged are sixties-style vérité documentaries, rarer and rarer now that video has co-opted the genre; newsroom-style reports on the plight of some person or animal or group of people or animals, such as homeless schizophrenics or the desert pupfish; and compilation films in which narrators intone on important events that happened mostly beyond the camera's view like the Yalta Conference, the Boer War, or the Reformation. Selection is a winnowing process, in which the 'best' of each type is gleaned from its fellows.

Once they've pronounced on what is a documentary, the old pros strike an unspoken compromise with the actors on the content question. Every year, besides a film on a historic event— preferably harking to the glory days of the civil rights struggle— the Oscar nominees include one film about the arts (a street-mime troupe, a famous or eccentric painter, Zubin Mehta conducting "Bolero"); one film about social abuses (plutonium shipping, selling small arms to small children); one film on the disadvantaged (retarded teenagers in love, wheelchair basketball); and one film on old people. The film on old people usually wins the Oscar, because when the whole Academy votes, the "content-blind" rule is ignored, and members vote for what they relate to. Occasionally a crossover film emerges (about a legless sculptor who welds confiscated small arms into activist art, or retarded old people in love kept apart by abusive laws); then a slot opens up for a more whimsical film. On the kudzu vine, perhaps, or sushi chefs who serve the poisonous fugu fish.

In order to preserve the committee's sanity, each member is given a white three-by-five card. Five minutes into the film a bell rings, and members who have seen enough raise their cards. If two-thirds have seen enough, the committee moves on. As the night wears on, patience grows short, and white cards fly.

Homer's film appeared at an unfortunate moment in the proceedings. The committee had been in their seats for almost four hours, and they'd watched only two complete films. The technicians insisted on sitting through a whole plodding hour on the Geneva Convention, and the actors had retaliated with ninety fervent, excruciatingly explicit minutes on Patagonian cattle blinded by the ozone hole. Both factions were tired and annoyed, and they'd been fencing for forty minutes, flagging films ruthlessly, when *Granite Plywood* was finally screened.

The first five minutes of Homer's film were his paean to plywood: woodland nature set to Schubert, and Silas Grant speaking his philosophy of plywood, and the myriad-uses-of-plywood montage. The more tolerant pros saw it as an earnest work, well photographed and well edited though technically primitive; the more caustic actors couldn't tell if the film was for real or a brilliant send-up of the genre, but either way it made them laugh. When the bell rang, enough cards went up to make the staffer take a careful count, but she let the film continue.

One crotchety fellow, a former audio mixer, demanded a recount. The sound was piss-poor, he said. It sounded like it had been recorded on a single-system Auricon and mixed in somebody's living room. He said he refused to watch film-school bullshit, and wanted to know how it had even qualified for consideration.

They stopped the film, and the Academy minion checked her paperwork. Yes, she said, *Granite Plywood* had won the Gold Medal at the Mucklinburg Festival of the Arts, attested to by the associate dean of the arts at Mucklinburg College in Vermont, a Ms. Bonnie Mamalok. The crusty fellow said it sounded like a shuck to him, a two-bit jerkwater trumped-up fraud, but one of the actors—who thought the film was a gas and was fed up with the old fart—said it was the premier arts festival in Vermont; he remembered doing *Measure for Measure* there with Burt Reynolds and Loni Anderson. When the Academy woman remarked that the film was only forty-two minutes anyway, they decided to watch the rest.

Homer had no ax to grind, no point of view beyond a general sense of wonder at whatever he was filming. Consequently, his portrait of Silas and the making of plywood, told straight, in Silas's own words, was at once acerbic, insightful, and funny, as only a film can be in which real people try to act themselves. The committee, starved for amusement, started to have a good time.

With the tree-spike scene in the plywood factory, the film took on another dimension. Here was commerce and the environment head to head, but shown with empathy for the blue-collar guy. The actors could relate to that. The technicians had seen a lot of film, and they hadn't seen much where the cameraman had almost been killed.

When Homer tracked down Trent Lockwood and got him to as good as confess on camera, *Granite Plywood* seemed poised to join that small group of activist films that doesn't merely expose, but uncovers. By the time Homer brought Lockwood and Silas together face-to-face, the audience had forgotten they were watching a documentary and were just enjoying the movie.

Then came the Shot: the plywood plant exploding outside Silas's window, Silas and his tattooed nemesis flailing away at each other, and Lockwood's panicky revelation that he was FBI. Gasps were audible.

The actors were knocked out by the double drama of Silas seeing his life's work go up in flames and the tattooed Green doing a sudden, radical character transformation before their very eyes. This was real-life crisis to treasure, a one-shot Method course in behavior under stress.

The old pros recognized it as a once-in-a-lifetime shot. And because Homer just showed what happened, without taking sides, they felt for the aged Silas and knew that Homer did too. Fed up with films on the spotted owl and acid rain and nuclear winter, they reveled in the defrocking of an uppity eco-saboteur before their very eyes.

EIGHTEEN

Jason pulled his XJS close to the voice box and buzzed. While he waited, he looked at the eight-foot iron gates, filigreed with the Hapsburg coat of arms. Beverly Hills had a six-foot height limit on fencing, but Darius, or, rather, one of his wives, had extracted an exception from the Planning Commission on the grounds that the gates were a historical monument, coming as they did from the castle of Charles II in Seville. Jason had to admit they were pretty imposing. But they made him think of dynasties, and that made him uncomfortable.

Jason had no illusions about the dinner invitation. In his taciturn manner, Darius was known to host scintillating soirees with Hollywood's wittiest and most talented; from these, Jason was routinely excluded. But once in a while his father would entertain people who he felt would be impressed by Darius the Family Man, father of a well-bred son who'd gone to Harvard—not members of the creative community, but Wall Street types in from Connecticut with their wives. Then Jason's secretary would receive a call from Darius's secretary, and Jason would traipse over to his father's house for a dreary dinner in their stuffy overdraped dining room, where he made conversation with the wives while they tried to catch the eye of someone more important.

Jason considered not going this time. He was sorely tempted. Since working on *The Agonizer,* he'd felt the leaden yoke of filial obligation lift from his shoulders. *The Agonizer* was his chance, and he was making the most of it. Sure, there had been frustrations working with Parrott and his crew. He wished he could be more creatively involved. But he was a big boy now. He knew that respect had to be earned. Once he had *The Agonizer* under his belt, his opinions would carry a lot more weight. And he had a lot to be proud of already in the way he'd nursed along the project. Respect was an intangible, like the ozone count, but he could feel his standing rise among his peers.

Lately he'd had an image of himself in a hot air balloon, "The Agonizer," wafting above the balloons of other producers in the eyes of the agents, writers, and execs craning their necks from the ground. It was a giddy feeling, looking down from that height.

On second thought, Jason decided to attend. It was the produceorial thing to do.

The gates hummed open, and Jason cruised up the drive, on past the big Mission Renaissance palace to the gardener's cottage at the back of the estate. With half-timbered walls quaintly awry under a droopy peaked roof of free-form shingles, it looked for all the world like the witch's house in "Hansel and Gretel," with stucco for icing. Helena, Darius's mother, lived here.

As a child, Jason had assumed that Darius had built it on purpose to look like a witch's house, but that was not the case. It had been put up by the previous owner. When Darius's actor father died of a heart attack, having squandered his fortune moviemaking while his cannier contemporaries were buying real estate, Helena moved in with her son. She'd insisted she wouldn't be any trouble. She wasn't.

It seemed an uncharacteristic act of benevolence for Darius to support his mother this way. How many studio heads had their mother in residence? But his detractors pointed out that Darius had gotten the better of the bargain. He didn't have to buy her a condo in Florida, and she'd raised his son as wives came and went. His partisans replied that Helena provided valuable emotional continuity for the boy, that a granny's love is more nurturing than the services of even the most highly qualified nanny. His detractors noted that the savings on child care were considerable. Darius, in his usual fashion, never commented on the arrangement.

Helena kept to herself. When Jason knocked on her door she was in robe and slippers, watching *The Lucy Show* on Nick at Night in her elfin living room. She invited him in to watch with her.

"Stay for some Stouffers. Their lasagna is very good. I bought one last week and didn't notice it was a double portion. I've been saving it for company."

Jason noted ruefully that she was genuinely pleased to see him. It reminded him how rarely he dropped in. "Thanks,

Mom, but I'm having dinner at the big house." He'd always called her Mom.

"With Darius?" Helena was incredulous, and a bit hurt.

"It's business."

"That's not business, it's highway robbery."

"It's what I do. You know that." Now he remembered why he didn't come more often.

"Your father I can understand. He grew up here. He doesn't know any better. But you went to Harvard."

Jason felt the undertow sucking him in. "C'mon, this is big business. Don't you read the papers? We're a major exporter."

She looked at him skeptically, then padded to her tiny kitchen for a beer. "Of what? Dog poop."

Jason pointed at her TV. "How can you say that? You've got that thing on all the time."

"That's TV. That's different."

"Yeah. It's product. I'm an artist, Mom. Think of me as an artist."

"You could have been a doctor. You can be a doctor anywhere. A doctor feels good about what he's done at the end of the day."

"I've got to get to the big house, Mom."

She gave him a kiss. "It's still not too late. I read that Harvard Medical School takes people in their thirties all the time."

Jason tried to regain his equilibrium by reminding himself that Helena just had a blind spot about the business. He put it down to bitterness from being married thirty years to a world-famous movie-star philanderer with not even a nest egg to show for it, and tried to be tolerant. But resisting her negativity was always draining.

When he had these arguments with Helena, he couldn't help but ask himself what his real mother would think of him. He was pretty sure her name was Roxanne. She had disappeared suddenly, utterly, and without explanation, when he was one and a half, and subsequent wives had purged the house of all pictures of the woman. Darius, of course, never talked about her. Jason thought he could remember her warm, talcy smell and her soft biceps, but he was never sure if his memories weren't just early sensations of Helena scrambled with Johnson & Johnson commercials.

Sometimes Jason thought his real mother would agree with Helena about the horrors of Hollywood—that she'd run away from this place, broken and disillusioned, to build a new life for herself on the outside. In this scenario she'd never tried to contact him because she couldn't afford to imperil her new life, like someone in the witness protection program. But other times he'd invent more exotic, operatic explanations for her sudden disappearance. Tragic death. Overpowering passion. A formidable scandal, triggering a dark conspiracy by Darius featuring some Mafia-like agreement she'd been forced to sign, which visited fearful consequences on her if she ever reappeared. This last possibility was his personal favorite. If that was his mother's story, wherever she was now, whatever she was doing, she'd be impressed with all he'd managed to accomplish.

Tonight he had the nagging suspicion his mother was in Helena's camp. Jason dragged himself to the big house.

When he entered Darius's big pink living room with its hand-stenciled beams, Jason's spirits brightened considerably. Not from the roseate glow of the quartz crystal chandelier, but because the room held two dozen of Hollywood's finest. Of course! Darius had just been east, so he must have met with all the money types on their own turf. But then, what was Jason doing there? Jason suspected Darius's secretary had speed-dialed the wrong number, but he resolved to make the most of it.

Casing the room, he was disappointed and a little surprised to see that Annette wasn't in evidence. He'd reconciled himself to the idea that their moment of passion had been a fleeting, impetuous indiscretion. Annette—any studio executive—had too full a plate to live a private life, and sex and business were a toxic brew. And yet . . . but clearly not tonight.

Jason saw a pair of dirctors sparring near the fireplace, and Melinda Toto orbiting between them and the hors d'oeuvres. How did she get herself invited? He steered the other way, toward the Bösendorfer. There, beneath the Rouault of a sad clown that reminded him of a painting by Keane, Redford, Schwarzenegger, and the Shriver woman were talking HMO reform with Bo.

Bo was the smallest of the four, but his presence dominated the group. He wore a long black silk mandarin jacket that tickled the floor. Transient currents rippled its hem, creating the impression that he was floating just off the parquet.

When Jason approached, Bo turned. He seemed the slightest bit unsure of how to greet him, so Jason put out his hand.

"Jason Fo. We're working together on *The Agonizer*."

Bo shook his hand and smiled. "Of course. Good to put a face with the voice."

"Is Klaus here?"

"Idaho, I think."

"Oh. Right." Damn! He knew that.

Bo gestured at the others. "Do you know Bob, Arnold, Maria?"

"We've never met." Jason shook their hands vigorously.

Redford's face crinkled in a smile. "Parrott's directing your picture, isn't he?"

"Yes."

"Does Parrott still do this—?" Redford tightened his neck muscles, drawing the ends of his mouth down in a masklike grimace. His sun-wrinkled skin formed contour lines, creating a wood-carved effect.

Jason laughed. "Yeah." He had to admit that was a pretty good imitation of the man when he was thinking.

Bob explained for Maria's sake: "Parrott does that when he can't make up his mind. Which is most of the time." He gave Jason a conspiratorial wink. Jason winked back.

Jason felt his body suffuse with the warm pink light of the room. He hadn't felt this way since the Oxfam benefit. But here he was, once more, at the center, the very heart, the omphalos. When his father approached to say a few words to Bo, Jason actually gave him a friendly pat on the back. Darius, who hadn't been touched by Jason in recent memory, gave a little start.

Throughout dinner Jason maintained his sense of cosmic well-being. The lobster was superb, the wine extraordinary, the conversation exceptional. Jason wasn't at the head of the table, of course, not with the likes of Bo and Arnold and Bob breaking bread, but among such distinguished company every seat was the head of the table.

When cognac and decaf cappuccino were being poured, Darius clinked his snifter with a demitasse spoon. The room quieted as all heads turned. Darius was not a man to speechify. Jason, nursing the cognac after his fourth glass of wine, saw the luminaries staring at his father and felt tears well up. Not tears of gratitude. No. He belonged there. Tears of pleasure that his father should finally give him a place at the table. Darius was an enigmatic man, to be sure, but he had to admit that he was also a compelling, complicated man. There was nothing wrong with being complicated. Complexity implied subterranean currents, hidden meanings. Jason asked himself if he was complicated enough.

Darius's speech was brief. He thanked everyone for being there and said he had a little announcement to make. Since they were all his friends, he wanted them to hear the news from him tonight instead of at the press conference tomorrow morning. "I am resigning as head of Studio Pictures to pursue other challenges."

Funereal silence.

"Running a movie studio has its compensations. But as a job, it's more difficult than important. For a long time now I've wanted to find work that puts me closer to the creative process."

Guests chimed in with their congratulations. Jason saw Melinda turn pink with excitement. So that's what she was doing here. She asked the follow-up: "What are you going to do next?"

"I'm afraid I can't discuss that at this time."

"Is there anything you can tell us?"

Darius and Bo exchanged a glance. "I'm investigating the possibility of assembling a significant investment fund from European sources."

That's what they all said when they got canned. The encouraging chatter got louder.

Jason was stunned. Briefly. Then it all made sense. Studio hadn't made much of a dent in the market, and Darius had just returned from a board meeting of the conglomerate. Still, he thought they'd have waited until *The Agonizer* came out. God, it was an unforgiving business.

Jason felt a warm rush of relief. Out from under! Then the cold fingers of reality clutched his throat. If the conglomerate didn't want Darius, why would they want him? He replayed the details of his producing contract with Studio, but he couldn't remember the cut-off provisions. Christ! The legalese didn't matter anyway. It all came down to who filled Darius's shoes.

Whoever it would be needed *The Agonizer*. And he was *The Agonizer*. Wasn't he? He tried to summon up the fine print on his *Agonizer* deal.

Melinda pursued her story. "So, Darius, have they named a successor yet?"

Darius nodded. "Yes."

"Can you tell us who?"

Jason leaned forward.

"Annette Foray. And may I say I think it's an excellent choice."

Annette didn't conspire to boot Darius. That wasn't her style. Jason decided this was a very good sign. Everyone knew she was totally committed to *The Agonizer*. Even if she wanted to, she couldn't back off her own project. Not that she'd want to. She'd been its biggest fan right from the beginning.

The more he thought, the better this seemed for *The Agonizer*. And for Jason Fo. By elevating Annette, the conglomerate removed the layer of bureaucracy that had separated him from the real decision-making. Annette had Yes Power now.

He understood why she wasn't at dinner. Inevitably, she would have become the focus of the evening, and that would have been woefully inappropriate. Jason guessed she'd bowed out herself, from her innate sense of tact. Darius must have invited her. He couldn't afford not to.

This news was too important to discuss across a table. By twos and threes people rose and huddled with Darius. With a twinge of sadistic glee Jason worked his way over to his father and put out his hand.

"Congratulations."

"Thanks."

"I'm sure you've been wanting to do this for a long time."

"I have."

Darius was distracted by another well-wisher. Jason watched his father, smiling faintly, shake the proffered hand, as if mildly amused by the whole situation. Jason could see the advantage of being a man of few words.

For the first time in his life, Jason felt genuine pity for the man. Darius's time had passed, and his was just beginning. Then it hit him. His invitation had been no fluke. Darius was saying, "Welcome to the table. I've made you one of us. But I'm leaving now. Now you're on your own." Darius was giving him wings!

Emotion clouded Jason's eyes as he watched his father, so calm, so brave, fielding the press of phony congratulations. Darius glanced in his direction, and Jason raised hand to eye in gentle salute. He thought he saw his father nod slightly in return.

The residential heart of Beverly Hills, between Sunset Boulevard and Santa Monica, boasts broad, straight, deserted streets, a twenty-five-mile-an-hour speed limit, and a population of automobiles capable of moving at one-quarter the speed of sound. The temptation to flout the law is overpowering. The Beverly Hills police, knowing this, have liberally salted the streets with stop signs. Doubling the speed limit is ticketed, but tolerated. Running a stop sign is not. When muscle cars meet late at night on Rexford or Beverly Drive, the chopped-up trip becomes a series of miniature drag races—gut-churning rubber-smoking hundred-yard sprints from sign to sign.

Jason's Jaguar was well suited to this sport, but tonight Jason wasn't playing. He tooled along with the top down at a smooth twenty-five, feeling the sentinel palms strobe by overhead, giant mutant pineapples on hundred-foot stalks lending the avenue an air of Egyptian formality. He was being very, very careful. He drank rarely enough to know he shouldn't be driving in his condition. Damn, he felt good! He didn't want any ugly encounter to break his mood. If ever there was a night for drinking, this was it!

He reached Santa Monica Boulevard. Checking the signs while he waited for the light, he noticed he was in the turn-either-way lane. Why go home? If he went home, it would all be over. When the light changed, instead of turning right, toward West L.A. and home, he impetuously swung the wheel left toward Hollywood.

He cruised along Santa Monica into West Hollywood, where even now life spilled onto the sidewalks near the Sports Connection. Gay life. In both senses of the word, he thought, ruefully. Jason had lunch with a lot of people, he got laid a fair amount, but he didn't have any real friends. Nobody he'd walk down the street joking with.

He thought about Annette. The news of her ascendancy hadn't broken yet, though he could think of a few car phones that were seeing heavy use. She was probably sitting tight at home, phones off, resting up for tomorrow's whirlwind. After tonight he might never have the chance to connect with her again. She'll be swept away in the tornado, like Dorothy. He'll be home knitting like Auntie Em. Why not give her a rousing send-off? At Crescent Heights he turned north, toward Laurel Canyon and Wonderland Avenue.

Jason parked and reached into the backseat for his karaoke machine. It was a present from someone with Japanese money trying to interest him in making a murder mystery where the audience sang along with the stars onscreen. He sorted through tapes and found one that would work, then picked up a handful of pebbles and tossed them at what he was pretty sure was Annette's bedroom window.

Violins wafted up Wonderland Avenue. Jason stood tall in the moonlight, jacket slung over shoulder, and crooned into the mike in his best Sinatra imitation: "Fly me to the moon." Coming from the boom box, his voice blended well with the strings.

Annette's window stayed dark. The song went on. Jason forgot the rest of the words, and hummed. He was beginning to doubt the wisdom of his serenade. This was his boss. Some less inebriated part of his brain warned he might be doing something incredibly stupid.

The window opened and Annette stuck out her head. Even in her nightgown, fresh from bed, she was a pale porcelain vision of perfection. Jason felt instantly reassured.

He bowed low. "Congratulations, milady, on your elevation to the throne."

"Shhh! Jason!" She seemed amused.

"Once the confetti starts to fly, I know you will have little time for such as the lowly I, a mere toiler in your vineyard. But I pledge my fealty, milady—these fingers exist but to pick your grapes, these feet but to crush them into wine."

She giggled. "May I always drink from your bottle."

Having scored, he gave her a graceful out. "Prithee, my fealty wroth I shall wend away."

"No, no. C'mon in." Annette disappeared.

Jason thrummed her doorjamb in anticipation. Could her bottle comment have referred to their poolside adventure? Was she going to drink from his bottle tonight?

The door opened. Annette ushered him in with a somber wave. No, this wasn't the night. "Actually, I'm glad you came by. I've been meaning to talk to you, but since New York, I've been so busy with all this . . ."

"Something the matter?"

"We're in trouble. Big trouble."

"On *The Agonizer*?"

Annette nodded. "I'm afraid you're the only one who can help."

"You know I'll do whatever I can."

"I know." She took his hand, her eyes large, dark pools of trust. "And I know you're one of the very best producers I've got. But what I'm going to ask is harder than anything you've ever done."

Jason could feel himself rising to the occasion. "Try me."

Annette sat him down next to her on her mission sofa. "Parrott screwed up. He didn't inform Klaus he was shooting on stage."

"Oh, that. Parrott said he'd call Klaus and clear that up."

"Klaus had a fit. He wants to quit the picture."

Jason's face went slack. "Christ. When did this happen? Why didn't anybody tell me?"

Annette waved that away. "I've tried everything to bring them together, but Klaus is furious. He says there's been a serious screw-up, and he's demanding Parrott's head."

"I'll talk to him."

"It won't do any good. *I* talked to him and it didn't do any good. Klaus says whoever ordered that set built has to go. Or he goes. And he means it."

Jason felt a pit open beneath him. He'd known it was a mistake to make such a big secret of that damn set—if only they'd made it public knowledge, Klaus and Parrott would have worked through this. But Parrott wouldn't talk to Klaus without the damn script. He should have pushed Parrott harder. Damn. "Maybe we could give him Marshall."

"Won't work." She shook her head solemnly. "Klaus knows telling him isn't the production designer's job. Besides, we'd never finish the set on time, and anyway, Parrott won't allow it. He's in a pissing contest now, and he's not about to let Klaus fire his old buddy. He has crew approval, remember."

"McGinty, then?"

"Pissing contest." She put her hand on Jason's shoulder. "There is only one person who can save this picture."

Jason swallowed hard. He noticed how small the room was, how dark. The wine that had buoyed his wits suddenly felt like a lumbering sea anchor, dragging him into stupidity. He fought to rise above the waves.

"Are you asking me to take the fall for Parrott?"

"You'd still be the producer. You'd keep your office, and your fee, and everything. You just couldn't go on the set or into the editing rooms or talk to Klaus or anybody."

"Not even Parrott?"

"If you talked to Parrott, Klaus would have a paranoid attack."

In his fog, Jason realized that Annette was actually being nice about this. As long as Studio paid him and gave him his credit, they were fulfilling their end of the contract. And yet . . . He looked at Annette. He couldn't keep the pleading out of his eyes.

"This is the only way?"

"You have every right to tell me to go to hell." She put her hand on his arm. "It's your call. *The Agonizer* is your picture. You can walk away and save it, or hold your ground and the picture will fall apart. It's up to you."

As Jason pondered his situation, he realized that Annette was right. Contractual niceties were irrelevant. Even if he had total control etched in steel, he'd have to step down. The picture had to come first. That's what producing meant. Putting the picture first. He began to feel better about the situation.

"I'd keep my credit?"

"Sole producer credit, single card, per contract." She touched his cheek, and he could see in her soft sable eyes Annette appreciated what he was going through. "I know I'm asking for the ultimate sacrifice. And when it's time to renew your deal, I won't forget you were the man who saved this picture."

So she'd owe him one. Not a bad place to be, having a studio chief owe you one. Jason had to admit that his *Agonizer* situation wouldn't be all that different from the way it was now. Parrott and all his fucking contractual rights. And he'd have more time to pursue other projects. Hell, he'd put *The Agonizer* into motion by bringing together the elements. That's what producing was anyway. Starting the chain reaction.

"Can we keep this to ourselves?" he asked.

"It's strictly between you and me."

"And Klaus and Parrott."

"As far as the world is concerned, *The Agonizer* is your picture." She gave him a peck on the cheek and led him to the door. "When it's envelope time, you'll be the man on the podium."

NINETEEN

Jason felt liberated, actually. Reenergized. Without *The Agonizer* to hold him back, he hit the development trail running, churning through treatments, spec scripts, and writing samples, conferring with playwrights and renegade federal lawmen and experts in cryogenics, lunching if not with top agents, then with the upper second echelon.

His secret, like any secret in Hollywood, was public knowledge within days, but Jason's nose wasn't rubbed in it. The agents didn't care. He was perceived as being close to Annette, a perception that Annette did him the favor of not denying. He'd started *The Agonizer,* they figured, and the agents had plenty of projects that needed starting. Within two weeks he had a couple of things that looked like they'd go into development.

So when the script arrived, it caught Jason by surprise. It was sent from Nantucket, addressed to him in Flaherty's own hand. He considered passing it on to Parrott unopened.

Inside, he found a brief note in Flaherty's scrawl, to the effect that this was the rewrite as per agreement. Delivery fee was now due and payable.

Jason surmised what must have happened. Flaherty and Parrott must have reworked the thing to the point where Flaherty said, "Send it in, I want to get paid," and Parrott had agreed, but Flaherty didn't trust him to actually make the submission, or was in too much of a hurry for dough to wait for Parrott to do it, so he sent Jason the script to get his check. Since he'd addressed it to Jason personally, it had slipped through the mail room net.

What pained Jason about this scenario was the thought that Parrott had never bothered to tell Flaherty he'd been taken out of the loop. He must have already been so far out, it wasn't worth mentioning.

Jason had a stack of scripts on his desk he'd promised to read

125

in the next forty-eight hours. By rights, this should go on the bottom of the pile. Something to leaf through during *Nightline*.

He folded back the cover page. The opening line crackled with the distinctive Flaherty style. Buried as he was under second-echelon stuff, upper second echelon, but second echelon nonetheless, he felt a frisson of pride as his eye swept the page. This was a Flaherty script. *His* Flaherty script. He tilted back and gave himself up to the pleasure of a top-echelon read.

Flaherty's weathered clapboard house, once a schooner captain's, perched high on an ocean cliff. Storm waves snarled at the rocks below and a dank sky crouched above. On the rickety balcony, a big man in a wind-whipped polo shirt leaned into the wintry bluster.

Klaus was staring out over the Atlantic. Slug gray. Cold. Like Flaherty, he thought. Why live staring at a fuckin' ocean too fuckin' hostile to use? Typical East Coast pent-up conflicted bullshit. Flaherty should study Sun Tzu. Master your foes, physical and mental. Or they master you.

He returned to the faintly mildewed study. Parrott stopped muttering to Flaherty. The two of them stared at him like a couple of cows.

"I'm gonna say this one last time." They didn't look too happy about going another round. Tough shit.

"You see, guys, I'm the hero. The hero is the good guy. He knows what he wants and he gets it. If anyone gets in his way, he kicks butt. What you've done here, you've made him a namby-pamby chump. Every time he kicks ass, he moans and groans about it. My audience will laugh this shit off the screen." He could see Parrott trying to figure out how to handle him. He didn't like being handled.

"Klaus," said Parrott, "your character murders seven people in the course of the script—"

"That's another thing. You've cut the action down to diddly-squat. Willis killed seventy-four in *Die Harder*."

"Let me finish—he kills seven people. He has to feel something, some remorse for all the mayhem, or the audience will hate him for it."

"Did Mad Max?"

"I haven't seen *Mad Max*."

"You haven't seen *Mad Max?* Well, I've seen *Mad Max,* and my fans have seen *Mad Max.* When Mad Max kicks butt, he feels like a million dollars. And *they* feel like a million dollars."

"Klaus, listen." Parrott's neck muscles clenched reflexively; for a moment his face tightened into a No mask. So Parrott was getting tired of dancing around. Maybe now they'd get down to red meat.

"Empathy,"—Parrott was putting on his best pissant East Coast voice—"empathy is a basic principle of drama. Since Aristotle, the hero is supposed to have a tragic flaw. Why? Because he's human, and we're human. He's better than we are, sure, but he has a human weakness we can all identify with. He's supposed to be telling us about ourselves. That's what moves people when they watch great drama. That a man—a great hero—struggles so bravely against the human weakness we all share."

"And the Agonizer's tragic flaw is he kills people?"

"Well, it's more complicated than that, but basically, yes."

"Two billion dollars."

"Excuse me?"

"Two billion says you're wrong."

Parrott was seated in a beat-up wicker armchair. The sprung seat forced him to slouch. Klaus approached and loomed over him, as if to prove his point by his sheer bulk. "I kick butt in *Black Death* and *Widowmaker.* I kick butt in all of 'em. And the more I kick, the more they love me. They don't ask how it makes me feel, 'cause they know how it makes them feel: They feel great. One hundred and ten percent. You start having me piss and moan about kicking butt, they'll start asking why they want to watch butt-kicking in the first place. Or they're too dumb to ask themselves anything, they just walk out of the movie feeling like shit. Then they tell their friends not to go, and the picture dies after week one"—here Klaus jabbed at Parrott, who slumped deeper in his chair—"and the next Frotner picture comes out, they say, 'Why the fuck should we watch him if it makes us feel like shit?' and they don't go to that one, and before you know it, Klaus Frotner isn't kicking any more butt."

Parrott hoisted himself up from the creaky wicker into Klaus's face. He was not a physically brave man, but he was a movie director. He could fight for a picture. Sixty pounds lighter than Klaus but two inches taller, he looked down at him with a hint of analytical amusement. "You're afraid."

"Bullshit."

"I didn't ask for this movie, Klaus. It was offered to me. You told me you wanted to make a creative leap. I thought you meant it. But you don't have the guts."

"Bullshit."

"You want to shoot another *Black Death,* that's your prerogative. But that's not what I signed on for."

"I already made *Black Death.*"

"If you want to make the leap, you have to trust me. Can you trust me?"

Klaus stared at Parrott, tight-lipped. Parrott softened his tone. "You have proven presence onscreen. That's not the same as acting. We both know that. It's not your fault. You haven't been allowed to act. I've studied your work, and I see tremendous potential. I'd stake my reputation on it. I *am* staking my reputation on it."

"I know what they want—"

"Forget what *they* want. Worry about what *you* want. As an actor, I'll trust your instincts implicitly." Parrott tapped Klaus's chest. "My job is to bring out what's in there. What's *really* in there. Keep you honest. Keep you on track. If I think you're cheating yourself, being lazy or lying to yourself or hiding your true feelings, I'll fight you every step of the way. Because that's my job. If you don't trust *my* instincts enough to let me do my job, you need another director."

Klaus could tell Parrott wasn't bullshitting him. The guy had too much at stake to dick around. He'd never been talked to this way, director to actor. It struck him that his directors had never trusted him, none of them. They'd feared him, they'd let him do whatever the hell he wanted, but they'd never trusted him like Parrott was talking about.

"You really think this can work?"

"We're very different, but I see that as an asset. We bring different values to the mix. If we can use the best of what we both have to offer, your performance—our film—will be raised to another level."

Parrott had a proven ability to deliver. Klaus grunted. "Like *Lawrence of Arabia.*"

Parrott nodded. "Or *The Godfather.*"

"Or *The Road Warrior.*"

"I'll run that as soon as I get back to L.A." Parrott tore a scrap from Flaherty's legal pad and made a note.

Klaus laughed. "Count the bodies in that one."

"We'll run it together. You can show me what you mean. But if it's as good as you say it is, I bet you I can show you the hero's a flawed human character."

Klaus gave a ruminant grunt. "This script needs more action. And I'm telling you—as an actor—this guy has to feel good about killing those geeks. Like he did in the first draft. Hell, they deserve it."

"I think we can accomplish that and still hold on to the basic values I'm describing." Parrott turned to Flaherty. "What do you think, Joe?"

Joe stopped writing. He'd been jotting something on a yellow pad—notes or doodles, Klaus couldn't see. He thought for a moment. "If Chris thinks we can do it, we can do it."

Klaus didn't like the way the two guys shared a look. "I'm gonna have to see something in the next two days."

Flaherty gave him a thin smile. "This is major surgery. I'll be lucky to have it in two weeks."

"I go pay or play in two days. I want to know if this is gonna fly."

"No can do."

Klaus stared at him, trying to read what was really going on.

"I'm not jerking you off, Klaus. Chris, tell him."

Parrott was uncharacteristically silent. "I go pay or play in two days too."

Flaherty's smile took on a sardonic twist. "I suppose you two will just have to take each other on faith. Unless, of course, you want to put off payday for a couple of weeks."

Klaus and Parrott sized each other up.

Sundays, Consolidated slept. Its agents worked still, on sparsely peopled beaches and crowded Beverly Hills brunch lines, but Sundays the soaring white needle was left to regenerate in peace, to stabilize its microclimate, cleanse its air of sweat, cigar smoke, and expensive perfume, and allow its weary carpets to spring back to life.

This Sunday was a little different. Bo, holding his antique split cane fly rod, stood by the stream in the deserted lobby, talking to a man in a plaid shirt with plastic pocket liner, who trailed a strip of paper in the water under Bo's supervision. The man straightened.

"PH content's fine."

"I know that, Preston," said Bo. "We have it checked every day."

"Just have to be sure before I make my diagnosis." Preston was the foremost icthypsychologist in Southern California, and not as awed by Bo as people in the movie business.

"Watch." Bo whipped the rod back and forth, ten o'clock to one o'clock, precise if not buttery smooth. The fly hit perfectly, in still water under hanging willows. A pair of trout eyed it speculatively for a second. The larger suddenly struck—and the smaller one took a bite from his tail. The larger trout turned, fly forgotten. A nasty fish-fight ensued.

"I told you it was a risk stocking goldens. What you have here is a case of territorial neurosis. Golden are a beautiful fish, sure, but they're a free-range species. Normally, the smaller fish loses out, he moves on, finds his own spot. Pile 'em on top of each other in this little bitty stream, the loser's got no place to go, gets psychotic. Liable to do anything."

"This little bitty stream is the biggest indoor trout stream ever built."

"You wanta tell the fish that? My advice is clear 'em out, introduce greenback cutthroats—"

"If we can't make golden work, I don't want trout. What if we stock females only?"

Preston considered this. "Never been tried that I know of. Wouldn't be surprised if they started humping each other. Why you so set on golden?"

Bo waved his arm to include the majestic lobby echoing with the deep rumble of the waterfall. "I'm in the myth business. Golden trout are wild, High Sierra creatures as Californian as the giant condor. They're the Moby-Dick of trout—"

Bo was interrupted by a chirping sound. Preston looked around to see if he could identify the insect. Bo whipped out his phone. "Bo."

"Joe Flaherty here. Reporting from the front." Flaherty was a client of Bo's.

Bo blanked out Preston. "How's it going?"

"We've reached an impasse. Or an accommodation. Take your pick."

"How so?"

"There seems to be general consensus that they need another rewrite."

"How big a job?"

"Big. Couple of weeks minimum. That's a hundred thousand a week, right?"

"I'll lock in the two weeks." Bo shifted to a more intimate tone. "How's it looking from a creative standpoint?"

"You're better off asking Parrott. He should be calling you any minute." Parrott was Bo's client too.

"What do you think?"

A pause. "You know Parrott. He whips up chaos and serves a soufflé."

"Can you give him what he needs?"

"Chris always needs more. You know that."

Bo looked at the wounded trout lurking under the willows. "What I'm hearing, Joe, is that you think he might not pull this one together."

"Ask Parrott. You'd better get Annette Foray at home, by the way. If I'm going to deliver in two weeks, I have to be on the job tomorrow morning."

Bo had barely snapped the phone shut when it chirped again. "Bo."

"Chris here. Calling from the grimmest damn day in Nantucket history."

"How's it going?"

Pause. "I always enjoy working with Joe. You know that. But it's trying having Klaus look over our shoulders. I don't think he understands the process."

"Want me to get him out of Nantucket?"

"That would be a big help."

"Once Joe delivered to the studio, you understand, I couldn't keep the script from Klaus."

"I know, I know."

"Joe says you need another rewrite."

Parrott's voice took on a testy edge. "Joe is a very talented man, but he thinks about money too much."

"What's your assessment?"

"Joe hasn't solved the script. It has some brilliant moments, but it hasn't come together yet. For what we're paying him, he should solve the script."

"Am I hearing that you think he can't do it?"

"It's hard to tell. The script's at that delicate point; it could go either way. God, I wish I had Klaus off my back."

"I'll take care of Klaus. Do you want to try another writer?"

Pause while Parrott considered this. "No. It'll take too long to get him up to speed. It won't do any good anyway." Parrott gave a plaintive sigh.

"If you want to bail out, now's the time."

Another long pause. "I need two weeks, Bo. By then I'll know if we're really on track."

"Do you want to put off going pay or play for two weeks?"

"Maybe. Christ, I don't know."

"You'll be getting four million. You've never got more than two point five."

"I know, I know."

"Annette will give you the time. But you're sending her a bad message. You're planting doubt."

"So she knows I'm worried about the script. When I like it in a couple of weeks, she'll be that much more convinced it's good."

"Will she? Will Klaus?" Silence from Parrott. "There is the momentum issue, Chris. Remember Darius. The conglomerate is cash poor and skittish. You ask for a two-week delay, they'll be only too happy to give it to you. Two weeks from now, when you love the script, it's that much easier for them to bail out."

A long pause. "This project has enormous potential."

Bo continued, calm, reassuring. Chris was hooked; now he had to let him run. He paid out more line. "If you want me to, I'll get the delay. From here, it's hard for me to counsel you properly."

Another long sigh. "I feel like my career's at stake with this one, that's all."

Bo kept the line taut. "You've said that before, Chris."

"But this is different."

"I haven't been in on the meetings. But I know that every project we've done together, you've had a period of intense doubt just before you commit irrevocably. It seems to give you a final creative boost."

Bo waited him out. He heard a faint rustling that he assumed was Parrott's chin rubbing against the mouthpiece as he contorted his face. Finally, Chris spoke in a voice thin with concern. "I suppose if I don't like the rewrite I can deal with that when the time comes."

Bo reeled him in. "Once you've committed, you've always felt a lot better about the project."

Bo had barely rejoined Preston when the phone chirped. "Bo."

"Klaus."

"How's it hanging?" With Klaus, Bo assumed more of a street persona.

"This is shuck and jive, man."

"What's the problem?"

"The problem is these guys are fulla shit."

"If you want out, say the word."

"That first script was a great fuckin' script. I don't see why Parrott has to jerk around with it."

"What does he say?"

"Some bullshit about deepening characters. He talks about motivation a lot."

"Do you want me to get him off the picture?"

A pause. "The pisser is, once he's on the set, I bet he's a fuck of a good director."

Bo let him chew on that for a while. "Tuesday I hit them up for your ten million dollars."

"But we have jack shit for a script."

"The usual shit. Harrison Ford dropped out of a David Peoples script at Paramount. They're in a tight place."

"Who's directing?"

"Cronenberg."

Klaus grunted. He was not impressed.

"I could get you pay or play in six weeks, maybe. Your deal will be back at your old level, though."

"So it would cost me, what, three million?"

"And points. And I got you a piece of gross video sales. You'd be back to net on that. That could cost you fifteen million."

Klaus whistled.

"Flaherty's good, Klaus. He might surprise you."

"He's nuts. Living in this toad hole."

"Get out of there, go skiing or something, clear your head. Give them a of couple of weeks."

Klaus didn't answer right away. Finally, "What the fuck. But you tell them I'm the fuckin' actor, Bo. I get on the set, nobody can make me say fuck-all I don't want to."

Bo reached Annette in her car. He was calmly upbeat. Yes, he'd talked to the principals. They were excited by the prospects of the project and eager to proceed. Chris and Klaus felt the script could use another polish, though. Bo presented this as something Parrott was doing to cement his relationship with Frotner, to make him part of the team again after the unfortunate misunderstanding about the set. Presented as a way to buy peace, Flaherty's two hundred thousand sounded like a bargain.

Bo explained that he knew Annette had until Tuesday to give the go-ahead to the project, but Chris needed to proceed with the rewrite posthaste. Before her phone broke up in the canyon, Annette okayed the rewrite, but she stalled on the rest until Tuesday, explaining that she wanted the conglomerate to feel they'd been fully consulted. Annette made it sound like a formality. Bo knew better. This wasn't about the conglomerate. The deals were in place. This was her call.

Monday night, nestled in her little hideaway on Wonderland Avenue, Annette turned off her phones and forced herself to reread the Flaherty script. This kind of movie was hugely successful, but she had to admit she wasn't instinctively a fan of the genre. How to tell if forty million Americans would pay to sit through this one? Yet this film would determine her success as head of Studio. She could root around, hope to dig up a cheapie sleeper, but she was *The Agonizer* in the minds of Hollywood.

The weight of the decision made it difficult for Annette to gauge how she felt about the script. Certainly the characters were more nuanced, more dimensional now. But even allowing for her distaste for the genre, she had the nagging suspicion that something was missing. She made herself a hot chocolate, using real shaved Italian cocoa and a froth inducer, and tried to summon up her initial response to the first draft. It was hard, after all the meetings and Flaherty's rewrite. She remembered being repelled but fascinated, like watching open heart surgery. She remembered flying through the script. But how much of her excitement came from knowing that Klaus was willing to commit? Maybe the demonic energy was all still there in Flaherty's version but she'd become inured to it. She looked around for a copy of the first draft, but couldn't find one.

Annette considered asking for a delay to see the new rewrite, but she knew Bo would never stand for it. She had a brief image of herself as a stoplight stuck on yellow. She had to flash red or green. Tonight.

The more she thought about it, the clearer it became that she didn't have a choice, really. To cancel out a Frotner-Parrott project—one she'd initiated, for that matter—would send absolutely the wrong signal to her peers. She'd go to the bottom of everybody's list. Particularly Bo's. And his list mattered most.

This was a people business, she reminded herself, and she was a people person. As she'd told *Variety*, everyone knew the movie business was a big gamble; her job was to find talented people and bet on their passion. Klaus Frotner and Christopher Parrott felt passionately about *The Agonizer*. Bo did too, or he wouldn't entangle three of his major clients in the project. She'd bet on a strong hand. Now she had to play it.

Tuesday, Studio cut a one-and-a-half-million-dollar check for Christopher Parrott and a ten-million-dollar check for Klaus Frotner and had them messengered to Bo's office. Now that their pay-or-play deals had been invoked, Studio was bound to pay another two-and-a-half-million to Parrott and another twelve million to Klaus according to a fixed timetable, whether or not the movie was ever made.

Over the next few days, McGinty locked in guarantees for the costume designer, the cinematographer, and the editor. An extras casting director joined the two casting people already on the job. The gaffer, key grip, prop master, wardrobe supervisor, first assistant director, unit publicist, stunt coordinator, visual effects coordinator, aerial coordinator, and transportation coordinator were put on payroll, and commitments tendered to lock in the rest of the crew. A special effects coordinator was assigned to design the climactic conflagration scene. Klaus's bodyguard and his personal trainer were charged to the picture. Lights, trucks, cameras, and camera cranes were contracted for, to ensure their availability during the shoot. A special casting unit was dispatched to the Amazon to find appropriate native people and arrange for their transplantation to Los Angeles. A second prop and costume crew accompanied them. Hotel arrangements were made for a ten day location shoot in Papua New Guinea, and the location manager and his assistant were dispatched there to track down the necessary transportation and native help, and touch base with local authorities. They carried forty thousand dollars in cash. Before the go-ahead, McGinty fought with Marshall over every additional species of butterfly and orchid, but now the set was given crash priority. Construction crews were doubled and working twelve-hour shifts.

In Marshall's search to make the rain forest lusher and more cinematic than the actual thing, he'd designed a place that blended the best of many ecosystems. Now the greens crew was increased to twenty-two, half to shape the basic infrastructure, half to chase down exotic rain forest flora: palms, deciduous trees and bushes, creeping vines, rare jungle orchids. Animal wranglers were put on notice: thousands of exotic insects were ordered from Brazil and Shanghai, scores of snakes, spiders, birds, monkeys, lizards, and bats from Panama and Belize and Burma. A trainer started working with the jaguar.

McGinty did a revised budget. The cost had increased from eighty-nine to one hundred and two million dollars. Forty-three million had already been paid out or irrevocably committed.

TWENTY

Dressed in Wellingtons and a lumberjack shirt, Homer squished daintily along the edge of his drive. Weeks of sunshine and tepid drizzle had melted snow and thawed topsoil, but the layer beneath was still frozen solid, trapping the runoff; with nowhere to go, slush had churned into gelatinous muck, neither solid nor liquid, and the dirt track with the hump in the middle that banged Homer's transmission was now a sinuous pool of sludge.

Homer liked the sucking sound his boots made when he switched feet. He felt kinship with the placid texture of the mud, and its odor of pregnant rot. He might have been wading through primordial ooze. Sliding along, he dreamed about making a mud movie, Vermont as world primeval. He closed his eyes to imagine the opening, framed so tight the mud looked like nothing but flat brown screen. Brown would bulge into a bubble dome of rising gas, bursting with a satisfying splattery "plop." . . . Homer's leg dropped up to the calf in muck and his foot pulled out, leaving the boot behind. Hopping on his other leg, he used both hands to wrench the boot loose and reinsert his foot without bemiring the sock.

He was pleased he'd saved his sock, but he wouldn't let himself think anymore about the mud movie. Instead, he thought about his ax. Homer hadn't been to the main road for three days, since his last expedition to town, when he'd bought a sack of oatmeal and milk and Tang and a new whetstone, and he'd left the whetstone in the car. His ax had been dull already, or he wouldn't have bought the stone, and over the past three days he'd been chopping a lot of wood with a blunt object, and finally he figured it was less work to slog the half-mile back to the car and swing a sharp ax again.

The Subaru was parked on high, dryish ground. Homer pried open the door and was hit by the heady pungency of moldy polyurethane foam. His backseat had split long before, and dur-

137

ing mud season it never quite dried out. He rooted around on the damp floor, and found the whetstone wedged under the driver's seat, behind an old film can. He slipped it into his shirt pocket and slammed the Subaru's door. Imagining the clean, hard thwack of a sharp blade biting green wood, he took two graceful glissades toward home.

Homer skidded up short. His spirits sank into the mud. Before him, inescapable, beyond a broad moat of muck, his mailbox rose in reproach.

Homer dreaded the mail. If it wasn't simply disappointing, it was full of bad surprises, or worse, reminders of things he was trying not to think about: bills, mostly, or letters about school stuff or tax stuff or ads he shouldn't ignore if he knew what was best. He couldn't think of a single good thing that ever appeared in that box. Except for when he used to get *National Geographic.*

But Frances had seen him leave the house, and she'd made him promise he'd retrieve the mail. If she didn't hate mud so much, she'd get it every day. The mailbox was her cave of wonders, crammed with flying carpets spiriting her away to New York or Hollywood or Europe, promising the magic lamp of a sweepstakes killing or a job offer. If he showed up with the whetstone, he'd better have the mail.

Homer asked himself, hopefully, if the mailman hadn't refused to deliver through such mire. But he saw tire tracks leading in and out of the mud pond. Betty's truck had four-wheel drive and giant Sno-Grabbers and she liked to challenge mud.

The mailbox was lashed with baling wire to a perforated steel post jammed into a finger of higher ground that dropped precipitously into deep mire. Clinging to the post, Homer tried to keep his footing on the ridge while he reached around front and lowered the box lid. Making a claw of his left hand, he poked around blindly inside. Not much. Finances being what they were, Frances had let her subscriptions lapse so long ago, the magazines had finally stopped coming.

Homer extracted a couple of window envelopes and stuffed them in his back pocket. Before going, he shook the box for good measure. Something rattled inside. Damn. Still clutching the post, he arched forward over the muck and tried to look in. He couldn't twist that much, but he shoved his arm in far enough to feel the edge of a small, square, fat envelope before it slipped back out of reach.

Homer straightened. Annoyed, he banged the back of the box with his fist; it wiggled on the baling wire, and the envelope shot out the front. Homer lunged for it. His legs slithered out from under him. Miraculously, his windmilling right arm caught the steel post, and instead of falling facefirst in the mud, he neatly speared the envelope with his free hand. But even as his fingers closed over the cream-colored paper, he felt something heavy slide from his pocket. The whetstone! He jerked upright, but too late. The stone made a lazy swan dive for the pond. Homer grabbed in desperation. As he clutched the stone, the letter went flying, Frisbee-style, into the middle of the muck.

Homer stared at the creamy little square afloat in the dark brown sea. If it was addressed to him, he'd let it go and good riddance. But he couldn't be sure. With a sigh, he waded in.

When mud oozed over the top of his boots, he stopped. He was still six feet from the letter, and the mire was deepening. His incursion had set up glacial ripples. They tilted the letter, and it slowly slipped under, like a torpedoed ship. He could finally read the address. It was definitely for him. But tilted as it was, he also read the return address, in bolder type than his own name: Academy of Motion Picture Arts and Sciences. Probably selling him something. Letters like this began "Dear Educator." But his name wasn't a mailing label. The top edge vanished, leaving only a faint indentation in the thick brown surface.

The mud was mid-thigh when he reached where the letter had been. Cursing his curiosity, he shoved his arm into the ooze. He felt something firm, and squeezed. Dead sparrow. The back of his hand brushed against smooth bond.

Standing there, his pants congealing around his legs, he brushed off the envelope with his elbow and ripped it open. The thick stock had kept out the mud. An embossed card was enclosed, and a self-addressed envelope with a real stamp. He unfolded the cover letter—mail-merged, maybe—and began to read. When he got to the end, he read it again. Then he started to shake all over.

"Frances!" Homer pulled ineffectually at his boots in the mud room. His fingers weren't working properly. Flushed, beaming, he was feeling the weight of the world's expectations descending upon him.

Frances poked her head in, and he stuck the letter in her face with a mud-covered arm. "Look! *Granite Plywood*'s been nominated for an Academy Award!"

Frances took the envelope and riffled through it. She wasn't as surprised as he expected her to be. "How'd they even know about it, Mom?"

His question annoyed her. "How do you think? I sent it in."

"Mom!"

Homer gave her a big hug, but she was busy with the letter. When she came upon the embossed card, she punched him in the arm. "Yes!" Now she sounded excited. "We're going to the Oscars!"

"We are?"

"Yes!" She waved the card. "You get two tickets!"

"How'll we get there?"

"I don't know. Take the bus. Who cares? We're going to the Oscars!"

"I mean, what are we going to use for money?"

"I don't know. We'll sell the Subaru." And Frances rushed inside to use the phone.

"Hell you will!" Ham's head poked through the front door. His cheeks were flecked with blood. He'd been out back, skinning squirrels. "Not my Subaru."

"I'm nominated for an Oscar!" Homer gave Ham a big kiss Ham didn't know what to do with.

"They give you any money for that?"

"No. It's not about money. You know that." Homer was still shaking lightly. "I made one of the five best movies of the year!"

"If you win, you get that statue thing. Must be worth something."

"You don't sell the Oscar, Ham."

"What do you do with it?"

"I don't know. Look at it."

"You're not selling my car for a piece of bric-a-brac."

Frances was back already. "The phone's dead again." She tugged at Homer's mud-caked Wellingtons. "I need the good boots. I've got to tell Bonnie about this."

Homer figured now that he'd been nominated, he should have a working phone. Maybe someone would call him about a job.

He was lugging the heavy spool that had fallen off his friend's phone truck, tracking down breaks in the line with Frances, when he heard honking from their access road.

"A bill collector."

Since Ham owned the farm outright and they weren't hooked into power or water, there weren't many people he owed money to who still expected to get paid. He stashed the spool near a distinctive tree and followed Frances through the mucky brambles.

Where the road dipped into a shady glade, a big Chevy Blazer stood over its axle in mud. Silas Grant was at the wheel, leaning on the horn. He rolled down the window when they approached. Homer waved.

"Mr. Grant!"

Grant didn't wave back. "Get a winch!"

"I don't have a winch. Isn't it great news about the movie, though?" Homer smiled proudly.

"That's why I'm here, young man." Silas didn't look as pleased with the news as Homer was. "The college said you didn't have a telephone."

Homer was glad he hadn't brought the spool. "You sit tight, Mr. Grant. I can walk to the road, hitch a ride to the Chevron station. They've got a truck that'll get you out in no time." He started up the road.

Silas called after him. "I drove out here to see you, young man!"

Homer stopped. He hoped Silas didn't want his money back.

"What possessed you to enter that film in the Academy Awards?"

"I didn't, my mother did."

Frances spoke up, cheery. "You'll be getting plenty of free publicity for Granite Plywood!"

"You had no right to do anything with that film. I own it. I will thank you to retrieve my property."

Frances was incredulous. "Don't you want a billion people to hear the name Granite Plywood?"

"We have a contract, madam. You have stolen property belonging to my company. Return the property or go to jail."

"*You* should go to jail. You still owe Homer twenty-five hundred dollars."

Silas clenched the wheel. "We might be able to come to an accommodation on that."

Frances was not impressed. "This film has been nominated for an Oscar. It's worth a lot more now."

"It's worth a jail term for you and your son."

Frances glared at him. "Then you can sit in there and rot."

Silas hit his horn again, loud and persistent.

Homer wasn't worried about the honking. They were a good quarter-mile from the road. He'd been stuck there once himself, and had to wade out. But Silas had a point. It was Granite's movie. He waved to silence Silas.

"I'll get you the movie, Mr. Grant, but I can't do anything about the Academy. They've probably already voted anyway. After the Oscars are over, you can rent it out and make your money back, I bet."

Silas ground his teeth in hard thought. "As soon as it's over, the film comes straight back to me. Straight back."

"And we'll take that twenty-five hundred!" said Frances.

"I'll get the tow truck." Homer headed for the highway. He wouldn't have to listen to Ham and Frances bicker over selling the Subaru. And maybe they could get some real orange juice next week instead of the perpetual Tang.

TWENTY-ONE

Parrott sat in the back of the cab, staring blindly at passing palm trees, basking in the peace of isolation. Cars used to be the only place you could be alone to think in L.A.; now, with car phones, cabs were the absolute final haven. He was thankful once again he'd never learned to drive.

Usually, Parrott's best ideas came to him in cabs, or on elevators, somewhere he was moving publicly but alone. Tonight his mind was a black hole. A question would materialize in his brain—about the third act, or casting, or scheduling, God knows there were enough things to think about—but by the time he was aware of it, the question was gone, crowded from his consciousness by a welter of related complications.

Admittedly, he had reason to be tired. In from Nantucket late the previous night, with the concomitant plane-changing, then meetings all day today, now the prospect of trekking back to Nantucket tonight on the red-eye. Christ. Even the red-eye had phones now. But Parrott was a man of great energy and had lived through a score of preproductions. Other times, the panic and the deadlines had cleared his head and helped him focus. This time all the tumult just tired him out.

He knew the real reason he was feeling so tired. He was depressed. He'd expected that once he committed to *The Agonizer*, really committed, his doubts would evaporate and this project would condense into its distilled essence, as they always did. Not this time. Instead of seeing the project hard and clear, as only he could see it—getting that reassuring click in his head that told him only he could do this movie justice—the project hung there, suspended in fog, lumpy and amorphous. He couldn't shake the nagging fear that someone else could do it better.

Working with Marshall, who'd done this kind of picture, and Flaherty, who hadn't, he came to suspect he'd never make a movie that grossed a hundred million domestic. Maybe it just

143

wasn't in him. He didn't feel demeaned by the perception—in fact, it was comforting to know that his sensibility outstripped the bounds of popular taste. But it was cold comfort. Particularly with Klaus breathing down his neck and a budget past one hundred million dollars.

He knew what lay in store. Long days on the set waiting helplessly for animal wranglers and pyro guys. Plotting storyboards with stunt jocks who thought he was a New York pencil-necked fagola. Arguing character with Klaus Frotner. God forbid, sitting in an editing room with him, fighting him cut by cut.

Parrott wasn't afraid of presiding over a disaster. He'd had his share of failures, like everyone else. Why is it after a movie is released, its failings suddenly become so obvious? But he was enough of a pro that his failures were honorable ones, well crafted, if misguided in retrospect. No, he'd surrounded himself with the best in the business, and he knew that even if this film never quite gelled, moment to moment it would be executed at the highest level. This might be *Godfather III,* but it would never be *Hudson Hawk.*

What scared Parrott deep down, more even than the prospect of a miserable year, was the growing certainty that it would never be more than that. To have made *Godfather III* without ever having made *The Godfather* was a prospect he viewed with profound dismay. Parrott had a keen sense of his own career, and he'd carved out a respectable if very specific niche in the world of cinema. Now he was breaking out. If he failed this time, what had been his self-assigned place in film history would become his pigeonhole. That aura of indefinite possibility that surrounded the great ones, Ford or Hitchcock, or even—though this pained him to admit it—his contemporaries Kubrick or Martin Scorsese, would forever be denied him. Everyone would know exactly what he was good for. And that's what they'd make him do for the next twenty years.

He reached Morton's all too soon. A parking valet held his door, grinning broadly. Parrott smiled back, thinking the attendant might have recognized him, until he realized that this man who parked Rolls-Royces without a second look thought it remarkable he'd arrived in a cab. Parrott didn't give him a tip.

Inside, Darius was awaiting him. He rose when Parrott approached, the tablecloth catching on his ample thigh, and held out his hand. They shook and sat.

"Julia sends her best."

"Excuse me?" Parrott drew a blank.

"Your wife. I ran into her last night at Lincoln Center. She said to say hi."

"Oh. Who was she with?"

"Harriman."

"Oh." Julia's name made him feel a pang for New York. He scanned the smug, nut-brown faces in the phony clubbiness of Morton's, and conjured up the urbane pallor of a Park Avenue dining room crackling with caustic wit.

Parrott didn't think about his wife much when in preproduction. She was a cool, self-sufficient, wealthy woman who devoted her considerable talents exclusively to perfecting her private life, and since they'd married, his. They'd found each other when he was old enough to value such things. When he was home, his life ticked like a Swiss watch, thanks to her. When he was off fighting his battles, she offered him a sympathetic ear when he called late at night to unload the latest creative crisis. If she was there. When she said she missed him, she gave a convincing reading.

She was seeing a lot of Harriman. How much? He eyed Darius, wondering if he knew more than he was saying. But Darius sipped his martini and studied the menu with scrupulous exactitude.

Parrott ordered a Cutty and water. When it arrived, Darius toasted *The Agonizer*.

Parrott didn't like the Four Seasons very much, but he stayed there. All the New York people did, though its appeal lay in being brand-new and looking old, which meant more to L.A. people. Parrott thought it was road-company Plaza. He'd switched over with everyone else when the Beverly Wilshire was redecorated. He missed the naive, red-carpet California pomposity of the old Wilshire, but he was a realist in such matters. The Four Seasons was geared to the industry.

Gardens, the hotel restaurant, was now the meeting place of choice for agents and their talent in from New York. The food was dull and heavy, but between seven and nine a bicoastal agent might eat two or three breakfasts there. Parrott was drinking coffee in a banquette, trying to divine whether the velvet cushions were gray or beige, when Bo arrived at seven sharp. He clasped Bo's hand hard, genuinely glad to see him. "Thanks for coming."

Bo nodded. He'd shined on the CEO of Pepsico to be here. "What's up?"

Parrott was uncharacteristically manic. Maybe it was the coffee. "I had dinner with Darius Fo last night. He was telling me about that revolving fund you set up for him."

"The Alliance Superfund."

"Right. He said the money's in the bank." Parrott looked to Bo for confirmation, and Bo nodded. Parrott's eyes twinkled. "He wants to do *Precious Things*." He looked to Bo again. Bo's face was bland, noncommittal. "He says he'll make it with unknowns if I can keep it under fifteen below the line, and McGinty already budgeted it out at eighteen when we thought we had Sean Penn and Alicia Silverstone. I can use those two from Steppenwolf—I wrote it for them—remember?"

Bo's voice was carefully neutral. "What's he paying you?"

"He says he'll meet my *Agonizer* price." Parrott read Bo's blank look as surprise. "He says it doesn't need stars. I'm the star. I should be able to make my kind of movies, my way." He clasped Bo's hand with a rare display of boyish fervor.

The waiter appeared, and Bo ordered orange juice and sliced fruit. He made it a rule to have only fruit for breakfast. It aligned his gastric juices for the rest of the day. He turned back to Parrott. "Sounds like you've done my job for me."

Parrott waved that away. They were grown men here. "This is about credibility, Bo. Alliance needs instant credibility. I give it to them." Parrott gave an impish grin. "In most walks of life, credibility's nontransferable. Here, executives claim credit for everything, so they're given credit for nothing. They have to buy credibility on the open market, in a bidding war. Darius needs credibility. He bids on mine." Here Parrott got serious and leaned close to Bo. "But I give him credibility only if I go into production immediately."

The orange juice arrived and Bo took a sip. "You are in preproduction on a hundred million-dollar movie."

"You'll have to call Annette and tell her I respectfully withdraw."

Bo put down the juice. "This is a very serious step you're proposing."

"I'm aware of that."

"You will be sued."

"Not if you handle it right. I haven't signed anything."

"You never sign anything until you're in post. But you've taken one-and-a-half million dollars of their money."

"I'll make them whole on my fee."

"You're going to make powerful enemies."

"If *Precious Things* is a hit, they'll be my friends again." Here Parrott hunched forward, and his perky manner slipped. "If I try *The Agonizer* and don't pull it together, will I have any friends left?"

"It's falling all to shit, isn't it?"

"I wouldn't say that."

But Bo could see the depths of Parrott's panic. He'd never known Parrott when he wasn't courting disaster. Disaster had finally caught up with him. "As your agent, I can understand why you'd jump to *Precious Things*. It's risky, but it may be your least risky option."

"It's more than that." Parrott had to make Bo see what a break this was. "It's the movie I was born to make—"

Bo cut him short. "As Klaus Frotner's agent, though, I must tell you my client will feel betrayed. He took a chance on you—" Parrott started to protest. Bo wouldn't let him. "Yes, he did, he got you *The Agonizer*."

"I took a chance on him too."

"If the movie falls through, he'll probably want to sue you. As his agent I'd say he has a case."

"I'm doing *Precious Things*."

Bo stared at him, stony. "People in this business will never look at you the same again."

"You can help me or you can fight me." Parrott stared right back. "I am doing *Precious Things*."

Bo nodded. "Okay. But you tell your pal Darius he'd better sit on this until the end of the week, or he just might discover his financing isn't as solid as he thinks it is."

Annette was one of those lucky people who eats whatever she wants without gaining weight. The first thing she did every morning when she reached her office was have a bowl of strawberries and heavy cream while she reviewed the latest cost reports on *The Agonizer*. The cost reports were intimidating but thrilling. It was like having a dangerous lover, someone you'd given yourself to completely, who could beat you up, maybe even kill you. She was still spooning out strawberries when Bo's call came in. She took it cheerfully, looking at a small abstract oil beside her desk, her job-warming gift from Consolidated.

"Thanks for the Klee, Bo. It makes the room."

"It reminded me of you. Playful precision. First class."

"I'm decorating around it. Why aren't you in some breakfast meeting?"

"We have a problem."

Annette could tell from his voice that this was serious. "I'm sitting down."

"I'm going to be completely frank with you. Parrott's in over his head."

"What do you mean?"

"I've never seen him this way. He's blocked on this one, Annette. Dried up." Silence. Bo sighed. "Between you and me, I don't think he'll pull this one off."

"What are you telling me, Bo?"

"This isn't happening, Annette. Chris is going through some sort of personal crisis. He's vapor-locked. If you want to save *The Agonizer,* we have to find another director."

This hung in the air. Annette's firm cheeks went drum-taut. A tiny crease appeared between her eyebrows. Her voice lost its musical lilt and became hard and dry. "Does he have another job, Bo?"

"Personal problems, Annette. He has no business making films out here. He's like Woody Allen. A creature of New York. And his wife's back there, cheating on him."

"You're swearing to me he doesn't have another job."

"On my mother's head."

"Your mother's dead."

"That's irrelevant, Annette. The problem is *The Agonizer.* It's just not clicking with him."

"It was clicking two weeks ago when he cashed my check for two million dollars."

"You'll get that back."

"Tip of the iceberg. You know that." She flipped to the last page of the cost report. "We've got forty-two five irrevocably committed—a large chunk of that in a set that was Parrott's bright idea."

"You can hold him to the contract, but what good will that do? He doesn't see this one. It's not there for him."

"Twenty-two million's going to your client Klaus. Is he giving it back?"

"We'll find someone he'll be happy to work with."

"Will Klaus give me a few weeks grace to find him?" Klaus's contract had a locked-in start date.

"His contract provides for that."

"At a million a week."

"Klaus has other commitments backed up, Annette."

"You were frank with me. I'll be frank with you. You know our slate. *Agonizer* is all we've got. It's the studio, Bo. And it's not just the studio. It's me. For better or worse, I'm the *Agonizer* lady. If I cancel, how long will I be sitting here admiring your Klee? I'm not pulling the plug on this picture, Bo. I'm making *The Agonizer,* and I'm making it first class."

"I'll do everything I can to help. You know I will. But Parrott's not your answer. Believe me."

"Has Klaus heard the news?"

"He's in Montana somewhere. We're tracking him down."

"If he drops out, you're going to have one fucking great lawsuit on your hands, Bo."

"Parrott wasn't part of the original package. I'll find you a director that's ten times better than Christopher Parrott for this film. When we preview, you'll be sending Parrott a magnum of champagne for dropping out."

"Don't bullshit me, Bo."

"I've got some ideas I'm working on already."

"In absolute secrecy."

"Absolutely."

"When we announce, we'll be touting the new director. It'll be 'creative differences' and 'the good of the picture,' and you'll give me a supportive quote for the trades."

"Whatever you think you need."

Annette picked up the last strawberry and snapped off the stem. "And, Bo. The crew is bought and paid for. Whatever Parrott's up to, the crew's mine."

TWENTY-TWO

A black '60 Lincoln Continental, the longest production car ever built, careened past cheap cars constricting a narrow hillside road into a single lane, bucking like a stallion on its bad shocks through blind corners, lucky it didn't meet itself coming the other way. The morning freeway roared like an angry rapids below.

Jack Doberman was at the wheel, pushing hard, swearing at the lack of street numbers. He was fresh-shaved and Armani-suited, if a trifle shiny in the seat. He'd been up all night, driving and thinking. The last months had been rough for Jack, since Consolidated gave him the boot. No more. Jack's back, he thought with grim pleasure as he spun the wheel, Jack's back and that's that.

The road dead-ended against a high blank wall. Jack steered through a broken iron gate and pulled up beneath a tortured gargoyle flanked by gray spearpoint leaves of decades-old agave. Clutching a paper bag, he pounded up steep steps toward a large, lumpy, stone and stucco monstrosity, an unholy blend of Moorish minarets and Gothic arches.

The studded oak door was open. Jack's pounding was smothered by gunfire and rending metal, so he walked right in. He followed the noise through a domed entry tiled like a Turkish mosque, to a large, barren room with a shiny wooden floor and freeway view. The leaded windows were open to the traffic, but the vehicles moved in pantomime to the bone-jarring reverb of a tanker-truck explosion in four-track surround. At the far end of the room, flanked by piles of laser discs, a projection TV threw up a creditable image of a five-foot ball of flame. A thin, pale form sprawled on pillows close enough to be seared by the heat.

"Elmo! Elmo! It's me, Jack!"

Elmo didn't respond, so Jack came closer, bag in hand. Elmo's flesh was the color and consistency of poached sole. His eye sockets were dark, pebbly smears. Pubic fuzz crawled over his chin, and his lips were red and raw from nervous chewing. Christ, Jack thought, his mouth looks like a gangbanged cunt.

Jack turned off the video. Traffic growled through the room. Elmo blinked at the empty screen.

"It's me. Jack Doberman. *The Agonizer.* Remember?"

Elmo stared at him.

"Jesus. You should see yourself. You look like shit on a skillet."

Elmo's eyes came into focus. "I'm just stuck, that's all. When I'm stuck I watch movies until I get unstuck."

"How long you been stuck?"

"I don't know. It went real well for a month or so. Then . . ."

"We talking hours or days or weeks or what?"

"I don't know. What day is it?"

"Christ." Jack held out the bag. "Here. Have an onion bagel."

Elmo stood with difficulty, swaying as the sudden movement sucked blood from his skull. Jack steadied him and handed him a bagel.

"Thanks."

"Some place you got here. Looks like it was built for Boris Karloff."

"Vilma Banky." Elmo pointed toward the windows. "Still got my freeway."

At the other end of the room an ogre's head held a pair of andirons in its gaping maw. It was heaped with script pages. Elmo staggered over to a card table beside it, and sat on a folding chair in front of a slim black notebook computer. He stared at the screen. Jack had vanished from his mind.

Jack grabbed his shoulder and shook him. "Elmo! Elmo!"

Elmo returned to earth. Whatever he was looking for he hadn't found. "What?"

"Look at yourself, Elmo! You are in deep shit."

"I'm all right."

"You're turning to puke. You ever been stuck this long?"

Elmo closed his eyes and thought about it. He shook his head.

"You are in deep shit. But today's your lucky day, 'cause I am the man with the shovel."

Elmo looked at him foggily. "What do you mean?"

"The Agonizer! The Agonizer!"

Elmo covered his ears. Jack raised his voice. "You think I've

forgotten about that? Well, I haven't! It's yours, Elmo! It's
yours! Bo fucked you out of it, we'll get it back for you! I swear
on my left testicle, we'll get you *The Agonizer*."

Elmo's features scrunched shut. "Don't start on that!"

"Listen to me." Jack pried Elmo's hands from his ears. Elmo
resisted, but it was no harder than pulling the wings off a butterfly. "Parrott's out."

"Parrott's out?"

"Parrott quit the movie, and we're the only ones that know!"

"How do we know?"

"He told me."

Elmo lost interest again. He turned back to his laptop.

"All right. All right. Lately I been parking cars at Morton's. I
figured it's the best place to make something happen. Drai's is
too full of phonies. Well, last night it happens. Last night I open
a cab door and Parrott steps out. I think maybe I say hi, but I
figure better I keep my mouth shut. I just make sure I'm the one
gets his cab when he leaves. Which was easy—he was the worst
fuckin' tipper all night. So he comes out of Morton's, all boozy-
sweet, arm around Darius Fo, swearing on the fuckin' muses
he'll start on *Precious Things* next week."

"What difference does that make?"

"Don't you get it? Parrott's doing *Precious Things*! *The
Agonizer*'s got no director! I thought you wanted to direct the
thing!"

Elmo looked sad. "They've already turned me down."

"Big fuckin' deal! You gonna quit 'cause someone says stop?"

"Klaus . . ."

"That was then and this is now. Now they got themselves in
production and no fuckin' director!"

Some hint of hope crept into Elmo's voice. "You really think I
have a chance?"

Jack glared at him, indignant. "They'd be damn lucky to get
you. You know it. I know it. All we gotta do is convince them."

Finally Elmo gave Jack his full attention. "How'm I gonna do
that?"

"Do you want it?"

Elmo hesitated.

"You gotta make it happen. But I got ideas. You still got those
pictures you made? Those *Agonizer* drawings?"

Elmo rose, and Jack followed him up a tight spiral staircase to a tiny domed room atop a minaret. The windows were blacked out. Jack stumbled over something soft and lumpy in the dark.

"Watch out for the mattress." Elmo flicked a switch. Dim lights glowed green. Jack made out cargo netting overhead, twined with ropy leaves. Withered tropical plants crowded the bare pallet. But one arc of dome was clear and there, framed by vines, were tacked Elmo's drawings.

"Shit on a stick!"

Elmo punched a button and the room filled with jungle sounds. "I come here sometimes, when I want to watch *The Agonizer*."

"Maybe . . ." Jack weighed if this room would fit into his plans. Something skittered along the floor.

"Watch where you step. There are black widows."

No way. Too weird. They'd have to take the drawings downstairs.

The Jaguar squeezed next to the Lincoln Continental. Jason eased himself out, checked his paint job for agave scratches, and sprung jauntily up the sloping steps. This was a coup in the making. After the *Agonizer* deal, Elmo'd been pursued by the whole town. The script had been kept under wraps, but the money spoke for itself. Elmo dropped from sight, though. Bo said he was working on another original, and hinted there'd be another auction in a few months. Now, from the blue, Elmo calls and wants to talk to Jason. No reason why the man who produced *The Agonizer* shouldn't produce Elmo's next film. But Jason knew it all depended on creating rapport. Elmo was an artist, clearly, and Jason's job was to forge a bond of trust and respect. Jason relished the challenge. He enjoyed working with artists, and knew his Harvard training had given him the tools to put them at their ease.

Jason knocked. A compact young man in an Armani suit answered. Jason took his hand. "You must be Elmo Zwalt. That's a terrific old Lincoln you've got out there. A real writer's car."

"The name is Doberman. Jack Doberman. That's my car."

"Oh. You live with Elmo?"

"No fuckin' way."

Jason followed the mystery Jack to the living room. There, backed by the throb of the freeway, a tired, pale young man sat on the only chair in the room. Jason thought he recognized him. He strode over, Jack forgotten.

"Elmo! Let me shake the hand that wrote *The Agonizer*." He pumped Elmo's hand. "This is a privilege and an honor."

Jason took in the video projector and its banks of speakers. He whistled, impressed. "A liquid matrix Nakamichi! That's a theatrical installation." He walked over to browse through the piles of laser discs. "I don't think I've ever seen so many laser discs outside a video store. *The Sorcerer!* Now, that is an underrated movie."

Elmo spoke in a thin voice. "I've seen it eight times."

Jason laughed and held up the disc. "Could I borrow this?"

Elmo nodded. Jason continued. "You know, you've got a terrific place here. I think I saw it in a book about silent-era Hollywood. Didn't Vilma Banky build this place?"

Elmo pointed. "Her lover fell out that window, impaled himself on the cactus."

"They never found out if she pushed him, did they?"

Elmo shook his head.

"Do you think she did?"

Elmo looked blank.

"Any ghosts running around?"

Elmo thought about this. "Come to think of it, that might explain some stuff."

"Oh? Like what?"

"Oh, stuff. noises . . . things moving . . ."

"Far out! Sounds like good material. You writing about it?"

"No." Elmo gave him a tenuous smile, and his eyes lost focus as he considered the story possibilities.

Jason clapped his hands and plunked down on a pillow with a sigh, still holding the laser disc. This was going very, very well. "So. What's up?"

Elmo looked over at Jack. Jack settled between them on the corner of the card table. "We want to talk *The Agonizer*."

Jason smiled noncommittally. "What do you want to talk about?"

"What if I told you you don't have a director?"

"I'd say you were nuts."

"That's what I figured." Jack wasn't perturbed. "You don't."

Jason looked pleasantly blank. "So?"

"So you don't have a director. We're offering you Elmo."

"You're his agent? Bo's his agent."

"Not on this. We have a preexisting agreement." Jack looked at Elmo, who nodded.

Jason rose. "Look, Elmo, it was great to meet you. But this is ridiculous."

"The news'll hit the trades in a couple of days. I'm offering you a way back in, Jason. Don't you want back in on *The Agonizer?*"

"What are you talking about? I'm the producer, and I'm telling you—"

"Yeah, yeah," Jack cut him off. "We know what that means. It means you're the pot Frotner pisses in."

Jason flushed. "Look, Elmo, I don't know who this guy is, but you're making a serious mistake to let him represent you."

"So I'm an asshole. I'm giving you the straight shit. *The Agonizer* is Elmo's movie. Dumbest thing in the world to bring in some preppy East Coast fag like Parrott. All he'd do is screw it up. Elmo sees this movie in his head." Jack tapped his forehead hard. "In there. He's got it all figured out. You don't believe me, just listen to the man."

Clearly, these people were crazy. Jason knew he should walk out then and there. But he didn't.

Elmo knelt on the floor cradling a sheaf of drawings. He gently laid one down. The wind skittered it along. Elmo chased it. "Get the windows, will you, Jack?"

Jack closed the windows. Freeway roar ebbed. Elmo put down the first drawing again. It was brushed in ink with a vivid, forceful line. Jason knelt to admire it, and Elmo started to tell him the movie.

Elmo's voice thickened and dropped a register. He wasn't pitching product, he was bearing witness. Like a Delphic oracle, Jason thought, or a visionary prophet of the Book of Revelations.

As Elmo spun the story before Jason's eyes, Jason felt a peculiar sense of shame and excitement. This was moviemaking. He'd been a fool, sucking up to the big names in the business, blinded by a little-boy need to play with the grown-ups. Now he saw with dazzling clarity that the only place he'd end up riding the big guy's coattails was holding their coats. He had to do what they'd done to break through. Champion youth. Champion untested genius. And Elmo was the real thing.

Jason felt dizzy, but giddily alert. For the first time in his life, he wasn't game-planning and balancing options. His future—his destiny—depended on landing Elmo this gig. His skin prickled with anticipation. He ached to get out there and start pushing.

Pinsky strode into Bo's office and discovered him crouched in contemplation by the stream. "Hello, Bo." The voice rang with cheerful authority. First impressions were important.

Bo rose. Pinsky held out a firm hand. Pinsky was naturally flabby and soft, but he worked out. He liked to think he radiated vital energy. Though Pinsky had the bushy beard and sensual features of a biblical scholar, he was draped not in tallith and tefilin but in soft silks and exotic animal hairs. He had the script in his fist, wadded in a scroll like a club.

"I'm glad you could read on such short notice—"

"For you, Bo, anytime, you know that."

"I've been looking for the right project for you for a while now."

That was true enough. Bo was nominally his agent but hadn't spoken to Marvin in a couple of years, since the last time he needed someone to pitch late-inning relief. Marv was a film-school wunderkind who'd peaked seven years before, when he'd worked with Frotner on the sequel to *Dead Run. Dead Walk* had taken in sixty-five million domestic but had been widely viewed as a disappointment, conventional wisdom holding that Frotner in an environmental impact report would gross sixty-five million. Pinsky had been tagged as a guy who was only as good as his material. Consequently he'd been given progressively weaker material, mostly action pictures without action stars. The last couple of years he'd been the chattel of Consolidated's TV department, banished to eight o'clock pilots and prime-time soaps.

Marvin laughed and slapped Bo's shoulder with the script. "You're sending me into a train wreck, aren't you? Maimed egos everywhere. I'll have to spend the first month as shrink."

"Nothing you can't handle, Marv."

"I know, I know." Marvin said it with the zest of a man who loved conflict resolution. He often thought if he hadn't become a movie director, he'd have been a group therapist.

"What do you make of the material?"

"Loads of potential. Loads. I'd have to meet with Klaus, of course, gauge his take on it." Pinsky remembered the pang when he'd read in *Variety* about the screenplay sale, and then of Parrott's attachment. Parrott had the breaks. Parrott had come up when there was still enough of a studio system that directors didn't have to be auteurs to get good scripts.

Pinsky knew he was better than the average A-list guy, certainly better than James Cameron or John Hughes, say. As a director. When he analyzed the problem, and he analyzed it often, it always came down to one variable: good as he was at his chosen craft, Pinsky was not a writer. Those guys were. In a twisted way the critics were right, he was only as good as his material. Now into his lap falls an A script.

"Studio is one hundred percent behind this movie, Marvin."

Marv grinned good-naturedly. "But they've spent their budget and it opens day after tomorrow."

"No, no. The tap's still open. First class all the way. Annette calls herself the *Agonizer* lady. You know."

Marvin didn't, but he couldn't repress a hiccup of glee. Then his face became sad and thoughtful. Philosophical. "How does Chris feel about being replaced? Is it an awkward situation?"

"No, no, this is coming from him. You'd be doing him a favor."

Pinsky smiled, relieved. He was a man who valued his integrity. Though he'd never stabbed anyone in the back, he'd stepped in over enough directors' still-warm bodies to acquire something of the odor of studio scab. It bothered him. This time he wouldn't have to wrestle his scruples to the mat.

Pinsky smoothed out the script and hunched over it talmudically. "Screenplay still needs a little work. Nothing I can't sort out with Klaus in a couple of weeks. He trusts me. He'll tell you *Dead Walk* was an excellent experience. I can pull it together. I've done it before."

Bo looked at Marvin, eagerly flipping pages. Pinsky's a rabbi selling used cars, Bo thought, only the used car he's selling is Pinsky.

What is as solid as a redwood? Annette rubbed the rough, rusty bark. Tannin came off on her hand. Redwoods live practically forever, she thought. They don't have to worry about option years and cut-off clauses. Except for these guys. Sprinklers fail, they're dead.

"Aren't these beautiful? They were too big to be trucked in. They were helicoptered into place." Crystal, the real estate woman, patted the tree as if it were a cute pet. Crystal was the best-dressed woman over forty Annette had ever seen in Los Angeles. She'd once been married to a studio head and claimed she sold real estate as a hobby. "I'm told Hannah spent three million on this grove. She went to school at Berkeley."

"Homesick medicine." Annette was feeling a trifle homesick herself. Except home for her meant a seedy split level in Cicero, Illinois. She missed her dog, though. Pebbles.

Searching for directors wasn't like searching for oil. No surprises. The possibilities were all too obvious. And tied up. She'd known they were tied up when she went with Parrott. In desperation, she faxed a script to an Australian in self-imposed exile back home. Celia was talented, she had the heart and the edge, but she didn't export well. Her Aussie films all worked better than her Hollywood efforts. Would Klaus ever go for a woman? If Celia took it on, she'd want to throw out the preproduction, start from scratch. Annette would be paying Klaus a million a week while Celia fiddled with the script. What if she didn't want to shoot on stage? Annette had always been conflicted about that decision. But McGinty'd convinced her it was a way to rein in costs—big front-end investment, but total back-end control—

"Annette! Annette!" She looked up. Jason was tramping toward her through ferns. This she did not need. She'd been very explicit about keeping him off the bus—

"Jason!" She held out her hand, palm down, like royalty. Jason touched it lightly. He was panting from the chase. At moments like this she regretted she ever let him lick her ass.

"Annette. Am I glad I found you. They said you were out checking houses—I had Stacy call every real estate broker in Beverly Hills—"

"Sit down. Take a breath."

Jason sat on a rock. He looked like he needed an appendectomy. Annette wondered if he might be on drugs.

"Should I call a doctor?" Annette reached for her purse phone.

"No, no. I'm fine. I feel terrible, though. I mean, I feel terrible you're in such a mess. I feel responsible, really."

Her bell-like laugh chimed. "I will call a doctor."

"No, listen—" He stood suddenly, turned, and shouted through cupped hands, *"Over here! Over here!"*

Crystal closed on them. "Those are delicate ferns, young man."

Jason led Annette away, speaking low and fast in her ear. "Listen. I've been a fool. I talked you into Parrott. I talked myself into Parrott. It was stupid. It made no sense. He has no feel for this material. I was crazy."

"Jason, Jason, what are you talking about?"

"You don't have to play dumb with me, Annette. We're in this together."

"If this is *Agonizer* business, Jason, we have an agreement—"

"We have an obligation. I have an obligation."

"No. You don't. You've fulfilled all your obligations. You don't have anything to worry about—"

Jason looked at her, and his look shut her up. "You don't have to reassure me, Annette. This isn't about reassurance. I acted like a baby. But that doesn't matter anymore. What matters is *The Agonizer*. I've solved *The Agonizer*." Jason waved to a skinny young man dressed all in black stumbling through foliage, backed up by a heavyset little guy in a dirty Armani suit. His bodyguard, perhaps.

Crystal called to the intruders. "Get out of the ferns or I shall call security!"

Jason focused laserlike on Annette. "Did you ever meet Elmo Zwalt? He wrote *The Agonizer*. And he's going to direct it."

The pale young man staggered onto the path. He gave her a shy smile.

"Listen to his take on the movie. If you don't like what he's got to say, I'm taking my name off the picture."

"Is that a threat, Jason?"

"It would be a pretty stupid threat, wouldn't it? Simple statement of fact. Go on, Elmo, tell her the movie."

Elmo climbed on a rock. He liked the cool, damp air. The moss and ferns, so much greener than parched southland palm and scrub oak, reminded him of the rain forest where Xavanti prowled. Annette stared up at him, serious as a fawn with her huge, liquid eyes. Vulnerable, but strong. The *Agonizer* nun incarnate.

Elmo didn't have to use his drawings. He was already in the Zone. He centered his skull on his spine with great care and inhaled three times from his nostrils to the pit of his diaphragm, the Shabu ghost breath. The spirits of the movie filled his lungs and seeped through three hundred million alveoli into ten thousand million red blood cells. They tumbled through his heart and brain and liver and spleen and larynx to flow from his lips, each soul distinct in timbre and inflection—the nun, and the Agonizer, and the riverboat captain and the cruel *commandante,* and Itangi, the witch doctor, and Xavanti warriors, the brave and the not so brave, and their wives and children. Elmo was not a narrator but a vessel. The movie filled him like thick jungle honey, and he poured it over Annette.

Annette had been away from the first draft for a long time. Hearing it like this, she was gripped with sure resolve: She was the *Agonizer* lady, and this was the *Agonizer* she was going to make.

When Elmo finished, he collapsed on the stone like an empty sack. Crystal spoke in hushed tones. "You sign that young man."

Annette was silent. When she spoke, she spoke to Jason, her Cicero accent peeking through. "He can sure tell a story. But can he handle the visuals?"

Jason was carrying a slim folder tied with black satin. He plucked at the ribbon. "Let me show you something pretty amazing."

TWENTY-THREE

Academy Awards day is an undeclared holiday in Hollywood, but Annette got to her office at seven-thirty as usual, planning how to cram in a day's work before she left at two to get her hair done and make herself beautiful. Normally she loved looking beautiful, but given her current plight, she wasn't relishing a long evening being gracious to the assembled grandees of her profession. Her charm reservoirs were dangerously low.

Nibbling on her strawberries, she picked up *Variety*. Academy Awards day is the ultimate slow news day, but the headline caught her full attention: FO'S "PRECIOUS" PARROTT.

Bo took her call in his car. Her voice had a nasal twang he hadn't heard before. Suburban Chicago, he guessed. Maybe Cicero.

"Have you seen *Variety*, Bo?"

"No."

"Your clients are plastered all over the front page."

"Oh?" This wasn't unusual for Bo.

"Fo's announced his Superfund slate. Parrott's out of the bag."

Bo pulled his NSX over to the side of the road. "I was going to tell you—"

"Bo, I have to go out tonight and smile and be charming to everybody, and they'll all be looking at me, thinking, 'That poor bitch, she's dead meat.' "

"I think you're overstating the situation, Annette."

"Am I? Do you have a director for me this morning?"

Bo thought fleetingly of Pinsky, but he knew better than to bring him up with Annette in this mood. Pinsky was no Parrott. "We're actively pursuing a number of possibilities."

161

"I'm a reasonable woman. But you've put me in an impossible situation."

"Hang tight for a couple more days."

"I'm making an executive decision, Bo. I'm hiring Elmo Zwalt this morning."

Bo made it a point of honor always to know what the other person was going to say before he said it. Not this time. "Zwalt?"

"I heard him last night. Very impressive presentation. This isn't Ibsen, it's an action picture. He'll make it fly like a rocket."

"He's a very gifted young man, Annette. As a matter of fact, I represent him, but—"

"Not on this deal. He says a guy named Jack Doberman's his agent."

"Doberman?" Bo dredged up an unpleasant picture of a tough guy in an overgrown suit, and began to piece together what must have happened. "Who represents him is beside the point, Annette. He's never directed a picture."

"He's got a solid script, a clear vision. He'll be surrounded by the best in the business. We can thank Parrott for that."

"You might not be aware that Klaus had a run-in with the young man. Elmo physically attacked him. Elmo is quite possibly the last person on earth Klaus would agree to."

"Check the contract. Klaus doesn't have director approval after he cashes our check. He approved Parrott. He doesn't like it, you get Parrott back."

"It never pays to push Klaus, Annette."

"If Klaus gives me any trouble, I'll hit him for all we're out. That's pushing forty-five million, Bo. Parrott, maybe I needed Parrott's soul, maybe I can't make him do a good job if he's not committed. But all I need from Klaus is his body. He can't act anyway. You know it, I know it, he knows it. He shows up, he does a day's work, or we sue his ass. It'll all be over for him in a couple of months."

"You are being extremely shortsighted, Annette."

"I'm fighting for my life, Bo. We'll make it as easy on Klaus as we can. But Elmo's directing this movie, and Klaus is the Agonizer. I'm calling Melinda Toto. When people come up to me at the Oscars, they won't be measuring me for a coffin, they'll be saying, 'Tell me about this Zwalt guy.' "

Bo saw disaster looming. Klaus would rip into him when he found out about Parrott, which was any minute now, since he was due back that day for the Oscars, but he'd positively skin Bo alive if Annette stuck him with Elmo at the same time. Bo would be blamed for getting Klaus in bed with Parrott, then for not controlling the situation at Studio. That's how Sue Mengers lost Streisand; where's Sue Mengers now?

Bo saw with diamond clarity he'd be in a no-win situation if Elmo got the job. Elmo blows the shoot, and Klaus leaves Bo for sure; Elmo pulls it off, he's the hottest director in town, in Jack Doberman's pocket, and Klaus'll probably jump to Jack. Bo remembered when he broke away—did he have as strong a hand as Klaus and a successful Elmo?

"When Klaus feels he's being jerked around he's not a rational man, Annette. He's perfectly capable of acting against his own best interests. There is enormous potential for chaos here."

"Don't muscle me, Bo."

"If you announce without letting me bring Klaus around, you'll have a war on your hands. Give me a couple of days to work on him."

Silence.

"These Oscars are going to be hell for you, Annette. But don't blow the picture for a party."

Bo wasn't just stalling. There was truth in what he said. Unlike Darius, who didn't care what anybody thought of him, Annette had a horror of being perceived the fool. Her fear of looking bad had been a tremendous asset. It had driven her to develop her grace, her style, her charm. But it was her Achilles' heel as well. If she thought she was coming off wrong, she was capable of doing the kind of damage that would make it damn hard for Bo to pick up the pieces.

A long beat of silence. Finally. "Tomorrow's *Variety* will be all Oscars anyway. I'll call Melinda tomorrow."

"Zip it up already!"

It is difficult to shave in a Porta Potti. The water is cold and the sink is small and there is no place to put your shaving brush. But Homer took his time. He ignored the angry guy pounding on the door and did a pretty good job, only a couple of nicks near his Adam's apple which he stanched with toilet paper. He had more trouble changing into his tuxedo without rubbing against the urinal.

When he was done, Homer examined himself in the metal mirror embedded over the sink. Ham had been forced to purchase the tuxedo fifty years before, as the result of an unfortunate accident at his own wedding; the pants had a large purplish blotch on one thigh, but it didn't show if Homer kept his legs together. Ham's old patent leather shoes had long ago been eaten by mice, but Homer's Nikes were mostly black, so they went pretty well with the ensemble. He liked the jacket. Padded shoulders and spearpoint collar gave him a rakish forties air, like the owner of a gin joint in a Bogie movie.

Homer left the Porta Potti with a crime lord's swagger. He picked his way along Hope Street, through massed parking valets and security forces, to the bleachers that formed Celebrity Canyon, the gauntlet walked by stars from limo to the Dorothy Chandler Pavilion. When the guard saw Frances waving at him from a middle row, he let Homer in.

It was a pretty good spot. They'd gotten in to L.A. the day before on Greyhound, and Frances made him rush right over to get a place. He'd have opted for a motel, but she insisted. If she was going to the Oscars, she wanted to wring the last drop from the experience. They'd curled up in their sleeping bags with the other fans, and awoke stiff and dewy but well positioned that morning. It seemed like an okay way to save the cost of a room.

Frances had preceded him to the Porta Potti, and she looked very stylish in a low-cut satin sheath. Homer couldn't remember the last time he'd seen her shoulders. They were pale and smooth, but belied by her rough red neck. She wore a boa to soften the transition.

Her fancy attire did not attract attention. The bleacher fans were equally divided between those dressed for comfort, in blue jeans or pastel shorts, and those making a fashion statement. To reach Frances, Homer had to clamber over a Tin Woodsman and three rouged and wrinkled Scarlett O'Haras.

"You missed Joel Grey!" Homer had never seen Frances this excited. "Look! Look! George Hamilton!" She started to wave and shout with all the others.

The red carpet between the bleachers was clogged with media. A grinning emcee stood at the head of the phalanx, introducing celebrities as they debarked from their limousines. Hope Street was blocked off to regular traffic; by three o'clock limousines were five deep. The celebrities jammed together, some taking half an hour to walk the red carpet, posing for screaming photographers and TV cameras.

Homer watched with his usual curiosity. He appreciated the urgent bustle, the emergency room air of the limos disgorging their patrons to be rushed onto the carpet. It seemed every celebrity who passed beneath them was possessed of a condition requiring immediate attention. The paparazzi, like good nurses, tended to all, but the TV reporters, like surgeons at a massive catastrophe, practiced a brutal triage, selecting only the most critical cases for their attention.

Except when the celebrities were women long of limb and high of heel, robed in hummingbird feathers or fishing nets, Homer didn't find them very interesting. They all seemed to be hiding something, and talked only about their clothes or how it felt to be nominated. Homer knew how it felt to be nominated. He liked to watch the plebeian escorts. They were less practiced in handling the press. Their faces displayed real emotions. They were proud of their mate, or resentful, or bored, or impatient to get inside. Homer looked for pride most. He could tell the ones proud because they were with a famous person from those proud because they loved their escort and felt good for him. Those last were the rarest. They were the ones Homer wished the interviewers would talk to. They never did.

Toward six o'clock, at the height of the crush, Homer recognized the large, liquid eyes of the woman he'd seen on television when he'd just been fired from Mucklinberg College. She was draped in shimmers. Basic black stitched with ten thousand ebony beads. Frances said it was designed by a Japanese who lived in Paris. She was the new head of Studio, and her escort was a millionaire Washington lawyer who owned the Baltimore Orioles. A telejournalist reached for her, but she sidestepped him gaily. Her laugh tinkled in Homer's ears.

Finally Frances had seen all she could see, and rose to go. Homer grabbed sleeping bags and duffel and followed, bouncing his burdens over bleacher bodies to the bottom. Frances unhooked a velvet rope and they stepped onto the red carpet. The bleachers cheered.

A guard was upon them before she could replace the hook. Frances held out their invitation.

"We're invited!" she said.

"They're invited!" half a dozen fans echoed. Frances waved at them.

The guard had been primed for every screwball eventuality. Terrorist attacks, obsessional assassinations, process serving, shouted accusations of paternity, self-immolation by frustrated actresses, proclaimed invasions from alternate realities. He wasn't about to be fooled by something as mud-stained and bent as what Frances shoved under his nose. "If you don't want to lose your seat, lady, you better get back up there."

Frances waggled the card at the nearest video camera, which had already strayed in her direction in its constant vigilance for conflict and color. "Read. My son's been nominated for an Oscar."

More cheers from the bleachers. The blond reporter tugged her camera crew over. "And you are?"

"Don't talk to me. Talk to him." She yanked Homer closer. The guard kept a firm hold on both of them, waiting for the camera to lose interest.

Homer dug in his pocket for his driver's license, displayed it for camera. "I'm Homer Dooley. I made *Granite Plywood*."

"And it's nominated for an Oscar?"

"That's right. Best Feature Documentary."

"What were you doing in the bleachers?"

"We spent the night up there."

Frances chimed in. "Now we're going inside to watch the show!"

The camera moved on to Goldie Hawn, and the guard led Homer and Frances to the closest security point. Their identities were double-checked. They were waved through.

The Dorothy Chandler Pavilion is poorly designed for awards ceremonies. It is wide and has no aisles. Each year at great expense the Academy removes chunks of prime seats so that winners may march photogenically down a center carpet, grasping the hands of fellow celebrities. Favorites are seated near this aisle, and the show producers pray they win. Otherwise, nominees must push past their crinolined compatriots to the end of the row, then circumnavigate the hall. When sleepers sweep, they can add as much as fifteen minutes to the broadcast.

Homer and Frances were far from the center aisle, about halfway back. Frances figured the seats were worth about a grand each. The performance seemed small from there. The view was better on the monitor placed near the end of their row, but watching the real thing was a lot more fun.

Growing up with Frances, Homer had seen plenty of Oscar-casts, and they'd always seemed tacky and forced. Cheap Vegas glitz, symbolized by those huge gold sword-hugging statues guarding the stage like giant bouncers at God's casino. Frenzied, regimented dance routines, a parade of drunk, belligerent, or mawkish honorees. The host was usually the best part of the show, and he was a lot funnier doing his regular job. But tonight Homer found the jokes hilarious, the costumes dazzling, the sets impressive, the dance routines paeans of balletic grace. Time flew by on iridescent wings until his moment of reckoning.

Klaus was the presenter for Best Feature Documentary. He would have conferred a more prestigious award, Editing or Special Effects, but Inga had insisted on being his partner. She looked stunning, dressed entirely in aluminum tab tops—mouth watering, if you weren't afraid of slashed gums. Klaus was imposing, dressed in seamless black: Norma Kamali zip-up tuxedo over black-on-black Roman-collared body shirt. He'd arrived in town that morning and hadn't yet talked to Bo, but the *Variety* headline had been called to his attention by a score of fellow Academicians. It had not pleased him. He ignored his first cue card. Surveying the crowd with gimlet eyes, he spoke his first line in his patented flat tough-guy snarl: "Anybody know a good director?"

Applause exploded. Hilarity cascaded in its wake. The TV screens filled with close-ups of Annette laughing gaily while the announcer explained her dilemma to one billion people.

Klaus and Inga launched into their TelePrompted speech, Inga flawlessly pronouncing a Polish filmmaker whose name had only Y's for vowels, Klaus lending a faintly Japanese inflection to a Latino surname. Klaus spoke Homer's name, sliding through with relief at having such an easy one.

Homer didn't hear the other nominees. The names didn't mean anything to him, since he'd never seen their movies. Only a hundred and seventy-three of the three thousand assembled filmmakers had. But had they been his best friends, he still would have heard no names. When his was voiced, time stopped. A black hole opened, a palpable void in space-time sucking all sound and light into the stiff envelope in Klaus's hand. Klaus fought with the seal. Inga took it from him, ran a razor nail under the flap, and pulled out the paper.

"Homer Dooley. *Granite Plywood!*"

Frances jabbed him in the kidney. He stood up. The orchestra played the Schubert sonata that started the movie, and Homer trotted along the red carpet to the stage. Every minute was worth hundreds of thousands of dollars. He was glad he wore his Nikes.

An usher guided him to the podium, where Inga kissed him and Klaus handed him the heavy statue. He clutched it hard enough to crush baser metal.

Homer had not prepared a speech. He didn't want to tempt fate. But he'd speculated long and hard on what he might say, if he had prepared. He'd have to thank Frances, of course, and Bonnie, and Silas Grant, and probably Dean Planck for firing him, and Ham, whose constant carping had hardened his resolve to see it through. And he was duty bound, in fairness, to sing the praises of plywood, and thank Jedediah Sprague, its inventor, and Samuel Fargot, inventor of thermoelastic glue. Now that he'd won, he wished he had fifteen minutes to sort it all out on paper.

But he didn't. Golden seconds dripped away. He looked out at the mob of faces, mildly interested in who he was and what he might have to say. He raised the statue and smiled. And stepped down.

Applause, greater than he expected or thought he deserved, buoyed him up and wafted him offstage. He had a hazy glimpse of people standing in tuxedos and gowns, actually cheering, before hands pulled him into the wings toward the press rooms.

It was indeed a first. Never before in the decades of Oscar awarding had any of the more than two thousand honorees ever accepted a statuette without giving a thank-you speech.

Bo stood with the rest, laughing and cheering. But his mind was elsewhere. On Klaus's opening crack. That was more than a joke, it was a threat. If Bo couldn't land a director for *The Agonizer,* Klaus would find someone who could.

Bo slipped into the aisle and out the hall. He knocked on the wood paneling in the vestibule, two long, two short, and a hidden door opened. The guard recognized Bo in his trademark mandarin jacket. Bo glided through the backstage chaos, looking for Klaus.

Presenters' dressing rooms were on the fourth floor, next door to the interview room, to satisfy the celebrities' and the media's mutual thirst for proximity. Klaus, however, had shut his door on the press. He was savagely removing makeup, grinding swabs of cold cream into his jaw and neck. He was in no mood to discuss the *Agonizer* situation. He felt more than angry about Parrott's abdication. More than betrayed. He felt disappointed.

Klaus was a very focused guy. He defined his goals and achieved them. He'd been hoping the next step for him would be into something more serious. Like Clint. He needed help to get there. Parrott had been perfect. Now he had to rethink his priorities.

Bo knocked and stuck in his head. "May I enter?"

"Suit yourself."

Bo entered. They eyed each other warily and kept the room between them. It was small, fluorescent lit, beaver-board-paneled. The sink, Abbey Rents sofa, and easy chair filled it up. "I tried Montana and Idaho—"

"Snow was shitty. I met a bush pilot, he took me up to the Brooks Range."

"That's in Alaska, isn't it?"

"Five hundred fuckin' miles of it."

"You really had them laughing out there."

"Yeah, well, I'm laughing on the outside, crying on the inside."

"Your instincts were correct, Klaus. Parrott lacks the cojones for an action picture."

"I figured that motherfucker might have surprised me."

"He talked the talk."

"Well, fuck him. He never got it anyway. I looked at that first draft again." He gestured at a dog-eared script by the sink. "That's a motherfucker first draft. Flat-out high-voltage Frotner."

"Good writer for you."

"Yeah."

"Ever think he might be the guy to direct this after all?"

Klaus's face set.

"I won't lie to you. Annette met with the guy, wants to take a chance on him."

"No shit? Well, I got another idea." Bo had expected an explosion. Instead, Klaus's tone was ominously mild.

"What's that, Klaus?"

"She can take a chance on me."

"You want to direct *The Agonizer*?"

"Why the hell not? If Steven Seagal can—"

"Klaus, you get twenty-two million dollars for four months work. You really want to spend six months in a windowless room putting together this movie? For what, another three hundred grand? You really want to eat all the shit you're gonna eat along the way?"

"I'm fed up having my cock stepped on by some conceited shit just 'cause he's got a viewfinder hanging around his neck. I tell you right now, Elmo Fuckhead waltzes on the set, starts telling me what to do, I'll take his viewfinder and shove it up his ass. They can film that and send the dailies to fuckin' Annette."

Bo knew Klaus wasn't speaking metaphorically. He had a brief flash of Annette reclining in her Eames chair in the beige-on-beige executive screening room at Studio, watching Klaus pull the pants off a bloody and helpless Elmo Zwalt.

There was a knock. The knob turned and the moon face of Melinda Toto shined from the door. "Klaus—oh, Bo."

Klaus gave her a taciturn nod.

"Oh, you're talking directors."

"Anything we can do for you, Melinda?"

"I wanted some color commentary from Klaus. About Homer Dooley."

"Who?"

"You gave him the Oscar for Best Feature Documentary. He's the sweetest guy. You know he spent all night in the bleachers last night 'cause his mother wanted to see the movie stars?"

"His mother?"

"You should sign this guy up, Bo. He's a doll."

Next door, in the interview room, Homer was having a grand time. It reminded him of teaching, except these people paid more attention to what he said, and he could make them laugh. The Academy guy told him he had five minutes. He kept his answers short and to the point, and the questions kept coming—about Mucklinberg College, and the farm, and Silas and the tree spikers, and making the film in his living room with only a car battery for electricity. They seemed to want to know everything about his movie and his life. One lady in particular, the blond reporter who taped him leaving the bleachers, seemed very excited about "her little drama" as she called it, and kept pumping him for more. When the next winner was brought in, she and her cameraman even followed him offstage. She stopped, though, when she saw Klaus Frotner approach with a bland-looking man in a long Chinese jacket. She turned her cameraman on the two of them, and asked the bland guy if he was there to sign Homer. He smiled ambiguously. The reporter told Homer he was a very lucky young man, and made him promise to talk to her as soon as they finished with him.

Homer followed the two men away from the reporter. "What did she mean, sign me up?" he asked the bland guy.

"I'm an agent. Name of Bo. I represent Klaus."

"Oh. Homer Dooley." Homer shook his hand. He was disappointed. He'd hoped the guy was offering him a job.

He smiled at Klaus, hoping for a smile back. Klaus just looked over at the bland guy. It was strange to see Klaus Frotner let someone else take the lead. Bo looked grim, like he was going to give Homer bad news.

They entered a tiny dressing room. Bo didn't say any more until the door was closed. And locked. Homer felt trapped. He wished he was out front seeing who won for best actor.

"You gave a good account of yourself out there, Homer."

"Thanks."

"What do you think of Klaus?"

Homer smiled at Klaus. That was an easy one. "Mom's not so hot on him, but I think he's great. I watch all his movies—I mean that make it to my part of Vermont. I live pretty cut off."

Klaus handed Homer a script. The pages fanned out from being bent back. "Take a look at this. Tell me what you think."

Homer pressed down the pages, but they sprang back up. "What's this? Your next movie?"

"Why don't you read it, then we can talk."

Homer sat in the Naugahyde easy chair, put his Oscar on the floor, and read. Bo and Klaus sat on the sofa, inches away, staring toward him. Homer felt self-conscious. Then he realized their eyes were focused six feet past the wall behind him. They were practicing some form of meditation. They sat absolutely still, and Homer concentrated on the pages.

Homer made documentaries and taught documentaries. He'd never read a feature script before. But five pages in, it didn't matter where he was or who he was with. Back home, Homer spent a lot of time in his own head. Now he was inside someone else's. It wasn't like reading a book or watching a movie. That was someone all tied up in a neat package. This was like fighting off a paranoid, gibbering crazy pushing his life down the street in a shopping cart, who sucks you so deep inside his own demented world you're afraid you'll never crawl out.

The script ended. Homer was released to the plastic furniture and deathly fluorescent glare, the two men in deep trance almost touching knees with him. When he stirred, they surfaced.

He returned the script to Klaus. "Thanks."

Bo eyed him seriously. "What did you make of it?"

"It's great."

"Think so?"

"It'll make a great movie."

"If you were going to make this into a movie, what would you do to it?"

"Do to it?" This was beginning to sound like a job interview after all.

"How would you change it?"

"Why change it? It's great."

Klaus spoke up. "You mean shoot it as is?"

"Why not?" He looked at them pleasantly.

Bo persisted. "If you were to make this into a movie, and we asked your vision of the picture—"

"My vision?" Homer remembered Dean Planck. This felt like a trick question.

"What you think the movie will look like, feel like. How you see the movie."

That was easy. "It's a big Klaus Frotner action picture."

"Meaning?"

"It's real exciting, Klaus does a lot of athletic stuff, there's plenty of action and suspense, explosions . . ." He turned to Klaus. "I'm not about to tell you what a Klaus Frotner picture is."

"Excuse us for a minute." Bo beckoned Klaus. They went into the hall.

Bo went right to the point. "My gut tells me you can work with this guy."

Klaus was dubious. "He seems okay."

"I've learned to trust my gut, Klaus."

"He doesn't know fuck-all."

"He made a movie that won the Oscar."

"For fifteen cents."

"So he knows the value of a buck. He'll make the script. He'll listen to you."

"That would be a fuckin' relief for a change."

Bo held Klaus's eye and quoted *The Art of War:* "Sun Tzu says, 'If thou would be victorious, attack without being the attacker.' If thou would direct the movie . . ."

"He also says, 'The best way to court defeat is to rely on a false champion.' "

"It's him or Elmo."

"You'll never sell him to Annette."

"That's my problem." Bo gave Klaus a look that reminded Klaus whatever he was now, he had once been Bo's personal trainer.

They came in from the hall. Bo looked very serious. "Mr. Dooley, how would you like to direct this script?"

Homer laughed. "Sure!"

"That's not an idle question, Mr. Dooley."

"Homer. Are you offering me the job?"

"I can't do that. I'm only an agent."

"Would you be my agent?"

"If you wanted me to."

"Sure." They shook on it. But Homer was uncomfortable. He wasn't being entirely honest. "I have to tell you, I don't know much about directing big movies like this. When I make my movies, I'm kind of a one-man band."

"That means you have experience with all the different aspects of filmmaking."

"I know how to use a camera and run sound and cut negative and stuff."

"How many big directors can say that?"

"I don't know. I don't know what a director does."

"The truth is, Homer, big movies are designed like spaceships. They've got many levels of redundancy built in. A good actor directs himself. A good crew could make a movie without a director. Matter of fact, most crews would prefer to do it that way."

"Then why have a director at all?"

"Why have an astronaut on the space shuttle? Computers could fly the ship without him. But he's there in case a system breaks down, or something needs tweaking."

"And to do experiments."

"That too."

Homer thought about that. "I could do that. If the crew was good."

"This crew is the best in the business. You'll have Speilberg's editor. Your cameraman worked for Fellini."

Homer blushed. "I'm no Fellini."

"How many directors are? I haven't known you very long, Homer, but I can see you've got character. You project a quality of calm good humor that makes people like and trust you."

"Thanks." Homer wasn't used to being complimented. It made him uncomfortable, but it felt good.

"In my experience, character is what counts. I've put together a lot of movies, and I handle a lot of major talent. For nine directors out of ten, character matters most. Cast and crew have been trained to be part of a team. They look for a leader."

"Like a coach?"

"Inspire the actors and the crew to do their best, then get out of the way. Phil Jackson would make a hell of a director."

Bo made it sound a lot like teaching. Homer figured he could do that. Be astronaut-coach. Sounded like fun.

The Governor's Ball, the official post-game festivity, was held beneath a large tent immediately outside the Dorothy Chandler Pavilion. The tent was an elaborate affair, enclosing not only the plaza but its computerized fountain and monumental Lipschitz sculpture. Annette looked at the doughy nudes piled in a thirty-foot heap, meant no doubt to symbolize striving in the arts, and thought of Hollywood, all those people stepping on one another to get to the top. Except Hollywood people were in better shape. To banish the thought, she remarked to her escort a trifle too gaily that the sculpture looked like an R. Crumb group grope. He countered that the water jets programmed to spurt orgasmically completed the image. They laughed, and Annette took his hand under the table, trying to block out the hubbub to her left.

Normally the powerful put in only a token appearance at the Governor's Ball on their way to more exclusive festivities. Annette had counted on hanging out there until the wee hours, with the below-the-liners and the celebrity tourists, avoiding the lethal sympathy of her peers without seeming to turn tail and run. But her plan had developed complications. Weeks before, when seats were assigned, some thoughtful administrator had placed her on the right hand of her then boss Darius Fo. Annette had spent many evenings making both sides of a witty conversation while Darius carefully loaded peas on his fork, but she wasn't about to do it tonight. She talked baseball with her escort, waiting for Darius to leave.

Unfortunately Darius, as part of his credibility campaign, had arranged to be given the Jean Hersholt Humanitarian Award. Instead of leaving after five minutes, as Annette had every reason to think he would, Darius held court at their table. His peers flowed by in a steady stream, paying homage to his humanitarian efforts on behalf of the film industry and invariably congratulating him on his more tangible coup, the capture of Parrott. Annette was obliged to smile and make nice with each well-wisher, who would remark sympathetically that Parrott had no doubt been the wrong man for a Frotner picture anyway, and she was sure to have *the* big Christmas picture in *The Agonizer,* to which Annette would respond with a modestly optimistic tinkle.

Annette's throat was dry from tinkling by the time Bo appeared. Bo shook Darius's hand mutely, more partner than praiser, then murmured in her ear.

"Can I borrow you for a few moments?"

Annette made excuses to her escort and followed him toward the limos stretched along Grand Avenue. She was in no mood for small talk.

"What's up, Bo?"

"I think I may have a solution to our problem."

"You've talked to Klaus?"

"I've talked to him. I want you to keep an open mind, Annette."

"You know my mind is always open."

"Besides the fact that Klaus will refuse to work with Elmo, I see other difficulties in using him."

She started to speak, and he cut her off. "I'm not talking about his inexperience. I'm talking about his emotionality. He's an artist. He's a loner. Can he communicate? Can he bring people along with him on his vision of the picture?"

"He's got the whole movie storyboarded. All he has to do is point."

"We both know it's not that simple. It's a question of personality. He's a storyteller, not a leader. Can he inspire loyalty? Can he drive men to their best work? Not Klaus."

"He impressed me. He'll impress them." Annette wasn't sounding so confident, though. "He can make a great movie."

"Maybe. Maybe he's a great artist. But Godard said a great movie that's also a great success is the result of a misunderstanding. You have two problems here. One is finding a person who can pull off this movie. Fact is, there are lots of people in town who could do that, given the support you've lined up. Even someone like Pinsky."

She laughed bitterly. "Bet the studio on Pinsky. I won't last till the movie comes out."

"That's problem number two, the tough one: finding a name that'll earn the respect of the industry. You'll take a chance on Elmo because he's such an unknown, you'll look like a visonary to the rest of the town. That's bold, and smart, but there's a flaw in your logic. Everyone knows Elmo wrote the script. They'll think, 'If he wasn't good enough before, how come he's good enough now?' It'll smell like desperation."

"And you have the answer to my teenage prayer."

He was getting to her. Good. "I have the man who fits your bill. He's completely unknown, yet he's already sparked tremendous interest. I think you know who I'm talking about."

"No, I don't."

"Homer Dooley."

"Dooley?"

"He just won the Oscar tonight. He was the fellow who didn't give a thank-you speech."

"Him?"

"The media love him. I saw his press conference after he won. They wouldn't let him go. Melinda Toto's doing a color piece that's front-page Calendar. Channel nine's working up a minidoc for their post-Oscar telecast."

"What did he win for?"

"Best Feature Documentary. Something on eco-saboteurs in the Maine woods. Thematically related to our picture."

"Has he ever worked with actors?"

"Has Elmo? This guy knows camera, he knows editing—he even knows sound. He loves the script—"

"You showed him the script?"

"I wanted his take on it. He loves it. Doesn't want to change a thing."

They'd reached Bo's big black smoked-glass limo. Bo stopped with his hand on the door. "Just talk to him. Judge for yourself." He opened the door and gave her the closer. "Klaus thinks he's a very good choice."

Homer was watching pro snowboarding with Klaus off the satellite dish, enjoying the stiff leather of the limo seat, when Annette's head and shoulders blocked the screen.

"Room for one more?"

He couldn't help but gasp. Up close, Annette had a luminous, faintly alien presence. Pale as snow on a sunny day, she shimmered insubstantially in her glittering black beads. Her aura filled the limo, but didn't weigh it down. She breathed not air, but something lighter, more refined. Helium, maybe. "May I?"

She reached for his crotch. Homer started. Then he realized she was going for the Oscar in his lap. She stroked it reverently. "That's the first Oscar I've ever touched."

"It's heavy."

The limo was big enough that it had banquettes facing both ways. She sat across from him, perkily erect with her knees together and her hands cupped over them. A fairy schoolgirl paying close attention.

"So. Tell me all about yourself."

Bo entered and zapped the TV to channel nine's Oscar wrapup. "Annette Foray. Homer Dooley. Annette is head of Studio Pictures."

"I know." Homer wanted to know everything about this creature, and he wanted her to know everything about him. "What can I tell you?"

"Bo says you want to direct our *Agonizer* picture."

"It was Bo's idea."

"Oh?"

"But I think it's fine. I like the script a lot."

"So do we."

"If I'd known I'd be having a job interview tonight, I would have brought my CV."

She smiled. "I don't need to know what high school you attended, Mr. Dooley."

Bo's timing was good. The minidoc came on. The blond reporter opened with Homer and Frances being cornered by the security guard in front of their bleacher pals, and her perspicacious interview, then seguéd to Homer's magnificent mute acceptance before a standing ovation, and snips of his press conference about life without electricity or running water. The piece ended with a tracking shot following Homer as Klaus and Bo closed on him, hands out in greeting. "Another rags-to-riches Hollywood story."

Homer was delighted. "I wonder if I can get a tape of that? Frances would love to see it. That was Frances. My mother."

"She looks like a charming woman. Where is she now?"

"Oh, still out there dancing. She's seated at a table with Art Buchwald!"

"So what makes you think you can direct a hundred-million-dollar movie?"

Homer thought. "I wondered about that too. But Bo says I can do it."

"I say he can too," said Klaus.

Homer had the feeling that wasn't enough. "All that money's being spent on good stuff, right? Great crew and actors and scenery and stuff? They're all hired, right?"

"That's true."

"So all I have to do is let them do their job." Homer leaned back and smiled. "It sounds a lot easier than doing it yourself."

Annette left the party as early as face allowed. In the limo on her way home, she flipped among Oscar wrap-ups. It had been a particularly uneventful ceremony, even by Oscar standards. The Best Supporting Actor wept, the Best Original Writer thanked her lesbian lover, the Best Director used the podium to defend himself from charges of child abuse. And there was Homer. In that mysterious fashion that proves the power of the free market, the invisible hand of the news had selected Homer's saga as the consensus human-interest story of the evening. His was the humanizing tale chosen to bring the Oscars home to the little man. Radio stations even risked the horrors of dead air to play the silence of his non-speech.

Next morning Homer was front page in Calendar, as Bo had predicted; also the late edition Living Arts section of the *New York Times*. *Good Morning America* aired the channel nine footage and featured a telephone interview with Homer from his suite at the Four Seasons Hotel. He charmed his interviewer by telling her he'd slept on the couch in the sitting room because his mother said he snored. When the interviewer asked why they didn't get separate rooms, Homer said Bo'd offered to, but it seemed like an awful lot of money, and this one had twin beds, and the couch was very comfortable, much better than the bleacher benches the night before. *Good Morning America* ate it up.

When Annette reached her office, even before strawberries and cream, she took out a yellow legal pad, put Homer's name at the top, and drew a line down the center with her Mont Blanc pen. On one side she wrote Assets, on the other Liabilities. On the assets side she wrote:

Good buzz in town
Good national publicity
Bo's gratitude and support
Peace with Klaus

She couldn't think of offsetting liabilities. She wrote below, on the liability side:

Unproven commodity
No experience

But she countered that on the asset side with:

Fresh face
Will let crew do the work

Then she frowned, and penned more liabilities:

?Leadership?
?Vision?

Against which she placed more assets:

Eager to please
Looks like he'll listen
Will shoot script

She paused for a moment, then added more assets:

Knows value of a dollar
Not yet egomaniac

She couldn't come up with balancing downsides.

Annette capped her Mont Blanc. Looking at the paper, she had to admit she was in a most unlikely situation: choosing an unknown commodity was actually playing it safe. If she named Homer, she'd have it both ways—she'd be hailed as bold, while actually being prudent. The thought appealed to her executive instincts.

He might not work out. That would create a messy situation, but that was down the line. Right now the project needed momentum in a serious way. Naming Homer just might give it escape velocity. That would buy her time and credibility to launch other stuff.

Annette had no problem reaching Bo and Klaus. She put them on the speakerphone. Let them hear her remote and resonant. The voice from on high.

"Klaus? Bo? I've slept on our little meeting. Before I go any further, I want to be sure we understand each other. You're both telling me that you want Homer Dooley to direct *The Agonizer.*"

"That's right," said Bo.

"I suppose so," said Klaus.

"I want to be absolutely clear on this, Klaus."

"Let's give it a try, Annette."

"That's my second point. We'll give him a try. If he doesn't work out, I replace him."

"What do you mean, doesn't work out?" said Klaus.

"You'll know if it happens. We'll all know. But it's my call."

"You'll pay him off, of course," said Bo.

"If he doesn't work out, I'll probably bring in Elmo. I don't want any trouble from you if I do, Klaus. That's part of the deal."

Silence. Finally, "This Homer guy'll shoot the script, Annette. That's all I ask."

"That's all I'll need, Klaus."

Homer was sitting in his sitting room with Frances, eating the free fruit that came with the suite, when Bo called with the news. Homer was very pleased. A job! He felt funny asking Bo what he was being paid, but he thought he should. Bo said two-fifty, and Homer thought that was okay, but he was hoping for a little more. How much more? Maybe three hundred. Bo said he should view this as a tremendous opportunity, and not get hung up on fifty thousand dollars. Homer then realized that Bo meant two hundred and fifty thousand dollars, not two hundred and fifty dollars a week, and he shut up. When Homer got off the phone, Frances made him open the champagne that came with the suite. He'd never had a whole half bottle of champagne before.

Next day, the *Variety* headline read: "AGONIZER" HOMERS.

It is worth noting that Homer got his job without any of the principals involved actually seeing his film. Later that week he retrieved *Granite Plywood* from the Academy and sent it back to Silas as he'd promised. Silas promptly burned it, as he had burned the negative when Homer gave it to him in exchange for his final check. *Granite Plywood* no longer existed.

Had he known, Homer would have been distressed. But he wouldn't have been devastated. If anything, watching the film was more pain than pleasure for him, because the projected film never lived up to the one in his head. No matter how sincerely he resolved to just enjoy it, he'd watch with mental body English, hoping this time a certain shot would stay in focus a few beats longer, or the sound would be clearer, or a certain scene would have richer blacks. Homer would have been relieved to learn he'd never have to sit through his movie again.

He'd even be relieved to learn he'd never have to show the film to anyone again. Sharing his movie with audiences made him very uncomfortable. Words of praise didn't make the movie any better, but any criticism, even random body movement, defaced it beyond repair.

It would not have occurred to Homer to mourn the fact that

critics and filmmakers would never be influenced by the brilliance of *Granite Plywood,* or moved to awe for its creator. He did not share the burning conviction of a Christopher Parrott that he owed the world great things, and that this debt must be collected by the world at all costs. Deep down, he wasn't even making the film for Silas Grant. He made it because it gave him great satisfaction to have a thought and work it out with film. That felt like accomplishing something, even more than hauling water or chopping wood.

In this respect, Homer and Elmo were much alike. They had no urge to prove their greatness or wield power over men. The difference between them, though, was that Elmo lived entirely in the world of movies, and Homer spent most of his time just trying to make ends meet. For Elmo to give birth to a film and not to have it in his hands forever would be disaster. The death of a child. For Homer, *Granite Plywood,* even stillborn, was a great success. It got him his next job.

TWENTY-FOUR

George Marshall, like the rest of the crew, learned of Parrott's abdication in the trades. He tried to reach McGinty, but the production manager had gone underground. That figured. So Marshall kept his crews working triple shift, not only on the rain forest but on the torture chamber, cantina, bordello, river boat interiors, piranha tank—eleven other stages in all. He wasn't going to be the one to turn out the lights. Oscars were on a Monday, as always; a major production meeting had been scheduled for Wednesday, when McGinty had to come up for air.

They met Wednesday morning outside the conference room. McGinty's face was splotched with purple blooms the size of prize delphinium. He'd packed too much rage, anxiety, and Cutty Sark into the past two days, trying to jump with Parrott and finding his feet nailed in place. When Marshall drew his finger across his throat in a quizzical gesture, McGinty responded with a twisted smile and handed him that morning's *Variety,* screaming the news about Homer.

Marshall tried to decode the article. "Who is this guy? Does he know what he's doing?"

"Hey. Annette Foray says he's got vision. Bet that means he looks up her skirts. But we'll straighten him out." He gave Marshall a conspiratorial poke.

Marshall saw two men leave the commissary a block away and head in their direction. He checked the photo above the fold. "That him?"

"Nah. This Homer guy walks a foot off the ground."

"Isn't that what's-his-name Fo with him? The guy who used to be the producer?"

McGinty squinted. "Mary Mother of God."

Jason was telling Homer how lucky Homer was to live in Vermont, how he was always making lists of places to escape to. The problem was, every haven of peace and foliage had one movie theater at most, and a couple ethnic restaurants if he was lucky, and maybe some college culture, but not the hip-hop pulse of real life. Jason embraced life.

Jason had every reason to embrace life. He was back in the loop. Yesterday, the day after Oscars, when Jack Doberman tried to close Elmo's deal with Annette, he'd scavenged the news that Homer was being tagged instead, so he'd sicced Jason on Annette to straighten her out. The new Jason, the dynamic, driven Jason, had charged in with an impassioned paean to Elmo Zwalt. Annette hadn't contradicted him. She'd said she thought Elmo might even end up directing the picture. But for right now she wanted to go with Homer.

Jason hadn't backed down. That surprised and impressed her. He'd pointed out the manifold pitfalls awaiting Homer, a man with no proven sense of character or narrative, so astutely and in such detail that Annette had deputized him then and there to guide Homer around them. Homer, she'd said, was a sensible man who listened to advice. His job was to make sure Homer had proper guidance to make the right decisions. Homer would be in charge of the movie, but he would be in charge of Homer.

He'd asked, delicately, how Klaus would feel about the arrangement. She'd just smiled and told him to let her worry about that. Jason had been scapegoated. Now that Parrott was gone, the blame could be placed where it belonged. All she asked of Jason was to keep her fully informed of the course of events on the set. Not her spy, more her Johnny-on-the-spot. This project had given her enough surprises already.

Jason's commitment to Elmo's talent was great, but his joy at becoming a fully functioning producer was greater. He told himself his duty to the picture was clear.

It really was his picture now. As a sign of his new level of responsibility, Annette had him guarantee the budget against his fee. Part of any overages would come out of his pocket, until his pocket was empty. But that was fair. It only underscored his level of responsibility.

He'd plunged into preproduction with Homer. They'd spent an afternoon together, going over the picture with Griffith, the assistant director. Jason liked Griffith. He was young and can-do, and he treated Jason like a real producer. Jason's first act as real producer had been to make sure McGinty was not informed of their meeting.

While Jason talked about the beauties of Vermont, Homer was thinking about the pancakes he'd had in the commissary. Homer wasn't a particular eater. He considered dinner in a restaurant more trouble than it was worth, what with choosing what to eat, and waiting for it without getting bored or changing your mind, and making a good impression on the waiter. But he did like the idea of an all-American restaurant breakfast, fresh orange juice, crisp bacon, tangy maple syrup seeping into fluffy buttermilk pancakes. At home he could never whip up a big enough batch to get them right. Restaurant pancakes made him feel part of a larger, nurturing culture.

Unfortunately, the commissary had renounced its cultural aspirations years before. Its bacon was matted grease jerky, its pancakes flannel soaked in dextrose. Homer felt vaguely betrayed. He vowed tomorrow to try the Cuban place on the corner.

But Homer had more important concerns. He'd spent a dizzying afternoon going over what Jason called "the big picture," long computer printouts of narrow strips encoding data scene by scene, like who played, and what special props were needed. His assistant director, Griffith, had prepared it all very thoroughly. At first Griffith asked Homer for guidance about how long things would take to shoot, but when Homer admitted he hadn't the faintest idea, Griffith was happy to fill in the numbers himself. It was nice to have an assistant.

Jason was a nice guy too, very supportive and enthusiastic about everything. Homer liked that. Everything he said sounded important too. But when Jason burbled on, he had trouble listening.

Jason was running through the crew list as they left the commissary, giving Homer clever thumbnail descriptions, which Homer immediately forgot. Until he met people, names meant nothing to him. He let the impressive titles wash over him, and thought about Mack Planck, his old boss at Mucklinberg College. He'd wanted Homer to show some initiative. What would Mack think of him now, presiding over a production meeting of department heads? He tried to imagine the production meeting and conjured up a bomber command war room in a Battle of Britain movie, attentive aides with hoelike sticks pushing markers around a map table big as his vegetable garden, while de-

partment heads debated in muted tones urgent issues of tactics,
logistics, and supply. Best make his entrance with a brisk mili-
tary stride. He rehearsed his pose as he walked, hands clasped
behind, bent at the waist as if leaning into a stiff wind. Jason
gave him a funny look, and he realized he was giving a passable
imitation of Charlie Chaplin in *The Great Dictator*.

Homer was surprised, then, and a little relieved when Jason
ushered him into a house trailer jacked up on cinder blocks.
Four cluttered desks were shoved together under the lone window. The rest of the trailer was taken up by twenty people
sitting on brown metal folding chairs around a couple of big
plywood tables. The plywood seemed to greet Homer like an
old friend.

Homer smiled at the twenty faces. Most smiled back, neutral
time-buying smiles. Like his students the first day of class.

Jason introduced Homer, and they went around the room
introducing themselves. Jason made an impassioned speech
about the wonderful work they'd all done, and the studio's high
hopes for the film, how he personally couldn't think of a script
he'd read that excited him more, and how they were the crème
de la crème, creatively, and Klaus was the number-one box office draw in the world. Then he brought up Homer.

He didn't have much to say about Homer, except that Annette and Klaus were both very impressed with his take on the
movie. He knew they were loyal Parrott men and women, and
the sudden change at the helm was a big surprise—no, make
that a blow—for all of them. He asked only that they give Homer a chance. He was sure they'd find Homer a great guy to
work with.

While he talked, Homer picked over the pile of Danish pastry
beside the coffee urn. After he'd made sure there weren't any
cherry Danish, he settled for apricot. But then he switched for
another near the bottom with more icing.

McGinty nudged Marshall and grunted in despair. Jesus, the
grunt said, this guy'll be making all the decisions, and he can't
make up his mind about a fuckin' piece of coffee cake. Marshall
nodded noncommittally.

McGinty knew he needed allies. Homer alone he could handle, but Jason stuck to Homer like slick on snot. How the hell
did that shit eater come back from the dead? Maybe he was
fucking Annette Foray. No, she could fuck whoever the fuck she

wanted. Hell, how Jason got there didn't matter. He wasn't spending six months changing Jason's diapers.

Jason must have caught his look. He continued, straight at McGinty: Because of Homer's lack of experience with big productions, he said, the studio asked him, Jason, to be more involved than under Parrott. He'd sat Homer down with Griffith and they'd gone over the situation in detail.

McGinty scowled at Griffith. The beefy A.D. put his nose deeper in his Powerbook. He and Jason looked like frat buddies. The Judas. He'd never trusted him. But Parrott had insisted on a first A.D. who knew computers, since McGinty hated the goddamn things.

They had their backs to the wall, Jason said. The mining company was torching four hundred thousand acres of rain forest in just three weeks. That was the climax to their movie. They were going to shoot that climax. They were leaving for New Guinea as planned. In one week. The jungle village that doubled the one on the soundstage would be done by then. Spend a week shooting big vistas around the village set, then get the climax as it burned to the ground. Spend another ten days shooting river exteriors for the riverboat sequence. Then back to L.A. As planned.

Words were muttered. Bodies tensed. François, the costume designer, called out.

"We haven't heard Mr. Dooley's plans in the way of changes."

"Call him Homer. Homer's very pleased with your work. He doesn't plan any changes."

There was a gentle rustle of legs crossing and uncrossing and an audible exhalation. Somebody cracked a joke and a couple of people laughed. McGinty echoed "nothing" ironically. They all knew what a director meant by "changing nothing."

Jason looked to Homer. "You tell them."

Homer looked up from his Danish. "You're all real good at what you do. It all looks great to me. Besides, we've already spent the money, haven't we? I'm sure it'll be fine."

Incredulous silence. Marshall raised his hand. Homer pointed at him.

"You're . . . ?"

"George Marshall. I'm your production designer."

"Sorry. I'm terrible with names. Your rain forest looks great."

"Thank you. I wanted to know what's happening with the script."

"What's happening?"

"Chris Parrott was working on the script, and I've been waiting for revisions."

"The script looks fine to me."

Jason interrupted. "We're going with the original script."

"You mean Flaherty's original?"

"No, the original original. The Zwalt version."

Marshall paled. "I designed the sets for the Flaherty version."

Everyone looked at Homer. He looked back at Jason. "They have a different script?"

People were stirring in earnest, poking through satchels and book bags and briefcases for the Zwalt script. Jason could see by the way papers were shuffled and clasps snapped that he'd made a serious mistake not bringing Homer up to speed on the Flaherty situation. But it had been ancient history, and painful to contemplate.

"Maybe I should look at the script they're using."

Jason waved his hand dismissively. "Parrott got sidetracked. Forget about it."

McGinty spoke up, his voice raspy with glee. "You're not changing anything, but you're changing every fuckin' thing. We can't do half the action pieces in the first script on the set we've got."

"We can't?" said Homer.

McGinty chortled and poked Marshall. " 'We can't?' "

Marshall shook his head no.

Griffith, sweating lightly, was doing some quick number-crunching on his notebook computer. "It's not as bad as all that. We were all working from the old script until a couple of weeks ago. Characters are the same. Eighty-seven percent of the locations are the same. Day out of days is different, but that's just scheduling. It comes down to . . . four big set pieces."

Homer brightened. He turned to Jason. "Let's just get Elmo to make his script fit the set."

"I'll get right on it." Jason made a show of being attentive and obedient, hoping it would rub off on everyone else.

Homer turned to Marshall. "Mr. Marshall, why don't you get together with Elmo, maybe walk him through the set, explain what you can do and what you can't."

"Just tell me when and I'll be there."

"Work it out with Elmo."

"When's good for you?"

"You need me for this?"

George was caught short. When Parrott had made him build a rain forest this scale on a soundstage, he'd thought it was a profligate, impossible idea. But the damn thing was coming together very nicely. It wasn't often you could build a really big set anymore. He'd come to think of it as his monument. It would ensure him a third Oscar, but more than that, he'd always be the man who built the *Agonizer* set. Now Homer was asking him to tell the writer how to show off his set to maximum advantage.

"I'll come along if you want me to," said Homer. "But you'll have a much better idea of what needs doing than I do. And the guy who wrote that script doesn't need any help from me in thinking up action. Good grief no."

The department heads laughed. Marshall smiled too. Designing the set had in fact given him some very concrete ideas about how action sequences could exploit it. But he was used to keeping such ideas to himself. In thirty years, he'd never talked script with a writer without a director's hand at his throat.

"No," said Marshall. "I guess not. We should do all right on our own."

"Don't forget to tell Elmo he's got three weeks," said Mc-Ginty. "And every day he's late costs us eighty thousand dollars." McGinty looked around for backing from the rest of the crew, but most of them had dug out their copies of the Zwalt script and were already scanning for changes. He nudged Marshall. "That's what happens when suits plan a movie."

Marshall nodded absently. He was already thinking about his set, and the old version, and what he'd need to bring the two together.

The top was down on Jason's Jag and the sun was high and white. Homer stared straight ahead, enjoying the cliffs whipping by on his right and the ocean spread flat and slow on his left. He'd never been in a convertible before—there weren't many convertibles in Vermont—but he'd sat in the back of plenty of pickups, so he knew the feeling, how the wind attacked you from all sides but where it should be coming from. Hair buffeted his eyeballs. He squinted shut, then blinked open, closed for a second, opened a blink, closed for a second, opened, closed for a second, opened—

Jason broke in. "Something in your eye?"

"No." Homer sped up now: black blink black blink black blink—

"You're not a convulsive or anything?"

"You should try this. It's like stop motion."

"I'm driving."

"I do it when I'm driving sometimes. It would make a neat movie. *Blink Movie.* Black leader with one frame of picture cut in every once in a while. But in real time, so each frame's exactly where it would be if the picture was running the whole time."

Homer blinked happily like a broken sleeper doll. He tried jerking his head from side to side and grinned. "Neat! Maybe we can use this in *The Agonizer.*"

"We'll see."

"It'd be easy to try. We have all those editors—"

"Homer?"

"What?"

"Do me a big favor. Don't discuss this with Klaus."

"Why not?"

"It's kind of experimental, isn't it?"

"I thought that was my job. They're the space shuttle, I'm the astronaut. I do experiments."

"You're the astronaut, Homer. But Klaus is the main thruster. He powers the rocket ship. If he won't go into your orbit, you have to find another orbit."

"He wouldn't like the blink idea?"

"Maybe later. Right now he needs to know you'll take him where he wants to go. That's what this meeting is all about. Trust me on this. I know."

"How'll I know where he wants to go?"

"I don't think that will be a problem."

"I hope not." Homer stopped blinking and brushed hair out of his eyes. He thought of the *Challenger* astronauts, sitting on their thrusters.

"Don't worry about it. I'll be there to steer things in the right direction." Jason patted him on the knee, smooth and reassuring. "I've been there before."

Jason knocked confidently on Klaus's door. The woman who'd given Homer his Oscar answered it. She was dressed in a loincloth and painted all over with bright red dime-sized polka dots, impasto at the nipples, which poked at him. He tried not to stare. She put out her hand.

"Congratulations again."

"Thank you."

They shook. She had an iron grip and a saucy smile. Maybe she was sticking out her chest on purpose.

"Normally the houseboy gets the door, but I was up here taking a leak. Everyone's outside."

They passed through a living room that looked to Homer like it had been blasted with a flamethrower. Anything soft was vaporized down to twisted metal skeletons. Before he could ask if Klaus had been firebombed, Jason nodded approvingly. "Love your Denovis."

"Surgical steel."

Homer followed bouncing polka dots onto the catwalk. Below, a small crew huddled around a camera. Homer perked up. This was moviemaking! He clanged down the steps.

A long-haired assistant was changing film. Homer watched with interest.

"That's an Arri S, isn't it?"

"Yep."

"We have one at school, sixteen millimeter though."

"Stanton's had this since *Zabriskie Point*. He keeps it around for tests. We're Panavision for the shoot." Homer had never seen a Panaflex, except in pictures of directors standing beside their cameras. He found the prospect of standing beside a Panaflex intimidating.

Jason pulled Homer away. This wasn't the time to talk f-stops. Klaus was closing on them. He was polka-dotted and loinclothed to match Inga, and he wore a straight greased wig clipped in bangs. Homer did a double take. Klaus picked up on it.

"I look like shit, don't I?"

François, the costume designer, followed him, waving a large book. "You want real, Klaus, this is real."

The makeup woman sniggered. "He looks like Louise Brooks with Karposi's sarcoma."

"Oh, shut up, Denise." François turned to Homer. "He's just

not used to the look. In context, he'll be a knockout. See?" He
handed Homer the book.

The crew stood silently, observing with clinical interest as
Homer leafed back and forth under Klaus's irate eye. The costume test had become a director test. Make-or-break time for
the new man. But Jason wasn't too worried. Homer had an easy
call.

The book contained photographs of Amazon tribesmen in
jungle finery. Homer pored over it, fascinated by their dignified
ferocity. Some hair was short, some long, some greased, some
curled, some hacked in strange patterns; warriors were painted
in dots from dime-sized to dinner plate, in straight lines or
squiggles or circles, in ochre or black, in bright red and yellow
and blue. Homer felt humbled by the tremendous variety of
human invention.

Finally Klaus grew impatient. "What's the verdict?"

"There are so many here."

"But the Xavanti have the red dots. Look." François turned
him to the page with a yellow Post-it.

Jason tried to slip Homer a pointed hint. "Is it critical that we
use the exact tribal colors? Can't we give ourselves a little artistic leeway?"

"And be deluged with postcards from angry Xavanti?"

"Button it, Denise."

Denise looked startled. She thought she'd been taking Klaus's
cue. Klaus glared at Jason. "First you tell me we shoot on a
fuckin' soundstage, now you tell me we don't use a real tribe."

"We are using a real tribe, Klaus. We have the Xavanti all
lined up."

"And I'm polka-dot Moe, Stooge of the Amazon."

"Maybe Denise has a point. Maybe we should bend the rules
a little—"

"Maybe we should do something right for once!"

"Whatever you want, Klaus, either way—"

"I want it fuckin' right! This is a fuckin' Klaus Frotner picture!"

"We'll do it real or we'll massage it a little, whatever you
want—"

"I want it to be right!"

"So, tell us what's right—"

"Hey, I'm not directing this thing, am I? That's what the
director's for!"

All eyes shifted to Homer. All hearts gave thanks they were not in his shoes. Jason in particular watched in suppressed panic. This was bad. This was soundstage payback. Klaus had Homer's head in a vise and was about to squeeze. When his eyeballs popped out, what on God's earth would Jason use for a director?

Klaus's voice took on the tough, flat tone of his movie persona. "So what do we do, Herr Direktor?"

Homer, oblivious of the drama, was deep in the notes at the back of the book.

"Herr Direktor?"

"You know, Klaus, these are all Xavanti patterns."

"Bullshit."

"No, it says here, Xavanti is the main tribe. Each village paints itself in distinctive colors. The pictures are listed by village, that's all. Except for the polka-dot one. They don't know the village for that one, so they call it Xavanti."

"So they're all Xavanti?"

"Right. Look."

Homer pointed to a paragraph and Klaus glared hard at it, trying to make him a liar. Finally:

"What village are we?"

"The script doesn't say. Does it?"

Jason led the firm and unanimous agreement that on this, the script was mute.

They spent the rest of the afternoon filming Klaus and Inga as inhabitants of assorted Xavanti villages. Homer found the variations a source of profound fascination. Klaus, at first suspicious, finally let himself believe that Homer was as open and patient as he appeared, and threw himself wholeheartedly into a subject he always found compelling: his look onscreen.

Jason knew a producer's job was to have opinions on such things, but after Klaus's soundstage crack he opted to stay in the background, watching the proceedings with barely concealed glee. When Stanton Frye, the cameraman, looked at his watch conspicuously, or Griffith muttered anxiously about the casting session Homer was missing, Jason waved them off. This was more important. His director and his star were forging a creative bond.

At the end of the day Jason was so ebullient, he allowed himself to approach Klaus and remark how pleased he was they'd found a director on Klaus's creative wavelength. Klaus looked at him coldly, and noted they'd spent all day picking polka dots; when they were shooting, they wouldn't have time to fuck around like this, and Homer had damn well better be a man who could make up his mind. Jason saw an opening, and pointed out how shooting on a stage wasn't so bad after all, because it freed up time for creative decision-making, and allowed the kind of fine-tuning Klaus seemed to value. Klaus replied that first they had to pack six months worth of exterior reality into two weeks on location. Jason shut up.

II

Narak-a-la-ok

TWENTY-FIVE

The mining camp location was at the end of a tortuous chain of supply: Sydney to Brisbane by rail, containership across the Arafura Sea to Port Moresby, small plane or leaky freighter around the impenetrable forested crags of Pegunungan Maoke to Wewak, soggy provincial capital of five thousand souls, where goods not pilfered were offloaded onto mining company barges and sent up the Sepik River, again offloaded and trucked along a raw, dusty scar through the Amboina jungle, dodging gigantic earth movers crawling to the mine like mutant termites homing in on a new nest. Theft was assumed to be thirty percent of cargo, and perishables arrived in varying states of decay.

The movie people had an easier time of it. McGinty had chartered a fleet of helicopters and small planes he dubbed Agonizer Airlines, which leapfrogged from Sydney to Port Moresby to Wewak to the mining camp. Cast and crew still arrived from Los Angeles exhausted and confused, foggy from time shift and engine whine and dead airline air, hobbling on legs phlebotically bloated from forty hours buckled in a BarcaLounger.

Homer had never been a traveler. There was plenty to investigate within a mile of his house. Why move on? He'd tried New York once; one bus ride down Fifth Avenue exposed him to more than he could absorb in a week. But this trip was different. No onslaught of guerrilla rappers and belligerent dowagers and abusive preteens and blind Nintendo players. He was shielded from all such plebeian hassle. He didn't have to decide where to sleep or what flight to take, and people made a career of shepherding his luggage and putting him on the right plane. Jason managed the people who took care of everything. By the time they overflew Honolulu, he'd discovered he could nod and smile at Jason without actually listening to his barrage of helpful advice. Homer cruised along, the happy tourist on the ultimate package tour, enjoying first-class service and reading up on New

Guinea during the long hours over the Pacific. Klaus traveled with his own entourage and kept to himself.

The movie schedule had been built around the birth of the mine. When fully operational, the mine would produce a half million tons of copper and a quarter million ounces of gold every year, culled from the one hundred fifty thousand tons of raw rock bulldozers would skim each day off the hills. Camp and refining equipment were in place, but the earth movers were dormant: first, forest had to be cleared. The film company, in a remarkable stroke of luck, had located a well-equipped, empty camp deep in virgin jungle ripe for burning.

Of course, the Papuans had to make accommodation. The moment the construction crew clears out, normally miners move in, but for fifty thousand dollars a day McGinty bought the camp for a week. Normally, land was cleared as needed, but judicious negotiations and substantial bribes convinced the locals of the wisdom of a twenty-five-year burn. Four hundred thousand acres.

To Homer in the chopper, the jungle was so dense, it looked less like carpet than like thick green fur. He saw the Jet Ranger as a mosquito flitting over a huge beast, looking for a place to suck its blood. The chopper would land, he and Jason and Klaus would emerge like mosquito spit, poison raising a pimple on the jungle.

Homer spied the mining camp, a canker in the pelt. It grew larger and more mottled as they approached, now more like a cancerous area prep-shaved for surgery. The tumorous bruises became mills and refineries and camp compound and cooling ponds and helipad. People and vehicles moved in all directions. The place seemed very busy for a deserted mining camp.

Griffith and McGinty sweated on the glare of the helipad, steaming in the jungle heat. As the chopper settled they rushed in, cringing under the rotor, tired partners in adversity. They were bursting with bad news, but the sight of Klaus leaping from the chopper shut them up. Klaus stretched and scanned the tarmac with a movie star's radar. When no one recognized him, he turned to Griffith and McGinty, relieved and disappointed.

"You look like two kids who cracked up Dad's Porsche."

The two men squirmed and waited for each other to speak.

"Come on, kids, out with it."

"Complications, Klaus." They talked at once.

"Things are tight—"

"Things are fucking tight—"

"We've been double-crossed—"

"This was bought and paid for—"

Klaus looked pained. He hated it when people couldn't do their job. Jason nimbly cut in. "Go, track down Inga. I'll handle this."

Klaus gave them a veiled look and ambled off. Inga had come on an earlier chopper with Johnny Palermo, the heavy of the piece.

When Klaus was well out of earshot, Jason picked up the ball. "What's the scoop?"

"Refinery's waiting on Korean turbines—"

"Two hundred of the refinery gang—"

"That would fill half the place—"

"But that's not the problem—"

"It's the miners—"

"Four hundred miners—"

"They've got rooms for three hundred—"

"Six hundred peons on site—"

"And us. We've been fuckin' sold down the river—"

"This was bought and paid for—"

"We are royally fucked—"

Jason held up a hand. "Peace, guys, I'm sure we can work something out."

"They're expecting you."

Griffith was leading them toward the closest building. A dark man in a dark suit stood patiently in the shadow of the tin roof, waiting for them to come in from the sun. He was strong and squat and bearded and crinkled, with clear eyes and an open smile, and most of his face was given over to a broad flat nose that lent it a simian quality that reminded Homer of stone age men in museum dioramas. A black dwarf Neanderthal Santa on steroids. He pressed together his palms in greeting.

"*Narak-a-la-ok.*"

Homer and Jason raised their palms back. McGinty didn't bother.

"Nahum here is our official government snitch."

"Please. Facilitator."

"He facilitates screwing us."

Nahum looked abashed. Homer thought he saw his shiny black skin pale to ebony. "No big deal. Everyone make happy."

"We've been getting the kiss-ass runaround."

"Chief talk chief. Now chiefs come chopper. Chief talk chief."

McGinty looked pained. Jason smiled. "Makes perfect sense to me."

"That narak thing. What does that mean anyway?" Homer asked.

"Highland hello."

"But what's it mean?"

Nahum looked blank. "Hello?"

The trucked-in building was two wide loads wide. They followed Nahum down a narrow center corridor to a door at the far end. He knocked. They waited. A noise from inside seemed to give Nahum permission to enter.

The windowless room ran the full width of the building. Maps covered the walls. Half a dozen Asian men in Daiwoo hard hats and jump suits clustered around a slight, bespectacled fellow in horn rims and jogging sweats, arguing in staccato over topographic plans strewn down a long table. The jogger looked up at the the intruders and discussion abruptly stopped.

Nahum gave his palm-together greeting. "Narak-a-la-ok."

"*Anyong hasaeyo*," the man said in what must have been Korean.

"Jason Fo this, son Darius Fo, Homer Dooley, son—" Nahum turned to Homer.

"Abby Dooley."

"Jason son Darius, Homer son Abby, *Agonizer* chiefs."

The Korean guy nodded at them. "What's your problem?" He spoke perfect California English.

Jason flashed his charming smile. "We were told this camp would be empty for a week and we could have the run of the place."

The Korean squinted. "If you think you're taking over my camp, you must be crazy."

"Excuse me?" Jason's smile froze in place.

"I'm trying to get this turkey on line here."

Jason pursed his lips, hurt by the man's cavalier attitude. This was chief to chief. "This is a government project. You're working under contract for them. They've granted us use of the premises."

"I don't know who you talked to in the government, but they didn't clear it with me."

"We are paying the Papuan government fifty thousand dollars a day for use of this camp."

"This is a two-billion-dollar venture. Interest payments alone run half a million a day. You must have talked to the wrong guy."

Nahum grunted for their attention. "No problem. Miners sleep stars. Rainy no much."

The jogger spoke in Korean to one of his lieutenants. The fellow seemed to say yes.

"Check with the miners. If they want to sleep outside, it's okay with me. But don't try to buy 'em. We're paying five bucks a day. I don't want 'em getting a windfall and heading home."

"No problem. Like they no sleep room of eight."

"Eight to a room?" Griffith did some quick calculations. "That'll free up—what—fifty rooms—we're a hundred and ten, not counting the Amazon Indians—"

"Our casting director found them in packing crates outside São Paolo. I think they can handle a week under the stars." Jason smiled winningly at the boss. "We can live with that." He stuck out his hand to seal the deal. Nobody shook it.

"Don't worry about feeding us. We're catering for ourselves. You're welcome to join us, by the way. Have dinner with Klaus Frotner. That'll be something to tell your kids about."

"But that means we have two or three to a room," Griffith persisted, "contracts call for singles."

"We're in the middle of the jungle. I'll explain it to them. We're only here for a week."

An assistant rattled on in Korean. The boss translated. "In four days we get another four hundred men. You've got to be out by then."

Jason beamed back. "They'll just have to sleep outside too. We're staying until you burn down the forest."

"Oh, the forest will be gone by then."

Jason's teeth vanished from sight. "Excuse me?"

"We torch tomorrow, it should all be burned out in three days."

Jason started to stammer. "Tomorrow?" He looked helplessly at McGinty. "What does that do to us?"

"The crane's stuck in Port Moresby. The Panavision package with our A and B cameras arrives tomorrow night from L.A.

We're waiting for four cameras with operators coming in from Melbourne day after tomorrow, and the helicopter mount from Los Angeles won't be here till then."

"That's what we don't have. What have we got?"

"Fuck-all."

"You couldn't be ready by tomorrow anyway," said Griffith. "We've got to block action and rig effects and rehearse camera. We need four days at least. Absolute minimum."

Jason turned back to the jogger. "We have come halfway around the world to film your forest burning. We have spent six weeks building a replica Amazon village and imported a complete Xavanti tribe from the Amazon basin. We were told the burn would take place next week."

"You were misinformed."

"But you don't understand. This is the climax of our motion picture. This is the nexus of the story."

"So you'll change it. It's only a movie."

"It's a major motion picture."

Jason slung this like a mantra. The jogger returned to his maps. Jason growled. Nahum tugged at his sleeve. Jason shook him off.

"We're talking five days. Four." No response. "What do you want? Want a Range Rover? McGinty, get the man a Range Rover."

The jogger looked up, annoyed. "What is this crap? I'm not some muckety-muck in a grass hut in Port Moresby."

"This is a major motion picture—"

The jogger waved at his colleagues. "When we're on line we'll be generating a third of Papua's hard currency. Any one of these guys—any one of them—handles an operation with bigger capital investment than your whole movie company. A Range Rover." He seemed to find it funny.

"We absolutely must have five days to prepare for the shot."

The jogger shrugged. "Pray for rain." He turned back to his maps.

Jason glared but said nothing, his jaw locked in impotent rage. Nahum, trying to set an example, backed toward the door, palms together. "*Narak-a-la-ok.*"

Homer copied Nahum's lead. He didn't get Jason's rage. The mining chief made a lot of sense to him. Their movie was important, but so was the mine. "*Narak-a-la-ok,*" he said pleasantly.

The mining chief spoke without looking up from his map. "Don't say it if you don't mean it."

"Mean what?"

" 'I eat your shit.' " The Korean guys all laughed. Nahum giggled along apologetically. "Better 'I eat your feces,' " he explained.

Jason watched his hundred-odd crew members chatting cheerfully over plates piled high with ribs and angel hair pasta and Caesar salad and fresh fruit, and he thought ironically of the cattle corral and pig sty and dairy barn and chicken coop they'd erected in a remote corner of the compound. McGinty had bitched about cost, but Jason decreed that a film crew traveled on its stomach. Looking at miners squatting nearby, scooping up mashed yams and rice garnished, as a special treat, this being Friday, with a tough old goat a Jeep had backed over, he considered how right he'd been, and how little good it would do him. For the miners' mashed yams were as ambrosia compared to the shit he was eating.

Jason hadn't told anyone about their problem. He had to suss out a take on it first. It was worse than a catastrophe. It was a debacle. Anything else he could fix. He could rewrite, recast, reshoot. But find a rain forest to burn down? He tried to tell himself they could cover up with computer wizardry and miniature work, but his gut wouldn't buy it.

The knot in his stomach said this was a mythic screw-up. He thought of Bill Buckner, the Red Sox who let the ball through his legs for the winning run in the '86 World Series. A lifetime three-hundred hitter, but always just the guy who blew the Series. Whatever Jason did the rest of his career, he'd be the producer who spent three million bucks to watch a rain forest burn and forgot to bring a camera. If he had a career after this.

Maybe they could shoot the thing somehow. McGinty had experience in these matters. If there was any way out, McGinty would be chasing it down. He had as much at stake as Jason, he screwed up the deal in the first place. But McGinty was sitting across the table, halfway through a plate of spaghetti and a bottle of scotch.

Jason apprehensively checked out his star. Klaus eschewed the

ribs, as indeed all animal flesh, but grazed placidly beside Inga
on a big Caesar salad. They might have been at Spago's.

They shared their table with Johnny Palermo. Swarthy, pock-
marked, beefier even than Klaus, lineman to his fullback,
Palermo attacked a plate piled with ribs and nothing more. He
liked to tell people he was pure carnivore. Johnny had in fact
been the most feared defensive tackle in the NFL, as well as a
former "close friend" of Inga's. The three of them seemed
chummy enough now. Inga wouldn't stir up trouble. Johnny
had given her visibility when she needed it, but he wasn't above
the title. She'd never make such a dumb career move.

The forest was burning and Jason didn't have a camera. What
would Klaus say when he found out? He might not say anything. He might just haul back and break Jason's nose. Jason
rubbed the bridge of his nose, and wondered if a break would
make him more ruggedly appealing. Belmondo.

To hell with his nose. Whatever Klaus did to his nose, Jason
knew with sick certainty that when he was finished doing it,
he'd be on the next chopper to Port Moresby, along with Jason's
producer's fee and his hopes for the movie. It was still ski season
in the Bugaboos.

Jason turned to McGinty, sucking in spaghetti. "Daiwoo's
trying to buy up Studio. I read it in the *Journal*." Jason always
referred to the *Wall Street Journal* as the *Journal*. "This is an
elaborate plot to drive down share price."

"Bullshit," said McGinty, and he chewed ferociously, spaghetti strands squirming like earthworms on the hook. "The
fuckers just don't give a fuck. Right, Nahum?"

Nahum was devouring beef ribs with special gusto. "First animal ever see bigger pig when me two wives."

"No more film, no more barbecue," said McGinty, annoyed.
"You want more barbecue, you better figure out how we can
stall the slopes for a week."

"Stall slopes?"

"Stop the gooks. No fire. No burn."

"No possible. Except maybe rain."

"Remember Port Moresby?" said McGinty, scotch fueling his
hostility. "Remember Sebastian Kawaluk? Remember the sack
of hundred-dollar bills? He didn't tell me it was up to the rain
gods. He said it was up to him. He gave me a stack of permits.
With big blue seals. Remember?"

"Our country, no say no bribe. Rude."

"Our country, you take bribe and you no deliver, you end up facedown in your own blood."

Nahum smiled indulgently. "We ten-thousand-year garden. You young. Custom primitive barbaric."

Homer didn't join Jason. He'd spotted Stanton Frye, slim, gray, and aristocratic, eating with his camera assistants at a nearby table. Homer was impressed with the air of intimate respect that enveloped Frye, high priest surrounded by vestal virgins. Homer plunked down, and an assistant sized him up through watery, dissipated eyes. Well, maybe not vestal virgins, maybe temple prostitutes.

Frye, pouring himself a glass of wine, offered some to Homer. It made Homer's mouth burn. He looked at the bottle. It was French and old.

"This stuff looks good. Is it?"

Frye smiled. "Yes."

Homer was impressed. "Wine with dinner."

"He gets to pick the vintage. It's in his contract," the assistant explained. "Ever since he worked for Bertolucci in the Kalahari. It's in Bertolucci's contract, so Stanton figured 'why not?' "

"Wouldn't do me any good," said Homer. "It all tastes the same. I think it's 'cause I have a deviated septum."

They ate in silence for a while.

"You were cameraman on *Woodstock,* weren't you?"

"One of seven."

"My dad was at Woodstock. But he never got close enough to hear the music. Mom was nine months pregnant with me, and she'd walked in a couple miles, and she started getting labor pains, and they had to go home. I wasn't born for another week. If I'd been born at Woodstock, Mom would have named me Jimmy. Jimmy Hendrix Dooley. I rented the video and I looked for her. I think she was in the nude bathing sequence, but she says no, it was some other pregnant person. With all the mud it's hard to tell."

"I don't remember much about it myself. When I'm shooting, it goes in one eye and out the other."

"You did the Porta Potti sequence, didn't you? That was the funniest thing in the movie."

"How did you know I did that?"

"The moves. It was like the sewer sequence in that Fellini film
you shot on Rome at night."

"Yes," said Frye, pleased. "That's where Federico got the
idea."

Klaus and Inga and Johnny strolled over to Jason's table.

Jason stood up. He wanted more room to maneuver. "So how
do you like the food? Not bad, eh, for a thousand miles from
nowhere."

"Not bad," said Klaus. "What's on the agenda for tomorrow?
How come no call sheets?"

"Well, Klaus, there seems to be a little problem."

"No Xerox machine?"

"Um, they're burning the forest tomorrow."

"What?"

"The burn. It was supposed to be next week, but they pushed
it up."

Inga and Johnny laughed. Klaus's jaw set and he got tight
around the eyes. "So we're shooting the thing tomorrow?"

"We're working on it."

"What the fuck does that mean?"

"It means we don't have any fucking equipment," said Mc-
Ginty. "No cameras, no helicopter mount, no nothing."

"This is fucking unbelievable."

Jason took half a step back to avoid possible injury. "We had
it planned down to the last detail, Klaus, believe me—"

"I told 'em they should get stuff here a week early," said
McGinty with bitter glee, "but—hey—I'm just some old fart—"

"—Griffith used the latest last-in, first-out inventory analy-
sis—"

"So what the fuck are you gonna do?"

"We're studying the situation."

"This is breach. This is not 'highest quality first-rate major
motion picture' as stated in my contract. This is back-lot Jungle
Jim bullshit. I'm getting Bo on the blower."

"We're outside the Comsat shadow. Why don't you just wait
and listen to what we come up with."

Waiting was far from Klaus's mind. He tensed and crouched
slightly. Jason thought he recognized a karate stance. He raised
his arms nervously.

"Hi, guys."

Klaus turned to see Homer and Stanton Frye approaching. Jason leapt at the diversion.

"Well, Klaus, here's our creative team right now. Why don't we all have a meeting?"

"That's a good idea," said Homer. "We're going to need help."

Jason looked at him stupidly. "You are?"

"Stanton's figured out how to shoot this thing, but—"

"Great! Terrific!"

McGinty chortled.

"With no fucking camera and no fucking helicopter," said Klaus. "Great."

"We've got a camera," said Homer.

"I've got the Arri I shoot tests with."

"And we have a helicopter. We just don't have one fixed up to take a camera."

McGinty imitated a spastic holding a camera. "Great climax. Excedrin headache number one."

"Stanton thinks we can do it."

"I didn't say that. I said it wasn't out of the question."

"You can do it. I know you can." The shrunken head was still in Jason's gut, but it had stopped gnawing on his small intestine.

"Amateur night in Dixie." McGinty poured himself another drink.

Stanton stared him down. "I think I know what I'm doing."

Klaus surveyed the bunch of them. Homer was a rookie. Production was a bunch of paper-pushers. Frye was the man who'd put it on film. He focused on Frye. "We're talking 'highest quality first-rate major motion picture' here?"

"Well," said Frye, "that depends on a lot of things. But I'd like to give it a shot."

Dark morning. Dawn long gone, heavy clouds hung low over treetops, turning them more black than green. The cloud cover could have been slow-moving swamp reflecting the jungle roof: matted, dank, and fetid, drained of color, sky lurched across the hills.

The simulated Indian village was a cluster of woven grass lozenges. It sat in a clearing atop a rise, artfully sited so land dropped away, then rose into an impressive backdrop of jungle vista. No tribe would last a season in the wilds of the Amazon living this exposed, but as Chris Parrott remarked, there was no point in torching four hundred thousand acres of jungle if you couldn't see it burn.

Three helicopters perched like dragonflies near the grass huts, their shimmering rotors swirling dust devils across the beaten earth: a sleek bloodred Jet Ranger, the "practical" chopper that played in the scene; a fat, low-slung Hughes 500, selected by Frye to carry the camera because of its big, low doors, now stuffed with foam mattresses scavenged from camp for Frye to kneel on; and an old Sikorsky, the getaway car for the rest of the crew. If they timed the shot right, the clearing would be engulfed in flames minutes after they took off. It was the kind of chance they'd never take with time to plan properly, to bring in stunt people for cover shots, to change angles to make it look more dangerous than it really was. They had only one camera and one chance to pull it off.

Homer sat in the Sikorsky. He was tired, but having a great time. It was just like Bo said. He was the astronaut, along for the ride. Frye and his guys were mission control. He'd asked some questions, sort of got Frye started, and the rest took care of itself.

Homer waved at Frye standing in the clearing, resting his shoulder pod on an apple box. The rig had been built the night before, in the machine shop at the mine. It was an L-shaped bracket of tubular steel, a triangle from camera to shoulder to waist, braced where it touched his body with pieces curved to his form and padded with strips of quilted sound blankets. Homer thought he looked like a bionic man, half flesh, half steel.

Frye didn't return Homer's wave. He was looking the other way, watching the horizon behind the huts. In the distance, the burn had begun. Thin smoke streamers were spreading into milky veils, veils were thickening into curtains.

Not yet. More smoke. He had only one shot at this.

He'd been all night lighting and rehearsing the move. He craved a cup of coffee, but he feared it might make his hand shake. He didn't do it much anymore, but when he'd made his name shooting vérité documentaries in the late sixties, he'd been one of the best, many thought the best by far, at the complex dance of handheld cinematography. He'd combined an Impressionist's eye for light and composition, the smooth, steady hands of a surgeon, and a director's instinct for performance that showed itself in an uncanny ability to anticipate his subject. As one critic noted, he placed the camera where God would have, had He been at the eyepiece.

No, the camera didn't scare him. But helicopters were another story. Like anyone who'd filmed for long, he had good friends who'd died trying for that knockout chopper shot. When his last couple of wives had made him swear he'd never helicopter-shoot again, he decided to make it ironclad policy. Why was he pulling this crazy stunt?

With all Frye's experience, he'd never encountered a director like Homer. Frye had dismissed him as a simpleton at first, another bad studio joke. He'd nursed enough first-timers through the process to know the type. Full of vision but blind as a bat. Terrified of everything—of the studio geeks, of stars, of the mechanics of moviemaking, of making decisions, of not making decisions—in short, in love with the idea of being a director but panicked at the prospect of actually doing the work. Homer wasn't like that.

Homer wasn't stupid, and he wasn't afraid. He was a cheerful, attentive audience, charmed and fascinated by the details of the shoot. He was just astoundingly ignorant. Too ignorant to bully the crew to establish his authority, too ignorant to be furious with Jason for screwing him royally, too ignorant to panic at the tremendous risk he was taking by pushing ahead with the shot.

If they packed up and went home without trying the shot, it would be Jason's fault, a blunder of legendary proportion. If they tried the shot and it didn't work, it was Homer's problem. Actors could screw up, batteries could die, the camera could jam, the move could be jerky or out of focus, the chopper could take off with a lurch, or be blown the wrong direction. Frye could think of a hundred disasters—disasters that had happened to him. Of course, the usual way a director bailed himself out of a major screw-up was to fire the cameraman. But Homer didn't even know enough to do that.

Woozy but adrenaline-alert, Frye savored the anticipation of performance. For twenty-five years, the productions had gotten bigger and the risks smaller. The more money at stake, the harder it was to take a chance. "Film is cheap," the saying went, "might as well shoot miles of it." For his last big one-take scene, a building demolition in a Bruce Willis movie, Frye had used twelve cameras. Placing them, he'd felt like a middle-level manager ensuring Sony an explosion effect for its software stream. Some of the surplus footage even ended up in a Super-Nintendo game. They weren't getting a video game out of this one. This was like the old days. Him and a camera and one shot out of the box.

Frye had picked a wide-angle lens, a twenty-four millimeter, to minimize focus problems and shake. He was overcranking a tad, twenty-eight frames a second instead of twenty-four, to smooth out his moves and, he hoped, give a subliminal grace to the fight sequence. Fight scenes were usually shot from many angles, pasted together as a mosaic of cuts, a jolting new angle for each bit of action. This time he had one camera, one chance; his fight scene was going to be continuous, and the excitement would have to come from how his moves were choreographed with the performers'. Twenty-eight frames should help pace the dance.

He was pleased with the way Klaus and Johnny had laid out the scene. Whatever Klaus's ego problems, he knew how to fight, and with only one camera to fool with, Klaus couldn't overstage the piece like some damn Hong Kong chop-socky flick.

Acrid smoke drifted into Frye's eyes. The shifting white curtains in the forest were boiling white walls now, crawling toward them on a carpet of flames. Time.

He straightened. The camera assistant grabbed the apple box and ran for Homer's old Sikorsky. Frye shook the shoulder pod into place and signaled to the effects man already on the chopper. The effects man pressed a big red button on a shortwave detonator and the background huts burst into flame. Frye waved at Klaus, poised outside the main hut in loincloth and mud-painted tiger stripes: time.

Klaus saw the ready sign. He waved to Inga and the Indians and Palermo in the shadows of the hut. They signaled back. Sweat on his shaved pecs kept the mud paint damp and pliable, but it caked on his nipples, tickling him. He fought the urge to scratch. He took a *chi* breath to center himself, and saw Inga cat-stretch under her nun's habit. She was nervous. That gave him a kick.

She hadn't been nervous last night, when they shared a room. Contracts called for separate suites, but under the circumstances he couldn't refuse to double up with her. He wasn't about to admit he hadn't slept in the same room with the bitch for a month.

He was turned to the wall to get a few hours shut-eye when she crawled in his bed. Next thing he knows he's flat on his back, she's doing the squat and jerk on his Rodney. He hates the bitch, but Rodney's being real persuasive, and he's just figuring maybe she's worth the hassle, when she sticks her tongue in his ear like a fat wet pencil, starts hissing a blow-by-blow of life in the sack with Johnny Palermo—and in the pool and on horseback and in free-fall from fifteen thousand feet and hung by her heels from an iron hook. He's bucking like a Brahman bull, pissed off and turned on something fierce, when she climbs off, gives Rodney a playful swat, and tells him Johnny Palermo was so big and so mean, he was the only guy ever made her come. And she goes outside to sleep in a hammock with the Indians and the fuckin' miners.

Johnny Palermo was dressed in Ninja black. He returned Klaus's signal with the high sign, like he was his parachute pal about to be first man out the door. Klaus flashed a high sign back. Since dawn they'd worked together as good buddies, laying out the fight. Klaus knew well the words of Sun Tzu: "Be as a fox in your lair until the time of battle." Now Klaus repeated to himself the rest of the quote: "When battle comes, be as the tiger at the water hole—rend the jackal limb from limb and devour his intestines."

Stanton appeared behind Klaus and shoved the camera lens into the small of his back. He flicked a switch and the camera rattled. "Action!"

Sitting in the Sikorsky, Homer crossed his fingers.

TWENTY-SIX

Jason aimed the nozzle so it spat air straight in his face. Jet at last. Now that he could relax, he felt a spasm of produceorial guilt at abandoning his film crew in the jungle. Was he Lord Jim leaving the sinking pilgrim ship? The pang passed. He couldn't have stayed. It was physically impossible. With a weary sigh he stretched his legs, stubbing toes on film cases crammed under the seat. The twinge was reassuring. Those cans held his future.

Before he left camp he'd insisted Frye explain the care and feeding of his climax, and Frye had given him a lecture on the latent image which made it sound as delicate as frost lace on a windowpane. The film cases became traveling companions as squat, demanding, and delicate as three-year-olds, and like three-year-olds never to be left unguarded. Whatever calamity the most possessive mother could imagine for her infant—drowning, overheating, kidnapping for ransom, premature aging, bombardment by invisible rays—Jason fantasized for his film. To which he added visions of thieving goons in search of gold and jewels yanking open his cans under the noon sun. When the cases didn't fit under his feet on the Twin Otter from Port Moresby to Melbourne, and they tried to make him stow them in the hold, he bought them a seat.

Before the Melbourne flight, he'd missed connections and laid over two days in Port Moresby. He'd read in the *Wall Street Journal* how Port Moresby was notorious throughout Asia as a gangster city. The government ruled the countryside, said the *Journal,* but thugs ruled the capital's streets. The Mercedes dealership thrived selling armed teenagers cars for cash. Jason considered hiring guards, but feared the attention they would bring. And what was to prevent guards from heisting the film? So Jason spent two days and two nights in the Congress Hotel without leaving his room. He ate room service. When he went to the toilet he left the door open and kept his film cases in view.

He couldn't sleep. He lay in bed, staring at the stippled aluminum boxes winking in the moonlight. When he drifted off, a nightmare would wrench him awake. In one, McGinty, dressed as the bandito in *Treasure of the Sierra Madre,* ripped open his film cans, laughing hysterically. They were full of sand.

That was, of course, his abiding fear. Nobody knew what was in those cans but Stanton Frye, and Frye wasn't talking. He knew better. No matter how hard Jason pressed him, Frye would only say the film was worth developing. That could mean anything.

The film could have been processed in Melbourne, but Annette had insisted on Studio's lab. She tried to make a joke of this, ascribing her insistence on shipping undeveloped negative fifteen thousand miles to a simple case of corporate greed and insanity. Jason knew better. She wanted to see dailies first. No doubt she'd be less than overjoyed when he showed up along with the film, but he was fighting for his life here, not to mention his movie.

The second sleep-deprived night in Port Moresby, as Jason sweated to the asthmatic pounding of the air-conditioner and stared at his precious cargo, he dreamed of Pandora. She was operating an Arriflex. It jammed. Before he could stop her, she opened the camera. Horrified, he stared inside. Something black and crusty leapt at his throat. Terror splashed his heart and he was thrown awake, gasping. He gaped at the mute silver boxes, fighting a teeth-grinding urge to rip them open and get it over with.

Elmo Zwalt eyed the giant spider. With its skinny black body and chalk-white legs, it was a hairier version of Elmo in his black T-shirt and shorts. The spider scurried into a red orchid the size of a microwave oven, where it lived in the second tier of the jungle.

Elmo was twelve feet off the ground on a ladder pitched against a remarkably realistic Styrofoam baobab tree. He yelled down to Marshall.

"Klaus swings down on the vine and—whap!—the spider lands on his face. Then he sticks one hand in the orchid and—bam—another one grabs his hand."

"That sounds anticlimactic."

"Right, right. Better Klaus swings onto the tree, grabs the

orchid, and pulls out his hand with a giant spider attached. He's disgusted by the thing"—Elmo mimed total revulsion—"and a bigger one lands on his nose."

Elmo slid down the ladder and loped to a cluster of grass huts. He slipped inside the largest, where a card table held his ink and brushes and his notebook computer, and he sketched out the spider moment in three clean panels, then typed up the beats for the script.

Elmo hummed as he worked. Drawing and writing in the forest of his fantasies, he was a completely happy man. He loved everything. He loved the rain forest. He loved Studio. He loved Annette. He loved Marshall. Particularly Marshall. Marshall built Elmo's rain forest. Marshall really knew what it would look like on film.

Elmo had been suspicious at first. After he read in *Variety* that Homer was directing, he told them all to go to hell. He shut himself up in his little jungle room and tried to push through on his new project. He'd locked up. He was back where he'd been before Jack got his hopes up, but worse.

Before Jack wormed back into his life, he'd just been stuck. That was bad enough, but he'd been stuck before and broken through. It always came to him in the end. After Homer snatched his movie, he wasn't so sure. The power that once swept him into new worlds had turned against him. The harder he tried to think, the thicker the fog became, until his brain felt like pot roast in a pressure cooker.

He tried to blow the fog away with laser discs, but they couldn't cut through. For the first time in his life, sound and images were just annoying distractions. Desperate, he'd haunted a Stanley Kubrick festival at the Beverly Multiplex, sliding from film to film. If anyone could flush his head, Kubrick could.

Jack and Jason found him hunkered down in the first row of *The Shining,* spine flat against his seat cushion, skull cricked at an acute angle up the seat back. Jack did a double take, afraid Elmo'd broken his neck. Elmo didn't care. He let them think he was dead while he watched Jack Nicholson sink a fire ax into Scatman Crothers.

But they didn't go away. They started in on him loud enough that they were all dumped outside, Jason telling him sure, he felt cheated and betrayed, but it wasn't like that, it was business, movie politics. Elmo hadn't been forgotten or abandoned. Oh, no. Elmo understood the material like nobody else in the world. Annette had to do what she did or they wouldn't have a movie.

Jack jumped in. This was all about the Klaus problem. She couldn't push Elmo on Klaus just like that. He'd broken Elmo's nose. This Homer guy had nothing to bring to the party. He was flavor of the month. Annette sent him to the jungle to get the movie going. She'd see the first dailies and she'd can him, bring in Elmo to save the day, and what could Klaus say about that?

Elmo pointed out Homer was shooting the biggest scene in the movie. That was weeks away, Jason said. Believe me. First dailies will be shoe leather. Establishing stuff setting up the set. Indian kids picking their noses, hunters chasing birds with sticks, stuff like that. Annette'll have plenty of time to replace Homer before the big scene. But Elmo had to come on board now. He had to fix the script—*his* script—so they could shoot it on the jungle set, or they wouldn't have a movie. That was the crisis of the moment. Solve that, he'd be indispensable. When the inevitable happened to Homer, there'd be only one person Annette could turn to.

He'd squeezed his eyes tight, tried to shut them out. That Jack was real persistent. Jack said he'd never lied to Elmo, never misled him, he'd always fought for Elmo and believed in him. Elmo had to admit that was kind of true in a twisted way. Now Jack was telling him this was his last shot at *The Agonizer*. His best shot ever. He was saying if Elmo passed it up, he deserved the shafting he was getting.

Jason started in on how great the jungle set looked. He threw facts and figures at Elmo, how they weren't just building a set, they were designing a biome, using state-of-the-art self-regulating ecotechnology straight from Biosphere II.

If Elmo hadn't been so stuck, he'd have walked back into *The Shining*. But after all that time spent in his jungle garret, he was curious to see what Studio had wrought. He let himself be persuaded to visit the set.

Until he entered that set, Elmo had felt like the Tin Woodsman in search of a brain. None of the murk in his skull would firm into fantasy. Passing through the airlock double doors, smelling the damp earth, hearing the chatter of spider monkeys, he was stepping into his own story. Crowned woodnymphs flitting from tree to tree tore violet holes in the veils shrouding his mind.

Jack and Jason shut up and left him alone. Elmo prowled the

place, he didn't know how long. By the time Marshall joined him to lay out the script problems, the shrouds had been shredded into inconsequential wisps. Walking with Marshall, listening to him describe how he'd built bits of jungle to fit action Elmo'd written, the *Agonizer* vision flooded back.

With the vision came relief, the supreme relief of one who'd hurt for so long, he'd forgotten life without pain. With relief came peace, with peace came elation, with elation came tremendous gratitude toward Marshall and the world at large for returning him his soul. Out of pure excitement with the place, he set up shop in the Xavanti village. He lived in his jungle from when solar lights brought dawn until guards threw him out at night.

It was difficult, technical work. Elmo had composed a panoramic treetop chase. Even the biggest set wouldn't have enough sky for that. Instead, they orchestrated an intricate polyphony of action through the second tier, counterpointed with comic relief. To make their caper feel like a chase across miles of open jungle, they carefully plotted how to place the camera and redress the set to make one site do the work of four or five. It was sleight of hand, but Marshall was a master magician and Elmo was his old self devising action. They took great pleasure in each other's abilities.

Elmo was hanging from a vine, showing Marshall how the Agonizer could swing into the orchid spider, when Jason appeared below, absorbed with keeping his shoes clean. Elmo dropped down and Jason jumped back with a start. "Jesus!"

Elmo saw Jason close up. "You get some tropical disease?"

"Let's just say I learned why Parrott was so hot to shoot on stage."

Elmo looked at him with concern. Jason had always eaten well, stayed fit, kept a constructive attitude, and he'd had the face to show for it, smooth and fully inflated. Sleek. The sheen was gone now. Lack of sleep and surfeit of care had blotched his skin, hunched his shoulders, and bagged his eyes. He surveyed the jungle anxiously and spoke to Marshall, almost pleading. "Tell me this is going to work."

"We'll be ready for you." Marshall, usually slow to show emotion, sounded positively upbeat.

"You don't know how happy I am to hear that."

"Jungle trouble?"

"Ask me in fifteen minutes." He checked his watch. "Gotta go."

"What happens in fifteen minutes?" said Elmo.

"Dailies."

"Can we go?"

Jason hesitated. He looked at the two of them, eager and expectant. Maybe their enthusiasm would help the cause. "Sure. Why not?"

Marshall smiled reassuringly. "Don't worry. Whatever Homer's stuff looks like, you'll be all right." He nodded at Elmo. "If Homer can't cut it, you're covered."

"That's good to hear," said Jason. "Very good to hear."

Elmo looked at Jason and tried to imagine what Homer had put him through. Whatever it was, Jason didn't want to go through it again. He tagged along to dailies, wondering if they would be bad enough for him to take over right away.

The screening room was in the basement of Studio's remaining office complex. Clark Gable's dailies had been shown there, and Humphrey Bogart's. It was a small, remarkably businesslike place, a beige boiler room hung with sound-absorbent curtains. There were larger and more sumptuous theaters available, but tradition decreed this was where the chief watched dailies, and as this tradition was cheap to maintain and could not be sold on the open market, it was honored.

Darius had made one improvement in the room. He'd removed the back two rows of seats and replaced them with six rosewood and leather Eames lounge chairs, one of which Jason fell into, hoping he'd be at Annette's right hand. Marshall, conscious of screening room etiquette, chose a folding seat near the back and to the side, out of executive sight-lines. Elmo, oblivious, slumped in the front row.

"We should see this on a bigger screen."

"Help me out, guys." Jason thought about telling Elmo to move. But what the hell. His head never rose over the seat back anyway. There was a long stretch of pregnant silence as they waited for Annette to arrive and give birth to the dailies.

She showed up on time, and to Jason's surprise, alone. That was class. He stuck out his hand, she kissed him on the cheek, and nestled in the next Eames chair. She'd been very gracious when she learned he brought the film back personally, hadn't pressed him on why. "So. Anything I should know before we start the show?"

He'd planned to give the film the right spin, but now, back in the real world, he realized he'd better put some distance between himself and the material. He might need room to maneuver. "There's no sound track. It's MOS."

"Oh?"

"It's all easy to dub." Truth was, Frye's old Arri couldn't shoot sync sound. "The footage will have to speak for itself." Jason flicked the intercom switch. "Roll when ready." The room darkened, and leader flashed on the screen. Ten, nine, eight . . . God, thought Jason, please make this screening room Apollo Mission Control. Not ground zero at Alamagordo.

Elmo felt a tiny thrill as the first images hit the screen. Rain forest. The real thing. Miles of it. Overcast, though. Too dark, too somber. He'd imagined emerald green. Vibrant.

Bloodred chopper descends from the sky. Johnny Palermo emerges, heavily armed, leading a brace of fearsome Mabili warriors painted black and blue, hurrying on cat feet toward the Xavanti village. Just as he wrote it.

Shoe leather, guys going point A to point B. But it lifted Elmo to a new plane. No more words or drawings. The real thing. It didn't matter who directed it. As long as he could remember, he'd seen these images. Now the first one was out there in the world. This was more than giving birth. A baby was a burden waiting to become its own master.

Another shot. Xavanti Indians, back from the hunt, approach the huts. Same dark sky. For the same scene, no doubt, lead-in to the climax. Elmo thought he made out faint wisps of smoke in the distant jungle. That would be the burn beginning. Nice touch.

Annette was getting antsy. "Is it all this overcast?"

Jason didn't answer. The film rolled on.

First shot of Klaus. Back from the hunt, naked and striped, jogging fast toward the hut. Now smoke pours from the jungle. "How did you do that?"

"Do what?"

"Make that smoke effect way in the background."

"They're burning the jungle."

Elmo sighed, annoyed. Of course it was supposed to be jungle burning. How'd they get the effect?

Next shot. Not panoramic like the others. Tight on Klaus's back. Klaus pulls away. Camera follows him into the hut. Inside, Elmo instantly knew he was at the climax of his movie.

Xavanti lie dead on the floor. Mabili have thrown Inga across a hammock and tear at her nun's habit. Johnny, back to Klaus, stands between her legs. Camera catches up with Johnny as black wool gives way, pouring out Inga's golden body in the *tapa* loincloth and white mud stripes of a Xavanti maiden on her wedding day.

Klaus attacks both Indians at once, comic-book brutal, almost too efficient for fun. Inexperienced at mock battle, the Indians telegraph his quick, twirling blows, falling a shade too soon. Without the sound of impact, the blows feel phony. But Klaus's moves are hard and fluid and not overplayed. A stiff when he acted, fighting he's cruelly smooth.

In the background, with a simultaneity all too rare in these battles, Inga hacks at Johnny and breaks free, only to be felled by a neck chop. Her unconscious body slumps onto the hammock, swings in slow arcs, revealing various comely parts of her anatomy.

Elmo admired how the action was slightly slowed, tinging it with surreal grace. He figured twenty-eight frames a second. He tried to pick out which piece of the shot they'd use, tried to figure cover angles. That was hard. Action surged up to camera, filling the frame in close-up, then ebbed back to wide shot. The camera prowled like another character through the battle, catching critical moments from the perfect point of view. There was really no reason to change angles at all, Elmo thought. It looked like it was photographed by God.

Johnny clips Klaus from behind. Pretty good stage blow. Klaus stumbles well and turns into close-up. Klaus stares at Johnny, not with blank game-face or banzai attack grimace, but with real hatred, and real pleasure at the prospect of hurting him. The sudden injection of genuine emotion startled Elmo.

Klaus kidney-chops Johnny. Even without the sound man's spongy crunch of crushing organs, Johnny's reaction looks absolutely convincing. He falls, then rises, eyes dim with suffering. Disgust clears his gaze, fury restores its fire. Johnny lunges for Klaus with lethal intent, as he had lunged for so many quarterbacks in his time, looking to put him out of the game for good.

Elmo fully expected Klaus's spine to snap when Johnny hit him. Klaus sidesteps gracefully and catches a pressure point behind Johnny's knee.

Johnny's mouth opens in a roar of animal rage and suffering, all the louder for its silence on film. He swings for Klaus's head, more shrewdly this time. Klaus slips the blow, but it lands on his shoulder with enough force to stagger him. Elmo thought he saw a bruise form. Johnny closes for the kill, Klaus spins and kicks, catching him in the small of the back.

Elmo was spellbound. This wasn't the usual pop ballet, or revenge as Kabuki. This is bloody war. These men fear and hate each other and mean to do each other serious harm. Palpable loathing springs from the shadows of the dim hut, wraps them in its dark cloak, and pulls them toward destruction.

Johnny has brute strength, but Klaus is a master of the martial arts. As the fight progresses, Klaus controls the tempo. He's hurting Johnny, but not enough to drop him. He wants Johnny to keep coming back for more. Limping now, favoring his left arm, Johnny makes a final desperate grab for Klaus. Klaus fells him with a blow to the back of the skull. He topples into Inga's hammock as Klaus pulls her free, slings her behind his neck, head on one side, butt the other, shepherd with a lamb. She stirs. Her mud stripes smear on his sweat.

The camera backs with Klaus into a smoke-white day, tracking him as he runs for the chopper. Gusting wind parts the smoke: Huts are blazing torches, the jungle a seething bed of fire. Elmo heard gasps from the seats behind him.

The camera pans off Klaus, onto the chopper beating away smoke with its rotor; in the background, the battle hut where Johnny and the Indians lie explodes into flame. Elmo gasped along with the others before he realized the actors cleared out while the camera followed Klaus.

Klaus reappears, cleverly obscured by the helicopter door, tosses Inga into the chopper. Must be a stunt-pilot double. The chopper sits for heart-stopping moments, shimmering in the heat from the blazing village. Roiling smoke blankets the frame. Then rotors whip away the pall, and the bloodred Ranger rises.

Again flames and smoke fill the screen. Elmo feared the cameraman was burning. Then smoke slides by and the camera moves again, rising through the inferno. Airborne.

Camera rises above the worst of the pall. The red Ranger materializes a little below, floating over the village. The huts drown in a sea of fire.

Smoke seeds the cloud cover. The sky lets loose, pouring rain onto the fiery ocean. Columns of superheated steam shoot up through the smoke. Boiling thermals tear holes in the cloud cover; chrome yellow shafts of sunlight push through, impaling the vapor columns. The ruby Ranger is pinned by a sunbeam to the jungle, a dragonfly on a mounting board of fire.

The Ranger breaks free of its sunbeam just as rainbows form—one, two, three, four. Elmo could swear he saw them mirrored in the shimmering rotors as the chopper flits beneath.

Flicker. Light flare. Scratches, emulsion punches. Runout. Next roll: close shots of burning forest. No one watched. They sat immobile, collecting their thoughts.

"Jesus wept." Marshall spoke first. Etiquette ordained he wait for the execs, but this time etiquette didn't make a damn bit of difference.

"Those rainbows . . . We've got our one-sheet." Annette seemed dazed. "Play Klaus big in that loincloth, over that forest and those rainbows—"

"Rainbows, hell. It's better than the opening shot of *Touch of Evil*." Jason spoke fast, his words slurred with relief and excitement. "That's the greatest fucking single shot ever made in movies."

"What about coverage? Don't we have other angles?"

"Coverage?" Jason was incredulous. "Annette, trust your eyes. Where are you gonna cut into that? That is ten times more powerful than anything you'd stick together from a bunch of shots. It's *real* this way. I tell you, it's Homer's documentary background. He's broken through to a whole new level. The guy's fuckin' incredible. Have you ever seen Klaus give that kind of performance? I mean, the guy can act! And Homer got it out of him! I don't have to tell you, Homer was working under the most difficult conditions it's possible to imagine. Worse—"

Annette cut him off. "What's your feeling, George?"

Marshall was silent for a long beat. "That is an extraordinary piece of film."

"Extraordinary, bullshit. The guy's a genius. A fuckin' genius. He's reinventing the genre—"

"Will you let the man talk!"

"We've built the hut, Annette. We could reshoot the fight on stage, add cuts. But I don't see what you'd gain. You'd only diminish the scene."

"It's a fuckin' mind-blower. A mind-fuckin'-blower. We're gonna have a movie like you've never seen!" Jason was up, bouncing on his toes, beyond ebullient. "Let's get out of here. The rest is just cover shots of burning jungle. No principals. I'm buying the champagne. We're getting drunk, and I'm getting the next plane back so we can finish the greatest fuckin' action movie ever made."

Annette seemed amused by his enthusiasm. But she was excited too. "Maybe I should take this film to New York."

"That is a great idea. It'll sit them up. You'll be hailed as the next Thalberg. They'll name a building after you—" The padded door swung shut as Annette and Marshall followed him out of the room.

Onscreen, giant plows push charred logs into a smoldering pit.

In the front row, Elmo still slumped in his seat, staring at the stinking rubble. One shot. One shot. Who'd have thought? In the thousands of movies he'd seen . . . Never . . . In his mind's eye, Elmo flipped through his storyboards for the sequence. It worked so much better as a single shot, he squeezed his eyes tight shut to drive out the drawings. They wouldn't leave. They floated in his brain, mocking him. He opened his eyes to blot them out, and gaped at the dying rain forest. When did jungle become rain forest?

A smoldering bird flies from the burning trees. The beating of its wings fans its wingtips into flame. The bird tries to flee its own fire, but the faster it flaps, the brighter the flames blaze, until fire consumes the feathers and the wings lose their lift. The bird drops to earth like a smoking comet.

The hard sun bit into Elmo. He squinted up at the giant wall with the huge "1" painted on it. It seemed impossible that something so blank and industrial could conceal his vital, intricate forest. Their forest. Homer's forest.

He was glad the wall blanked it out. That made it easier to move on. He'd just walk on by, out the gate up into the hills. He'd just gather himself together and start over.

It sounded good, even noble. But the thought filled him with a terrible sorrow. It wasn't going to happen. He'd never come up with another *Agonizer*. The pictures in his head were blank, like the soundstage wall. The movie in his mind had been turned on and off too many times. The switch was broken.

The "1" loomed over him. Maybe he should go inside and say good-bye. He knew every spider, every bat, every orchid. In all his struggles, it was the one solid thing to spring from his brain. The movie would come from Homer's brain. But not the jungle.

"Elmo! Elmo!" Marshall poked his head into the hut Elmo used for writing. No sign. Not unusual. Elmo liked to wander. Marshall walked deeper into the jungle.

"Elmo! Let's nail down the spider sequence!" Marshall ducked as a butterfly the size of a bird zigged for his head. A monkey shried in the upper tier. Marshall looked up. Something white flashed among the leaves.

"Elmo?"

No response. The white must have been an egret, or the albino chingtu monkey from Borneo.

Marshall's toe nudged a soft bundle. A mangled macaw. He knelt, concerned; the forest was supposed to be predator free. But sometimes the monkeys took after the parrots. He decided to leave it in place. One more building block in the biome.

Marshall walked the length and breadth of the jungle without encountering Elmo. He wasn't surprised. The kid had taken a tremendous hit. Must be drowning his sorrows somewhere. He headed to the Culver City stages to check out the bordello.

TWENTY-SEVEN

While George Marshall was scrutinizing his bordello in Culver City, Stanton Frye squatted in a dugout canoe on the Sepik River, squinting through the eyepiece of his Panaflex. Bats rose in clouds from the umbrella trees, casting speckled shadows on a fat gray gunboat that steamed through the black river like a huge and complacent waterfowl, past tangled vegetation glowing emerald and jade and turquoise in the warm light.

The jeweled intensity of the colors gave Stanton great satisfaction. In his frame the gunboat, pocked with rust, loomed against the bat-pocked sky; when he tracked the action, the lush greens of the Xavanti's land would contrast sharply with the toneless filth and decay of gunboat civilization.

Above, an assistant director peeked over the gunwales. "Ready whenever."

Homer was sitting next to Frye. "What do you say?"

Stanton nodded.

"Let's start the camera, then."

Stanton flicked the switch. He was still handling his own camera. The moves were too subjective to entrust to the operator. Homer yelled "Action" at the gunboat in a loud voice. The assistant hung the slate over the hull and gave it a clack.

Sky and rusty gunwale. Then Klaus appeared on deck in stripes and loincloth, leading wimpled Inga by the hand. They leapt from the ship, landed with a splash, and two Xavanti pulled them onto Stanton's canoe.

The canoe rocked violently as they slid aboard. Onscreen, this would have a distinct effect, for the camera was solidly bolted to the boat: While the world around the canoe pitched and spun, the canoe would sit securely at the bottom of the frame, providing an anchor for the action. Stanton, peering through the camera, approved of the effect. You were supposed to give the audience a nice safe earthbound frame of reference, but this was right for the picture.

It felt good to know what was right for the picture. Every film he worked on used to speak to him, tell him what it should look like, but that stopped years ago. Like chatting up women in bars, he'd done it so many times, he found it harder and harder to listen, and when he did listen, they gave him the same old line. Often now he changed things just to make them different, or, even worse, just copied himself. This movie had a look. It had been forged that first day, in the flaming hut.

He had to hand it to Homer. Having the fate of one's movie decided in a lab fifteen thousand miles away would turn most directors into anxious, temporizing wrecks. But Homer'd sailed on in complete serenity, taking each day as it came, finding fascination in every setup. "Maybe the dailies are shit. Nothing we can do about it now," he seemed to be saying, "let's have some fun out here."

Homer's enthusiasm freed up the crew. They worked with the loose, go-for-it attitude of a young ball team twenty games out of first. They moved fast, they came up with fresh ideas, they gave anything a try.

Of course, this could all change now that Homer was an anointed genius. That morning, Jason, airborne and bursting with adjectives for the brilliance of Homer's work, had caught Griffith through the Comsat window over Hawaii. Homer was now a visionary who could do no wrong.

Stanton felt a transient pang. Maybe he should back off, make Homer tell him where to put the camera. That would stop this genius talk damn quick. But he was having too much fun. He just hoped the crew wouldn't tighten up now that they were working for a movie immortal. Depended on Homer.

Stanton, shooting from the prow of the canoe, held the Xavanti in foreground, Klaus and Inga behind, paddling hard. As they pulled away from the gunboat, Johnny Palermo trained its forward cannon on their canoe and fired. A plume of water rose beside them, drenching Klaus.

Klaus spat a mouthful of water and glared at Inga. The bitch thought it was funny. Klaus had a brief paranoid flash that Johnny might be using real ammunition.

Each paddle stroke brought to mind a blow he'd landed on Johnny Palermo during their big fight scene. He cheered up. He gave Inga a screw-you look and dug deeper into the water. She looked right back, her paddle flashed in unison. The end of every stroke she gave a special twist. Then it hit him. Every stroke, she was jerking Johnny off.

He pulled furiously. She pulled harder. He was glad to be rid of the bitch for good and all. She needed the shit kicked out of her. Let Johnny do it, save him the trouble. He was glad they hated his guts. It helped the work. The work was fuckin' primo.

Homer watched Klaus and Inga in a state approaching bliss. They were giving him everything they had. Everyone was giving everything they had. This wasn't like teaching at Mucklinberg. People cared, and they worked hard, and they knew what they were doing. They radiated competence, and he basked in their glow.

It got better. When he made a suggestion, they listened with rapt attention, then focused all their skills and intelligence on doing it his way. He never had to argue about it. People took it for granted their job was to give him what he wanted. It was like he'd found a magic lamp—he'd make a wish, and this band of genies would make it real. He'd been cautious with his magic power, afraid he'd run out of wishes. Afraid the next suggestion he made, everyone would just ignore him like people used to. They didn't need him to do their work. He knew it, they knew it. But they never let on.

Commanding such powerful forces had its obligations. Genies expect wishes. Though they tried not to show it, they felt let down when he didn't have an opinion, which was most of the time. He was sorely tempted to have opinions just to make them happy, but so far he'd resisted temptation and let them work it out. The great thing was, they always came up with something better than if he'd told them what to do.

In the last few hours, though, he'd felt an odd new stirring. Since the news about the dailies. Jason said he was a genius, Jason said Annette said he was a genius, Jason said they were making the greatest action picture ever. He'd gotten in the habit of tuning Jason out, but these words had barbs. They lodged in his mind, creating little cankers of expectation. Just now, when he'd wanted more bats and Stanton said there were plenty, they couldn't wait or they'd lose the light, he'd had a sneaking suspicion Stanton was holding out on him. He'd felt stirrings of pique that this genie wasn't more obedient or more powerful. But he hadn't let on. He knew the dangers of disputing with genies.

Basically, things were going great. Stanton's canoe shot, for instance. Homer felt privileged to sit beside him in the prow of this golden canoe skimming the black river, hearing the tight beat of paddles slashing water, watching smooth, shiny bodies strain up and down like chrome push rods in a V-8.

Homer hung on as they veered around a hairpin bend. The sun swung full in his face, throwing the paddlers in silhouette. Homer squinted. Current pushed them toward the bank. He heard a light buzzing. Lines flashed by. For a moment he thought they'd paddled into a swarm of exotic insects. Then a Xavanti cried out. One line had stuck in his arm. They were being bombarded by small featherless arrows. This wasn't in the script.

Homer yelled, "Cut!" Nobody heard. They were listening to Klaus call "Pull! Pull!" loud and cool, while he steered them out of range into the middle of the river. With Klaus calling beats, the paddlers dug hard, even the fellow with the arrow in his arm, and clawed the boat back upstream around the bend.

Xinu, the wounded warrior, was a stout, strong young man. The tiny arrow sticking from his arm looked no more lethal than a soda straw. By the time they reached safe water, the arm had swollen to the size of his thigh and was cycling through the colors at the blue end of the spectrum.

While poison arrows rained down on the Sepik River, electronic sunset settled on Stage One back at the Studio lot. Because karaka toads and vampire bats set their internal clocks by solar duration, the full-spectrum sky pans were timed to exactly mimic spring in Belem. Each morning they would illuminate four seconds earlier, in phased-array step-voltage imitation of dawn; each evening they would extinguish eight seconds later, the same way. This particular evening, sunset began at approximately six forty-four, and extended for eighteen minutes and sixteen seconds. At six fifty-two, as bats stirred and darted off to hunt, massive humidifiers kicked in, providing the twelve thousand ferns essential twilight fog.

Leaves rustled. Bats dodged a pale form dropping onto the dim forest floor. The form unfolded into a crouching creature so thin and pale, he looked like a rising patch of mist. Dark rings the color of crushed hashberries speckled his body. Bright yellow macaw feathers, proud mark of the Xavanti warrior, crowned his head, still bloody from plucking. Small beasts scur-

ried away as the warrior slipped through the jungle, clutching
the broken parrot.

The warrior stood in the village compound, confused. He bit
his ragged lip, more nervous than a warrior should be. The tribe
had vanished. No wives or children met him with clucks and
giggles. The stones that lined the fire pit were cold.

The warrior was patient and resourceful. He scavenged fallen
branches. He searched out a length of sisal vine and shredded it
into lint. He selected a hard, pointed branch, and he placed a
flat bit of bark in the fire pit. He laid the sisal lint on the bark
and he ran the stick back and forth through his hands. When the
lint smoked, he blew with high, rapid breaths.

The warrior was clumsy at fire-making, but he rubbed and
blew undaunted until lint curled and flashed. He piled on twigs,
then sticks, until the fire found its own life. Then he turned
away to pluck the parrot.

The fire pit was planned to be practical. Carpenters were
scheduled to insulate it and install the firewall to bring it up to
code next week. But when the pale warrior made his cooking
fire, the fire-pit stones were made of AB foam sprayed over two-
by-fours. As sticks caught fire, they ignited the foam. The foam,
a petroleum product, fumed cyanide and flared like a Kuwaiti
wellhead, combusting the two-by-fours.

The roof of the nearest hut dangled a few feet away. The roof
was made of Mexican grass ponchos, which laid on top of each
other gave an excellent thatch effect. When the pine lumber
popped, a chunk of flaming foam landed on the roof, igniting
the dry grass with the whoosh of a prairie fire.

The small trees around the hut were natural, and slow to
burn, but the big ones were sculpted from the same AB foam as
the fire pit.

The gunboat, churning wake, returned the anxious film crew to
their cruise ship, the *King of Saxony*. Named for a particularly
rare and alluring bird of paradise, she was a rusted, mildewed
hulk, but still queen of the river. She was moored beside a small
cluster of palm-thatch huts, each protected from flooding by
stilts and from evil spirits by a fierce mask.

McGinty was very proud of this site because he had discovered the only Yawaba village with an airfield. Decades before,

during an antiterrorist sweep of the region, villagers had been press-ganged into building an airstrip at an army camp. That strip had long since been swallowed by jungle, along with the camp, but witnessing the stream of materiel flowing through the landing site, one visionary elder experienced Epiphany: God told him if his tribesmen followed suit with an airfield of their own, He would treat them with equal largess. God would send their ancestors to Sydney, and the ancestors would forward to them planeloads of meat, bags of rice, steel tools, cotton cloth, tinned tobacco, and a machine for making electric light.

The elder was charismatic and persuasive, and with labor they would otherwise have spent carving ancestral totems, he and his fellows leveled and cleared an acceptable runway for a DC-3, and constructed a reasonable approximation of a conning tower. Time did not prove out his vision, and his tribesmen reverted to totem carving and less technologically sophisticated scenarios for salvation; McGinty came upon their airstrip as it was about to be reclaimed by jungle, and refurbished it. Now the strip was indeed bringing forth a steady flow of goods, and for Xinu, the wounded Xavanti, it again promised salvation.

As soon as the gunboat reached the *King of Saxony,* the wounded Indian was rushed by his comrades to the ship's dispensary. The film crew doctor removed the arrow and tried to drain the wound, though he told Homer and Klaus it was probably too late, the poison was thoroughly absorbed into the system. As for the antidote, he was stumped.

The doctor, an expert in tropical medicine, was perplexed by the patient's reaction. The color of the arm had stabilized at purple and the swelling had subsided to twice normal size. The man was conscious, and his muscles were soft and pliable, but from the neck down he was completely paralyzed. Xinu thought he'd been poisoned by curare, but when the poisonous vine was described to Nahum, he said it did not grow in his country.

Xinu's compatriots were upset they hadn't brought their own healer on location, foolishly agreeing to rely on the white man's lore. After much discussion in Xavanti, they declared their colleague should be moved at once to the Yawaba village, to be cured by the local sorcerer or die on dry land.

The film crew held a hasty meeting. Griffith and McGinty, fearing legal complications if word reached Los Angeles that a witch doctor was treating cast members, in a rare spasm of unanimity insisted on airlifting Xinu to Wewak. But Klaus wouldn't hear of it. He thought doctors were full of shit. A staunch believer in homeopathic medicine, he trusted tribal wisdom.

Ultimately, location triage was the producer's responsibility, but Jason was suspended over the Pacific. All turned to Homer. This, too, was finally the director's call.

Homer left the choice up to the doctor. The doctor said he doubted Xinu would survive the flight, or what passed for a hospital in Wewak. Besides, he was curious to hear what the locals knew about the poison.

The huts were arranged like five fingers picking up a flat stone. They faced inward on a small clearing, and where the flesh of the palm would be, a ceremonial arch of woven grass marked the entrance. When film people and Xavanti, bearing their comrade on a pallet, approached the arch, half a dozen men ran forward, pulling spears from a cluster near the main hut and shouting menacing imprecations in Yawaba. Like the Xavanti, they were half a foot shorter than the film people, but they were blacker than the Amazons, with Nahum's flat nose, and they had less body fat. Their muscles stood out in sharp relief, like a skinned dog's. Save for the occasional woven armband or feather necklace, their only clothing was a horim, a stalagmite-shaped gourd that encased the penis.

Nahum tried some gruff words of pidgin Huli, the lingua franca of Papua New Guinea, but to the Yawaba it might as well have been Demotic Greek. After some confusion, they summoned a bent old man, his sagging skin ridged with ancient scars like crocodile scales. He listened to Nahum's explanation and barked a reply.

Nahum turned to the Amazons. "Down. Put down." He indicated the litter. "Yali say leave here."

"This isn't going to work," said Griffith. "Let's get out of here."

Klaus glared at him, and spoke to Nahum. "We can't leave him here. We have to go with him."

"Okay you. Them no." He pointed to the Amazon Indians.

"Why not?"

"You white men. They—" Nahum shrugged. "They what?"

Given the menacing stance of the Yawaba, the Xavanti didn't

need much persuading. They said a few words of encouragement to their terrified compatriot, handed the litter over to Homer and Klaus and Griffith and the doctor, and squatted on
their haunches by the gate.

Once inside the compound, the litter bearers were surrounded
by people and pigs. The women pushed to the fore, shoving the
children aside, laughing and chattering, more concerned with
the Xavanti's skin color and bone structure than with his pre-
carious condition. Woven nets slung from their foreheads down
their backs held babies and sweet potatoes. Otherwise they were
naked as the men. Instead of horim, a net sash wrapped their
loins well below the waist. Homer didn't see what kept it up.

Klaus, huge and bulging in his tank top, attracted as much
attention as the patient. The women reached out to stroke his
ham-sized biceps with stumpy hands missing fingers. Klaus bore
it patiently, hiding his distaste for their stubby touch.

Crocodile-skinned Yali shooed them away and led the litter-
bearers into the depths of the largest hut. The village men followed, stacking their spears at the door, but the women hung
back. The place was dim and sooty, and smelled of rancid pork
and male sweat.

"Men only, huh?" Homer asked Nahum.

"Women dirty. Live with pigs."

Yali had Homer and the others put the litter down by a
banked fire bleeding smoke through a hole in the middle of the
roof. He went to the darkest corner of the hut and returned with
a heavy palm-leaf bundle. Muttering to an invisible partner, he
ceremonially peeled back the leaves to reveal a boulder the size
of a teapot, which he placed beside the litter. Klaus asked Nahum what was going on.

"Ancestral stones maybe. Protect."

"Protect him or protect Xinu?"

Nahum shrugged. Yali placed six more stones in a ragged
circle around the wounded man, then picked up a feathered
stick and poked at the Xavanti's arm. The biceps wiggled, loose
as jellied aspic. Xinu babbled at him in a voice tight with terror,
but Yali paid no attention.

Starting at the toes, he waved the feather over Xinu's limbs
until he spotted the wound, now oddly dry and shriveled. He
spoke more words to his invisible partner and poked at the
wound with the feathered stick. Homer expected Xinu to
scream, but the Xavanti's stream of scared talk didn't ripple,

Yali spoke to Nahum. Nahum translated: "Yali say angry spirit enter body."

"We know that," said the doctor, waving the arrow at Yali. "It entered him on this. Ask him if he has an antidote."

"Dote?"

"Cure. Medicine."

Nahum translated. Yali looked at him blankly, scratching his horim, and returned to waving his feather.

Shouting voices came from outside the hut. Homer watched the men slip out, picking up spears as they went. Were the Xavanti getting into some sort of scrap with the locals? He spoke urgently to Nahum.

"Is there something he can put on the wound, or feed Xinu? Not just feathers and sticks."

Nahum spoke to Yali. Yali ignored him. The shouting outside grew louder. While Homer wondered if he should do something, Klaus went to reconnoiter. Bending low to fit through the door, he almost bumped his chin on the forehead of a square, muscular fellow sticking his head in the hut.

The man smiled apology and shouted something to Yali. Yali kept working his feather, but he shot back an answer, it seemed to Homer rather huffily. They argued for a few minutes, until Yali threw down his feather and went outside. The film people followed.

The Yawaba were gathered around a man with a cassowary bone stuck through a hole in his lower lip. He was talking fiercely, and the heavy bone waggled ponderously, giving an air of majesty to his pronouncements.

He was no friend of the tribe. The Yawaba were shaking their spears at him, and a few of the younger men even mimed running him through. But though he was unarmed, he did not seem afraid. When he saw Homer and Klaus, he yelled in their direction. The Yawaba yelled back, ominous; the intruder backed out of the compound, shouting something threatening.

Yali ignored the hollering, prowling the yard in search of something in the dank crawl spaces beneath the huts.

Klaus, stirred by the excitement, pulled Nahum aside. "What's going on?"

Nahum asked Yali.

"War tomorrow Mang." Nahum mimed the bone through the lip.

"War!" Klaus was impressed. "Did those jokers ambush Xinu?"

Nahum and Yali had a staccato conversation.

"Road belong cargo."

"What?"

"Yawaba ancestors bring sky men come destroy Mang. Take land."

Homer was listening with mounting distress. "You mean us? War because we used the airstrip?"

Nahum nodded.

"But we're not men from sky. We don't want their land."

"Not you. Him." Nahum pointed to the hut where Xinu lay.

"War!" repeated Klaus.

Yali found what he'd been looking for. He pounced, cat-quick, and came up with a rat, which he displayed proudly and carried into the hut by the scruff of its neck.

"They can't fight over us," said Homer. "We'll be gone in a week."

"Fight over steal pig. Fight over rape wife. Is no big deal."

Back inside the hut, Yali found a sharpened sliver of bamboo. Standing over Xinu, he tilted the rat on its back, squeezing the skin behind the neck so the belly stretched tight. Then with great care he split open the skin over the rat's stomach. Pleased, Yali held it up for their inspection. Entrails pulsed, but they were still hidden from sight behind the abdominal wall.

"No guts. Good omen."

Yali spoke with new confidence to Nahum.

"He fix Xinu now."

"Great," Homer said uncertainly. "Tell him thank you."

"Yali say you ally Yawaba, he fix Xinu."

"We ally Yawaba, yes. And tell him we'll give him two pigs."

Yali's reply was gracious and formal.

"Yali say war, then feast pigs. Yawaba and ally fight Mang, win great victory."

"He wants us to fight in their war?"

"You ally Yawaba."

"We can't do that."

"Then no ally Yawaba. Yali no fix Xinu."

"But we no enemy Mang." Homer found himself falling into Nahum's pidgin.

"Mang hurt Xinu."

"That was misunderstanding. We clear up."

"Yes yes. Fight war, clear up."

"We fight Mang, Mang hate us more. Ambush us on river."

"Maybe. Depend war."

Homer looked at the wounded man. His arm appeared black in the dim light. "Do you think Yali can really save Xinu?"

"No problem maybe."

Klaus spoke. "If I fight in this war, is that enough? Tell the old man I am great warrior of his new ally."

While Nahum and Yali conferred, Griffith hissed and sputtered. "Forget it, Klaus. You can't do this. No way. Acts of war are expressly excluded from our insurance. Homer, tell him he's nuts! You're risking the picture here!"

"You gonna let that kid die, Homer?"

The terrified, paralyzed young Indian turned his head to look at Homer. He seemed to know his fate was being decided.

Homer gave him a thumbs-up sign.

"Yali say talk war chief. Talk Anaklek."

Klaus found Anaklek outside. He was the man who'd interrupted Yali's exorcism. Though barely up to Klaus's clavicle, he was bigger than the other men, and more heavily muscled. His horim reached above his nipples. He was straightforward and direct, as if he'd known Klaus a long time. No fancy front. Klaus liked that.

Nahum put the question to Anaklek. He shot back like Nahum had just grabbed his naked nuts.

"What's he saying?"

"Say Yali full shit. Yawaba fight Mang. No you."

"Tell him Yali says I must. Tell him I am a seasoned warrior. I know discipline. I will obey his commands."

There followed a protracted argument. Klaus loomed over the two and tried to follow it. "I know what he's thinking, Nahum, he's thinking I'm some muscle-bound stiff. Here. Anaklek. Get a load of this."

Klaus danced a balletic martial-arts riff. Anaklek watched impassively, then shook his head vigorously back and forth. Griffith took it for an emphatic no, and gave silent thanks.

"Anaklek say okay."

"Tell him thank you."

Griffith cursed silently. Nahum said something; Anaklek spit at the ground by Klaus's feet.

"He say you're welcome."

"Homer, stop him. The movie's at stake."

"Klaus—"

"Butt out, Homer. This is personal business—"

"It's not, Klaus, it's about the movie. It's my responsibility."

"I'm fighting the fucking Mang."

"I'm in charge. I'm responsible."

"You may be a fucking genius, but war is not your department. War is my department."

Homer had the weird feeling if Jason hadn't called him a genius, Klaus wouldn't be declaring war on the Mang. So he was responsible two different ways now. "Nahum, tell Anaklek, Klaus is our great warrior, but I am chief. If he fights, I fight."

"Two fight?"

"Right."

Griffith drove his fist into his forehead. "Jesus Christ, I don't believe this."

Nahum conversed with Anaklek. Anaklek shook his head brusquely back and forth.

"Yes."

Griffith groaned and grasped at a straw. "Maybe if Stanton films the thing, insurance'll cover us. Maybe. Jesus Christ."

Homer spat at the ground at Anaklek's feet, and Anaklek spat back. "Tell him we're going now, Nahum, if it's okay with him. We'll leave Xinu with Yali."

The film people took their leave of a confused but vaguely reassured Xinu, explaining in pidgin sign that they'd return the next day. As they left the compound, they passed a crowd of women gathered around the warriors, stoically watching them boast and brandish their spears. Anaklek held his out to Klaus. Klaus grabbed it and flashed an explosive kendo move. The Yawaba were impressed. Nahum whispered in Homer's ear.

"Him bloody great big fast."

"How dangerous is a war like this, Nahum?"

"War much running, shouting. Act big. Scare women. No big deal."

The women did indeed have a somber air. "If it's no big deal, why are the women scared?"

"Is women. Want men garden."

Homer looked at the women waving their stumpy hands at the menfolk. "Do they lose their fingers digging in the garden?"

Nahum laughed. "Heaven no." He mimed slicing off a finger. "Father, brother, uncle die war, women cut finger."

Homer tried not to count the missing fingers. He looked back at the men's hut, and saw the doctor behind him. "Do you think Yali can save Xinu?"

The doctor shrugged. Nahum smiled.

"Cure. No problem. Anaklek say arrow poison wawa-bird feather."

The doctor perked up. "Did Anaklek say what the antidote was? The cure?"

"No."

"But Yali knows," said Homer.

"No cure."

"What's Yali going to do, then?"

Nahum smiled and shrugged. "Nobody die wawa-bird feather. Two, three days Xinu okay no problem."

"So why am I fighting?"

"You say Yali you ally Yawaba."

"But I don't need to be ally Yawaba if Xinu doesn't need their medicine."

"You ally Yawaba. Ally no fight, ally enemy Yawaba. Yawaba fight enemy. Better fight Mang."

Fingers black with pig grease and fern ash, Homer scratched his scrotum. His penis sheath fit fine, but the string around his balls tickled. He was plainly adorned as warriors went, in a single turquoise macaw feather from the costume department. He eyed his fellows, hung with snail-shell bibs and pearly chunks of cowry, and crested with elaborate confections of white egret, blue bird of paradise, and brilliant red and yellow larakeet, with a certain sartorial envy. But his skin was shiny black with the magic grease that would turn aside enemy spearpoints, and he'd been given a spear of his own to carry. He tried hanging from the spear with one foot crooked against his thigh like the others, and stumbled. One of the warriors laughed, and helped him put his legs in the right position.

Warriors had been trickling in for hours. Newcomers would look at Homer, perplexed, until one of Anaklek's men explained things in their rapid, clicking tongue. When Yali's name was mentioned, they reacted with amusement and a touch of fear, and stopped asking more. But they seemed to accept him. By now Homer found himself shoulder to shoulder with two hundred excited, chattering men. They stared across a gentle valley at the gathering Mang, from this distance merely colored feathers shining through swaying spears, a flock of birds in lethal river reeds.

Homer wasn't as scared as he expected to be. The men around him didn't act like death was staring them in the face. Tension hung in the air, but it felt like tension on a Sugarbush ski lift on the way to a double black diamond run.

Unlike skiing, though, this was not an optional diversion. They didn't choose war any more than they chose eating or sleeping. And there weren't newfangled improvements to contend with. They'd been fighting with the same weapons on the same hill for ten thousand years. Their spears, their ornaments—the men themselves—were as much a part of the landscape as the bamboo and the bats. The way Homer liked to think of himself and the farm. Except Vermont had winters. Rattling his spear with the laughing warriors, Homer basked in their glorious certainty of being.

"Wa, wa, wa!" The warriors waved their weapons and shouted at the Mang. Homer waved his borrowed spear and shouted along. The Mang charged. Laughing and whooping and pointing, Homer's colleagues leapt away down the hill. Homer leapt with them, and his voice merged with theirs, shouting "Kip! Kip! Kip!" and "Hoo-r-ra! Hoo-r-ra!" The soft earth rumbled beneath their pounding feet.

Homer was not a joiner. He'd never truly felt a part of any group he'd been attached to, as student or teacher or at the plywood factory or even with the film crew. The groups always felt illusory to him, lopsided, incomplete, and part of him always lay beyond their embrace. But these warriors rushing into battle were their own universe, total and all-inclusive. Bouncing down that hill, yelling and waving his spear, Homer finally became piece of a perfect whole.

Homer's army stopped where the slope tapered off, across a flat marsh from the Mang. Homer could see the cassowary bones waggling in their lower lips. They must have been just out of bowshot. Boasts and insults flew back and forth. Gibes drew laughs from Mang and Yawaba alike. Homer laughed along too.

Men from both sides pranced forward, twirling white egret wands or black cassowary whisks, feinting with spears, snapping bow cords, gyrating splendiferously. They were admired and jeered. Though well within bowshot, no one showed any more inclination to snipe than would an audience at a Mucklinberg College ballet.

Homer was considering giving the dancing a try, when Anaklek and a dozen warriors, crouching like crabs, dashed across the no-man's-land, dodging from one clump of grass to another. Arrows arced. One slab-sided warrior seemed twice the size of his fellows. Klaus.

Suddenly Homer's movie obligations weighed on his greased shoulders like a leaden snail-shell bib. McGinty and Griffith had threatened to bring in the army to shut down the war unless Klaus swore on his mother's head he'd stay out of trouble. Klaus had sworn. He'd seemed sincere. Nahum explained these wars were ritual, not killing. Klaus said he knew what wars were.

Klaus was tight on Anaklek's ass, bent low enough to smell marsh gas seeping through the matted undergrowth. His eyes flicked left and right. Any flutter of Mang movement gave his nerves an electric jerk. Damn. This was it. Fuck yes. This would blow the Inga-Johnny shit out of his head.

An arrow sailed toward him. He sidestepped it. Smaller than a fucking number two pencil. No feather shafts, no compound bows. Dangerous, but hardly lethal if you kept your eyes open. Just as well they didn't use poison in war, though. He scanned the whole field of fire, keeping tabs on the chief.

So Klaus was keeping low and out of trouble. Homer took heart. From his vantage point at the rear, the fighting had none of the coordinated mayhem of football or hockey. If Klaus hugged the grass and kept his cool, he'd be okay. Homer was more distracted by Stanton Frye, back with the second wave of warriors. Not that Stanton would take any foolish risks—before Woodstock, he'd free-lanced on the Mekong Delta—but his

Kevlar shirt and his intricate machinery blighted the prehistoric purity of the battlefield. He turned timeless into primitive. Homer tried not to look at him.

Homer was not alone at the rear. About a hundred others kept him company on the fringe of the battlefield. Some howled threats and shook their spears, but most were as unobtrusive as Homer. Apparently it sufficed for them to show up dressed for battle. They watched and rooted with the cheerful attention of diehard fans.

But it wasn't a ball game. Soon warriors were returning with arrows stuck in arm, or thigh, or torso. One young man had an arrow in his butt, and had to crouch on his hands and knees while one of the cheerleaders dug it out with a bamboo sliver. Another had an arrow tip broken off in the shoulder. A comrade rooted in the wound for fifteen minutes before he came away bloody-lipped, the point clenched in his teeth. The more badly hurt were laid on the ground, their wounds packed with moss and bound with purple strips of fresh banana leaf. Yali appeared, and cut their stomachs with bamboo while another man blew in their ear, "Ou-phoo, ou-phoo." If they didn't bleed enough to suit Yali, he would stick the bamboo into the cut and work it around. The wounded never cried or complained, though they might sigh in agony, or grind their teeth and claw the ground with their toes, especially those Yali bled. Though Homer suspected some would die from wounds or Yali's treatment, no one was killed outright. Homer sensed a death would end the battle.

To his surprise, the grisly surgery didn't seem barbaric or grotesque. He couldn't tell if the warriors believed in a soul or an afterlife, but there was a matter-of-factness about the whole undertaking that belied questions of fate and justice. To them, the battle was a natural process, like a lightning storm; people caught in it might die. They didn't think to comprehend the cause, or try to stop it: They didn't blame lightning, or expect it not to kill. Homer was struck with the remarkable rightness of it all. Below, Anaklek lived out his warrior instincts; up here, the less warlike watched, above the violence but still part of it.

Fat black clouds were rolling in. Klaus had been dogging Anaklek, staying out of trouble like a good boy. He was in damn good shape, but he was pushing now, fighting a ten-pound hammer in his solar plexus. He took a breather with a bunch of gasping Yawaba behind some tall reeds. When Anaklek passed, bent double like a spider, yelling at them, they shouted tough back but stayed put. They were losing their hots for battle.

Not Anaklek. Klaus had played blood crazy plenty of times, but he'd never actually seen it for real, in combat, until then. Anaklek had the fury. He fed on war. The longer they fought, the more jacked up he got. He was taking crazy chances now, he didn't give a fuck. Hell, he wanted more. He was a fuckin' blood junkie. Just watching him made Klaus want to leap out and smash heads. But Klaus was a guest at this war. He kept cool, studied Anaklek's moves.

Ducking and feinting, Anaklek attacked a clump of grass. A gang of eight Mang sprang out. They had him eight to one, but his blood lust kept them at a distance. Like most of them, these guys liked war a hell of a lot more than they liked risk.

The chief backed toward Klaus's reeds, yelling at his men to come and get the Mang. They yelled back plenty of encouragement but kept down. The chickenshits. Anaklek was fighting the Mang and his own men now, and he was doing better with the Mang. They had him surrounded, but it was a paper circle. His spear could tear it up anytime. He couldn't get his own guys off their asses.

The longer they stalled, the more pissed off Anaklek got. Finally he gave a great war cry of frustration and flung his spear at the nearest Mang. The spear pierced the man's arm. They all backed off a few steps. Anaklek shouted for his men to attack. The men shouted back. The wounded man ground his teeth so hard, Klaus could hear him from the reeds. Klaus fought the urge to boot his fellow so-called warriors in their butts to get them into gear.

The Mang eyed their wounded comrade, sympathetic and embarrassed. Two, perhaps the victim's brothers, angrily called to the others and gestured at Anaklek. Klaus didn't need the lingo to get their point: Anaklek had no weapon, he was a great warrior, this would be a great kill. The circle started to close. Anaklek called a final time to his warriors. Klaus shoved one. He shoved back and muttered something that seemed like he was saying it was too late.

Fuck that. Klaus jumped from the reeds, shouting the kung-fu shriek of death. The startled Mang turned toward the sound. That gave him the two seconds he needed to bust into their circle, whipping his spear kendo-style over his arms and around his back, cold-cocking one feather head, catching his buddy in the crotch. All his skill and discipline on the line. Fuck, this was living.

Anaklek whipped around to face him when he broke through the ring. For an instant, the blood-crazed warrior glared like he was going to rip out Klaus's throat. Klaus tossed him his spear sideways. The chief grabbed it with a nod and swung to the Mang.

Klaus took a battle stance at Anaklek's back and prepared to kick some serious butt. Two Mang, seeing him unarmed, poked at him with their spears, high, hard, and fast. He chopped one, the other missed him by a fluke. Smelling blood, more Mang joined the circle. Angry fear stabbed Klaus. This could be it. But he was taking a fuckload of Mang with him.

Klaus heard a thunderous crack, like a giant spear breaking. Fat raindrops cooled his shoulders. Instantly the Mang broke ranks for the tall grass. Pumped and primed, he chased them for the kill, but he pulled up short when he saw Anaklek hanging back. All the warriors on both sides had dropped their weapons and were pulling up grass like crazy.

Klaus didn't get it. He stood alone in the middle of battlefield. The drops became sheets of water. Klaus's white parrot feathers sagged in front of his face. He pushed them out of his eyes and caught up with Anaklek.

The chief's head was cocked at an odd angle, so the grass he was holding could cover the long black plumes sticking out of his hair. When he saw Klaus's feathers hanging soggy by his ears, he clucked sympathetically.

That's why those fuckers didn't back up their chief. They didn't want to get their feathers wet. Klaus stood in the open, battle frenzy pissing through his veins like boiling sulphur, letting the rain ice him down.

Fuck 'em all. All but Anaklek. He could sure as fuck fight. Klaus put his palms together, sensei-bowed to the guy. Anaklek seemed to figure out it meant respect. He patted Klaus on the ass, then put the hand to his mouth. Ditto, Yawaba style. That pat on the ass was worth more than all the fuckin' Oscars ever made.

Homer sat with his friends, sheltering his feather with grass and wishing Klaus would get out of the rain. He liked the way they waited, calm, patient, and unconcerned. If he'd been shooting film, the crew would have cursed the rain and counted the minutes to hurry it along, and Homer would have picked up their anxiety and tried to make the rain stop. The bad part about ordering genies around was you had to pretend to be in control. These warriors knew better. Directing, he felt a little phony, but he didn't feel phony here. He belonged here. Of course, one reason he felt he belonged was he knew he couldn't stay.

Everyone squatted in place until the squall passed. When the sun broke through, the warriors uncovered their headdresses with great care, like unpacking crystal, and preened the feathers. Some shouted brave words, halfheartedly trying to revive the fury of war, but when Anaklek turned with Klaus and headed back up the hill, they all fell in behind, stamping the earth and shouting "O-o-A-i-i-A-y-y—WU!" and "O-o-A-i-i-O-o-WAH!"

"Wua, wua, wua!" Homer's companions sang shrill howling counterpoint. Homer joined in. They cavorted together, leaping high in the air, wildly twirling egret wands, driving heels hard into the ground. Homer and his fellows delighted in everything—the gleaming grass, the bravery of their warriors, Homer's game attempts at celebration.

The returning warriors thundered into their midst. Still pounding the rhythm, Anaklek grabbed a black cassowary whisk from the grasp of a young single plume. Stamping toward Klaus, he presented it with both hands, chanting "Hunuk Palin." Klaus accepted with solemn dignity. Anaklek slid into a lewd, taunting, funky shuffle, hips and pelvis thrusting, fornicating in place: Telling the Mang how badly they'd been fucked. Clutching his war trophy, Klaus joined in, grinding his hips with glee. The other warriors fell in behind, leaving Homer and his friends to bring up the rear.

Leaping, shuffling, twisting, singing, they all moved up the hill. At the top, the women were doing a dance of their own, a slow, sensual shimmy from the shoulders to the knees, arms shivering in and out. Homer noticed one young woman in particular, Mikak shell bouncing above her high breasts, rooted to the spot, swaying like grass in the wind. Homer leapt higher; he was her warrior, back from the battle, dancing with pride and victory.

One group wasn't dancing. Homer couldn't figure it. Then he made them out—it was McGinty and Nahum and an older guy who looked a lot like Jason. Wait. It *was* Jason. He looked like he needed serious cheering up. Homer danced over to the group and beckoned with his spear.

"*Wua, wua, wua!*"

They backed off half a step.

"Come on! War's over! Join the celebration!"

McGinty stared slack-jawed. "Jesus fuckin' Christ!"

"Oh. It's you." Jason didn't seem to notice that Homer was naked and smeared with pig grease. "We have to talk."

"Talk later. Dance now! *Wua, wua, wua!*"

"Talk now, Homer. We have to call Studio. We've only got a half hour Comsat window."

A bitter twang to Jason's voice sucked Homer back into the twentieth century. "I thought you said dailies were fine."

"The jungle set burned down."

"What? The what?"

"Whole kit and caboodle. To the ground."

"All those animals?"

"They're the least of our problems."

Griffith was already in the back of the jeep, unfurling the umbrella antenna for the satellite phone. Homer followed Jason over, pensively tapping his nails on his horim. They made satisfying clicking sounds. Nahum mimicked it with his teeth.

"So. You like war?" Nahum grinned at him.

"Huh? Oh. War great. You were right. Okay no fight. Plenty men no fight."

"Kepu. Plenty men kepu."

"That's what it's called? Kepu?"

Nahum spat yes.

"Kepu is a great idea. We should have kepu. I think it's great that it's okay not to fight."

"Kepu no wives no pigs."

"They don't have wives or pigs? Why?"

"Rape wives kepu, steal pigs kepu."

"Rape their wives and steal their pigs? Why?"

"Why not?"

"What's up? How's dailies?" Klaus had joined them, idly flicking his trophy whisk. Nahum pointed at it.

"Where you get?"

"A gift. Chief Anaklek."

"Hunuk Palin. You Hunuk Palin." Nahum spoke gravely, with respect.

"Yeah. That's what he said. What is that anyway?"

"You crazy son-of-bitch killer fighter."

Klaus stroked his chin with the black feathers, and smiled.

"Maybe you wife daughter Anaklek."

"Wife his daughter? Yeah. Why not?"

One calendar day later in Los Angeles, but exactly the same moment in planetary time, Annette was biting into a yeasty scone, savoring the tang of wild strawberries and the delicate fatty texture of clotted cream. She pointed her butter knife at the trivet.

"Fresh from Devon this morning. You must try some, Victor, it's heaven in a spread. Here."

"No jam, please. I'm allergic to strawberries."

Annette took a scone, slathered it with cream, and handed it to a tweed-suited gentleman with a handlebar mustache. She was giving Victor the Sofa Treatment: Concerned and maternal, she perched straight and alert on an Adams ladderback chair while Victor, dwarfed by the vast bulk of an overstuffed Regency sofa, wallowed in puffy cushions.

Victor took the scone. He leaned forward so he wouldn't dribble crumbs on the silk brocade, but the sofa sucked him back in, shoving his knees to his Adam's apple. He had to crane his neck to look Annette in the eye. She smiled graciously.

"I'll be mother." Annette removed the tea cozy and poured.

Victor looked at his watch. "The satellite window should be open now."

"Cream? Sugar?"

"Black. Two lumps, please."

Annette plucked them from a Queen Anne bowl with silver tongs. Tea was a ritual that deserved respect. Under her tenure, Studio had added tea to the daily round of double and triple breakfasts and two-hour working lunches and dinners, and agents had embraced it as one more way to do business over food. In no time at all, restaurants from Playa del Rey to Burbank were packed with tea-swilling execs debating the relative

merits of Keemun Fancy and Pumphrey's Blend. Sony top brass
professed a preference for green tea, and the Japanese tea ceremony, but that, too, was a compliment to Annette in a back-
handed way. Tea was her signature, the stamp she'd put on this
town. Tea was hot because Annette was hot. Annette was hot
because of the fire.

It had been well past sunset, the very tail end of magic hour.
She'd been in her office dressing for the annual Christopher
Reeve Ball (a fund-raiser for one of her charities, the Quadriple-
gic Foundation), zipping herself into a Jean Louis gown on loan
from Western Costume for the occasion, a bias-cut sequined
piece he'd designed in 1938 for Carole Lombard and which
Annette could wear without alteration, so close were her dimensions to Miss Lombard's, when she'd heard the fire Klaxon and
looked out her window to see thick black smoke pouring from
exhaust vents on Stage One.

She'd rushed to the stage as fast as stiletto heels would carry
her, racing the Doppler wail of fire trucks screaming down
Washington Boulevard. She arrived as a security guard, gagging,
stumbled out the stage door dragging an empty cage; coming
closer, she made out a lump of black shadow at the bottom, an
asphyxiated panther.

She heard the syncopated whine of a turbojet rotor and
looked up to see an Action News helicopter treading water,
trolling a high-intensity beam. It caught her in its circle of silver
light. Her body draped in hand-sewn sequins exploded in spar-
kles. She ignored the beam, and the guard's warning, and rushed
into the building.

Local news vans arrived with the fire trucks. When she tot-
tered back out, four camera-crew kliegs caught her in a brilliant
cloud of glitter, clutching an unconscious spider monkey like a
baby in her arms. She staggered into close-up, choking on
smoke, holding out the limp monkey to a waiting paramedic.
Tears painted porcelain tracks down her soot-clouded cheeks.

The image of this goddess chief executive in a Jean Louis
gown weeping like a Serbian peasant over her dead monkey
captured the imagination of the global village. It made four local
channels as a live feed; the networks picked it up for the national news, and CNN played it worldwide every eighteen minutes for a day and a half. Annette and the monkey graced the
covers of two hundred–odd tabloids in forty-three languages.
Vanity Fair took their Annette article off the back burner and

rushed it into their next issue, heading it "Style with Soul in Tinseltown."

Annette had broken through, but tragedy threatened Studio. The synthetic construction materials burned with intense chemical heat, generating a fire storm that puddled steel and vaporized concrete, leveling the entire soundstage complex. Experts agreed it was impossible to tell what started it. Arson was suspected, particularly once it came out that the conglomerate owning Studio had been secretly planning to raze the stages to build a Universal Citywalk–type shopping experience.

That cloud was dispelled when Elmo was discovered missing and unaccounted for, and Marshall reported seeing something Elmolike lurking in the upper reaches of the set. Investigators sifted the debris for his bones, but found only carbonized fragments that might have been spider monkey or chimp. Arson, all agreed, but a crime of passion, not profit. Studio was covered for the loss of the stage and its contents, and the conglomerate immediately announced plans to proceed with StudioPlace.

The movie was a different matter. The loss of the set was a fraction of the costs at risk. These costs would not be borne by Studio, however. They were Unamerica's problem, and Victor's. In exchange for a hefty fee, negotiated by Victor, Unamerica had guaranteed the movie would be completed on time and on budget. If it ran more than ten percent over, Unamerica would pick up the tab; if the production ran amok, Unamerica could abort and make Studio whole on their investment. "Whole" at this point meant approximately two-thirds of the ninety-five-million-dollar budget of the picture. It was Victor's job to decide if it was worth continuing.

Victor had sixty-four million reasons to keep them in production, but he had to have some confidence he wasn't throwing good money after bad. The worst scenario for him would be to pump more millions in and still be stuck with an unfinished movie, and as things stood they had no way to shoot the heart of the picture.

The most cost-effective solution would be to "suspend and extend": Shut down production, take a few months and the insurance money, build a new rain forest somewhere cheap, North Carolina, maybe, then pick up shooting again. The problem was Klaus. Klaus had a stop date and Bo said he could give them ten more weeks at a million a week but then he was booked on another project. Victor would have happily replaced

Klaus—they'd barely begun shooting, and he didn't care if the movie made any money. But Annette had him there. Unamerica was bound to deliver "essentially the picture specified" by "date certain." Klaus was an "essential element." Give us Klaus, she said, or give us what we've spent of our hundred million dollars.

Annette figured she was in a win-win situation. The project had already put her on the map. If Victor pulled the plug, the conglomerate would get its millions back and no one would call it failure of nerve on her part. She wouldn't be branded a loser. The growing legend of her dynamic, caring personality would gleam with tragic luster. Besides, she was about to start production on a terrific Keanu Reeves project about a cowboy who becomes a professional polo player.

Making the film was more of a gamble. Then the conglomerate's hundred million was on the line again. But the press they were getting from the fire was fantastic, and the climax was in the can and spectacular. If Victor canceled the picture and the conglomerate retrieved its millions, there was no guarantee it would spend them on more pictures. She was torn, really. She could go either way. She was glad she wasn't Victor.

Annette's secretary buzzed her. "New Guinea on one."

Annette picked up. She heard the dead air of static suppression. "Hello? Jason?"

"Hello, Annette." The voice had been digitally deconstructed and reassembled so many times en route, it sounded like Jason had his larynx removed and was speaking through a voice box.

"You sound like the living dead. Is Homer there? And Klaus? And production?" There was a delay, and an echo. In the background, two people argued violently in a tonally inflected language.

"All present and accounted for."

"*Narak-a-la-ok.*"

"That's Homer saying 'hi' in Huli."

"I'm here with Victor Zelin. His people hold the completion bond. I'm putting you on speakerphone so we can both hear what you have to say." She pressed a button and the bitter singsong argument crackled through the room. Victor was taken aback for a moment, until he recognized it for microwave crosstalk. "Hello. Victor here. I take it you know our problem?"

"They just found out. I filled them in."

"We've lost the big set, and we're searching around for ways to finish the picture without it. Klaus, we were hoping you could delay your next picture until we rebuild. Marshall says that would add ten to twelve weeks to our schedule."

"—Fucking agent!" Klaus had begun talking before Victor had finished, and the coder had clipped him out. But Victor got the drift.

"What are you talking about, really?" Jason had broken in. "I've been over it with Griffith. All the other sets are intact. We can build a bunch of huts on any soundstage in a few days. All we're talking about is the jungle stuff."

"Including a battle to the death with a jaguar, and a twenty-page chase sequence budgeted for five weeks shooting."

"You know, I could never figure out why they built that set in the first place."

"Who is this?"

"Homer Dooley. I'm the director. Hello, Victor."

"You spent eight million dollars on it. You must have had some reason."

"They told me that's how they did it."

Annette could see this response confused Victor. "It was already built when he came aboard."

Jason broke in. "What Homer is saying, Victor, is he comes from the documentary idiom. If he'd had it to do himself, he'd never have built that set. The film screams for the reality of the real forest."

"What about logistics? What about schedule? Are you telling me you can do it in the same amount of time you could have done it on a stage?"

"It's all do-able. I'll stake my reputation on it. It's Homer's look. Totally real. It'll be gangbusters. Has Victor seen film, Annette?"

"Not yet."

"When he sees film he'll understand what we're getting here. It'll blow you away, Victor."

Annette knew that the single most important issue hadn't been broached. "Klaus? Are you there?"

"Yeah. Sure."

"How does this sound to you? You think you guys can do a first-rate job on the fly down there? Think you'll survive a few more weeks so far from civilization?"

"This is civilization."

"That means it's okay by you?"

"If the set was still up, I'd go back to L.A. and burn down the fucking thing myself."

Klaus's lines were breaking up badly, but he'd said what Victor needed to hear. Annette spoke in a loud, clear voice. "We are losing our window, Klaus, Jason, Homer. We better sign off."

"Thank you!" Victor shouted. "I'll get back to you!"

They heard Griffith's voice for the first time, in broken bits sprinkled with static suppression. "What—we—meantime?"

Annette looked at Victor. Victor nodded. Annette called as loud as she could, "Keep shooting! Bye now!"

She punched off. "There'll be added costs, of course. That's an expensive location."

"The fire insurance in your production package covers expenses incurred incidental to a claim. I'll see how much blood I can squeeze from the turnip."

"We could get lucky. Documentary style's fast. The climax was scheduled for two weeks, Homer shot it in a day."

"I should see that film."

"Absolutely. Right away."

They both knew he probably wasn't going to bother. If Annette was satisfied the scene was "the quality of a first-rate major motion picture" as stated in the completion bond, that was all that mattered. He'd draw up a codicil stating he'd deliver scenes of equivalent quality, and the rest was her problem.

Annette shook his hand and silently thanked Chris Parrott and the late arsonist Elmo Zwalt. Between them, Chris and Elmo had done her a tremendous favor: For the cost of a set, she was getting a full location shoot in New Guinea.

Annette might have fought harder, might have been less sanguine about her fate, had she realized that certain hollow pops and clicks on the New Guinea phone patch were not electronic noise or the chattering of finches, but the sounds of her director and her star idly tapping their penis sheaths.

TWENTY-EIGHT

The first signs of trouble arrived with the next batch of dailies. Annette watched them bright and early, as was her habit, fresh from the lab, cradling a steaming mug of latte amoretto, with no other execs, her only company Marshall and Nancy, the assistant editor who wrangled the film.

Marshall was about to join the rest of the crew on location. He had taken the destruction of his masterpiece like a trooper. He'd suspected building a rain forest on a soundstage was a foolish endeavor, but Parrott had talked him into it. One more proof Parrott couldn't make an action picture work. Homer seemed to have a real feel for the genre. He was better off on location, not only because the look was better, but because he was trying something fresh, and instinct and experience told Marshall that was better done half a world away.

Annette sipped her latte in cozy expectation. "What's scheduled, Nancy?"

"Well, we were supposed to get river business with Klaus and the Indians, Klaus sneaking Inga off the gunboat. But that's not what they sent."

"What did they send?"

"Uh, maybe you better just look at it."

Film rolled: Klaus close up, bare-chested. Small black men, brilliantly painted and decked with feathers, show him how to smear his shoulders with grease.

"Who are those little men, Marshall?"

"They look like locals."

"But they're not in the movie. The movie is set in the Amazon. Where are our Amazon warriors?"

Camera pulls back enough to show a twisty pointed thing sticking up from the bottom of frame. It wobbles as the little men grease Klaus's pecs.

"What's that, Marshall?"

"What?"

250

"That thing that looks like a rhinoceros prick."

Camera follows the greasers down to the abs. The twisty thing is lashed securely over Klaus's penis by a strap around his testicles. "Ohmigod. It *is* a rhinoceros prick."

"It's a gourd, Annette."

"Where's his loincloth? Where are all their loincloths?"

"They don't wear loincloths. They wear penis sheaths."

"That's got to be an NC-17."

"I don't know, their cocks are covered."

"But their balls are waving in the breeze."

"I thought cocks made something NC-17."

"Nancy, call the rating bureau, find out if balls without cocks are NC-17."

Nancy made a note.

"It's their traditional dress."

"It's not Klaus's. We might get away with the locals, maybe, but I'll bet you anything Klaus is a guaranteed NC-17. What scene is this?"

Nancy checked camera reports. "Slate was marked X900. That's not scripted."

"Why are they shooting it, then?"

"There's no note on that."

"Great."

Short pieces, beautifully framed. Billowing egret plumes. Bouncing cowry necklaces. Flicking cassowary whisks. Swaying grass. Running bodies. Waving spears.

"What is this, the world's most expensive *National Geographic*?"

"You must admit it's stylish stuff."

"Where does it go in the story?"

Camera running with the black horde. Camera stops behind a clump of grass. Klaus and the black men dash ahead, shrinking in the distance, obscured by reeds and tall grass for long stretches of film. Distant bodies pop up, arrows fly, bodies drop from sight. More minutes of tall grass.

"What kind of coverage is this?"

"There are pieces there."

"The cameraman's hiding in a hole."

"It looks like real battlefield coverage."

"Battle? That's a battle? From here it could be dodge ball."

Grass parts. A black man staggers by big in the frame. An

arrow pierces the skin of his forehead and sticks in the root of his ear. The shaft tunnels beneath the dermis like a fat IV line.

"At last. A close-up."

"That looks real."

"You're telling me this is a real war?"

"It looks that way."

"Klaus is fighting in an actual war?"

"This is very interesting stuff."

"God. What if he catches a spear? We're not covered for acts of war. Nobody's covered for acts of war."

The camera pans the wounded man up a hill to where more greasy, feathered men hang out. One is taller than the rest, and carries his spear like a pool cue.

"That guy looks familiar."

"Who?"

"The taller one." Annette leaned forward. Maybe this was part of the missing story. "Ohmigod. That is Homer."

"It is?"

"Homer's fighting too."

"Maybe he's giving himself a cameo. Pulling a Hitchcock."

"He's pulling a Kurtz. We're watching *Heart of Darkness* here."

"This is remarkable footage, Annette. I'm sure Homer has a plan for it."

"How long does this go on, Nancy?"

"Eighteen reels."

"Eighteen reels? Three hours? Do we ever get any closer to the action than this?"

"Uh, not in the fighting. There's some dancing, and they kill a pig and cook it and eat it. That takes six reels."

"Six reels to eat a pig?"

"The whole pig thing."

"Any of the other principals involved? Inga?"

"No. Just these men. But Klaus kills the pig with an arrow. It kind of looks like his pig."

"Is Homer there, Jason?"

"No, Annette, he's out checking a location I found for the jungle chase. It's amazing—like nothing you've seen—beyond bizarre—"

"Shouldn't you be with him?"

"There wasn't room. Wasn't room for Griffith or Frye either. We're down to one chopper."

"How can he check a location without his cameraman?"

"It's a conceptual reconnoiter. Klaus wanted to check it out first. It's amazing, Annette, Homer's pulled the rabbit out of the hat—he's brought Klaus on board one hundred and ten percent. Klaus has totally cathected to this picture. We're breaking new ground here, Annette, a whole new look, a whole new level of reality—"

"But don't they need a cameraman?"

"It's a five-man chopper, and Klaus had to bring Anaklek, and Nahum to translate—"

"Anna Who?"

"Anaklek. Our War Kain. He's staging the chase sequence."

"Jason? Jason, describe what you are wearing."

"What are you talking about, Annette?"

"Just tell me what you're wearing."

"Uh, Patagonia shirt, Polo chinos, New Balance 580s—"

"So you're not in one of those penis things?"

"Of course not."

"Thank God. Then maybe you can explain the dailies."

"Oh, the war."

"Yes, the war."

"Don't worry, that wasn't planned. It just happened, so we thought we'd find a way to work it in."

"You're the producer, Jason. One of your jobs is to prevent your star from fighting in wars."

"I was in L.A. delivering the dailies. But it wasn't Klaus's fault. The Amazon Indians started it."

"The Indians started it?"

"Yes, there was friction there. But that's taken care of. We've shipped the Indians home."

"The Indians are gone?"

"We're one big happy family now."

"But the movie is set in the Amazon. It's about the Amazon Indians."

"Now it's set in New Guinea. Everyone's seen the Amazon anyway. That's yesterday's news. This place is virgin big-screen territory. It's beyond weird. It's unknown. I can't tell you how excited Klaus is about this."

"But the script, Jason!"

"We're sticking very closely to the script. Don't worry about that. This country's a cultural smorgasbord. They speak a thousand languages here. That's one fifth of all the languages on earth. We can find whatever we want right here; we'll make it fit the script like a glove."

"Indians are in every scene you've shot so far!"

"I know. That's why we didn't send the other dailies. We can't use them anyway. Not worth the cost of processing."

"But you'll have to reshoot everything!"

"It's only a few days work."

"But the climax—"

"We'll cut around them. Klaus was very insistent about this."

"What did Homer say? Couldn't Homer talk him out of it?"

"Homer said it made sense to him. He couldn't understand why we were pretending New Guinea was the Amazon anyway. And he's right. Ship Amazon Indians to New Guinea for a few days, pretend we're in Brazil, okay, that's show biz. Now we're talking major sequences. Annette, this is a unique ecosystem. We've established extraordinary rapport with the local cultures. Homer is getting amazing stuff, and Klaus is happy as a bat in a banana tree. That's a local expression."

"Tell me there won't be any more surprises, Jason."

"There'll be plenty of surprises, I hope. Good ones. That's the great part about shooting on location. We'll give this picture the texture of reality."

"No more big surprises, though."

"No. Not the way you mean."

"You don't sound absolutely positive, Jason."

"Well, I don't know if you'd count the jaguar hunt."

"What about it?"

"There are no jaguars in New Guinea. So we're substituting."

"What do they have? Tigers? Panthers?"

"There are no large mammals here. The biggest mammal's the spiny echidna. Looks like a duckbill platypus with its nose caught in a pickle jar. See, all the animals here came from Australia, so they're mostly marsupials. Except the bats. They flew in from Asia. There are some huge bats."

"Klaus fights a bat?"

"Heavens no. They're fruit bats."

"Don't tell me he's fighting a kangaroo."

"The biggest kangaroos live in trees, weigh only fifty pounds. Look like koala bears."

"What is he going to fight?"

"We're working on it."

"Well, give me an example."

"They have a very dangerous bird here. The locals are terrified of this bird. Called a cassowary. Striking animal. Crimson neck, brilliant blue face, yellow crest. Looks like a Technicolor ostrich."

"He's fighting to the death with a blue-faced ostrich?"

"They're pretty terrifying, believe me. They can rip open your chest with a single kick. The problem is, they're herbivores. They're harmless unless you attack them. Klaus feels the scene lacks drama if he slays an herbivore."

"If the herbivore's an ostrich, I'd agree with him. Aren't there any dangerous predators? Real flesh-eaters?"

"Well, yes. Their king of the jungle is the Salvadore's monitor. Twelve feet of ripping teeth and slashing claws. It's the world's biggest lizard. Think *Jurassic Park*."

"That sounds promising."

"Yeah."

"So what's wrong with the lizard?"

"Well . . . it moves at a slow walk. Kinda struts along, like a giant iguana. Except it looks more like a salamander. But think raptor."

He was breaking up. Annette rang off, haunted by the image of Klaus locked in mortal combat with a salamander. If only she'd seen these dailies before she'd patched Victor into New Guinea, she could have gotten her money out of this mess. Maybe she still could. Maybe the Indians were an essential element, maybe she could force Victor to pay off the movie if he couldn't deliver one hundred percent certified Amazon Indians. It was a comforting thought, but in her gut she knew Xavanti wouldn't be specified in the contract. Maybe if she had Victor to dinner over at her place, a Morton's-catered tête-à-tête, a little swim perhaps, she could make him see the logic in pulling the plug. She buzzed her appointment secretary.

TWENTY-NINE

The helicopter had left the lime-green grasses of the Sepik flats far behind. Waves of somber verdure, each crest higher than the last, rose from troughs filled with silver mist. Homer shouted to the pilot over rotor noise.

"The forest's so thick, it looks like you could put down right on the treetops."

"I tried. Wouldn't recommend it."

"Not many other places to put down."

"You see one, you let me know, I'll mark it on the chart."

"What if we get in trouble?"

"Could be worse. Trees break your fall. It's there you gotta start praying." He pointed ahead. Out of the mist loomed sheer, jagged cliffs.

The chopper sailed over the cliffs into a shattered landscape, spread to the horizon like the underwater vista of a dead coral reef. Clumps of trees clung like anemone to steep, pitted slopes with the spiny, porous look of wild sponge.

"That mother's limestone karst. Rain's leached out the soft stone. Nothing left but sharp bits hard like broken glass. Cut through your shoes like they was made of marzipan."

Homer looked for flat spots. He didn't see any. "Where can you put down?"

"That Fo fella found a spot. Around here somewhere."

The pilot searched the landscape. Sawtooth ridges gave way to slightly flatter terrain. The clumps of trees spread into mini forests among crusty peaks. White water foamed. Steam rose from hot springs.

Homer could see why Jason was so excited about the look of the place. He checked back to see how the others were taking it. Klaus waved his cassowary whisk at the window. He carried it everywhere now. "Far fuckin' out."

"What do you think, Nahum?"

256

Nahum's usual grin was missing. "Lizard teeth. Son-of-bitch god-awful."

"Ever been here before?"

Nahum shook his head up and down vigorously. "No way."

"Nobody's been here. See?" The pilot pointed to a map clipped to his visor. Homer followed his finger to a large blank space.

"Anaklek ever heard of it?"

Nahum found the idea amusing. "First time Anaklek go no walk."

Homer looked at Anaklek. He was examining the buckle on his seat belt. Since takeoff he'd been playing with the mechanism, clicking and unclicking with intense fascination. Homer felt a spasm of industrial pride. He was repaying Anaklek for letting him fight in Anaklek's war. Or was he corrupting Anaklek forever?

"Nahum, ask Anaklek what he thinks of this machine. Does he think it's a big bird? Does he think it's magic?"

Nahum spoke, Anaklek replied nonchalantly.

"Say beat walking."

Homer wanted to ask more, but he knew there wasn't any point. Since the war, Anaklek had been polite to Homer, but dismissive. He treated his questions like those of a less favored child, to be tolerated but not indulged. Homer understood. He had chosen not to fight. He was kepu. At the pig feast he'd sat with the other kepu men, far from Klaus and Anaklek and the fire, and he'd eaten what the warriors left behind. From the Yawaba point of view, it made perfect sense. Defenders of the tribe needed priority in protein. Risk must be rewarded.

The chopper banked and dropped. Under Homer's feet in the clear plastic nose, a blank dot clipped from the forest neat as a bullet hole rushed toward him. As they descended, Homer could make out more detail, but it was impossible to judge scale in such an alien, fractal landscape. The trees could be six feet tall or sixty.

He made out spear-shaped leaves. The bullet hole became a missile silo. Homer feared it wouldn't hold their rotors, but by the time they passed the treetops it had grown to the size of the Mucklinberg College parking lot.

If the hole was bigger, the drop was deeper. The helicopter fell through the black earth. Instantly the black pulsed to life and closed around them. Homer recoiled in terror. Throbbing black thumped and thrashed the plexi nose of the chopper, and he could see it was bats, millions of bats, beating their leathery wings fast and furious against the windstorm of the rotor wash.

"Motherfuck!" Fighting for control, the pilot settled his craft onto flat, sandy soil as far from the bat-clouded walls as possible.

Homer sprang the aluminum catch and swung open the flimsy door into a blast of steaming air. He jumped down into hot sand and looked up at the pilot. "Coming?"

"Nah. Better stick with the iron horse. Don't want those little mothers chewing up my wiring."

"I know. I have the same problem with squirrels back home."

"This hole blocks radio contact. No fun being stranded down here."

Klaus landed like a cat beside Homer, swinging his whisk. "At least we wouldn't starve to death. What say, Nahum?"

Nahum had shakily stepped down beside them. He looked distinctly queasy. "What?"

"Eat bat. Yum-yum."

"No no. Bat spirit dead man. No eat dead man."

Klaus grinned at his discomfort. "They're a damn useful source of emergency protein."

"Dead men eat dead men."

Klaus laughed, and pointed to one wall of the sinkhole. Slabs of basalt had peeled away along a diagonal fissure, leaving a rough path up to the surface.

"There. That's what Jason was talking about."

Klaus headed for the path. Homer started to follow, but was stopped by the sound of shouted pidgin behind him. Anaklek was yelling at Nahum from the plane.

"Nahum, tell him it's okay to come out now."

"Anaklek say not okay. Dead land. Dead men."

"They're bats, bats, he sees bats all the time."

Nahum translated. Anaklek shouted something Nahum didn't bother to translate.

"Tell him Klaus is already going into the forest. Tell him his warrior friend needs his counsel."

Nahum tried again, but whatever he was saying only resulted in more angry shouting.

Homer went back to the plane, stuck his head in the door. Anaklek was buckled firmly in place, staring into some parallel universe.

Homer's weight shifted the aircraft. Anaklek's spear rolled toward him. He reached for it.

"May I?" Anaklek mumbled something dismissive. Homer worked the spear from under the seats and held it up.

"Come on, Anaklek. War Kain."

This time Nahum translated his reply.

"No spear no good dead land. No spear no kill dead man."

Homer pointed at himself. "Kepu."

Anaklek shook his head back and forth.

Homer knew that meant yes. He pointed at himself again. "Kepu." He shook Anaklek's spear, pointed at Klaus. "Me go Klaus."

And he started off, carrying the spear. He'd walked halfway to the wall, when he felt a strong hand close over the spear and lift it from him. Anaklek, grim but determined, jogged ahead to catch up with Klaus. Homer hurried to close the gap, already sweating in the damp heat.

The climb up the sinkhole wall was a messy scramble. Centuries of bat shit had coated the limestone blocks in slimy drifts, a foot thick in places. Klaus moved with precise grace, always balanced and in control. Anaklek picked his way, using his spear for balance. Homer slipped once and coated the seat of his pants with gray goo. He had trouble regaining his feet until Nahum lent him a hand.

"Nahum, if the bats are your ancestors, what do you call this stuff?"

"Guano. Good garden."

"Very valuable in other parts of the world."

Nahum looked around him, fear and distaste now tinged with mercenary interest. "How much?"

"I don't know. A lot. You could be sitting on millions of dollars worth of fertilizer here."

"Son of bitch."

"The problem is getting it out, though."

Nahum clammed up. He looked like he was trying to figure logistics. Homer climbed the rest of the way in silence, trying not to slip. It reminded him of the walk to his mailbox in mud season.

At the top, the path ended in a spillway of broken rock pouring from a wall of foliage. Klaus was already running in and out of the trees, miming for Anaklek. The warrior leaned on his spear, one guanoed foot against his thigh, watching. Klaus shouted at Nahum as they approached.

"Explain we're doing a chase here. I want to know, if he was after me, how we'd be going through this forest."

Nahum spoke in pidgin and Anaklek replied.

"Say why?"

"We want to get it right. We need his input to make it real."

More pidgin back and forth.

"Why?"

Homer spoke up. "Tell him we make up a story. Yawaba are chasing Klaus. It's make-believe. Pretend."

More conversation.

"Pretend no get. Pretend?"

"He doesn't have make-believe?"

"Why make-believe?"

"Tell him it's a dance we do, a kind of war dance, to bring us success in battle."

Anaklek understood.

"Anaklek say make fine etai."

"Good. We're doing our kind of etai."

This confused Anaklek.

"Anaklek say why? Who you fight?"

"Other white people. Back home."

Anaklek clearly thought this was a big mistake.

"No etai here. Land of dead."

"Let's pretend we're not in the land of dead. Let's pretend we're close to the river."

This didn't fool Anaklek.

"Say river far away."

"Anaklek, you go to the forest, don't you? You hunt there often." Homer mimed throwing a spear. "Cassowary. Bird of paradise."

Anaklek agreed with a side to side shake of his head.

"Let's imagine this forest is where you hunt cassowary. Show me how you do it."

Anaklek didn't think this was a good idea.

"Anaklek say here no cassowary."

"Make believe here cassowary."

"Make believe?"

"Yes."

Nahum said a few words. Anaklek stepped into the forest,

torso bent, spear at the ready, acting the perfect hunter. Klaus copied his motion. Homer and Nahum followed.

"How'd you get him to do that?"

"I make believe Anaklek here cassowary."

"I thought you said he couldn't pretend?"

"No pretend. Make believe. Say you say cassowary for sure guaranteed."

Ten steps into the trees and Homer was in a new world. Not the sparse, cool rain forest he knew, where vines dangled in graceful arcs between big trunks and the ground was carpeted with a firm pliant rug of humus. This world was dank and greenish black, the color, consistency, and odor of sludge sucked from his clogged kitchen sink. Humidity coagulated into fetid drops and hung suspended in the stifling air, feeding vegetation that never saw the sun. A lush riot of ferns, mosses, and albino orchids fought for space between close-packed, stunted trees, bark coated green as the ground beneath with slime that squished like guano underfoot.

Each step Homer took triggered tiny skitterings and slitherings. A leafy branch moved in the dead air, morphing into a foot-long bulb-eyed insect. A crab dangled its claw out from under a rock. What crab lived so far from the ocean?

Homer saw a yellow gleam by his shoe. He knelt down for a closer look. A brilliant golden slug the size of a calabash crept through the ooze. He touched a puce antenna, sending it recoiling into the body. Was he the first man ever to see this creature? Perhaps he had discovered a whole new species. Perhaps its body contained a chemical that would cure hepatitis.

He straightened and looked around in delight. He hadn't thought about the chase sequence much. It had seemed kind of busy and perfunctory, with lots of racing through trees and sliding down banks. Now it was taking a shape of its own. He could see it as something out of *The Incredible Shrinking Man,* Klaus and the Yawaba trapped in a terrarium, slinking through this soft and murky world, watched by weird, tiny creatures big as houses on the movie screen.

He heard a crashing and squishing up ahead. Predator! He looked for a tree to climb. They were too small and slippery. Then he remembered New Guinea's only man-eater was a lizard he could outrun at a walk.

Ferns parted. Anaklek, spearless, slipped and slid into sight, ricocheting off trees in his haste to escape. Nahum put out an arm to slow him down. "*Mel! Mel! Anaklek!*"

"*Yahno Welegat! Welegat leklek!*" Anaklek shook Nahum off and disappeared toward the sinkhole. Nahum grabbed Homer's sleeve.

"Run! Dead men! Run!"

"What? Dead men? You mean bats? Giant bats?"

"Dead men! Damn dead men! Come or what!"

"What?"

Nahum took off after Anaklek.

Homer watched him go. His gut twitched with excitement. Klaus! He'd been with Anaklek up ahead. Homer pushed forward fast through the trampled ferns.

He didn't have to go far. He scrambled up a short rise and almost tripped over Klaus belly-down in slime, not hurt, hiding, spying through the sphagnum moss. Homer sprawled beside him and peered over the crest.

The hillock sloped into a small black pool. Across the pool crouched half a dozen creatures Homer took at first to be an exotic form of golden monkey. They were men, small and scrawny and completely naked, their skin thick and cracked and glowing yellow ocher. Homer guessed they'd coated themselves with sulphurous mud. Long threads of mucus hung from their noses. A tropical disease, perhaps, or permanent colds from the incessant damp. They didn't brush away the dangling strings.

One of the men was drinking from the pond, splashing water into his mouth with a hand that moved like a dog's tongue lapping. Water dribbled in soupy green rivulets down the clay of his chin. Beside him a smaller creature—it must have been a boy—was gnawing on the carcass of a bat. On the ground, bats squirmed in heaps, alive but tethered in bunches by lengths of vine shoved through their wings.

Homer could certainly understand what made Anaklek freak out. If he'd seen ghost-men eating his ancestors, he'd freak out too. But Homer felt more excitement than terror. This was first contact! It had to be! He had discovered a new tribe of humans, never encountered before, not even by the other native tribes! They made the Yawaba look like yuppies. Save for the mud that coated their bodies, they had no dress or ornament of any kind. They carried no spears or bows and arrows, only a single stone ax between them. Homer was looking twenty thousand years into the past, back to where it all began.

He stood up, jubilant, hands open, palms out in what he'd heard was the international sign of peace.

"Hello! I come in peace!"

"Get down, you asshole!"

Homer paid Klaus no attention. He walked down the hill, smiling broadly to show he had no evil intent. The mud men watched, not especially surprised by his appearance. They grunted to each other. The boy, who looked to be about twelve, put down his mangled bat and approached, his mouth smeared with blood, swinging something in his right hand. A talisman perhaps.

"I come from sky." Homer pointed up and made the "brrrr-chopchopchop" sound of a helicopter, figuring they must have heard it come in. "Friend." He shook hands with himself, smiling and nodding.

The boy flung out his right arm and sent a stone into Homer's forehead.

Homer didn't remember hitting the ground. He looked up to see Klaus's legs above him and the mud men rushing forward. Klaus strode out in his battle stance to meet them. Homer feebly tried to stop him, but he was just as glad when Klaus ignored him, and sent one man flying with an efficient roundhouse kick. Four leapt at once, like wolves or jackals, all claws and teeth. Klaus chopped one to the ground and stomped another's spine, but two landed and closed their jaws around Klaus's biceps, big and meaty as their own thighs. Klaus shook and cursed, trying to beat them off against a tree trunk, but they hung on like pit bulls.

Homer staggered to his feet and went to help Klaus. He pulled at the men and pounded on their backs, but they paid him no attention. He looked around for a weapon, not sure what he'd do if he found one, and caught a glimpse of the boy loosing his sling from point-blank range into the base of Klaus's skull. Klaus staggered and fell facedown in the moss, unconscious, bringing his attackers down with him.

Homer knelt to see if Klaus was breathing, expecting to be bashed himself at any moment. Nobody bothered. They unclamped their teeth from Klaus's biceps and jumped on his back, twisting his arms behind. When Homer tried to stop them, they shoved him rudely into the gelid black pool, making a noise that might have been laughter.

When Homer surfaced, the boy was disentangling a vine from

a gaggle of captive bats. The maimed bats fluttered into the ferns, and the men held Klaus while the boy trussed him neatly hand and foot with the vine. Every time Homer climbed the slippery lip to stop them, a mud man kicked him back in. Four of them picked up Klaus by his bonds, two grabbed the strings of bats, and they moved off, trailed by the boy swinging Klaus's cassowary whisk.

Homer finally hauled himself out of the pool, stinking and desperate. He couldn't go back for help. The mud men would dissolve into the forest. He had to track them himself, somehow signal the chopper. They ate bats, so they must live nearby, close to the sinkhole. He set off, dripping algae, after Klaus.

Klaus was alive when they'd carried him off. That was a good sign. They could have killed him—could have killed Homer— but they didn't. Of course, they hadn't killed the bats either. Come to think of it, if you couldn't refrigerate meat, or smoke it or jerk it, you didn't kill your prey until you ate it.

But if Klaus was meat, why didn't they take Homer too? Was he just too much to carry? There were six of them, and the boy . . .

Homer's head ached from the slingshot stone and his ribs burned where he'd been kicked. His strength was sapping into the damp fibers of his clammy clothes. He skidded through the slime, stumbling on roots and sliding over mossy slabs, desperate to keep the mud men in view. They moved at an easy pace, slow but steady, with a gliding gait well suited to the slippery floor. Homer figured he must be working twice as hard as they were, and making more noise than all of them put together. They must have known he was following them, but they didn't seem to care.

As he struggled along, he would hear a rumbling roar and come upon violent waters slashing through the undergrowth, which the mud men forded with care. They seemed to know the crossings, stepping from rock to rock as if they'd placed the boulders themselves. Homer had a much harder time of it, but they stayed in sight. Did they slow down so he wouldn't lose them? Perhaps he was cattle on the hoof being led to market. If they'd thrown a vine around his neck, they'd have to leave some bats behind.

For the first few hours Klaus would rouse himself periodically. When he stirred, the boy would borrow the stone ax and clobber him on the skull, and Homer would hear the snap of bone cracking. Finally Klaus didn't wake up, or if he did, he'd learned not to show it.

Once they stopped by a rotten log. The man with the ax hacked it open to reveal a pullulating mass of maggots big as thumbs. The men grabbed handfuls and popped them in their mouths one by one, biting off their hard brown heads and sucking out the juices in their fat white bodies. When they moved on, the log still seethed.

Homer didn't know when he'd have another chance to eat, so he grabbed a handful as he passed. He was sucking on a maggot, thinking it tasted a bit like squirrel liver, when he heard the faint mechanical buzz of a helicopter rotor. He looked up at the mat of leaves. Even if he got in the clear, which he couldn't, he didn't have a mirror to flash. He didn't have matches for a signal fire. If the chopper saw him, there was no place to put down. He hoped it kept searching. When the mud men reached camp, he'd find a way to flag it down.

The forest was fading out. Sunset. Greenish-black became black, but Homer could see the mud men still, their sulphurous bodies glowing faintly like fluorescent fire engines. When they passed into dense ferns he'd lose them, but he never lost their trail. The moss underfoot sparkled with phosphorescent algae. Their footprints were shining pools leading him on.

The footprints ended abruptly. Homer blundered ahead, hoping to catch sight of their yellow bodies, and the soft sludge underfoot gave way to scaly points jabbing his Vibram soles. Homer lurched onto a broken-bottle wasteland gleaming in the moonlight. Spiky hills and fractured ridges of karst rose to the stars, softened only by hanging pockets of volcanic steam.

Homer gaped at the fat moon. Of course. They'd hunt in the full moon if they liked to travel by night. He scanned the jagged, empty landscape, suddenly conscious of how cold it had grown. He stumbled ahead, trying not to think what would happen if he couldn't find the mud men.

A steam veil parted; to his great relief, he spied yellow bodies not far off, gathered around a volcanic spring. Soggy and shivering, he picked his way toward them. He crouched behind a steaming rock, trying to get warmer but not wetter, and watched. Was this base camp?

There were no huts or caves, no families to greet them. They were squatting by the spring, shoving their hands into holes in the limestone, not to warm them but to pull out round white

eggs, which they cracked open and ate raw. One of them un-
strung a bat and broke its neck with a practised twist. They
handed it around, chewing on the flesh while warm blood still
flowed. They threw a bat into the boiling pool.

They rested, not talking, but expertly wrapping their feet with
lengths of vine torn from bat tethers. When they were finished,
one of them retrieved the boiled bat from the hot pool and they
pulled it apart with gourmet pleasure.

Did they know of fire? Homer'd seen no evidence of it. In
such a damp place, perhaps they'd never learned. They might be
as terrified of fire as lions or hyenas were. He tried to make his
weary mind come up with a plan for using fire to free Klaus.
He'd seen a competent Yawaba start a fire with twigs in half a
minute. Maybe when the time came he could copy the trick,
make a torch or something. But he'd never actually made fire
that way, and he didn't see much he could use for kindling.

The mud men started off again. Their vine-clad gait changed
from forest glide to precise, dainty prance over prickly stone.
They looked almost prissy lugging Klaus.

Beyond the hot spring the ground rose abruptly. The mud
men moved doggedly up the barren slope, following an invisible
trail, in plain sight of Homer, never acknowledging his presence
with even a backward glance.

It was exhausting work, and progress was maddeningly slow.
Though they inched along, Homer felt himself falling behind.
Pushing himself, he lost his footing and shot out a hand for
balance, slashing his fingers on the karst. He tried to imitate
their mincing gait, but no matter how carefully he trod, glassy
points sliced into his boots. His toes felt warmer; they were
soaked in blood.

It took most of the night to climb the slope. The moon set,
and for a while Homer worked by starlight, feeling his way step
by step, telling himself he could make out faint yellow forms
bobbing above him on the hill. His feet were bleeding more
now, and he slipped and tripped in the void; by the time the sky
lightened to a dim purple, Homer's palms and fingers were criss-
crossed with gashes.

When Homer could make out the crest of the hill, the mud
men were gone. He plodded on as the sky went from purple to
green to red, turning the karst to blood. Walking now required
such care, he forgot that he was cold and hungry. But he
couldn't forget that his hands hurt, and that each painful step

put him farther from return. He prayed he'd be able to spot the mud men from the top.

The karst was dead white when Homer crested the hill. He gazed down onto a volcanic basin hemmed in by prickly walls: a small, soft, self-contained world the same bitter yellow as the mud men. Cottony mounds sloped gently to a crusty beach, crazed by the sun. A steaming, bubbling lake of sulphurous mud lapped at the shore.

Homer spotted the hunting party as they left the karst slope and stepped up their pace on the mud. Homer tried to speed up too, so they wouldn't disappear on him again, but by the time he reached the bottom, he'd lost them behind a puffy hillock. He forced his aching legs and shredded feet to trot him there.

The hunters had stopped a few yards beyond. They were showing off Klaus and the bats to four women and two small children, naked, mud-smeared, and streaming snot like the men. They all seemed impressed by the haul. The men launched into what looked like an elaborate victory dance, leaping and grabbing at a huge imaginary beast who threw them off again and again. When the boy mimed using his sling and all fell to the earth, Homer decided they must be telling a suitably embellished tale of their battle with Klaus; when one jerked his foot oddly, making the others snigger and blow snot, he must have been shoving Homer into the pond.

The women enjoyed the display immensely, which pleased the warriors; several grew erections. The man with the ax grabbed the youngest woman, a teenager, by the hair and threw her to the ground. The others waited patiently while he mounted her doggy style, a brief and frenetic encounter. Then the men stretched out in the sun to sleep, and the women hauled off Klaus and the bats.

Was this Homer's chance? Weary and broken, nauseous from the fart stench of sulphur, besieged by clouds of vicious mosquitoes, he followed the women to a mud cave by the shore of the mud lake, where they dumped their burdens and departed, leaving the teenager behind with Klaus to attack what was left of his clothes. Buttons and zippers meant nothing to her, of course, and quite possibly she'd never seen any form of clothing before; the way she ripped off Klaus's shirt, she might have been skinning him.

Klaus's head lolled to one side, and in his ear Homer saw a pool of clotted blood. Now or never. Homer staggered forward.

The girl looked up from her work. He smiled weakly, then knelt to untie Klaus's bonds with his bloody hands. She stood, backed off half a step, and kicked him in the kidneys. It was a strong, well-placed kick; Homer felt like he'd been bisected by a chain saw. He collapsed in a heap. She returned to her work without a backward look.

Homer lay on the mud floor, blind and breathless with pain and exhaustion. When his wind returned and his sight cleared, he staggered to his feet and lurched toward Klaus once more. This time she didn't even kick him, just put her foot against his chest and shoved. Homer rolled to the mouth of the cave.

He lay there in a stupor, weighed down by a crush of images—Klaus twirling his cassowary whisk; the golden slug; the arrow piercing Xinu's arm; his last meal, a cottage cheese salad. The images were solid and reassuring, clean and pure; he wanted to lie there and savor them, but the buzzing hordes eating his eyelids and his neck and crawling inside his nostrils wouldn't let him. He raised himself, but could get no farther than his hands and knees. He willed himself to crawl toward Klaus, but found himself moving the other way. He had to help Klaus. But the damn mosquitoes. He was so tired. She hadn't been covered with damn mosquitoes.

Homer stopped crawling at the first mud hole. He slipped sideways down the slope and buried his head in the thick, steaming pool. The buzzing cloud evaporated. Hot muck soothed his puffy, welted skin. He shoved in his hands. The hot balm leached their pain, and he sank the rest of his body into the ooze, safe and warm. He was back in Vermont, skating along his access road in mud season.

When he awoke, he was half out of the hot pool. The sun had dried the mud on his face and chest to a thick crust. His hands and feet burned, his head throbbed, and his kidney felt like a foot still crushed it, but he was warm at last, and his upper half dry, and sleep had restored his congenital optimism. Yes, it was impossible to retrace his steps. Yes, Klaus was too far gone to walk out even if they could find their way. But this mud men— yellow world was the best possible marker for any airborne search. When Nahum saw the color he'd swoop down and save them. Unless there were many such sulphurous springs. Homer hadn't seen any on the flight in. He dared to think about breakfast, and then he realized he'd been woken by a high-pitched wailing scream. He crawled up to the rim of the mud hole and peered over.

The wailing came from the women. They were standing in a semicircle behind the twelve-year-old boy, who was sitting cross-legged, rubbing his crotch with what looked like a large, hairy coconut. The boy turned the coconut, and it wasn't hairy anymore; Homer could make out Klaus's face staring at him. The boy was rubbing himself with the severed neck now.

The boy continued rubbing himself first with the neck, then with Klaus's mouth, over and over, to the rhythm of the wail. Then the men started an answering cry, nasal and yodeling, and hauled on two vines that led into the mud lake. The vines were short. They brought Klaus's body, steaming, to the surface. The men dragged it over to the boy.

The boy surveyed the massive corpse before him carefully, with respect. The way Homer looked at a Thanksgiving turkey before he carved it. Then the boy rose, put Klaus's head back on his shoulders, and lifted Klaus's massive right arm. The boy solemnly took a bite of the meaty biceps. The flesh came away easily. The lake must have been much hotter than the mud hole Homer was hiding in.

The boy knelt at Klaus's beefy thigh and took another mouthful. Stone Ax reached between Klaus's legs and yanked off his egg sack. He presented it to the boy, who devoured the bag and its contents with sober gusto.

The yodeling shifted up an octave, and the boy picked up Klaus's head. He carried it to a scraggly stand of bamboo, the only greenery on the mud flats, and placed it in a hole at its base. Not burying it, Homer thought, planting it.

The boy stood over the hole. Stone Ax took the boy's foreskin in both hands, bent over, and bit hard. The boy shook, mutely fighting the pain. Stone Ax spat a gobbet of flesh into hole. The boy peed on it, blood and urine. The other men filled in the hole with their hands.

The wailing stopped. The boy plastered mud on his wound and they all returned to the massive pile of protein that had once been Klaus. They dined with diligence and enthusiasm, the teenage girl showing a pronounced preference for gluteus maximus.

Homer felt duty bound to watch the whole procedure. These were Klaus's last rites, and he was sole witness. He tried to compose a eulogy for the man, but instead he kept asking himself, why Klaus, why not me? And he kept getting the same answer: Klaus isn't meat. They eat Klaus to absorb his strength and prowess and courage. I can't hurt them, so they won't eat me.

Much of Klaus remained when they'd eaten their fill. Homer watched them haul it to the lake and throw it in. Then he slid back into his mud hole and closed his eyes.

He was woken from black, empty sleep by the staccato whine of rotors. He lay on his back, staring past the yellow lip of his hole at the blank blue sky. The whine became a roar, and blue was briefly blotted out by flashing blades and red aluminum and the glare of sun off plastic.

He blinked, and was staring at blue again, but he couldn't banish the hallucination: The roar persisted, shifting pitch. Wearily, he clawed his way to ground level.

The mud people were gathered in a bunch watching the machine settle tentatively onto the mud flats. They waited patiently for the rotors to slow. When the door opened and Jason appeared, closely followed by Nahum and a big man with an automatic rifle, they made no move to advance or retreat. Jason and then Nahum shouted at them from a safe distance, words buried under rotor noise.

Homer staggered from his hole. Jason looked at him in panic and the armed man raised his weapon. Bent with pain, shuffling and stumbling, caked with yellow mud, he must have looked to be an old and sickly member of the tribe. He stopped beside the other mud people. The two groups stared at each other in silence.

Homer made out Stanton Frye in the doorway of the chopper, peering at him through the eyepiece of a video camera. He waved. Stone Ax put his hands in the small of Homer's back and gave him a healthy push. Homer tripped forward into Jason's arms. Fear, disgust, and finally recognition lit up Jason's face.

THIRTY

Christopher Parrott sat on his balcony wrapped in a terry-cloth robe, enjoying the fresh pastel twinkle of dawn over the Mediterranean as he geared up for a hard day location-hunting villas. The poached eggs were, as usual, perfect. Whites firm as a woman's breast, yolks thick as heavy cream. Hollandaise hovered over them, adding richness and warmth but no weight at all. It must have been whisk-whipped moments before. Normally Parrott knew better than to order eggs Benedict from room service, but the Hotel du Cap was a magical place, where food flew instantaneously to one's balcony from the chef's skillet.

He sipped the orange juice. One of life's delicious mysteries. How did the maître de jus squeeze oranges so gently and filter their nectar so selectively that his glass was devoid of pulp, but packed thick as spawning salmon with fat pods of juice? He massaged a school, round and slippery, with his tongue, then pressed harder, savoring the satisfying tingle as they burst, flooding his taste buds and leaving only the thinnest membrane behind.

Leafing through the newspapers beside his plate, Parrott's eye was caught by the screamer on yesterday's *Variety*: ADIOS KLAUS. Had he sent his eulogy telegram? He couldn't remember.

He picked up the paper. A photo filled the middle columns above the fold. Rare for *Variety*. The picture was an aerial shot of a few miles of narrow, winding canyon road completely clogged with cars. Apparently, Bo and Inga held the memorial service at Klaus's ashram, the lamasery at the top of Topanga Canyon, and the hundreds of thousands who came to say good-bye gridlocked in a day-long traffic jam. Los Angeles had not seen its like since the earthquake shut the Santa Monica Freeway. *Variety* portrayed it as the town's ultimate tribute. Hence the photo.

Parrott liked to view *Variety* with amused contempt. It embodied a world obsessed—no, consumed—with the biz. He always said he subscribed only to check the grosses and remind himself of how lucky he was to be living in New York. In truth, he viewed it with a certain morbid fascination. The news never interested him—if important, it would show up in the *Wall Street Journal*—but he found himself scanning the doublespeak in the articles, decoding them simply because he knew how. He honed his Hollywood instincts on *Variety* the way people practiced their French by subscribing to *Le Monde.*

This was a Klaus Frotner memorial issue, fat with farewell ads from Klaus's friends and colleagues using the occasion of his death to remind the film community they were still in the game. Universal had a full-page photo of Klaus in Ninja action, bordered in black, with the words "Two-Billion-Dollar-Man" and a list of his Universal movies. Studio had a double-page spread, a location photo of a greased and naked Klaus from the waist up, towering over fellow warriors, with only his dates for text. Better a full-length picture, but all told very simple, understated. He could see Annette's touch there. The photo hinted at the glories of a film destined to enter Hollywood lore as a great unfinished masterpiece, and subtly recalled the media excitement around their discovery of a new tribe, the first in fifty years. Overleaf was Studio's announcement of the Frotner Foundation for Man and the Environment, endowed by Studio, with a tear-off coupon soliciting donations. Its logo was a stylized cassowary whisk.

Parrott smiled. Perfect. Just perfect. Annette had wrung the most from the situation. Whatever it cost her losing the soundstage had been neatly recouped by losing Klaus. He was the essence of "essential element." She was whole. Better than whole. To her growing aura she'd added the mystique of an unfinished masterpiece, which Parrott suspected was considerably more of a masterpiece unfinished than it would have been in release. She'd certainly pleased her bosses, the board of the conglomerate. They'd bought Studio for the name and the real estate. She'd added luster to the logo, and razed their soundstages without personally committing arson. Annette had style and she had luck. It was a killing combination in that town. Parrott knew they'd be working together again.

He flipped on. That young producer fellow, Darius Fo's son,

had bought a page, simply Frotner's name in stark Helvetica and the quote from Yeats's epitaph:

Cast a cold eye on death, on life,
Horseman pass by.

That's the Fo kid. Too smart for his audience. Parrott flipped on. On page fifteen, a three-inch article trumpeted half a dozen new projects for the young Fo's company, Argonaut Productions. A true desperation move. You'd think he could have waited a couple of issues. Not that it mattered, it was bullshit pure and simple. When you lose the world's biggest set and the world's biggest star on your first major outing as producer, you are either monumentally inept or monumentally unlucky. Either way, you are bad news waiting to happen. The silver screen had seen enough of the younger Fo. If Darius wanted to pull strings, he might be able to land his son in syndicated TV.

A half-page ad below the article froze his jaw in mid-chew. A cheap-looking mishmash of computer type styles and a snarling Doberman proclaimed "LET THE MAN WHO DISCOVERED *THE AGONIZER* DISCOVER YOU." Below, a grainy photo of a serious young man holding the old *Variety* screamer: $3 MIL AGONY. In smaller type: "AGGRESSIVE REPRESENTATION. I can make it happen FOR YOU." In smaller type still: "Submit scripts with one-hundred-dollar processing fee to Global Worldwide Talent." P.O. box, and nine hundred number for script consultation. Chris laughed. In the Frotner memorial issue. Talk about tacky audacity. In a town without taste, there is no such thing as tasteless.

Parrott returned to the front page and scanned the lead story on the memorial service, half searching for a mention of his own message. They ran a long list of well-wishers, but Parrott's name was not in evidence. He hoped he'd forgotten to send it.

He noticed that Homer Dooley, his replacement as director, had appeared at the service, and had been hissed by many of the mourners. Parrott found their fury amusing. In this age, fans knew their idols' drug problems and sex partners and when they had their tummies tucked, and—poof!—the biggest star of all just disappears in a puff of yellow smoke. Nothing but cassowary whisk. There was bound to be a massive surge of voyeuristic frustration. The diehards, of course, maintained Klaus never died at all. Parrott had read a *Wall Street Journal* article on

Frotner memorabilia that said the hottest-selling item was a
Frotner-MIA bracelet.

It was bad enough that Klaus had disappeared. But there had
been a witness, and the witness wouldn't talk. That just didn't
happen in this age of star journalists and special investigators.
Parrott had watched the news spots on the "Frotner affair," as it
was called, with a certain clinical interest, as a student of character. They never featured Dooley. He must have been pressured
by the best, from the attorney general to Ted Koppel, but he'd
kept his mouth shut, even when accusations flew that he might
have had a hand in Klaus's demise.

The sensible majority dismissed such talk as contrary to all
logic and common sense. This wasn't a *Twilight Zone* situation.
Nobody, certainly not a first-time director, ever told Klaus
Frotner what to do. But Parrott imagined there was more than
one macho nut out there looking for any excuse to off the man
who cost the world Klaus Frotner. And still Dooley did not talk.

That was the stick; think of the carrot. Dooley couldn't have
made more than a quarter million directing the movie. An exclusive to the *Enquirer* or the *Sun* would be worth two hundred
thousand at least. If he didn't go the tabloid route, the book
contract would probably reach a million. But the guy wouldn't
talk. Alone among all the ghouls and the self-promoters, he was
showing proper reverence for the dead. Parrott had to hand it to
Homer Dooley. A true man of principle. He couldn't be bullied
and he couldn't be bought. Parrott felt a stab of guilt. This man
didn't subscribe to *Variety*. Christ, it would be good to forget
the biz—just pack up, move to Vermont, smell the roses.

He took another sip of orange juice. Soft flavor torpedoes
exploded against his tongue. On the other hand, he'd played his
Agonizer hand very well. He'd trusted his instincts in spite of the
law and his advisers and the tremendous momentum of a movie
in active preproduction. He'd bailed out safely and hit the
ground running. He owed Bo an I-told-you-so call.

Christopher Parrott put down *Variety* and picked up the *Wall
Street Journal*. Homer Dooley, he decided, was too good for the
business.

Homer was curled in a sweaty fetal ball when the bus pulled
into Burlington at nine o'clock at night. He'd spent eighty hours

and forty minutes in transit from L.A., seventy-one hours and twenty-five minutes in buses, the rest making connections in Chicago, Cleveland, Albany, and Montreal. It had cost him one hundred and forty-three dollars. He was spending his own money now, and he didn't see the point in blowing a couple of hundred more for the plane. What was he going to do with the extra time that was worth two hundred dollars?

The bus wheezed to a halt beside Ham and Frances. Homer unfolded, stretched, and stepped off, holding his day pack gingerly in torn fingers. Frances gave him a hug and Ham gave his hand a big squeeze. Homer yelped. As usual, they both talked at him at once.

"Glad to see you're not wasting your money on airplanes—"

"So, what happened to Klaus—"

"How about 'Hello, Homer,' Mom?"

"What happened to Klaus?"

"I told you on the phone, Mom. It's not important."

"Then why won't you tell anyone what happened?"

"Because it's not important."

"Then why not tell?"

"Because then it would become important. Can you help me with my bags, maybe? My hands are kind of cut up."

The Greyhound man had already opened the luggage compartments. Ham picked out Homer's old duffel. Homer pointed to a triangular packing tube normally used for skis. Frances grabbed it.

"It wasn't ski season down there?"

"Momentos. You'll see." The tube held some bird of paradise feathers and his horim. They didn't quite fit in a shorter one.

Ham lugged the duffel to the Subaru and threw it in the trunk. They waited while he fought the door handle.

"Damnation! Maybe you can buy us a pickup now."

"I don't know."

"A used one."

"New tires, maybe." Homer wasn't planning on going out much.

They all slid in the front seat, Homer in the middle straddling the shift. The packing tube barely fit diagonally front to back.

The car started right up. Ham and Frances did too.

"Your boss at Mucklinberg stopped by the house, dear—"

"The sucker wants you back. Says you're fundable now."

"I'm not going back, Ham."

"It's the only decent job in a hundred miles."

"I've figured it out. After taxes and my agent I've got about a hundred forty-seven thousand dollars, plus about twenty-two thousand per-diem money I never spent. I figured I'd stick the hundred forty-seven in the bank or buy bonds or something. I bet I could get eight or ten thousand a year in interest, maybe even more.

"You gonna live on that?"

"Yeah."

"Eight grand a year? Don't you have any gumption? Don't you want to make your way in the world?"

"I tried that."

"What are you going to do with the twenty-two grand, then?"

"I thought I'd spend it fixing up the farm. Put in running water, get us a septic field, maybe insulate another room."

"We could sell the place. You could get work in L.A."

"No, Mom. We talked about that."

She didn't argue. They both knew she was disappointed, and they both knew he wasn't going to change his mind. They rode for a while in silence. Ham tapped a drumbeat on the steering wheel, pleased.

"I'da bet for sure you were gonna blow your dough on some damn fool movie thing."

"No, Ham. I'm through with movies."

"Well, good news at last!"

"I don't think I'll be picking up a camera again."

Frances found the utter assurance of his tone disturbing. "Whyever not?"

"Because he finally came to his senses!"

"It's all you've ever liked to do, Homer."

"Not really. There are plenty of things I like to do."

"But why stop doing something that means so much to you?"

"It's too dangerous."

Two hours later they reached their turnoff. Mud season was long gone, and the mire had congealed into a dry, hard obstacle course, washboard on the flats, ridge-backed on the rises, potholes like tank traps in the gullies. Ham knew the terrain, though, and the headlights etched it all in high relief. Bouncing along violently in the middle seat, dodging the packing tube, Homer felt the warm comfort of home.

Coming down from a particularly big jolt, he thought he

spied the place he'd lost his boot in the mud, that day he'd gotten the Oscar letter. He remembered how excited he'd been when he opened it. The world wanted to heap him with glory! He hadn't sought it out. He would never have sought it out. But there it was, waiting for him!

He knew better now. He knew he was kepu.

Homer looked down at the palms of his hands. They were scabbing over well. With luck, they'd be in shape for him to dig water-pipe ditches before the ground froze.

The U.S. of A. was a pretty good place to be kepu. Especially Vermont.

Romulus, Michigan, is a grid of small frame houses with fuel oil tanks in the front yards. They were built without basements, cheap and quick on concrete slabs, and they lie within a mile of Wayne County Airport, directly on the descent path for the northwest heavies. When Greater Detroit shrank, these blocks were the first to lie fallow.

Among the empty shells shedding shingles and peeling siding, one house clad in tar paper bricks showed signs of life. Its newly patched roof vibrated crisply under the coruscating roar of Rolls-Royce turbofans. Clean black blinds blocked light from open windows.

Inside, in the ghostly glow of a Silicon Graphics work station and four gently buzzing Quadras, a thin figure in a black T-shirt bent over a vector graphic sphere. He typed awkwardly. Scar tissue welded his left hand into a claw. The left side of his face looked like a raccoon had wadded it up and chewed on it.

He was officially dead. He liked it that way. Nobody bothered him. His mother knew he was alive, of course, and sent him what he needed from the inheritance he'd left her. As long as he was happy, she let the world think whatever he wanted it to think. And he was happy. He had time and money to do his work. He didn't want the distraction of an identity.

He called it work. That was false modesty. He was building a world. All by himself. He and his machines. Not just pasting images on a screen. Building a world took a long time. He had to shape each rat cat, each hyena assassin and vampire bee and turbo terrorist in three dimensions, from pure geometry. He stretched and squished cones and spheres and cubes into living creatures, like one of Plato's gods deriving the specific from the absolute. Then Mandelbrot fractal randomization multiplied his singular beings into a varied species.

Sometime, months or years from then, he would combine his creatures on a three-d bit map he was generating on two of the Quadras. Parallax software and binocular displays would create all the depth and substance of fully dimensional space. He would don his helmet, slip on his power glove, and roam at will. Nobody could stop him.

In his world, scientists had improved humanity and everything else through gene surgery and nanomechanical implants. Nothing was passive any longer. Nothing was rooted in place. Computer intelligence evolved into conscious will. Automobiles became four-wheeled centaurs. Toaster ovens hunted rye bread. Trees took prisoners. Homo sapiens had succumbed to the inevitable Darwinian pressures and vanished from the earth.

He gnawed with anticipation on what was left of his lip. Today he was starting his masterwork. The Mole. A terrifying combination of animal aggression, machine malignance, and the supercerebration of post-sapiens wetware. He summoned two more spheres from his Alias program, seeds for the torso, and consulted the drawing beside him.

It showed a sleek hybrid, part tubes, lenses, and steely carapace, part fluid, palpitating organism. The torso was humanoid. Its bulging synth-chrome pecs looked a lot like Klaus Frotner's. The head was also quasi-human. It resembled a hardened, bolder version of Elmo Zwalt.